WORTH EVERY *Moment*

HAWKSTON BILLIONAIRES

RAE RYDER

Author's Note

Please note this book is written in British English and will include British variations on spelling and vocab where applicable.
You'll find pavements, lifts, tubes (as in metro/subway), boots (of the car), a lot of S instead of Z, and an extra U in places you might not expect. Sometimes an E for an A, too.
Finally, Mr and Mrs appear without the .
Trigger warnings can be found on my website at www.raeryder.com /content-warnings.
This book contains mature content and is intended for those over 18.

To anyone who has ever wanted to tell their narcissistic parents to go
fuck themselves.
I hope you find the love you deserve.

1
ERICA

Five Years Earlier

The most handsome man I've ever seen is asleep on my new sofa. Okay, so he passed out there, but that's beside the point. I'm still allowed to feel a little pride in the fact he's here at all.

Seb Hawkston. The youngest son of William Hawkston, hotel magnate, and one of London's most eligible bachelors. Seb has featured on Tatler's list of the most eligible men under 30 in the UK for the last few years, and right now, he's on *my sofa*.

It's nearly 9 am on Saturday, and Seb and the scattered detritus from last night are the only remaining signs that I threw a party. I stare at him, delaying the moment I have to wake him up.

Broad shoulders, a suit that's definitely bespoke, and shoes that scream hand-stitched Italian leather. Strong jaw, full lips, thick brown hair with a slight wave to it. He's so good looking that my examination of his face feels compulsive; his presence has unearthed some addiction I didn't know I had and now I have no choice but to feed it. There's a shadow of stubble over his jaw, which I want to stroke with my fingertip, but that would be *properly* creepy. And I'm not there yet. I'm on the border, peeking a toe over the line like a teenager obsessively perusing a celebrity's social media, but not daring to leave a comment. *A teensy bit creepy, but not fully committed.*

I hadn't met him before last night, but occasionally, someone walks into your life and you get a strange 'knowing' that they're important. That's what happened when he walked in. He didn't look at me, but my body reacted to his presence, as if part of his soul reached out to mine and said, *'Hey there, I'm the one you've been waiting for. Sorry it took me so long to find you'*. Even if we never see each other again, I'll remember that feeling *forever*.

He's lying on his side, one arm draped off the edge of the sofa. *He has beautiful hands.* He was drunk last night, and it's a miracle he's not snoring. I imagine he'll feel dreadful when he wakes.

As much as I'd like to keep him here, or at least let him rest a little longer, I need to clear up and head to a casting before my mother shows up. I'm not expecting her, but she has a habit of appearing whenever she wants, especially if she suspects I might have sullied my virginal reputation in her absence. If she finds a man on my sofa, she'll probably have a meltdown. It doesn't fit the brand—*Erica Lefroy, top model and fashion entrepreneur, and a paragon of untouchable chastity*—to have men strewn across the sofa, even if they do look like Greek Gods.

Crap. I'll have to wake him.

I put my coffee on the table and crouch beside him. He's beautiful, but he smells like alcohol and I wrinkle my nose.

How am I going to do this? He's out cold. I could shout in his face, but who wants to be woken up like that? I'll have to touch him. *Just have to.* Gently, of course.

I tap the tip of his nose with one finger, and an energetic jolt zaps down my arm. *Did he feel that? How is he still asleep?*

I run my fingers over his cheekbone, finding his skin softer than I'd expected. He sighs and shifts, but doesn't rouse fully. I blow into his face; his eyelids flutter and he waves his hand like he's batting away a swarm of flies.

Opening his eyes, he catches sight of me and his hand halts in midair. He lets it fall slowly, and then he just... stares right back at me. His full attention blazes like the force of a thousand fires against my skin. *It's hot in here.*

I hold his gaze, taking in the sharp blue of his irises, which are framed by dark lashes that curl. *I'd pay good money for those.*

"Wow," he breathes, sounding almost like he's in a trance. "You're even more beautiful in the morning."

My stomach flutters. *Oh, boy am I in trouble.* I need to get him out of my apartment before I do something I regret.

I shift back from the edge of the sofa and perch on the perpendicular one where I can calm down without looking like I'm running away.

"I bet you say that to all the women you wake up next to." I aim for playful, but my tone must miss the mark because he looks away, and the loss of eye contact hits me like whiplash.

"Fuck," he groans, flopping onto his back and staring at the ceiling as he rakes a hand through the thick wave of his hair. His eyes flick to mine through a wince. "Please tell me we didn't have sex, because I have no memory of it and that would be the fuck up of all fuck ups."

I want to laugh at the distress on his face. "That was a lot of fucks."

He groans again.

This time, I put him out of his misery. "We did not have sex." *Of course we didn't have sex.* I've never had sex with anyone, but Seb Hawkston doesn't need to know that detail.

He blows out a breath and lowers his legs to the floor so he can sit up. The movement releases a burst of expensive cologne, which fans the flames of the heat roaring through me. He's still wearing a jacket and tie, and although I suspect he's feeling like shit, he looks nearly pristine and devilishly handsome. *Impressive.*

"Hi," I say, intending to introduce myself so we can start over. "I'm—"

"I know who you are," he says, his voice husky and low. The sound makes my heart race a little too fast. "Erica Lefroy."

I'm relieved he said my name instead of reeling off a load of my recent accomplishments. It makes me feel more like a person and less like a brand.

"Ah, so you do remember last night," I tease.

"I remember *you*." He doesn't echo my playful tone, and the emphasis he puts on the final word sends those flutters in my stomach spiraling like confetti caught in an updraft.

The air feels loaded, and while I'm breaking into a sweat and trying not to gawk at him, Seb casually takes a packet of chewing gum from his pocket, offers me a piece, which I refuse, and pops one in his mouth before pocketing the packet again.

He glances at his watch. "Damn. I missed my gym session. I never miss the gym."

That explains why his shoulders and upper arms fill out that expensive suit to perfection. My mind conjures a perfect sculpted male body beneath, golden skin smooth over taut abs that ripple right down to—

"Am I the only one here?" He takes in the empty flat.

"Yeah." I smooth my skirt with one hand, hoping he can't tell what I was thinking about. "Everyone else left last night."

"Nico?" he says, asking for his brother who brought him. I met Nico at a fashion show afterparty a few months ago, and Mum hounded him until he agreed to accompany me to a charity event where we would be seen together publicly. I guess you could say it was a date, but it was never sexual. I never felt anything for him, as handsome as he is. It was more about Nico Hawkston being good for the brand. A *serious* businessman. Discreet with the women he dates. Elegant, sophisticated. *Powerful.* Different to Seb, who's more flirtatious and fun-loving, but nonetheless, there's a gravity to him that reels me in. I've never felt a magnetic pull to another person the way I do with Seb. He's attractive, but also easy-going, which makes it seem like he's not trying to be anything other than he is. No pretenses. No phoney charm. Not that I really know. I can't judge him on one drunken night, and today, in sobriety, his gorgeous smile and the dimple that usually pops on one cheek have yet to make an appearance.

"He left around midnight," I respond, remembering that he asked me a question. "You refused to leave."

He curses under his breath. "Sorry." His brow furrows as he waves a finger between us. "And we definitely didn't... do anything? Nothing happened?"

I should probably be insulted that a guy thinks he could have no memory of something happening between us, but the edge of devastation in Seb's voice checks the impulse. I pick up my coffee again and take a sip, trying to appear way cooler about this than I feel. "No. You tried, though."

A smile pulls at his mouth. "Obviously."

His tone is all amused, with not a hint of sleaze, but I gasp in mock horror anyway. "Are you objectifying me?"

He hums a laugh and scratches at his throat, fingertips rasping over the stubble. "No. Just admiring."

I bite my lip to stop the goofy grin that wants to spread across my face. When he was drunk, he told me over and over that he thought I was the most beautiful woman he'd ever seen. People are always telling me things like that—it comes with the job—and while it's lovely to be complimented, most of the time I suspect they're running a calculation in their heads at the same time. *How can we leverage this face? How can we make it work for us? What can we use it for? How much money can we make here?*

But the way Seb said it was different. Awe lit up the edges of his words, like I'd sprung fully formed from his dreams, and he wanted nothing more than to be in my presence. I know it's silly, but I'd love to hear him say it again. Sadly, he doesn't seem inclined to repeat himself the way he did last night.

He glances around the messy apartment. "Why didn't you kick me out?"

I put my mug on the coffee table between the sofas. "You're a cute drunk. Plus, someone out there could have taken advantage of you." I nod at him. "That pretty face has to have got you in trouble before."

"I hoped *you* might be the trouble." The lopsided smile he gives me makes his dimple pop. *There it is.*

Sparks burst against my skin. "Drunk guys are not my thing," I say, hoping that my voice doesn't reveal the fact that his proximity is causing a myriad of physical reactions I can't control, and his every gesture is internally unravelling me. I don't think I've ever been this attracted to someone, *ever.*

"I'm sober more often than I'm drunk." He levels a serious look my way. "I'd like to get to know you in sobriety."

An ember of warmth flares in my chest, but a chill of fear quickly snuffs it out. Mum always told me men are animals, who are only interested in sex and food, and as Seb sits there watching my reaction to his words, I can't help wondering if he's nothing more than a well-dressed, handsome animal.

But if he is, I'm not sure I mind as much as I'm supposed to.

"The thing is," I say with caution, "I already told you my life story last night, and if you can't remember it—"

He tips his chin. "I remember that you hate your mother."

I gape. "I didn't say that."

"Maybe not exactly. I'm paraphrasing. If I remember correctly, she's effectively your agent and manager. You're very grateful for everything she's done for you, but she's got greater control over your life than you'd like. You're resentful, but you feel guilty about it because now you're on the cusp of super-stardom, and it's because of everything your mother pushed you to do."

I'm speechless. He's recalled everything I said to him last night when he was slumped on the sofa, the last one here. I didn't think he was even conscious, let alone paying attention to every word I said.

"You listened," I blurt.

He pushes off the sofa and stands, running both hands through his hair before he adjusts the knot of his tie. "Yeah, it stuck in my head because my dad's a raging narcissist too."

This brings me up short, and the nonchalant way he announces it only amplifies my confusion. I'd never thought of Mum as a narcissist. Ambitious? Absolutely. Bitter because Dad left her for another woman when he found out she was pregnant with me? Definitely. But a narcissist? I'm not even sure what it means, and there's something about the word that sounds almost evil. I don't want to expose my ignorance so I say, "Is he?"

"Sure." He shrugs like he's unmoved by what he's saying. Either he's resigned to the idea of having a raging narcissist for a father, or he's so deep in denial that he can't feel any pain attached to the idea. "He built a global hotel chain from nothing. You don't get that kind of success in one lifetime unless you're prepared to bulldoze everyone in your way. It demands the subjugation of everything and everyone else."

"Oh." I sound surprised, but I have no idea what else to say. Should I comfort him? He doesn't look like he needs it, and before I can decide upon a course of action, he shrugs again.

"People want what they want," he says. "The people who get it are the ones who are prepared to go further. Push harder. Sacrifice more. I don't think anyone truly successful isn't at least a bit of a narcissist. They say a lot of billionaires are psychopaths. Or sociopaths. One or the other."

"Aren't you... you know..." *Stop talking. Stop talking, Erica.* "Worth a lot? Tatler said you—"

He raises a brow, a smile ghosting his lips. "Tatler?"

A blush rages over my cheeks. *Definitely should have stopped talking.* "Sure." I nod at the coffee table where the latest copy lies. There's a picture of me on the front, but there's an article inside about Seb and his brothers, and the teaser headline is on the cover in gold lettering next to my face. *'The Hawkston Billionaires. Meet the men who changed the way you sleep at night.'*

"That's a great picture," Seb says, indicating the magazine cover before he lazily waves his hand in the air. "But you shouldn't believe everything you read. I'd have thought you would have learnt that by now."

The condescending tinge to his voice pisses me off. "So you aren't worth two billion dollars? The ladies will riot when they find out."

He tilts his head ever so slightly as his gaze drops to my mouth. "I'd like to see *you* riot."

The air fills with sexual tension, which seeps through my skin and settles between my legs like a hot, pulsing ball. I lower my head and stare at the floor. Turns out, I can't give as good as I get with this man and maintain it. I take a breath and glance up, trying to keep my cool. "So you don't—"

His eyes narrow. "Why do you want to know?"

I sit a little straighter, meeting his gaze head on. "I'm just trying to work out if I'm alone in the house with a psychopath."

His laugh is loud, and I get a heady rush knowing I elicited that beautiful sound from his mouth. "I didn't have to bulldoze anyone to get what I have, but let's not talk about money." He rolls his shoulders. "I'll get out of your hair. I'm really sorry about..." He gestures to the sofa. "You should have kicked me out. I'd have survived out there."

"You could hardly walk."

"I would have been fine. I've got a driver waiting in the car outside." He winces and groans, his voice full of regret when he speaks. "Fuck, he probably had a worse night's sleep than I did." He drags a hand down his face, but cuts the gesture short, letting his hand fall to his side as he looks around at the mess. "You need a hand clearing up?"

"Nah, it's okay."

"Is it? Because I remember you freaking out about your mum turning up this morning and finding out you threw a party."

I clasp my hands between my knees. Even if I do go to the casting, Mum could still let herself in. She has her own set of keys and she mentioned wanting to come and see my new apartment. So I need to clean before I leave, and I'd really like to leave *before* she gets here.

Seb, reading my hesitation as the doubt it is, removes his jacket, chucks it on the sofa as if it's not the finest Savile Row tailoring I've ever seen, loosens his tie, and whips it free from beneath his collar. The *whoosh* of it has heat unfurling in my lower belly. *This man*. He throws the tie on his jacket and begins removing a pair of cufflinks that look like solid gold. He slips them out with nimble fingers, dropping them into his trouser pocket.

I hold my breath, watching as he methodically rolls up the first shirt sleeve, exposing a tanned, muscled forearm inch by inch, like some cruel striptease. I'm so captivated by the ripple and flex of his tendons and the veins that slip through the muscles that he might as well be stripping naked.

That hot pulse returns between my thighs, and I press my legs together, continuing to stare with my mouth open. It's only when I feel his attention skate my skin that I look up to find amusement dancing in those blue eyes.

I didn't think I could get any hotter, but much more of this and I'll be using that copy of Tatler as a fan.

He moves to the second sleeve without a word, his attention back on his task, but the curve of his lips tells me he's still thinking about catching me gawking at him and enjoying the recollection.

I don't know how to feel about that.

"Come on," he says when he's finished, grinning at me like we're already the best of friends as he holds out a hand to pull me off the sofa. "If I help you clean up, can I come back?"

Come back? Huh? "To fuck?" I cup my hand over my mouth as soon as the words leave it, and he laughs so loud and warm that it heats my stomach and diffuses through my body like clouds of steam.

"If you want," he says with a grin that's wider than any that came before.

I shake my head, but I can't help mirroring him with a smile of my own. "I don't."

His hand is still outstretched, and I take it. A minor shockwave pulses up my arm at the strength of his grip and the skin-to-skin contact. We stay that way for a fraction of a second too long before he pulls me to standing.

"Okay." He releases my hand and slides his into his trouser pocket. "Just to hang out then."

"Why would you want to do that?" The question comes out sounding as though I think he's insane to want to. As if the idea that he might want to spend time with *me* is crazy. I guess the fact someone like Seb is here at all is a sign of how much my life has changed in the past few years. I've gone from obscurity to fame and fortune in under eighteen months. And, regardless of whatever I said to Seb last night, I have my mother to thank for that.

He lifts a shoulder. "Why not?"

I narrow my eyes at him. "Are you asking me out?"

He narrows his eyes right back, mimicking my suspicion. "Would you like me to?"

That flush of warmth hits again, and a bubble expands in my throat; a giggle desperate to be released. I swallow it down. "No. I don't date."

"Ah. Mummy says no?"

I cringe. "No. Well, yes. Kind of."

The clock on the wall ticks loudly in the silence. It feels like I'm in a therapy session.

"How old are you?" Seb asks.

"Twenty. How old are you?" I know exactly how old he is, but I repeat his question anyway.

"Twenty-five." He rubs a hand along his jaw. "So can I see you again? I know you don't date but... as friends?"

Friends. The word leaves a buzz in the air, like the ringing in my ears after an alarm has shut off. It's a seemingly innocent request, but there's nothing innocent about this man or how he makes me feel. He's not like Nico, the professional businessman. He's... *different.* To me, much more appealing, and that's the risk. Could I maintain a friendship with someone like Seb Hawkston without crossing that dangerous line?

And then there's Mum to consider. She definitely won't like me seeing him, even if it's just as 'friends'. He's everything she dislikes in a man. The charm, the sexual energy, the money, and the power. He's her worst nightmare; the type of guy who'd lead any woman astray, or worse, abandon them and publicly humiliate them. Thing is, she might be right because Tatler didn't just list his estimated net worth. It listed all the women he's been seen with over the last couple of years. And it was a *lot*. My brand—*Erica Lefroy*—is valuable. It's not just my name; it's our company, and Mum owns fifty per cent of it. Now that I'm more established in the modelling world, she has plans to expand into fashion, perfume, and cosmetics. And I guess I'm going with her. Me being associated with the ultimate playboy, when my whole brand is based on purity and innocence, wouldn't work for the business plan.

I should say no. That's the right answer. We'll inevitably see each other again either way. London is a small place when you move in certain circles. But to see him *privately*? Just the thought of it has nerves cascading through me like water through a broken dam. He shouldn't even be here now, let alone come back *again*.

And yet the thought of not sharing another private moment with him feels so wrong, it's almost frightening. Maybe I can step out of Mum's shadow just a tiny bit. I already threw the party, although the longer I sit here not clearing away the mess, the more those nerves cascade, raging like a river that could drag me under. But maybe enduring them would be worth it, and I can have this one thing *for me*. A friendship with Seb Hawkston. I'll have to clear away all the evidence that such a thing exists, like I'm covering tracks in the snow with a fallen tree branch. *I was never here*. And I'll never date him; that's a line I won't cross. But friendship... I could do that, right? Well, I want to try, at least.

I swallow hard and say it quickly before I can stop myself. "Yes. You can see me again. I'd like that."

2
ERICA

Present Day

"This *fucking* shoe." I groan as I bend over to fix the patent leather strap that's tied around my ankle like a shackle. A high fashion, three thousand dollar shackle.

I'm on the runway first tonight, opening the show for Dominic DeLacey, the fashion designer of the moment. And I think he's trying to kill me with these shoes. They're a cross between something a dominatrix would wear and a melting Mr Whippy ice cream. The heel is nearly as long as my forearm, and it spirals like twin streaks of brightly coloured carnival candy.

I'd never sell anything this wacky in my own fashion line.

With the strap in place, I totter a few steps. I should have practised this more, but as it is, I have fifteen minutes before I'm going out. *Shit.*

The frustration is a good reminder that I'm making the right decision. I want to quit modelling and move to the big screen. Become an actress. If I'm honest, I always wanted to do it, but what Mum wanted came first. She was—*is*—the engine behind my career. And sure, modelling has always been good to me, but it felt like I was living my mother's unlived life. It was her dream, not mine, and I've tried to shake that feeling off for years. I might be twenty-five, but this move into acting will be the first thing I've really, truly done for me. Not for my mum or anyone else. Just for me.

I can't wait.

Dominic's going to lose it when he finds out his muse—*England's Rose*—is abandoning him to break into the movie industry. He's been by my side for years, ever since he saw the Claudia Kirchwood photo shoot that made my career. He said I had an 'inspirational face', but I'm sure he'll do just fine without me. I give a little shrug for my own benefit. I'll think about that later.

I inhale deeply, taking in the familiar smells of hairspray, nail polish, and perfume. As much as I want to move on, I'll miss the chaos of fashion shows. The energy behind the scenes is fraught, but I've thrived here. I've been doing this since I was a teenager, and I'm right at the top of my game. *Hot property*. It's the perfect moment to make a change.

On the dressing table, my phone pings and I drop into the nearby chair as I swipe to open it.

Mum: Not feeling well so I can't come see you walk this time. Keep your back straight and your eye on the prize. Every step you take now is crucial to our next move with the company. DO NOT LET ME DOWN.

My blood pressure rises. *Thank God Mum can't come.* I'm pretty sure this is her version of being supportive, but it feels like crap. I loathe having her judgmental glare on me when I'm working. You'd think I'd be used to it by now, but knowing she's out there scrutinizing me always adds an extra layer of tension I don't need.

"Erica!" Marni, one of the new interns, rushes up to me, and I'm relieved to have a reason to stop thinking about Mum's harsh critique. "There's some gorgeous guy looking for you." She fans herself with her hand. "He's been asking where you are." I don't know for sure who she means—it could be any number of people—but there's only one man who shows up reliably every single time I'm on the runway.

Seb Hawkston. I glance down at my phone, swiping away Mum's message and returning to the GIF Seb sent this morning. He sends one if he knows I'm feeling down or nervous about something. This one is a cartoon roadrunner in high heels with the words *STRUT YOUR STUFF* pasted across it. A fizzy sensation pops in my stomach and I bite my lip to stop from smiling. But as I look back at Marni, I remember I'm supposed to be a professional. "Did you tell him I'm working?" I ask, hardening my voice. "This is not a good time."

Marni blushes. "No. I didn't say anything to him." Her hands go to her cheeks. "I can't talk to men who look like that."

I let out a small laugh, taking pity on her because Seb used to make me feel exactly that way. "Oh, honey. You work in fashion. You'll have to get used to it."

She glances at the floor, the colour in her cheeks deepening. "Easy for you to say. I bet you can talk to anyone you want. You're the most beautiful woman in the whole world." She fans her face again, except this time I think it's more about me than the mystery man, and I can't help smiling. Mum might think I'm riddled with imperfections, but not everyone does.

"You're too kind," I say, squeezing her arm. "Relax. You can talk to anyone. You're gorgeous. But you know that's not a prerequisite for engaging other human beings in conversation, right?"

"Oh. Yes. I know. It's just…" The poor girl turns pink all the way to her cleavage and I pass her a glass of water from my dressing table. She takes a sip, eyes wide with thanks.

My phone buzzes again. *Mum*. Probably pestering me to undergo some spurious treatment in the pursuit of perfection before I walk down the runway, like getting the underside of my kneecaps lasered or some shit. *Nope. Not today.* I lay it down on the dressing table face down so I can't see her name flashing at me.

"Everything okay?" Marni asks as she sets the water glass back down.

I blow out a breath. *I will not worry about my mother.* "Yeah. We've got a big cosmetics launch coming up," I explain. "It's a bit stressful."

She nods at the phone. "Your mum?"

Does the entire industry know about my mother? I guess we are business partners and she's *always* poking her nose where I don't want it.

"Yeah." It comes out sounding too severe, but I don't want to open up this line of questioning. I lift my foot off the ground, and the torture device masquerading as a shoe dangles from my ankle. "Can you untwist this strap?"

Marni gets on her knees and sorts the strap in seconds.

"Thank you so much," I say with a smile. *Business as usual.* These shoes are insane, but I've never been one to complain about what I'm made to wear on the runway, and I'm not going to start now.

"Erica!" Dominic's voice booms through the backstage hubbub as he runs towards me, sending Marni scampering in fear. Poor kid. She's going to need tougher skin if she's going to make it in this industry. "You look exquisite. Perfect."

Perfect. Sometimes it feels like all anyone needs from me is perfection. *Who would stick by me if I fell short?*

He blows me a kiss, even though our mouths are only a few inches apart. With trembling hands, he picks at a few strands of my hair and tweaks the tulle collar I'm wearing. Excitement buzzes off him. He's high on the near success of this show and his pupils are blown wide with it. I've been at this long enough to know that Dominic's work is something special. Everyone at London Fashion Week is going to be talking about this collection, and I'm the model wearing the key pieces.

He steps back to observe his work, drawing his chin in and letting out a sigh of appreciation. "I'm blessed to have the great Erica Lefroy as my muse. I cannot believe you're single, darling."

"No one's good enough," I joke.

"I'll say." He lifts his hands to cup my face but stops as he takes in my makeup. *Can't mess that up.* His hands fall. "Wonderful. Go make me proud."

Still smiling, I say, "I'll do my best."

Dominic moves away to micro-manage the other models. The music is thumping and I can feel it in my feet through the shoes. I imagine all those people out there in the audience. The rows of celebrities and high net worth individuals taking in the show and deciding what they want to buy. Or the fashion journalists and social media influencers planning their write up.

Reappearing at my side, Marni grips my arm, her voice rising two octaves as she squeaks right in my ear, "That's him." With her free hand, she points towards the door where there's a kerfuffle of sorts occurring. She emits another tiny squeal, and the hand that's wrapped about my arm tightens like a tourniquet.

As I look closer, I realise it's not so much a kerfuffle as an energetic ripple. Whoever has entered is drawing a lot of attention, and the models, assistants, and hair stylists are smiling and nudging one another, greeting the newcomer.

The crowd parts and I catch sight of the person causing the disturbance. *Seb Hawkston.* Right on schedule and dressed, as usual, in a navy suit that reeks of cash. The fabric is molded to his form, and beneath it is a pressed white shirt and pale blue tie. There's a timepiece on his wrist that probably cost as much as a London starter flat.

But his face... that's why everyone's excited. There are handsome men, and then there's Seb Hawkston in a league all of his own. Sharp cheekbones, blue eyes so bright they could illuminate the night sky, and a strong jaw with just the right amount of scruff on it.

Poor Marni hasn't been around for long enough to know he turns up at all my shows, but the other models know, and they're not concealing their enthusiasm. Arms are thrown around his neck, kisses pressed to his cheeks, and he's all smiles and kind words, giving them each the attention they deserve. I bet they feel really special for the brief moment that his focus falls on them. He's like Midas, but rather than gold, the merest touch turns women all gooey, falling hopelessly in love with him. I know because plenty of them have asked me about him. *Is he available? Can I ask him out? Do you mind if I do?* I always try and warn them off because he'll never take any of them seriously. It's not his thing, and I don't want to be responsible for anybody's heartbreak.

He's carrying the biggest bouquet of white lilies I've ever seen. Dominic will lose his shit when he sees them. *Are they for me?* I hate to admit it, but if he hands them off to someone else, I'll be devastated. Jealous is the word that springs to mind, but I push it away. I can't be jealous because of Seb. He's my *friend*. I have no claim on him, and I wouldn't want to have one. *Would I?*

"Lefroy." His voice is deep, and it causes a tremor somewhere behind my breastbone that I refuse to acknowledge. I want to be annoyed that he's not treating my work with the respect it deserves by showing up right before I'm about to go on, but the sight of his gorgeous face and that one-sided dimple, which only deepens as he takes me in, has my lips twitching to break into a smile. I can't even pretend to be annoyed that he's here.

Standing to greet him with these bizarre shoes on, I'm nearly as tall as he is.

I affect a scowl and muster up an angry tone as I say, "I'm working. You shouldn't be here."

Pat on the back for Erica. That sounded almost convincing.

He gives me a quick once over as though he's trying to work out if I'm serious. He must decide I'm not because he smirks and says, "Couldn't stay away."

That damn smirk will be my undoing, and my false anger melts away under its glow. *It's just Seb.* Flirting and teasing me as he always does. He does it to everyone, but somehow, when he does it to me, it makes me feel like I'm truly desirable, and not just in a model-perfectly-photo-shopped and highly made-up kind of way. In a *real* way. He's good at convincing me that he would like me even if I didn't look like *Erica Lefroy*, top model. And no one else *ever* makes me feel like that. I love him for it.

"Must you flirt with *everyone* though?" I ask.

His head quirks and he jerks his thumb back towards the door. "That wasn't flirting. That was just being friendly. You should try it sometime."

"Hey, that's not—"

"Get that man out of here."

Oh, crap. Dominic's yell cuts across me, and Seb turns to the voice, eyebrows rising as the designer barrels towards us from the other side of the room. Dominic is shorter than both of us and something about the way he's approaching Seb—face contorted with rage and hands fisted at his sides—strikes me as hilarious. I snort.

"Erica," Dominic shrieks, his face turning puce. "Get away from the lilies. Who brings lilies to a fashion show?" He waves me away from Seb with both hands, and I step back. Dominic focuses on Seb. "You didn't take the stamens off. That pollen will stain anything it touches. Get them away! Get them away, you beastly man."

Seb doesn't move. "Did I fuck up here?"

"No, you're fine. Dominic's just having a fit. We always get at least one before a show," I reassure him, then notice Marni nearby, wide-eyed attention fixed on Seb like she's never seen a man before. I nod my head in her direction. "Give them to my assistant. She already thinks you're the hottest man she's ever seen. It'll make her day."

Seb frowns. "But they're for you."

"Please."

He gives me an indulgent smile, half rolling his eyes. "Anything for you, Lefroy." Without hesitation, he beams at Marni, who gazes at him like a chocolate rabbit melting in his headlights. "Anyone who has to put up with Lefroy all day…" He side-eyes me before whispering in her ear. A red flush works its way up her cheeks, and when he pulls back, she looks buoyant enough to float away.

She takes the bouquet from Seb. "I'll put them in water," she mutters at the floor, as if his face is down on the ground rather than a foot over her head. She takes a few steps backwards, and Seb turns to me, a bemused look on his face as he dusts his hands off.

"That went well, I think," he reports. "Next time, I'll bring you roses."

"Away from the clothes," Dominic yells as he reaches us, looking near apoplectic, and Marni performs an odd curtsy before she rushes away.

"Love the vibe back here," Seb jokes, but his attention snags on my cheek, and his eyes take on a darker hue. Before I can stop him, he grazes it with his thumb, but he might as well have struck a match on my face because something I've struggled to keep in check for years sears right beneath my skin. "Sorry. Pollen," he explains and then leans in to kiss the spot he wiped, his lips skimming the makeup that Dominic didn't dare touch earlier. It's a formal cheek kiss; there's nothing sensuous about it, but his lips are so soft, the kiss so gentle, that my breath catches in my throat. I stiffen, which is the opposite of what I want to do. I want to let out a satisfied sigh and melt into him.

Wait. What?

The rough graze of his stubble scrapes my face as he moves away, trailing his familiar cologne. It's masculine and rich, a mingling of spice and wood, underpinned by something that's uniquely Seb... catching his scent this close feels intimate, and the thought stokes the fire in me. *Ugh.*

What is going on? I am losing my mind here. It must be the pressure of the show, and knowing I'm going to disappoint Dominic when I finally gather the courage to tell him I'm quitting. Nothing to do with Seb. He's been my friend for years, so whatever is happening inside me, I push it right out of awareness. I cannot start sweating. My makeup will melt. I'll be all shiny for the cameras.

"Don't touch her," Dominic screeches, sinking to his knees and tweaking the underside of my skirt.

Seb's gaze follows the motion, and his eyes widen with his smile. "Another man falls to his knees for Lefroy," he declares like he's commenting on a football match.

I laugh. "But never you."

Seb raises a brow. "Do you want that?"

He moves as if he's actually going to kneel on the floor beside Dominic, and I can't help but giggle. He's always making stupid jokes. Dominic reappears, fast as lightning, scowling up at Seb. "Stop it. Every time you show up, it knocks her off her game. If you get on your knees, I'll have to deal with unparalleled levels of distraction. You should stay home."

Thanks, Dominic.

Seb straightens, blue eyes sparkling at me. "Is that so?"

"No, it's not so," I say, popping a hip.

Dominic huffs. "Don't touch her. I mean it."

"I wouldn't dare," Seb replies.

"Good. Keep your hands off. You can touch her after the show. If you must. And only if she says you can."

"She says no," I cut in, but I'm grinning. Seb always brings out the tease in me. "Keep your handsy hands to yourself."

Seb knocks his shoulder against mine. "Such a party pooper, Lefroy," he mutters so quietly that I think I'm the only one who hears it. But then he steps back, appearing to forget about everything else as his gaze does a full sweep of my body. "Your legs are as long as the Nile with those shoes on," he says, voice all amazement.

"Is that a compliment?"

"Absolutely." He shakes his head while looking at my feet. "Killer shoes. How the hell do you walk in those?"

Before I can reply, Dominic is standing and shunting Seb away. "Unless you're buying my whole collection, you need to fuck off. We're about to start."

Seb slides his hands in his pockets, looking breathtakingly casual as he says, "How much is it?"

Dominic pulls his chin in. "How much is what?"

"The whole collection," Seb deadpans.

I can almost see the dollar signs appearing in Dominic's eyes as his jaw slackens. We all know Seb could buy it ten times over.

"He's not going to buy the whole collection," I say, interrupting Seb's peacocking.

"Why not?" Seb says, nodding at my feet. "Then you won't have to walk in those death traps and we can go out for dinner instead."

Dominic tips up on his toes, fingers steepled. "Perhaps we could come to some arrangement after the show, Mr Hawkston." His voice has turned oily. "It would be an honour to sell—"

"He's not buying it," I repeat, and Dominic's shoulders sink. "Go on," I say to Seb, shooing him with one hand. "If you don't leave, you won't get back to your seat in time to watch."

"And I really do want to watch," he purrs suggestively. I roll my eyes at him, but even though I know it's all a joke, my heart beats oddly in my chest. *Too fast.* "Break a leg. I'll be in the front row," he adds, his tone much more platonic. He winks and saunters back the way he came.

When he's gone, the final minutes pass in a whirlwind of activity as we gather and line up, ready to process down the runway. Dominic kneels at my feet, fiddling with my shoe. He taps my ankle to get my attention.

"Watch this," he says, warning me about the fragile strap on the shoe. Maybe if he hadn't designed something so crazy, I wouldn't have to watch it. I grit my teeth and take a preparatory breath as Dominic stands and clasps my shoulder, tipping his head towards the curtain. "Go be perfect."

Be perfect. Always.

I am so fucking tired of being perfect.

3
SEB

I stride down the front row to my seat. *Fuck, it's loud in here.* Fashion week isn't normally my scene, but I come for Erica. I've been so many times now that I've lost count. I'm never entirely sure if she appreciates it or not because she scolds me every time. But then she gives me that gorgeous smile—the one she never uses in public—and it feels like all is forgiven.

My knee knocks against a woman I recognise, but I can't recall her name. She scowls, her gaze jerking up to me, but when I smile and whisper an apology, warmth fills her face, heat rising to her cheeks. "Oh, Seb."

Shit.

I've slept with her, and I can't remember her fucking name. I inwardly cringe, hating myself. I don't do it deliberately; I'm not that much of an arse. It's difficult for me to retain information about the women I sleep with; the things they tell me filter through my brain like rainwater through a sieve. Sometimes, the sex is blurry too. It could be the fact that my nights out are fueled by alcohol and the occasional drug-taking, but I suspect it's deeper than that, and I don't want to dig because I'd probably uncover a black void of shame that would swallow me whole.

No, thanks. I'll keep my shit buried.

On the plus side, I'm always honest that I'm not interested in anything serious. I keep it casual and consensual, and everyone's happy. Sort of. Most of the time, afterwards, I'd prefer to rewind time and go home and fuck my fist instead, because there's only one woman in the whole world I actually want.

Erica Lefroy.

Sadly, my feelings aren't reciprocated. It's painful, knowing she doesn't care the way I do, but I'm prepared to numb it with an array of other women. It's not healthy, but I can't quit because leaning into my playboy image invites fewer questions. I can't possibly be in love with my best friend if I'm sleeping with other people, can I? Besides, Erica would prefer to focus on her career than anything else, and who am I to stand in the way of her goals?

I first saw her in a high street clothing catalogue the housekeeper accidentally left on my kitchen island seven years ago. She was wearing a forty-quid beige jumper and jeans, and that was it. Her image lodged itself deep into my psyche, and I couldn't stop thinking about her. But it wasn't just her face or her body—both of which are fucking fantastic and appeal to me on every level—it was her eyes. There was something in them that resonated with me... a sadness that jumped off the page. And all I could think was, how could someone so beautiful ever be sad? It was a question I needed to know the answer to.

We didn't meet in person until two years later, by which point, her career had taken off. The girl from the catalogue was world famous, and I would have knelt at her feet and kissed her toes if I didn't know it would make me seem unforgivably odd.

Instead, I got blind drunk and tried to impress her. I must have succeeded to some degree because here we are, five years later. *Friends.*

"Good to see you again," I say to the woman whose name I can't remember, tilting my chin as I move past. I knock her other knee. "Sorry."

"Of course," she mutters, gazing up at me as though I'm entitled to barge past her. As though I could spank her six ways to Sunday and all she'd do would be smile and say 'thank you'.

The adoration in her expression makes me feel fucking guilty. I need a sign around my neck—*or my dick*—that reads, 'Emotionally unavailable. Proceed with caution'.

Her gaze lingers on me as I continue to my seat, but then another woman grabs my hand.

This one I do know the name of. Harriet... *something*. The daughter of one of those old aristocratic English families. Freckles on her nose and cheekbones, and hair the colour of straw.

"Seb, hi," she whispers, her face lighting up.

I nod and smile—*nod and smile*—as I keep moving.

"Call me," she mouths.

I add a wink to the smile because, *why not*? She looks delighted by it, which goes some way to soothing the guilt I feel at not remembering her surname.

I catch sight of my brother, Nico, further down the row, leaning forward in his seat to watch my progress. He shakes his head, disapproval etched across his face. Shame slithers somewhere deep and uncomfortable, but I roll my eyes like his opinion is nothing but a minor inconvenience.

"How many women in this row have you fucked?" Nico hisses as I take my seat beside him. On his other side sits his fiancée, Kate.

The question riles me, but I don't let it show. I tug on the lapels of my jacket and loosen my shoulders. "A gentleman never tells."

Nico glares before flipping his phone from his pocket and flashing the screen at me. There's a picture from last week of me stumbling from one of our clubs, Martini Gems, with a woman under each arm. I'm kissing one of them, gripping the other's breast over her shoulder with my opposite hand.

"You look debauched," Nico hisses. "Dad's not happy."

I wave a hand to dismiss the comment and lean back in my seat, affecting my most nonchalant posture for Nico's benefit. He can sit there all smug with his perfect fiancée, but we both know he wasn't that much better than me a couple of years ago. A bit more discreet, sure. I don't think there are any photos like that of Nico in circulation. He cares more about appearances than I do. And he'd probably make the photos disappear if they existed anyway.

"I don't give a fuck what Dad thinks," I mutter. Nico side-eyes me and I know what that look means. It means, *Don't be an idiot. We have to care what Dad thinks*. "And neither should you. You're the CEO now."

Nico's expression hardens. "I might wear the crown, but we all know who's on the throne. The board is in his pocket. He won't give it up until he's six feet under."

"Old bastard should know when to step back," I mutter.

Nico emits a dry laugh. "Ha. It would take an almighty scandal to dislodge him. But that's hardly the point. If you keep messing around, it fucks with business." He subtly points across the runway, where an older man is seated with a young blonde girl. "That's Antonio Marchetti. Dad's trying to do a deal with him so we can build the mega hotel. Whatever you think about Dad, we have a front to maintain, and it does not include being the dick who fucks anything that moves."

I'm not in the mood for being reprimanded, even if Antonio Marchetti is sitting right opposite us. Dad's been trying to win him over for access to that land for years, but honestly, I couldn't give a shit about the plans for business expansion. It's not as if we don't already have hotels all over the world. But then, Dad is a greedy fucker. If he could own every hotel in the world, he would.

Amy Moritz, legendary pop star and one of Erica's closest friends, leans around from Nico's other side, giving me a view of her bright pink hair. "Thought you were going to miss it," she hisses, saving me from responding to Nico.

"He'd never miss Erica," Nico states without looking at us. He's focused on the runway, and there isn't a hint of mockery in his voice. He might not be teasing me right now, but I know he's found my crush on Erica amusing for a long time. I've always played it down, maintaining that I don't feel anything special for her, because there's nowhere it could go anyway, and I'm not about to let anyone in on the hopelessness of my situation. We're friends, and that's it. But Nico thinks he knows me better than that, and, as much as I hate to admit it, he'd be right. I just wish he wasn't so condescending in his amusement.

Perhaps it's a good thing that Erica doesn't want me, because she would unwind me. Take me apart, brick by brick. Not that I haven't tried to let her do exactly that. When we first struck up a friendship, I tried. Really tried. She said no. And now, I joke about it, asking her out now and then, to prove I'm totally okay with rejection. If she ever said yes, I'd probably keel over and die from shock.

Apparently, my image doesn't work for the perfect English Rose. She outright rejected me with some marketing bullshit spiel about my 'public persona'. I can still remember exactly how the conversation went down.

"We're friends. Let's not ruin that."

"Who says it would ruin anything?"

"Seb. Please don't push me on this. Aside from the fact I don't want to date you, I could never do it because your reputation would damage my brand."

"What reputation? I'm pretty eligible. Actually, I'm a fucking catch."

"Sure. But not for me. You have that whole arrogant playboy thing going on, and it just doesn't work with what I've built. Mum and I have carefully managed this brand for years. Erica Lefroy is elegance, sophistication, and purity. It's not random sex on a Friday night with a hot dude in a suit."

"Hot dude?"

"Yeah. You're a hot dude in a suit who likes to party and have casual sex. We don't match. I'm sorry. Let's just be grateful for what we have."

Cut and dry. Erica Lefroy was choosing her career over me. And maybe she was right to do so because she's risen to become the most famous model in the world. Britain's most lucrative export, after the Royal Family. She certainly had her eye on the prize, and it wasn't me.

While rejection quietly devastated me, I was grateful for whatever she would give me. Movie nights on the sofa. Drinks at parties. She's always the one I gravitate to in a room, and our social lives overlap a fair bit, so there's been no shortage of opportunities to get to know each other. She probably wouldn't say the same, but Erica Lefroy is my favourite person in the whole damn world, even if she's determined to control the circumstances of our every meeting to make sure her business doesn't take a hit. Fuck knows what will happen to me when she finds someone she actually wants to be with. I'm not sure I could handle becoming the third wheel in that relationship. I'd probably have to step away entirely.

"Where were you?" Kate whispers, a worried expression on her face as she drags me from my somewhat unpleasant thoughts.

"Wishing Erica good luck," I explain.

Kate shakes her head. "You'll distract her."

Amy, on the other side of Nico and Kate, pokes forward again. "Erica doesn't get distracted."

I roll my eyes. *Don't I know it.*

Amy leans across and grabs my knee with a claw-like hand. Kate and Nico tilt back to give her access, amused expressions on their faces as they share a glance. "You're so adorable," Amy coos. "I wish I had a fan like you in my corner." She scrunches her nose as she smiles at me.

I'm pretty sure they're all laughing at me. *Fuck it.*

I settle in my seat as the models stream out; orderly, rhythmic, evenly spaced like aeroplanes lifting off the ground. Choreographed. There's a predictability to it that pleases me.

When Erica appears at the end of the runway, my breath stalls somewhere between my lungs and my throat like it does every fucking time I see her. She's impossibly beautiful. More so in real life than in any static image. Her face is everywhere now, on posters around the city, rotating on billboards at bus stops for whatever perfume she's the face of. *Erica Lefroy.* World famous for her perfect face, her cheekbones, her eyes... all of which are seared into my mind. If our friendship ever went south, I'd be haunted by visions of her face.

She doesn't even look my way. Not that I'd expect her to. She's a professional, her gaze fixed on the mid-distance. She begins the walk, all toned legs, high heels, and shimmering tulle skirt, so short it's barely there at all. Everyone in the room is looking at her; the other models become completely inconsequential because Erica's presence takes up every ounce of space. She might think she's channelling grace, elegance, and purity, but there's a lot more going on. Each step emanates feminine power as she strides down the runway in time to the music like some otherworldly beauty who's deigned to visit the lowly humans, only to take up residence as their queen.

Erica Lefroy.

The one woman I can't have, and the only one I truly want.

4

ERICA

The runway never ceases to get my adrenaline going; the thumping music and bright lights; the audience's rapt energy tingling over my skin like magic.

Seb is sitting in the front row. I can't look, but I sense his presence like the pull of a magnet I have to resist.

Is he paying attention, or is he flirting with someone else? Is he watchin—

Snap.

Almost inaudible over the music, the crack jars up my leg. It happens in a split second, my brain struggling to catch up. *Is that my foot or the shoe?*

My ankle twists and my knee buckles. Pain surges through me, panic wrenching at my chest.

My arms fly out to break my fall, but I'm going sideways, not forward.

A piece of the twisted heel skitters across the runway as my body slams to the ground.

Pain splices my hip, but it's not nearly as bad as whatever has happened to my ankle.

I can't look up. *Can I hear gasps?* I don't want to see the faces in the audience staring at me. I can't move; my ankle is agony. *Could I have broken it? Is that possible?*

A clammy sweat breaks out over my body, and the harsh thump of the music resonates through my bones as though I'm lying on top of a speaker.

The model behind me is approaching, which means I've only been down here a second or two. She'll likely walk around me. Or over me. I'm roadkill. Runway kill. *Shit.* I'm out of time, out of rhythm. I'm messing it all up. I try to stand, but my ankle gives in. I can't walk. Panic roams through my mind like it owns the place.

Will I have to crawl back? Maybe I could roll off the raised runway and hide out of sight until it's over. But I can't do that. I have to finish the walk.

A figure lunges from the seats, his hands slamming onto the runway before he hauls himself up. It's impressive, how limber he is. How easy it is for him to push up here in his suit. The watch on his wrist. *The watch?* I hone in on him through the pain. I'd recognise those hands anywhere. Gorgeous, masculine hands...

Seb crouches beside me and his concerned eyes meet mine. I'd love nothing but to throw my arms around him, but we're already making a scene. Ruining the show. Dominic will be furious. Seb reads my face for a second, maybe two, then nods, realising I won't abandon the runway.

"I didn't mean *literally* break a leg," he hisses.

I try to smile, but it warps into a grimace as pain lances through my ankle and up my leg, and Seb winces at the sight. He leans towards me, his mouth close to my ear when he whispers, "I've got you." He eases a hand around my waist and loops my arm around his neck. "Lean on me."

He helps me to my feet and lets me use him like a crutch as I steel myself to walk the rest of the show, all evidence of pain shoved down so deep that you'd never know I was suffering.

He walks the runway like he's done it a million times, looking every inch the model even with me hanging off him. In another life, he could have done this too.

When we reach the end of the runway, and we're finally hidden from view, I collapse, slumping against Seb.

"Jesus," he mutters.

Dominic runs over to us, looking Seb up and down, without so much as a glance at me. "Who designed your suit? What a shame it wasn't one of mine. That would have been perfect."

Seb looks horrified. "Perfect?" I try to communicate using only my eyes that this is how Dominic is. The clothes and the show are the number one priority. I never expect more from him.

Dominic huffs. "I'm just saying, you would look fantastic in one of my suits." He plucks at Seb's lapel. "This one is not quite—"

"Get your hands off," Seb growls, and Dominic springs back in alarm. "What the fuck were you thinking, making Erica walk in those stupid shoes?"

Dominic's lips purse and he turns to me. "Erica. Shit, darling. That was messy. Can you get up again? Can you walk?" He grabs a silk dress from the nearby railing and holds it out to me. "I need you in this in thirty seconds."

I've never missed a show or pulled out. Not once. My body revolts at the idea of abandoning a show halfway through. I try to keep the pain out of my voice as I say, "I... I'm not sure."

"What the fuck is wrong with you?" Seb accuses Dominic. "She's in pain. She's not walking again tonight. And it's your fault. It's barbaric to have women walking around on those things." Seb indicates my broken shoe.

Dominic's mouth falls open, his brow creasing. "You... you..." he stammers, hardly able to say a word in the face of Seb's fury. "You know nothing about fashion." He turns back to me, waving the dress in my face. "You need to get it on. Now."

Seb yanks the dress out of Dominic's hands. "If you don't take this fucking thing away, I'm going to tie it round your neck and hang you with it." Dominic's hands fly upwards and he reaches out for the dress, a terrorised expression on his face, but Seb isn't finished. "She could have broken a bone. Look at her." He points aggressively at my ankle, which is swelling up like a balloon.

"Seb, don't," I say through the pain, digging my fingers into his arm. His jaw clenches and he gives a little sideways jerk of the chin as though he's mentally telling himself to settle. He shoves the dress back at Dominic, the silk now all crumpled.

Marni appears with a bottle of water and painkillers. She helps me take two and then produces a plastic bag full of ice for my ankle.

"Erica, Erica," Dominic frets. "The show must go on. It has to be you. The show *is* you. You and me, Erica. What can we do? Can we get a shot? Some painkillers injected right in there? Steroids? Someone?"

"Shut the fuck up," Seb says. "She's done. She's not going back out."

Dominic presses his lips together, furious, as he surveys me. Then he lets out a breath and turns to Seb, fingers steepled. "If you still want to buy my coll—"

"I don't want to buy your fucking collection," Seb says through gritted teeth. "I want to make sure Erica is okay. If you aren't going to help me, fuck off."

Dominic backs away, half-cowering. Once he's put some distance between him and Seb, he starts barking orders, redistributing my outfits to other models, and making sure the rest of the show isn't a second out of time.

"You fashion people are nuts," Seb mutters, making me laugh, even through the pain. "It's too noisy here." Before I know it, he's lifted me in his arms, using his body to shield my ankle as he pushes through the other models and staff.

"What are you doing?" I murmur, surprised at how strong he is. He's not built like a gym monkey. He's limber like a tennis player.

"Taking you somewhere that arsehole of a designer isn't going to find you and drag you back out again. The bastard will have you hobbling out there with a gun to your head otherwise. Where's quiet?"

I nod at a doorway that leads to a quiet preparation room in the back. No one will be there now.

Seb strides that way. An inconvenient fizz of *something* bubbles through my core, and I find myself bracing, as though tensing every muscle might ward the sensation off. *Friends. We're friends. That's it.*

"You okay?" he says with concern. "Relax."

I nod, obeying his command and softening in his hold. I could stay right here all night. He pushes through the door and lets it swing closed behind us, shutting out the noise. Carrying me to a seat, he settles me in it, then kneels at my feet, unstrapping the shoe and wrapping my ankle with the ice. His touch is gentle, reverent. A shiver runs up my spine, making itself known through the discomfort. *It's the ice. Just the ice.*

I stare down at the top of Seb's bowed head. His hair is so thick that the glimpse of exposed scalp in the parting feels like a secret I shouldn't be witnessing. It's so intimate. I want to trace my finger down it, run my hands through his hair, and tip his face up to look at me.

I shake the thought away. Of all the men in the world, Seb Hawkston is not the one to be having these thoughts about. "You climbed on the runway. You ruined Dominic's show," I whisper.

"Ruined it?" Seb says, sounding amazed. "This will be all anyone can talk about. Dominic's collection is made."

I let out a husky laugh. "You might be right."

He glances up at me, and the sight of him steals my next breath. Those blue eyes, so full of life, his smile, his lips, his jaw... he's like a movie star, and coming from me, who spends my working life with some of the best-looking people in the world, the compliment is a serious one. But unlike those of us whose career depends on their looks, Seb is casual about his face. It just *is*. It's as though his good looks hold no weight for him at all, and that's incredibly appealing. To me, that sounds like freedom...

"How does it feel?" he asks, laying a gentle hand over the top of my foot, holding the ice to the ankle with his other hand.

I try to rotate my foot, but a fierce hit of pain strikes and I suck in a gasp. "Not good. But I think it's just a sprain."

Seb makes a low *hmming* sound as his hand rests on my foot. His touch is feather-light. A caress that's of absolutely no therapeutic use. I should tell him to stop. *I should.* This is definitely crossing some line. *Do friends do this?* This feels more than friendly.

His fingers continue up the front of my foot. It's not providing relief, but it *is* soothing. I shouldn't be letting him do it. Should put a stop to it. It feels like a strange type of foreplay, and given the tingles that are spreading up my legs leaving fields of goosebumps in their wake, my body is convinced we're doing something here too.

Can he see those goosebumps on my legs? I hope not. I need to put a stop to this. Say something to shift the silence away from my skin and his hands... and the way my body is responding to his touch.

"I saw you out there," I say. "With those women."

He stops, lifting his hand away. *Phew.* "Women?"

"On your row."

He doesn't look up, his eyebrows drawing together. "I didn't know you were watching."

My heart clenches. *Damn.* Maybe I shouldn't have admitted to that. He looks up at me and I give a little shrug, at which the tension in his brow eases. "There are always so many women," I murmur.

Seb is quiet before he offers me a smile that looks forced at first, but then eases into his usual charming grin. "You wanna go out with me instead? Just say the word and I'm all yours. I'll quit them all."

Unsurprisingly for Seb, his tone is jocular, but I take a sharp intake of breath anyway, feigning shock. It's our usual dance around the topic. "You're incorrigible."

"I'm serious," he says, and this time it gives me pause because it sounds like he means it. I scan his face, but I don't see the joke there either, and the lack of it makes every feature on his sculpted face look different... harsher, but even more handsome. But there's no way Seb would ask me out. Not seriously. Not after all these years. If he did, what would I say?

I refuse to think too hard about it, but if he's going to sound serious, I will too. "I'm not going to finally agree to go out with you just because you hauled me and my broken shoe off the runway."

He pulls back, the furrow between his brows reappearing. "Why not?"

"Come on, Seb. You know we'd never work."

A slight huff escapes between his parted lips, and the sound seems to suggest that he expected exactly that response from me. He drags another chair towards us and rests my leg on it. When he's sure I'm comfortable, he crouches at my feet again. "Do I?"

I swipe a hand in his direction, a playful thwack that he avoids by ducking and making a show of pretending he thought I really meant to hit him. *That's more like it.* "Yes. Have you ever had a female friend you haven't tried to sleep with?"

"Apart from you?"

"Yeah. Apart from me. And given you just asked me out, I'm not sure I count."

"There's a difference between a date and sex, Lefroy."

"Come on. Really. Do you have any female friends you haven't had sex with?"

He ponders this, and the silence feels heavy. I'm more invested in his answer than I should be. "Amy Moritz," he says finally.

Thank goodness. The relief that floods me is intense. If he'd had sex with Amy, one of my closest friends, I don't know how I'd feel. It's not as though I have any claim on Seb. I've never even kissed him. But if he and Amy... *Oh.* It would be awful, and I'd rather not know, but at the same time, I need to check. "I heard a rumour that you had a threesome with her and her backup dancer."

Seb guffaws. "Did Amy tell you that?"

"God, no." The answer comes far too quickly, and Seb's gaze sharpens. It's totally reasonable for him to assume Amy's my source. But Amy never mentioned it, and I never asked her. If it hadn't been Seb, if the rumour had been about someone else—*anyone* else—I would have asked her outright. But the memory of the gut-wrench that happened when I heard the story... *horrid.* Seb, my best guy friend, and Amy, my best girlfriend? No. I couldn't have asked her. "I'm asking you."

He looks at me that way he does, as though he's seeing all my thoughts and feelings at once, and my skin prickles. "I did not have sex with them." He sounds uncomfortable, making me feel bad for dragging the information from him. But then he licks his lips, and says, "I watched."

I splutter. "You watched Amy and her backup dancer have sex?"

He lifts a shoulder, signifying that it's no big deal, while I try not to reveal the gut-wrench that's suddenly back with a vengeance. "I did. I smoked a cigar in the corner of the room while they got it on. And in my defence, I was there first, having a quiet smoke. They came in all drunk and excitable, and I just... stayed. I mean, I made my presence known, but they didn't care, and I was too drunk to move. I'm not sure I could have got out of my chair even if they had told me to leave. So yes, I do have a female friend I haven't tried to sleep with."

I hinge at the hips, tilting towards him. "Veto. I veto that example. It doesn't count. Maybe you didn't have sex *with* her, but you were in the room while she was... I mean... when they... did you..." I fade off. *What am I doing?* I can't ask him if he enjoyed watching my best friend have sex. It's too messed up. *How did this conversation take such a lewd turn?* For all the hours we've spent together, this feels like the closest I've ever come to admitting that *maybe* he affects me. Maybe I'm interested in who he has sex with. Maybe, I care. Maybe, when we hang out, when we're being 'friends', my body suffers an onslaught of chemical and biological confusion. Hormonal urges I can't control.

Maybe that stuff is true.

He's watching me so closely, as if he's reading every shifting emotion on my face, that a rush of heat attacks me. *Okay, fine.* There's no maybe about it. I have an enormous crush on my guy friend. My guy friend who's dated more women than I have pairs of shoes. And I have a *lot* of shoes.

I'm definitely attracted to him, and he's so perceptive, so tuned in, that I'm sure he knows. Or at least suspects. If he took a moment to wonder why I'm asking... why I care... I couldn't bear it if he thought I *actually* liked him. It would ruin everything. How could we continue being friends? And what about Mum and my career?

He smirks, and that irresistible dimple deepens in his cheek. "Are you blushing?"

Instantly, the heat rises even more intensely to my face. He starts to laugh, but when it eases, he says, "I'll tell you this much. It's hard to be in the same room as people who are having sex, and not get turned on. Damn near impossible."

"Oh," I say, my voice so weak it's pitiful.

Awkwardness seeps into the air like a gas leak, and Seb's eyes dip as he clears his throat. "What are you doing later?"

I lean forward and poke his shoulder. *Friendly.* "Are you asking me out again?"

"I wasn't, but I could." *Thump, thump goes my heart.* "Would you like that?"

I let out a shrill laugh that sounds forced and makes him frown. "Not today." I gesture to my ankle, rapidly trying to divert the conversation from wherever it hadn't quite gone. "You'd have to carry me. But seeing as I'm unexpectedly free tonight, you can come home with me and watch a movie. Get a takeout? An Erica and Seb night on the sofa."

The smile that splits his mouth is so delicious, I have to rein in the crazy urge to bite it right off his face. "That sounds better than any date. I'll call my driver."

5
SEB

Erica's flat is huge. A great big pad in Vauxhall, with an enormous balcony that looks over the river. I've been here before, many times. This is where I first met her; at the party I begged Nico to take me to. I was determined to meet Erica Lefroy in person, even if I had to sell my left bollock to do it.

Occasionally, she still throws glamorous parties here where everyone gets drunk and makes out on the balcony as the sun sets. Everyone apart from Erica, that is. She doesn't drink, and I've never known her to date anyone beyond whoever makes sense for her PR at the time, and even then, it's normally a couple of dates and never more. Thank God for that, because having to stand by and watch Erica seriously date someone else, pretending to be happy for her... I don't think I could do it.

The fact that I've never had to gives me the tiniest flicker of hope that maybe... *maybe*—

Ding.

The lift signals that we've reached her floor. She's leaning almost all her weight on me, not putting any pressure on her bad foot at all.

"Let's go," she says, hopping on one foot to leave the lift.

"Oh no, you don't." Before she can object, I scoop her up in my arms and carry her down the corridor.

"Oof. Are you going to carry me everywhere today?"

"If you'll let me."

I take a few more steps, but I've already carried her a lot today and this corridor is long. The urge to forcibly exhale creeps up on me, but I hold those fuckers in. *I will not pant.*

"You sound like you're straining."

"I'm not," I reply through gritted teeth.

She sighs. "I get it. I'm tall. I'm heavy. You can put me down."

Absolutely not. "You," I say, summoning a burst of Herculean strength as I hike her up and over my shoulder in a movement so smooth it would make the London Fire Brigade jealous, "are perfect." Making sure there's no danger of hurting her ankle, I secure her in place with one forearm over her thighs, the upper half of her body hanging down my back. "I could do this all day."

She squeals, her hands thumping against my shoulder blades. "Oh, my God. Put me down."

"Nope." I take the last few strides towards her front door. "I'm carrying you over the threshold." I chuckle at the bad married couple joke, but Erica doesn't laugh. *Awkward.* "Where are your keys?"

I take another step and a huffing pant escapes me. *Nearly there.*

Erica prods my lats. "Are these muscles just for show, big guy?"

I deliberately jerk her against my shoulder, and she puffs like it shunted air from her lungs. "Fuck off, Lefroy. My muscles are decorative *and* functional. Where are the keys?"

"Pocket," she says, shifting awkwardly against my shoulder.

I hold her tighter. "Which pocket?"

"Put me down, I'll get them."

"Nuh-uh." Trying to avoid grabbing her arse, I shift my free hand on her hip until I hear the jangle of her keys, hidden in a pocket of her grey tracksuit bottoms. I tap them with one finger. "I'm going in. Any objections? Speak now or forever hold your peace."

Ah, fuck. Stop dropping wedding shit into normal conversation. If I don't watch it, I'll start accidentally humming the wedding march.

"You are so bad," she says on a laugh. "Do not put your hand in my pocket."

I try and slide a finger in, but given how she's pinned against my shoulder, it's impossible to gain access. "Fuck. I gotta put you down after all."

"Damn," she laments, thumping my back one more time. "I'm just starting to get comfy up here."

"Shit, really?" I spin and start walking back the way we came. "Because I can keep going."

She giggles. "Stop, Seb. Put me down. I get it. You're very big and very strong. Big man Seb can carry woman all day."

"And?" I say, prompting her for more.

"And you're my best friend in the whole world."

My grin splits wide. "Good girl." Turning back to her door, I set her gently on her feet and she offers me the beautiful smile she rarely reveals in public. We must look crazy, standing here grinning at one another. She laughs, I laugh, and *fuck* I love this woman. "Really wanted to carry you over that threshold though."

Her eyes gleam a little. "Oh, yeah? Why?"

I ruffle a hand in my hair, and that strange, awkward feeling washes over me again. The silence stretches a bit too long before I answer. "Because I'll probably never get married, so this is as close as I'll ever get."

Erica frowns, takes the keys from me, unlocks her front door, and pushes it open. "Why do you think you won't get married?"

Because you'll never have me. "Because then I'd have to give up all the women."

"You wouldn't be giving them all up. You'd be choosing the one you want the most. The one you love."

The silence feels potent, and she looks away as though I've just stripped naked in the middle of the hallway and she doesn't want to see. I wish I knew what she was thinking. Sometimes it feels like she's trying to tell me something. Other times, I'm convinced I'm delusional. "Pfft. Sure," I say to dismiss the sentiment that's clogging my airways.

She grips the doorframe with one hand and hops into the flat, and I edge under her arm so she can lean on me again.

She winces. "Thanks."

I kick the door closed behind us and walk her over to the sofa, lowering her gently so she can sit, and then I pull over a stool so she can prop up her sore ankle. "Can I get you anything?"

"No." She takes off her baseball cap, and all that long, dark hair falls out. She shakes it like a mane, releasing a wave of scent, and then scoops it all up and ties it back. My body tingles watching her do it, but Erica is oblivious as she pats the sofa next to her. "Just sit with me."

I flop down, all too ready to relax, even though I'm still wearing a full suit. I undo my tie and top button, take off my jacket, and sling it over the back of the sofa before I kick my feet up on the stool next to hers. I pull my tie free from my collar and toss it nearby. *Casual.* I hope she can't tell I'm not nearly as relaxed as I'm pretending to be. I love hanging out with Erica, but there's an edge to it. A simmering energetic *frisson.* Maybe it's me. Maybe I'm broken. Maybe I really can't just be friends with women. But friendship is all I'm getting from Erica, so I'll damn well try and do it.

I grab the remote from where it's next to me on the sofa and point it at the huge TV, but before I turn it on, I say, "Have you heard back about that movie you auditioned for? Are we gonna be sitting here watching you on screen someday soon?"

She looks down at her hands, wringing them in her lap. "I didn't get that one."

I place one hand over the anxious movement of hers, and she looks up at me. "You really wanted it, huh?"

She pins her bottom lip with her teeth and looks down at where my hand rests on hers. "There's a role I want even more."

"Oh, yeah?"

She nods. "You know that *Taming the Beast* book?"

I only know it vaguely. A big bestseller, apparently. "Yeah?"

"The role of Vanessa. I think I might be in with a chance because they've been fan-casting me for it on social media for ages. The auditions are coming up soon, and I *really* want it."

There's a depth to her answer, and it feels heavy with emotion I'm not ready to pick up. I thread my fingers between hers, not missing the tiny catch in her breathing as she watches me do it. *Fuck it.* Now I'm sitting here, stuck to her side, my fingers tangled up with hers, having to pretend I didn't just notice the way her chest shifted when she did that tiny gasp. But I can't ignore it because the one little intake of breath set my whole body aflame and I am roaring with heat. I let go of her hand like she burnt it. Her brows flex, but she makes no comment.

Is there something going on here, or am I stuck in some awful delusional limbo-land where I'm so desperate for a sign that she might like me too that I'm making stuff up? Yeah. That must be it. *Fuck's sake, Seb. Keep your head screwed on.*

My dick gives a tiny throb.

Not that head.

I nudge Erica with my elbow. That seems *safer* than actually holding her hand. I keep my voice light when I say, "Then you'll get it. When has Erica Lefroy not got exactly what she wants?" She smiles and, as though to prove I really am super casual and can handle anything she might throw at me, I add, "Just promise you'll take me up the red carpet if you don't have a real date."

Her big eyes flick up to mine beneath the heavily made-up lids and long, black lashes, and there's a seriousness there that I glimpse for a second before her lips tug up at the corner. "I'll put you on the waitlist," she teases.

I chuckle and before I think it through, the words pop out like a reflex. "Treat them mean, eh?" She flinches and I imagine she's doing exactly what I'm doing: filling in the rest of the catchphrase. *Keep them keen.*

I swallow, awkward *again* on account of the way her expression shifted. *Is it just me, or is there extra tension today?* I point the remote at the TV again with my other hand. "What are we watching?"

"I don't mind. You choose." Erica nuzzles into me, resting her head on my shoulder, and I can hardly breathe. *She is my friend. Friend. Friend.*

But being friends with someone is not supposed to be this damn hard, is it? If she were anyone else, this would be nothing. Fuck, anyone else could get naked and ride me all night, and I'd barely bat an eyelid. But Erica Lefroy, sitting next to me on the sofa and resting her head on my shoulder, confuses the fuck out of me.

I pretend to give the choice serious consideration before I announce, "Porn, it is."

She slaps me gently, and her head shifts against my shoulder as she laughs. "Incorrigible. That's what they'll write on your gravestone. Here lies the Incorrigible Sebastian Hawkston."

"Tomb. My tomb. We have a Hawkston family tomb." Erica snorts and I correct, "Actually, it's more like a mausoleum."

She slides the remote out of my hand. "Your family is ridiculous," she says, as she clicks the TV on.

We settle on a movie, and I try my best to focus on the screen, not the woman next to me, despite the fact I'm half hard because she's so close to me.

After forty-five minutes, my phone buzzes in my jacket pocket. I ignore it. But it goes off again, and again; an influx of messages disrupting this moment with Erica.

She sits up, shifting her body away from mine and pointing the remote at the TV to pause it. "Can you get that? Someone obviously wants to get hold of you."

I grab my jacket and pull the phone from my pocket, unlocking it. I click to the messages and when I open them, a selfie of a naked woman appears. I click the screen off, turning it dark before I even have a chance to work out who it is. My heart is racing, and beside me, Erica has gone very still.

"Do you need to answer it?" she asks, her voice quiet.

"No." I put my phone face down on the coffee table, where it sits like a landmine. *One wrong step and that fucker's going to explode.* "Let's keep watching."

"Who was it?" Erica asks, nodding at the phone.

"I... I'm not sure."

My phone buzzes again. *Now? Really?*

"Whoever they are, they really want your attention." Erica leans forward to grab the phone and hands it to me. "Just deal with it."

The phone starts to ring. *Unknown number.* Erica raises her brows, nodding at it.

Okay. Fine. I swipe to answer. "Seb Hawkston speaking."

"Seb. Where are you?" comes a woman's voice I don't recognise. "I'm here. Waiting. In the hotel. Room 346. You're late. Are you coming? There's champagne on ice."

Erica is inspecting her nails, but I know she can hear every word of this woman's verbal onslaught.

I push off the sofa, pacing away from her. "Who is this?" I whisper into the phone.

A giggle comes down the line. "Who is this?" she mimics. "How rude." She doesn't sound remotely affronted. "It's Emerald, from the other night." I say nothing, having no idea which 'other night' she's referring to. It could be any number of 'other nights', and she could be any number of women. "At Martini Gems?"

Oh, right. One of the women in the photo that Nico took objection to. I had no idea her name was Emerald.

"I'm staying at the hotel," Emerald continues. "The Hawkston Mayfair. I told you when we met, and you said you'd swing by my room tonight. I've been waiting for half an hour... did you get my pictures?"

"Yes," I hiss, sounding as angry as I would if she'd just shat on my doorstep. "I got them."

"Good. So... are you coming?"

I glance over at Erica again. She's watching me, so I quickly turn away to prevent her lip-reading. "No. I'm busy tonight. I'll cover the cost of your room. Feel free to enjoy it with someone else." I hang up and make my way back to the sofa, but Erica doesn't lift the remote to play the movie.

"You're supposed to be on a date, aren't you?" she says, her voice tinged with annoyance, and the question makes me halt.

"I wouldn't call it a date."

"A hook-up? A booty call?" Her annoyed tone only increases, eyebrows rising with it. "Is there a naked woman waiting for you in a hotel room somewhere?"

I take a step back. "How much of my conversation did you hear?"

Fuck, I all but confirmed it.

Erica sighs, lowering her head and running a hand over the back of it before she points at the door. "Go on. Go."

I raise both palms like she has me under fire. "What? No. It's not important." I let my hands fall. "I'd rather stay with you."

Erica's narrowed eyes latch onto mine. "I don't want you here if you're supposed to be elsewhere. You can't leave her hanging like that. And I don't want to sit here with you, knowing that some woman is waiting in a hotel room for you to show up. And that maybe you'd prefer to be having sex with her than sitting here with me."

I rub a hand over my jaw as I stare down at Erica's impossibly beautiful face. I'd rather sit beside her all night, *every night*, than go and find Emerald-whatever-her-name-is back at the Hawkston. "I have no memory of arranging anything with her. I don't even know her full name."

Erica's face scrunches, telling me that this is absolutely the wrong thing to say. "Maybe you should go and find out then," she snaps.

"Erica... come on, don't—"

"I'm serious. I really don't want you here if you're standing someone else up. Please. Just go."

"What about your ankle?"

"I'll be fine. Please." She flicks the back of her hand at the door. "Go have sex. I know you want to."

At the sound of her condescending, slightly repulsed tone, I straighten, puffing out my chest. But beneath the instant defense mechanism, I'm aware of an unpleasant sensation, like my blood has turned to sludge. "Why are you saying that like it's disgusting? Like me wanting sex might be disgusting?"

"I'm not."

"You are. Why are you being so weird about this? It's just sex. It's human. Everyone does it. It's like wanking—"

She covers her face with her hands and lets out a groan. "Gross. Can you just go? Please?"

I hesitate, then point at the door. "Do you *want* me to go and meet her?"

She crosses her arms over her chest, and when she speaks, her voice is devoid of emotion. "I don't care what you do, but I don't want to sit here knowing you have a hard-on because a woman in a hotel room is sending you naked photos."

Fuck's sake. "I don't have a hard-on." I gesture at my decidedly not-hard dick. Except... it kind of is a bit hard, like it knows Erica's talking about it, and now *staring* at it, and it wants to say hello. *For fuck's sake.*

Erica's gaze shifts to my crotch, where there is an unmissable bulge, and her eyes widen. "Get out."

Fuck this shit. I shove a hand in my pocket and adjust things down there. "That's not what you think it is."

"Oh, no? You got a sock down there? Or is it just your big fat wallet?" she says with cruel derision.

I press my palm to my forehead. "Erica—"

"Out. I am completely serious. I don't want you here right now." She nods at my crotch again. "Not like that."

Shit. This can't be how tonight ends, with me looking like a sex pest with no self-control, and her rejecting me for a misplaced semi, which is absolutely all for her.

I wait for her to say something else, but all she does is give me an ice-cold glare. I assess her for a few seconds, but her expression is hard. She's made up her mind. I snatch my jacket off the back of the sofa and shrug into it, and when I look back at her, she's studiously avoiding eye contact.

Fine. If that's how she wants to play this. "Have a good evening," I throw out. "I know I will." I have no intention of going to find Emerald, but if Erica thinks that's where I'm going, then so be it. Without another glance in her direction, I pace to the door, my shoes slamming on the tiles like the repeated crack of an air rifle.

I resist the urge to slam the door on the way out, but once I'm in the hallway, all I can think is that there is no way I can ever explain to Erica what happened tonight without admitting that I really, *really* like her.

And I'm a fucking idiot for ever sleeping with anyone else.

6
ERICA

The door closes, and I sit in a stupor for a second, hoping against hope that Seb will come back. Any second now, he'll knock on the door and walk in again.

The longer I sit there, the clearer it becomes that he isn't coming back. He's gone to the hotel. To the woman with the naked photos. I pushed him out. I sent him straight into her arms.

Good riddance. How dare he come and sit on my sofa and pretend to give a shit about me, when he's half hard because of some woman in a hotel room?

But I can't convince myself I actually feel angry when I don't. I'm devastated that he couldn't have concentrated on me for one evening. That I couldn't have been enough for him, just this once.

But I'll never be enough for Seb Hawkston. Not when he has women throwing themselves at him like that, and he's not shy about taking them up on what they offer. And me? What can I offer? If he got his dick out, I wouldn't know what to do with it.

A horrible urge to cry cramps my throat and it has nothing to do with the ache of my sprained ankle.

I pull out my phone and put his name into the search bar. It's a stupid thing to do, and yet I can't stop. Picture after picture comes up of him with different women. Sometimes two of them, sometimes three. A gaggle. And he always looks so happy… like he hasn't a care in the world. That handsome smile and his little dimple…

The ache in my chest increases, and my breathing hitches. I type in Erica Lefroy and Sebastian Hawkston, and a bunch of pictures of him carrying me down the runway pop up. I quickly scroll past them, but what remains is sparse. There are hardly any pictures of us together. Of course there aren't, because I made sure there weren't. When we hang out, it's in private. At his place. At mine. Seb Hawkston, lothario, Casanova, ultimate player, does not look good with Erica Lefroy, and I tend to my reputation so carefully. If he knew how deliberately I avoid being seen with him, I'm sure he'd be devastated.

Sure, we meet at parties and public events, but when it's just the two of us, I've always made sure it's private. I had to, to keep my mother off my back. I'd rather spend my time with Seb than anyone else, but now, looking at him and all the women, I know I was right to do it.

Erica Lefroy, the UK's top model and soon-to-be movie star, is not one of those women. She could never be one of them, casually hanging out with Seb Hawkston, his arm slung around her shoulders, laughing as they leave a club together. She doesn't do *that*. And she certainly doesn't get romantically involved with men like Seb Hawkston.

But she is me, and I am her.

So why the hell do I feel like I want to wrap my hands about her neck and throttle her until she dies?

I wipe my eyes with the heel of my hand. *Crap.* I have *actual* tears. Maybe it's the disastrous fashion show. The ankle. Dominic being so disappointed in me.

It's all too much.

But it's okay. My ankle will heal and I can make this right with Seb. If he's off having sex, which he almost always is, then that's his business. It shouldn't bother me. I'm not that judgmental. *Am I?*

Why are you saying that like it's disgusting? Like me having sex is disgusting?

Argh. He was right. I said it with utter disdain. I don't even know why I sounded that way. Is it because I don't want him to be out sleeping with people? Or maybe it's just that I feel so trapped by this whole persona I've created that I don't even know how *I* feel versus how *Erica Lefroy* feels?

I smash my hand into the cushion next to me, letting out a strained, frustrated sound that ravages my throat. At this rate, I'm going to splinter my soul into pieces that I'll never be able to put back together again.

Maybe I should call him. Tell him I'm sorry. I scroll to his number, letting my finger hover over his name.

He's probably there by now. At the hotel. In her room. Touching her. Kissing her... getting undressed...

Fucking her.

A distressed whine leaks from my lips. I can't call him. What would I say?

Agony tears through me, and I curl over my chest, clutching my phone. This is my fault. *I'd rather stay here with you.* He said as much and I still forced him out.

If he spends the night with her, it'll be because I all but gave him my blessing.

Regret doesn't even begin to cover it. I feel so pathetic, sitting here alone in my tracksuit, ankle throbbing. I try to remind myself of *Erica Lefroy* and all she's achieved. *Be grateful, be grateful, be grateful.* My dreams have come true one by one, toppling like dominoes as Mum and I ticked them off the list. *Be grateful.*

But I don't feel grateful. I feel trapped.

My phone buzzes, and my heart shoots against my ribs like it's on a G-force rollercoaster. *It's him. It's going to be okay.*

But my leaping heart crash lands when I see a message from Amy flash on the screen.

Amy: You okay? I'd come and check on you myself, but I'm flying back to the States tonight.

Me: I'm okay. Thanks.

Amy: Saw Seb rescue you. That man is sex on legs. And he clearly adores you. Tell me again why you aren't screwing his brains out already? I bet he'd know just how to give a lady a good time.

My gut ties itself in knots at the sight of his name on my screen. I can't escape him. And in this context? The worst. Because she's right. He *would* know. He's probably doing it right now.

Amy: My advice? Bang him bang him bang him. ASAP.

I let out a groan. I wish she wouldn't talk like this, especially seeing as now I know he's been in the same room with her while she's been banging someone else. She's always been more sexually free than me, and she's fascinated by the fact I'm not out there having sex. She lost her virginity on a one night stand when she was drunk at a party ten years ago. *Fifteen.* So young. I can't judge her though. I very nearly did exactly the same. The only reason it didn't happen was because the guy didn't have a condom, and he cared more about himself than I did about me. I'd have let him fuck me bare my first time and hardly have remembered it. I don't think I even knew his name. I didn't give a fuck about anything apart from escaping Mum's strict rules.

The next morning, I woke up in my bed at home, stinking of booze, makeup smeared down my face, suffering the hangover from hell, all of which were made a million times worse by the fact that Mum was sitting on the end of the bed, watching me. And boy, was she furious that I'd snuck out. Even back then, she was adamant that any action I took could come back to bite me on the arse when I got famous, which was absolutely, *definitely*, going to happen. *Erica Lefroy* was a brand before anyone ever knew her name.

After that night, Mum controlled every aspect of my life, including who I dated, with an even firmer grip.

Me: He's my friend. Friends don't do that.

Typing the words and sending the message makes me ache, and I don't know why, but Amy's response only makes it worse.

Amy: Friends could do that.

Me: Not me.

She sends a succession of laughing-so-hard-they're-crying face emojis.

Amy: Of course not you. ROFL. Ice Queen. It's probably best you don't, because if you did the deed, your mum would crawl in there and sew your hymen back together.

Me: That's disgusting.

Amy: You know it's true.

Me: It's not.

Amy: It is. Erica Lefroy doesn't have sex. No man is worthy of such perfection. Mummy's guarding the entrance.

I scrape a hand over my forehead. This Ice Queen nickname has been haunting me in the press lately. It's like the whole purity thing went too far, and rather than pure and chaste, they think I'm aloof and frosty. I might need to take action if it's spread so far that even Amy is using it.

I sit there staring at my phone for a few minutes before another message pings in.

Amy: You there? I'm kidding. Chill out. But I do think sex would be good for you. Loosen you up a bit. MELT YOU! Hahahaha.

Oh, for fuck's sake. She thinks she's so damn funny. It's annoying, but I smile anyway because I love her. I still don't know how to respond though.

Amy: Are you angry with me?

Me: No. But you're a pain in the arse.

*Amy. *Blowing-kiss-emoji* Love you.*

I'm about to respond in kind when the sound of keys click in the lock of my front door. And there is only one other person who has keys to my apartment.

Shit.

7

ERICA

Mum is the last person I want to see because I know she'll have something to say about my fall on the runway today. Steeling myself for an inevitable attack, I tie my hair up and hobble towards the door, but before I get there, Mum swings into the apartment like she owns it. *I really need to get those keys off her.* Maybe change the locks. I'm a twenty-five-year-old woman whose mother has keys to her flat. Sometimes I hate myself for how pathetic this picture is. Sure, on the outside it looks great. I'm a multimillionaire model and part owner of a cosmetics and luxury fashion company. But beneath the surface... it's fucked as all hell.

"I thought you were sick?" I ask.

She casts me a fluttering eye roll. "I miraculously recovered when I remembered how you mess up when I'm not there." Sarcasm drips from her tone. No matter how old I get, or how much money I make, comments like that always sting. "We need to talk about these photos of you today. I'm seeing them all over my feed." She stills, tapping a finger to her lips as she ponders my face. I restrain the urge to look away. "At least you weren't smiling. Thank God for that. I can't fathom how it contorts your features. So peculiar." Shaking her head, she blinks and shifts into business mode, scrolling on her phone, barely looking at me as she walks past. Each click of her heels is a wordless reprimand that has me bracing. She's wearing a long black dress beneath a camel overcoat, and her dark hair is blow-dried to perfection. She's the epitome of middle-aged glamour.

I close the door and lean against it. Mum glances up from her phone to do the usual sweep up and down of my attire, her gaze as disparaging as ever.

"Tracksuit. Really? I hope no one saw you in that. It's not on brand. Erica Lefroy is the face of high fashion. Glamour." She inhales through flared nostrils, turns her palms up, and glances deliberately at her attire. "Look at me. I left the house to come here, but I turned myself out properly in case anyone saw me."

Guess she's not going to ask about my ankle then.

She steps towards me and teases down some strands of hair from my untidy up-do, assessing the effect, but a moment later she throws her hands in the air and lets out an exasperated sigh. "You shouldn't wear your hair up unless you really have to. Your ears are very prominent. Your father's ears. Dear Lord. We should have had those pinned back."

The familiar void drops through my centre, threatening to reduce me to a heap on the floor. She's always assessed me like this. And I am *always* found wanting. I steel my spine. "My ears are fine."

"Are they? Have you considered that they might be part of the reason you keep failing to get a role in any of those movies you're auditioning for?" I wince. *Shit.* I'd tried to keep this from Mum. "Oh, yes." She jabs an accusatory finger at my face. "I know you've been going behind my back. A rejection letter came to our joint email."

"And you opened it?"

"Think you're too good for modelling, do you?" Mum continues, thrusting her chin forward.

"No, that's not it—"

"You want to try and operate without me? Ha!" The pop of brash laughter makes me retreat, and I edge back against the door. "Think you can go it alone in a new industry, do you?" I say nothing because this is exactly why I want to shift into acting. I want something that's mine, not ours. Not Mum's. A career I can build myself, and be proud of.

"Yes," I say, trying to make my voice sound strong.

"You'd fail, Erica." She tuts. "An actress? You might have the looks, but you need actual talent for that." She exhales theatrically, and a lump rises in my throat. She always knows how to hit where it hurts. "I could have been a fabulous actress. I was on the cusp of great fame when I fell pregnant with you." She turns and marches further into my apartment without looking back. "Honestly, having a child ruined my life. I sacrificed everything for you. *Everything*." She spins back to me, her eyes dark. "And look where it's got me. A daughter who falls on the runway like an amateur." It takes all my resolve not to crumble, but I remind myself I can take this criticism. It's not new. I've been handling it for years. Mum clears her throat, and the rattle of it is full of derisive laughter. "You're a laughing stock." Her voice turns cold and deadly. "And I will not have it. If you pursue this acting thing when you haven't a scrap of ability in that department, you will make things worse. Do not shame me. Promise me you'll give this insanity up."

Never. But the word sticks in my throat, wedged behind the lump. I can't force it out.

Mum's mouth puckers. "I see you mean to say no. Well, if you are so set on it, let me help you." She does another round of inspecting me, this time walking around me as though I'm on display in a shop window, and I try not to shrivel in response. "The boobs." She waves her hand at my chest. "Far too small. All right for modelling, but if you want to make it as a female lead in the movies, you need bigger breasts."

I glance down at my chest. I've never had an issue with my boobs, but under her scrutiny the lump in my throat crawls into my mouth, and the back of my nose stings.

"Tiny, aren't they?" Mum's vigorous nodding tells me she assumes I'm in agreement. "I've thought it for a long time, but I've held my tongue. And it has pained me. But now, with this movie business, you've forced my hand. I can't keep quiet. Your breasts are far too small. Not like mine."

The tiniest flicker of anger bursts through the sadness that has been creeping up on me, but when Mum arches her back so her breasts stick out, and stares down at them with as much pride as another mother might look at her newborn, the sadness snuffs it out again. *I don't think she's ever looked at me like that.*

I press a hand over my chest. "I think they're fine," I say, but my voice sounds weak.

"They don't have to be huge, darling. Just a bit bigger. I'll book a consultation. I know the perfect surgeon."

I guess that's it then. Decision made.

As if she hasn't blown in here like a hurricane and torn me apart, Mum perches on the edge of my sofa, where Seb was sitting not long ago. I wish, once again, that I hadn't sent him away. If he'd been here, he might have been able to shield me from this. She smooths her skirt with one hand, then glances up like she can feel my stare. "Aren't you going to offer me a cup of tea?"

Fuck's sake. The tiny flare of anger burns a little brighter this time. She really doesn't care about the *me* beneath the body at all.

My ankle throbs but I hop over to the kitchen and begin making tea, which I do very quickly given the boiling water tap and its proximity to the fridge for milk, but even so, every movement I make is loaded with resentment. I shuffle across with her tea, being careful not to spill it. But I do anyway.

"Erica!" She stares at the puddle of tea on the floor. "So clumsy. No wonder you tripped over today."

I grit my teeth and hand her the mug. She peers into it. "Milk?"

"Yes."

"No. Not milk. Black. I like my tea black. How could you forget?" She holds the tea out like she expects me to take it away again. "I hope you haven't been having milk in your tea. We save so many calories by not adding it. Not to mention how bad dairy is for one's skin." Her eyes flash from the milky mug to my face. "Your complexion is looking a bit off. You need to watch what you're eating."

Fuck this. I'm tired. I feel dreadful about what just happened with Seb. My ankle is sore. I want to sit down, take the weight off it—*take the weight off everything*—but I don't want to get any closer to Mum. Those claws could draw blood. I take her tea away, moving back to the kitchen island where I settle on a stool, close enough to the open plan living area that I can justify the distance I'm putting between us. I sip on the tea myself, holding eye contact with Mum the entire time. A deliberate flaunting of her rules.

Her eyes narrow, and she launches herself off the sofa. "Don't push me, young lady," she says as she snatches the mug from my hands. She pours the whole thing down the sink, then turns to face me, leaning back against the counter. "We need to do damage control."

I blink. "Now? I'm in pain. I want to rest."

"Yes, now." She purses her lips as if preparing to say something, but then her gaze flicks back to the sofa and her eyes widen. *Shit.* The end of Seb's tie is poking out from beneath a cushion, as if I tried to hide the fucking thing. Mum lunges and tugs it free, holding it up between thumb and forefinger like it's a piece of dirty lingerie. "Is this his?"

Hot pinpricks spear my skin. "I... uh..."

"Erica." Mum snaps the tie taut in both hands. "Is this Sebastian Hawkston's tie?"

"Yes," I admit.

She tosses it back on the sofa and paces back to the sink, fury flashing in her eyes. She grips the edge with one hand, letting her lids close for a second before leaning back against it and staring at me. "I've spoken to you about your friendship with him, and I do not like to be ignored. If you start to disobey my rules, all this"—she wafts a hand over me, my apartment, the room in general—"starts to fall apart. I've seen it happen before, and you are not immune. Reputations can be destroyed faster than we can build them."

A weight presses down on my lungs, and it's hard to breathe. As much as I resent Mum and the control she has over my life, my reputation is important to me. I don't want to destroy it.

"I don't have a friendship with him," I begin, hating myself for denying Seb as though he's something to be ashamed of. But he pissed me off tonight and it makes me think that Mum probably has a point. He'd never be able to commit to anyone, and to look like another woman he could easily toss aside won't do me any favours. It's all optics. At least to Mum it is, and I've been abiding by her rules so long that it's hard not to see the world that way too. "He brought me home because of my ankle." Mum's gaze darts to my foot for the first time, but there's no sympathy or concern in her expression. "We only see each other at parties. We don't—"

"He doesn't fit with the brand. You know that. *Erica Lefroy* is elegant. Sophisticated. Pure. That's your USP."

"Don't I get to be a person occasionally?" My voice wavers. "Not just a brand?"

"No." She slaps her hand on the kitchen counter, and the crack of it makes me jump. "We've worked hard on this. Don't mess it up by hanging around with that boy."

The people-pleasing part of me wants to tell her I just threw him out. The other half of me wants to staunchly defend him. I settle somewhere in between. "He's hardly a boy. He's thirty."

Mum flutters a hand as though anything I have to say is irrelevant, and Seb will always be a boy, no matter how many birthdays he has. "You shouldn't have let him help you today. Those pictures of him picking you up... it's all over social media. It'll give people the wrong idea. Like he's Prince Charming to your Cinderella." She says it with such disdain that I physically recoil. "You do not need a man to save you, Erica. Neither of us do. We're a team, you and I. Say it after me. *We do not need a man to save us. I am Erica Lefroy, and I am an independent woman. I do not need a rich man.*" The mixing of the pronouns makes me feel nauseous. *Am I a 'we' or an 'I'? Who the fuck is Erica Lefroy? Is she me or Mum?* Mum snaps her fingers in my face. "Say it."

"I am Erica Lefr—" I shake my head. "No. I don't want to say it."

Mum's face reddens, her eyes widening. If she were a cartoon, steam would be blowing out her ears. "Men only want us for sex, Erica. They're animals. Food and sex. Just like your father. Sebastian Hawkston is no different."

Nausea roils through me. I want to scream at her that she's wrong. How dare she compare Seb, who's always been such a supportive friend, to the man who walked out on us? But that's not the only way she's off the mark. Seb doesn't want me for sex. He wants some random woman in a hotel for that.

"Repeat it after me," Mum insists. "I'm an independent woman. I do not need—"

"Stop."

Mum's gasp is eons-long, and when it's run its course, she clenches her jaw before she speaks. "Tell me you're an independent woman."

I slump, shoulders rounding. "I'm not though, am I? Not when you're here telling me what to do all the time." I sound like a stroppy teenager rather than the empowered woman I was aiming for.

Mum inhales slowly and then exhales even slower. "I am looking out for you in a way that man never will. You do not need him and he will damage what we've built. I've put years of blood, sweat, and tears into this brand. Into *you*. And it's working. Our shoe line is taking off. The makeup is being stocked in major department stores up and down the country, ready for release. We're finally exactly where we need to be to blow this up. Do not jeopardise it by cavorting with Sebastian Hawkston. You cannot be associated with a man like that without there being serious financial implications for us."

Anger flares hard and fast in my chest, but I'm not in a position to fight her on this.

"By all means, once you're no longer young, or in high demand, have an affair with him, if that's what you want. But do not do it now. There is too much at stake. No one will take you seriously if you're dating someone like Sebastian Hawkston."

"Seb."

Mum's head quirks, making her look like a bird hearing a predator snap a twig in the forest. "Seb?"

"He prefers to be known as—"

"I don't care, and neither should you." She clicks her tongue against her teeth. "The only thing you should be concerned about is the launch of your new fragrance. The cosmetics line." Mum pushes herself off her resting place by the sink and comes towards me at such speed, and with such a vicious expression on her face, that I freeze. She taps my forehead with two fingers, each strike a violation that makes my body tingle with impotent rage. "That is all that should be in this vacuous head of yours right now." *One more hard tap.* "Stay focused."

My body tenses, as if I can transform my skin into armor that will fend off another attack. I can't sit here and say nothing. I've done it for far too long. "If I want to be seen with Seb, I'll be seen with him. He's not as much of a threat as you think he is. He's handsome, well-dressed, eligible—"

Mum steps back, her expression growing wary. "Do not start with me, young lady."

"It should be my choice," I say, loathing how it sounds like a desperate plea.

"If I'd left the choices to you, where would you be now? Knocked up by a teenage boy on a drunken night out, that's where." The statement winds me, pain blasting through my chest like she's actually hit me. "Mothering some bastard child in a council house, most likely. That you are anything at all is down to me and my choices. I *saved* you."

She saved me? "You're my mother." *You're supposed to love me unconditionally.*

Mum starts nodding, but in a way that tells me that I've confirmed whatever low opinion she holds of me. I should have known that throwing the idea of being a mother at her wouldn't hit. She's never been a mother. She's been a manager, a manipulator. A dictator.

"You think you're so special." She gestures to my face, my body. "Without me, you would be nothing, young lady. Nothing. You think that boy, that *Seb*, would be interested in you *at all* if you weren't *Erica Lefroy*." The air quotes she makes with her fingertips around my name are pure mockery. "World famous model?" Her laughter reaches a higher peak, becoming almost manic. "You little fool. Of course he wouldn't. He wouldn't look twice at you. No one would. You don't know how to count your blessings, you ungrateful little—"

She cuts herself off with another dramatic intake of breath, followed by a guttural groan that contains all the hatred I'm sure she feels for me. *It's fucking mutual, Mum.* "Let's stay focused. The brand. The perfume launch. The cosmetics." Her features settle into a stone wall. "Stay focused." She taps her finger on the end of my nose, and for a second I wish I were a dog so I could bite the tip of it right off. Swallow it, digest it, and shit it out at her feet. *It's what she deserves.*

"I am focused. I've always been focused. I would have been okay without you."

"Oh, darling," she says, all condescension. "I know what's best for you. For all of us. If the movies are what you want, I'll make it happen, like I always do." She tuts. "You really do need to work on that attitude of gratitude, Erica. An attitude of gratitude is a state of receivership. Resentment will get you nowhere. Be thankful for everything you have. Everything I gave to you. You should be on your knees, thanking me for sacrificing my life to achieve your success."

I bite the inside of my cheek to stop from screaming. I don't want more success. *I want to be free.* Free from the dreaded 'sacrifice' that I've worn like chains my entire life. Free from the control that Mum exerts over me. *There's no point fighting with her. I don't have it in me. This fight is bigger than me.* "Thank you, Mum," I mutter begrudgingly.

Mum smiles, seemingly satisfied with my thanks, despite it sounding as though it was dragged up from the depths of the deepest ocean like a shipwreck. "You're welcome." She arches a brow. "So, are we clear? Focus on the brand. The launch. Do not go out with or be seen with anyone who might affect your reputation. You're the face of this brand, and I am as deeply financially invested in it as I am emotionally.

And if you want this Hollywood career, then I will get it for you. First stop, breast implants. Then your body will finally match your gorgeous face, and we can take on the world."

We? She wants to take this from me too? I want to throw up. I want to destroy everything I've worked for. Take a match and burn every single photo that's ever been taken of me—*the legacy she created*—just to hurt her.

Fortunately, I have enough self-restraint and common sense to realise that fucking things up for Mum is the same as fucking everything up for me. I need this platform. This fame. This brand. I need all of it, so I can use it as a springboard to launch myself into Hollywood. Or at least as far away from my mother as I can get.

I *will* find success, and I will find it on my own this time.

8
SEB

I'm on my way to the opening of a new exhibition at the Tate Modern. Some fancy new artist. Nico owns a few of his pieces and we're sponsoring the show, but I couldn't give a fuck about it. There's only one thing on my mind tonight, and it's Erica Lefroy.

I haven't heard from her for six weeks. Radio fucking silence since the night she kicked me out. Not that I've tried to contact her—my stupid pride wouldn't let me—but it still feels like I'm being ignored because the absence of contact is a noticeable void in my life. I hadn't realised just how often I reach for my phone to share something with her. A joke. A stupid GIF. Something that someone said. Something that happened to me. A random *Good Night, Sleep Tight*, or, if I'm feeling like I want to piss her off just a little, an unacceptably early *Wakey wakey, eggs and bakey* when I leave for the gym.

I've been emotionally dependent on Erica for longer than I want to admit.

Maybe a break is a good thing. Maybe this whole 'being friends with a woman I find indescribably attractive' is bullshit anyway, and I'm kidding myself that we could ever maintain a friendship long-term.

But it's been five years, and we've somehow got this far. But I'm tired. Tired of pretending that I wouldn't prefer Erica to anyone else, and yet knowing I have no fucking chance. Tired of pretending that all I want is friendship.

Tired. Yeah. That's what I am. Tired of seeing my brothers and my friends getting together with women who adore them. Finding something serious. Finding love.

I want something that isn't completely meaningless. Something more than a vacuous physical connection with someone I hardly know.

But with Erica? I'm not foolish enough to think she'd really give me the time of day. If she can give me the silent treatment for six weeks, maybe this whole friendship doesn't mean as much to her as it does to me.

But then again, she could be thinking the same thing about me, having no idea that I've been tormented by the silence. Has it tormented her too? I have no way of knowing. A dark part of me hopes it has. Hopes she's fucking ached for me every day, but a more rational part knows she's probably been too busy to spare me a second thought.

Tonight, there's a chance I'll see her and our stalemate might break. She'll be at the event, and I'm as nervous as a teenager on a first date. Palms sweating, stomach rioting.

I have no fucking clue how to tell Erica that she's the one I want, so here I am, on my way to the event with Harriet, my date for the night, who's staring at me like I hung the goddamn moon.

As we get out of the car on the St Paul's side (I wanted to walk over the bridge to clear my head), a hint of spring warmth lingers in the air. It's unusual to have warm evenings in London in April, but this year we've been blessed with an early heatwave that makes it feel like we're in the Mediterranean. It's one of those blissful London nights where the air is full of the chatter of people out late, corporate suits spilling onto the pavement from the nearby bars. It makes me happy in a way Harriet's presence ought to, but doesn't.

"I was so glad you called," she says. "I'd been waiting to hear from you, you know, since we—"

Fucked. "Yeah. Sorry. Work was hectic." *God, I feel like a prick.* I'm not into this woman. I'm using her to soothe my bruised ego. I should tell her I'm not looking for a relationship or even a hookup, but I don't want to ruin the evening. Yet here I am, staying quiet and thinking about someone else. I hate that I'm doing this to her.

I should definitely tell her I'm not interested.

"I thought you'd forgotten about me," she adds, staring at me with those big, pitiful eyes, like I made her fucking year because I asked her out tonight.

Well, fuck. Could she have said anything worse?

I'm an arsehole. The worst type of man. But I'm fairly committed to the persona, and the flirtatious compliments are reflexive by this point in my life, so I flash a smile and watch her visibly melt. "Nope. Absolutely not. You're unforgettable." Harriet... *whatever your name is.*

"That's such a lovely thing to say," she responds as I offer her my arm and she takes it as we stride over the bridge.

I say nothing as we walk the rest of the way, the Thames churning, dull and dreary beneath us. But I fucking love it. London. The river. The Millennium Bridge. There's a power to this city that I can feel through the soles of my shoes, making my skin tingle. I ache with wishing it was Erica by my side. She's the one I want to share this moment with. Fuck it; she's the one I want to share every moment with.

The gallery looms into view, a great brick and glass building overlooking the river. My family has been sponsoring exhibitions here for years, and it's expected that I attend. My brothers, Nico and Matt, will be here too, and perhaps even my father. I know he's in London at the moment, but I haven't been to see him.

In fact, I haven't seen him since Christmas, and that's a fact I have no desire to change anytime soon.

Once we're signed in, we enter the party. We're a bit late, and the place is heaving with women in elegant evening wear and men in suits, a buzz filling the huge atrium. A waitress offers us both a glass of champagne, which we take.

"Shall we look around?" Harriet asks.

"Sure." I follow her through the crowd, searching for my brothers. Or Kate. Or Aries, Matt's fiancée. They should be here somewhere.

Harriet pauses before a huge nude of a woman sprawled on a bed, and I stand beside her sipping my drink.

"Do you buy art?" she asks.

"Sometimes."

She tilts her head at the enormous nude. "Would you buy this?"

I snort. "No. I see enough naked women in my life without needing paintings of them too."

Harriet frowns. "Oh."

Fuck, that was a dumbass thing to say. I'm completely at odds tonight. This is the first date I've been on since Erica threw me out. The same day I had my hands on her ankle. My dreams have been haunted by it. I wake in the morning trying to recover from the feel of Erica's skin under my hands, the feel of her body in my arms. She never kisses me in the dreams. I always try, but she never concedes. *My subconscious is primed for rejection.*

"Ladies and Gentlemen." A voice booms through the loudspeaker, and I turn to see the head of the gallery at a podium at the far end. "Welcome to our sponsors' drinks evening. We are so thankful to all of you, whose contribution to the running of this gallery cannot be overstated. We, and our artists, are indebted to you all. We wouldn't be here without you." Applause ripples through the building, and when it settles, he adds. "I'm here all evening, should you wish to revise your level of support."

The man smiles broadly and laughter filters through the foyer as he steps down.

A ruckus by the door draws my attention, and every part of me surges with electricity before I even turn to look. *It's her. I know it.* I concentrate on the champagne glass in my hand, the taste of the bubbles on my tongue, and Harriet at my side.

I can't stop myself from glancing over; the way Erica draws my attention is like an addiction. *I need a fix.* She's walking in on the arm of that damn designer. Dominic DeLacey. He's all puffed up, chest swelling as he greets people either side of him, acknowledging everyone who's making way for them to come inside. The arsehole probably thinks they're looking at him, but they aren't. They're looking at Erica.

Because, *fuck me*, if she isn't the most gorgeous thing I've ever seen. An emerald green silk dress cascades down her body to the floor, and her long dark hair curls over one shoulder. The dress leaves little to the imagination. It clings in all the right places... places I'd very much like to put my hands.

"She's so beautiful," Harriet murmurs, eyeing Erica with almost as much appreciation as I am. And that pisses me off because I don't want to be in the same situation as Harriet. I don't want to be swooning over Erica from afar, with no chance of getting close. I want to stake a claim on her. I'm not some random guy in a tux. I'm *something* to her, aren't I? I count, don't I?

The emotions dancing through me are confusing and unpleasant. I'm not enjoying this version of myself at all. I'm not used to wanting things I can't have. Other people might have to look on from afar, but not fucking me.

And yet here I am, an onlooker on Erica's glamorous life. An outsider. When really all I want to be is inside.

Balls deep inside.

I tip back the rest of my champagne and slam the glass down on a passing waitress's tray. Her eyes widen and she pauses to steady the glasses.

"Sorry," I murmur. I grab Harriet's hand and haul her away. "Let's find the canapes."

If I can't have Erica, maybe not being able to see her is the next best thing.

The next couple of hours pass with Harriet commenting on art, and me pretending to pay attention to her. I've introduced her to Nico and Kate, and Matt and Aries. For a while, they were all waiting for me to tie the knot with someone so I could join the happy-couple club, but that's not going to happen. They've stopped asking 'Is this the one?' when I introduce them to anyone because it never lasts longer than milk left out of the fridge.

Harriet is definitely not *the one*. But that never felt like it mattered before because the only one I wanted was off-limits, and it was easier to date other people than face the fact that Erica was never going to be mine.

But now, having Harriet dangling off my arm while Erica is on the other side of the room and we aren't speaking, it matters. Inviting a date and hoping Erica might notice, or, better yet, be jealous, is downright dirty and manipulative. And I don't want to be that guy.

Besides, Erica probably wouldn't even care. *Fuck it*. I'm tired of pretending that she isn't the only one I want, that I'm unmoved, that my sex life is progressing as normal when really it's ground to a fucking halt because she's not talking to me and the health of my friendship with her has far more influence over my life than I'd previously acknowledged.

I need to get things back on track with her.

A man's raised voice filters through the party. It's out of keeping with the happy chatter that preceded it. I'm immediately alert. I turn to see that damn designer making a scene, yelling at someone out of sight. My first thought is *Erica*.

"Excuse me," I say to Harriet, "but there's someone I need to check on." Her eyes widen, silently begging an explanation, and I restrain the urge to rush off. "I wouldn't leave if I didn't think my friend was in trouble."

She nods. "That's okay. I'll wait here."

I clench a fist, hidden at my side. She deserves the truth, so I give it her. "You don't have to wait. I've brought you here under false pretenses. I'm not available for a relationship of any kind. I'm so sorry. You deserved better than this." I bow my head, wishing I hadn't vomited the words like I'd been struggling to hold them in all night.

"Oh, Seb. I—"

Raising a hand, I cut her off with a gentle, "Please. Enjoy the rest of your evening. There's plenty more to see, but if you don't want to stay, my driver is outside. He'll take you wherever you want to go."

To her credit, she takes it well, and the tension in my shoulders loosens as I head in Dominic's direction. Not my finest moment, but at least I was honest with her.

I get a view of Erica, standing opposite the designer, looking altogether too passive for someone who's being screamed at.

"You selfish bitch, how could you do this to me?" Dominic squeals. Red-hot rage rises through me. *How dare he speak to her this way?*

Without stopping to think, I push through the crowd, but I'm still a fair distance away when Dominic throws his champagne over Erica, soaking the front of the silk dress.

"That's the last dress of mine you'll ever wear," he yells, before turning and storming towards the exit.

By the time I reach Erica, Dominic has vanished, escorted from the premises by security. She's surrounded by women attempting to comfort her, but I shove through until I'm right at the front.

"You really like to make a scene, Lefroy," I say, and she smiles before she's even looked at me. *God, that smile is something else.* I know it's all forgiven from our last encounter. We'll probably never talk about what happened when she threw me out, or why we haven't spoken. Maybe she never even fucking noticed.

Maybe all this is in my head.

"And you really like to be there when I do," she says, with a bitterness that's all pretense. It's more like a private joke, and internally I'm jumping up and down that I get to share it with her.

"I love it." I put my arm around her shoulder. She folds into me, resistance melting. She fits so perfectly under my arm that I don't know why the hell she doesn't just want to stay there. "Let's get you cleaned up." I have no clue how I'm actually going to do that, but any excuse to get Erica on her own works for me.

"You coming to the ladies' with me?" she teases.

"Aren't the bathrooms all gender neutral in these places now? So yes, I'm coming with you."

"I'm okay." She tugs at her dress. "It'll be dry in a moment. Stained, but dry. Let's go get another drink instead."

There's no way I'm letting her wriggle out of a moment alone with me. "I'd rather you were comfortable first."

"I am comfortable."

I draw back to peer at her. "You're not upset? That madman was screaming at you."

She rolls her eyes. "Oh, no. That's just Dominic. It's his way. It's annoying because it doesn't do much for my brand." I'm the one restraining my eye roll now. *Her bloody brand.* "But I was expecting it, to be honest. I should have told him in private."

"Told him what?"

"That I'm quitting modelling. I had to work up to it because I knew exactly how he'd take it." She glances at the stain on her dress. "I thought telling him in public might keep him in check. Stupid of me. But I finally did it."

Her words catch me off guard and I halt, turning to face her, unable to control the surprise that must be scrawled across my face. "You're quitting? But you..." *are the hottest woman on planet Earth.* "Is it the acting? Can't you do both? Loads of actresses do modelling campaigns."

"I want to do something different," Erica says matter-of-factly. "I've been doing this for over a decade. And I'm getting older, you know? I have to make plans for the future. Acting can sustain me for longer." She grips my arm, an inner light shining through her eyes. "I'm really excited to see where it takes me."

"Oh." Dread filters through my veins like ice, and as much as I want to match her enthusiasm, I can't. *Please say it doesn't take you away from me.* We continue walking, and the crowd filters out. Soon I'll have her all to myself.

"What about your date?" Erica asks, glancing around as if she's just noticed we're alone.

Something warm stirs beneath my ribs, replacing the chill. *She noticed.* There's no way I can admit that I ditched my date at the mere thought that Erica might be in trouble, so I mutter, "Fuck my date."

Erica does one of those fake gasps, striking her hand to her chest. "I'll leave that to you, thank you very much. And before you ask." A cheeky glint gleams in her eyes. "No, I don't want to watch."

My smile must be insanely big right now, and I let out a laugh that probably looks totally incongruous to anyone outside of me and Erica. She's just been yelled at and soaked in champagne. It makes no sense for me to be laughing, but when I look over at her, she's grinning too.

"Are we okay?" I ask, unable to resist asking for confirmation.

"Yeah. I'm sorry I threw you out that night."

I shrug. "Throw me out anytime. I'll always come back for more."

"Masochist," she says, a barely repressed smile on her lips.

"For you, yeah," I joke.

She stops and places her hand over mine, making my heart skip a beat. "I missed you."

My heart swells. "Missed you too."

For a few seconds that linger too long, we stare at one another, and I sink into the present, wishing it could last forever.

Erica blinks. "But really, you shouldn't leave your date."

I dip my head to recalibrate. "We won't be gone long. Harriet will be fine."

Erica's gaze drifts from mine. "Harriet," she repeats quietly, which makes me frown.

We pass a few smaller exhibitions on the way to the bathrooms, and an idea strikes me.

"When was the last time you saw your Claudia Kirchwood photo shoot?" I ask.

Claudia is one of the most famous fashion photographers in the world, and the shoot she did when Erica was eighteen became iconic. Black and white images of Erica dancing in an empty ballroom. It was part of an advertising campaign for a perfume, but the photos subsumed the campaign, taking on their own legendary quality. Romantic, ethereal, with an edge of intangible sadness. The same sadness that drew me to Erica in the first place. Even when she's with me and she's smiling, I can still see it in her eyes. Kind of haunted. I shake the thought off.

She muses. "I don't know. A few months after we did it. Maybe six or seven years ago?"

I take Erica's hand. "Come with me."

I lead her to the lift, relishing the feel of her hand in mine, and press the button with the other. The gallery's closed to the public tonight, and we shouldn't be up here, but no one's around. I know exactly where the exhibit is because I've followed it around the world. And right now, it's here in London.

We enter the gallery, and I switch on the lights. The exhibit has been perfectly curated. Around the walls, the enormous prints of Erica are spotlit in golden light.

"Oh, wow," she breathes, releasing my hand and walking slowly to the middle of the room, scanning each picture in turn. "I didn't know these were here."

I linger by the door, taking in the sight of her staring at the iconic images, and a heavy ache settles in my chest. Is it really awful not to come out and tell her how much I want her? Am I a total fucking arsehole for keeping it from her? I don't want to risk it and lose everything, but wouldn't it be better to tell her the truth?

I pace to stand beside her, my heart pounding. "Erica, there's something I—"

"I forgot what these were like," she murmurs dreamily, cutting me off and reminding me that I brought her here so she could have this experience. I can't trespass across it with my own feelings. "Time is such a funny thing, isn't it? I can remember posing for these like it was yesterday. I'd never be where I am today without this shoot. Without Arthur Knatchbull. He's the head of the luxury goods conglomerate that paid for this shoot. Did you know that?"

Of course I fucking knew. He's only one of the biggest businessmen in the world. "Yes. I knew that."

"He picked me out of obscurity. It was him, choosing me from a hundred other young models, that changed everything. Before that, I was a catalogue model. High Street stuff. But after this shoot, I started earning real money. I was able to leave home. Buy my own apartment. I owe him my career. My life. Everything." She scratches at her eyebrow. "Actually, it was my mother who took my portfolio to him in the first place. She got me the job. I have no idea how she got access to such a powerful man when I was a nobody at the time. Anyway, it was fate, I guess. And together, Mum and Arthur Knatchbull gave me my big break. I'll be indebted to them forever." *Her mother? That's what she told her?* Erica gestures around the room, blinking as though there are tears welling. She pinches the bridge of her nose and rubs at the corners of her eyes. "Sorry, you were going to say something?"

Having Erica's full attention on me once more sucks the air from my lungs, making me forget my annoyance that her mother is claiming credit for her success.

She assesses me, whatever contemplative sadness she was feeling seeming to disintegrate as she laughs softly. "You're not going to ask me out *again*, are you?" The joke is off-hand, as though she knows I'd never seriously ask her out so there's no danger in the teasing. I wish I could meet her in that space where it's funny to think I might ask her out, but I can't laugh. All I experience is the sensation of my stomach dropping.

She sits on the huge velvet banquette. I sit beside her, trying to conceal the fact that her ridiculing tone has stirred up my insides.

I brush my hair off my forehead with one hand. "I wasn't."

"Phew." She gives me a pointed look. "That would be terribly poor form, considering Harriet is waiting for you downstairs."

I'm pretty sure Harriet will have scarpered. "Actually—"

A noise outside cuts me off. Someone's coming.

"In here," comes a woman's voice, and I know without a doubt they're coming into *this* gallery.

I don't know why I do it, but a sudden impulse has me pulling Erica down off the banquette, the two of us crouching there on the floor in the semi-dark, hiding.

"Kill the lights," a male voice says, and we're plunged into darkness.

9
ERICA

My heart is racing as I hunker down in the dark next to Seb.

"God, you are so fucking hot," a voice growls.

Less than ten feet away from us, backlit by the moonlight streaming in the windows, a couple is kissing feverishly. They're tearing at one another's clothes, panting like they've been oxygen-deprived until this exact moment.

I don't dare look at Seb, but I'm acutely aware of him. The heat of his body, the strength of him beneath his suit, the scent of his cologne, and the sound of his breathing too close to my ear.

"I've waited far too fucking long for this," the man rasps as he hauls the woman's dress up, and she tilts her head back as he kisses her throat.

"Quick," she moans. "We have to be quick."

Seb tilts forward to see what I'm seeing. I've been blocking his view. His eyes peel wide, and, comedically slowly, he turns his gaze to me.

Please, don't look at me.

Too late. I can hardly breathe as my blood turns to rivers of fire. I don't know if it's the couple, the noises they're making, or the feel of Seb's attention on me while it's happening, but I'm burning up.

This is some great cosmic joke. It must be. I drag my gaze from Seb's, back to the couple who have stumbled against the wall. A trail of their clothes marks their path. Their passion is wild and uncontained;

the two of them unravelling mere feet from where Seb and I are hidden in the shadows.

The man turns the woman away from him and she braces her hands on the wall while he fiddles with his trousers. The little metallic clink of his belt is unmistakable.

"Quickly," she husks. "I need you now."

Seb lets out the most minuscule snort at exactly the same moment the man grunts and his dick springs free.

The woman whimpers, and a responding throb of arousal makes itself known between my legs.

He thrusts, filling her in one swift movement. It's carnal and raw, and I wish I could say I'm appalled or unmoved, but I'm neither. I let out a tiny gasp, staring in rapt fascination.

Seb leans closer. "They're defiling your exhibition," he whispers, and I'm thankful for the break in tension. I try to hold onto the amusement, but it dissipates with each hard thrust of the couple.

Tension wraps around us, and Seb shifts closer. "Told you," he whispers, his voice so deep and full of suggestion that it slides right beneath my dress. But my mind is so fogged up, my body so aroused, that I struggle to work out what he's talking about. And then I remember his words the last time we met.

It's hard to be in the same room as people who are having sex, and not get turned on. Damn near impossible.

Embarrassment flares in my chest, the heat of it mingling with the arousal I can't control. He *knows* I'm turned on. Of course he knows. He might be polite and charming when he wants to be, but that sexual energy is always simmering beneath the surface. Humming like electric wires. He can't help it. I can feel it emanating off him. Or is it me, doing that?

Rhythmic groans from the couple fill the space. The sound of their bodies slapping together is pornographic. I screw my eyes shut, trying to ignore the heat running through me and the gorgeous man beside me.

"Erica," Seb addresses me in a low whisper. "Is this turning you on?"

Opening my eyes, I expect to see him looking amused or smirking, but he's not. He looks deadly serious, his heated gaze on me.

Everything but Seb and the thrusts and moans of the couple nearby fades to insignificance. I'm hardly breathing, and for some inexplicable reason, it feels like we're the ones having sex.

"Do you want to leave? If you're uncomfortable, we can leave." He takes my hand in his and tugs it gently. I know he doesn't intend it, but because of what's happening in the room and inside my body, his touch sends electric bolts of desire racing through me. "On three." He tips his head towards the exit. "We'll get up and go."

"No."

He tilts his head at me and mouths, "No?" His brow furrows, but then his eyes widen. The hint of a smile on his lips tells me he sees right through me to every dirty thought and is ready to catch them in his hands and make them his.

"Your cock feels so good. So." *Thrust.* "Fucking." *Thrust.* "Hard."

My mind instantly fills with thoughts of Seb and his cock. *What does it look like? Is he hard right now? How big is it? What would it feel like to touch it? Taste it? If I got down on my knees, would it fit in my mouth?*

He raises an eyebrow, wordlessly asking what I'm thinking.

I might die here, in the flames of my own sinful thoughts.

Seb's eyes darken and he lets go of my hand, his fingers settling on the hem of my silk dress. He teases at it, his fingers sliding over my ankle.

Oh, shit. His touch burns. It's all I can do not to moan and throw myself into his arms, begging him to satisfy the painful need that's pulsing through me. *The need that I've denied for years, for the sake of maintaining my image.* But I will not be another woman Seb Hawkston takes to bed. I will not let him take my body and break my heart.

"Stop," I hiss. "Don't."

He nods, almost like a bow, and lifts his fingers off my ankle, putting a little space between us. We can't move too much or the couple will know we're here, watching them.

Their movements get more vigorous, the repeated cries of pleasure so ecstatic that there's no possible way to ignore them. Everything between my legs is throbbing, and jealousy for the couple going at it runs through me like poison. They're about to find release, and I'm stuck here, pent up and frustrated, because I always have to be so *good*. So perfect. An innocent English Rose.

And dating a man like Seb Hawkston has never fitted in with that.

Crouching in the dark, watching people have sex has never fitted in with that.

But... *fuck it.*

As the man withdraws and turns the woman around so they're face to face, I crack, splinters fissuring my perfect facade.

"Touch me." It's a soft plea, underpinned by a gritty determination. *I'm doing this.*

Seb's brow creases. "What did you say?" His voice is low and slightly hoarse.

"Touch me."

"Touch you...*where?*"

I can't form the words, but a quick glance between my legs reveals it all.

Seb doesn't hesitate. He slides his hand up my leg, running beneath the fabric until his fingers are on my thigh, his grip hot and hard. "Here?" he murmurs.

"Higher," I whisper.

He moans quietly as he leans towards me, and it might be the sexiest noise I've ever heard.

In the dim light, his bone structure is accentuated by shadows, and his blue eyes are dark and hungry. I've never felt more wanted than I do in this moment.

His face is so close to mine that when he speaks, his words vibrate along my skin. "You sure?"

My breathing is stuttered and shallow, and when I don't reply, he rests his forehead against mine. His breath is warm against my mouth, and all I want is to press my lips to his and swallow it all.

No man has ever ignited a desire in me like this. It's so strong that it's more like a compulsive *need* to be touched. *Taken.* Hovering on the edge of temptation with Seb is an exquisite agony I've never known.

He shifts his head a little, and his tongue licks at my upper lip, teasing at my mouth.

Oh, God. There is no way I can resist him. Not now.

"Are you sure?" he repeats, and somehow I manage to nod.

He doesn't waste a second before he kisses me. His lips are full and soft and his tongue slides into my mouth. The hot glide of it against my own sends my thoughts whirling.

His name is mantra that consumes my mind. *Seb, Seb, Seb.* I'm kissing my best friend. *And, oh, God. What a kiss.* It's passionate and desperate, as though he's been starving for me for far too long.

His hand comes to the back of my neck, fingers twisting into my hair.

The dominance of his touch unleashes something inside me that I've kept locked down, and now that it's out, I have no control over it. My hands are on his face, the scruff on his jaw rough against my palms as I force the kiss deeper, wanting to devour his mouth with my own.

Not far off, the couple are approaching climax, thrusting furiously, their moans gathering momentum.

Seb breaks our kiss, and I meet his gaze with alarm. *Why is he stopping?*

Seeing my panic, he smiles and whispers against my mouth. "I've wanted to kiss you forever." He shakes his head a fraction, then adds, "I need to taste you. Can I taste you?"

His words set me on fire, and years of self-denial go up in flames. I'm all libido and nothing else. It has me flat on my back in seconds, knees raised, murmuring *yes, yes, yes* so quietly that I'm not sure even Seb can hear as he positions himself between my legs, nudging them further apart.

He lifts my dress, his fingers trailing over my underwear, teasing at the edges. I feel like a teenager, letting someone touch me for the first time. That's pretty much exactly what I am. The only person who's ever given me an orgasm is *me*. My hands, my fingers. No one's touched me, and here I am giving it all away to Seb Hawkston on a meaningless Friday night. But if anyone knows what he's doing, it's Seb, so he's a good choice, isn't he?

He hooks his fingers into my thong and I raise my hips to let him ease it down my legs and toss it to the side. The air hits my pussy, and I'm deliciously exposed. He lowers himself to kiss my inner thighs, his lips working their way upwards, to the place I so desperately want him.

A moan rises in my throat, but I hold it back. If we make too much noise, the couple will know we're here.

He teases my entrance with a fingertip, taunting me as if to give me a chance to change my mind, but all I do is arch my hips. A low rumble of appreciation sounds in the back of his throat as he slides his finger inside. My body ignites, and I bite down on my lip to stop from crying out. Closing his eyes, his free hand tightens on my hip as if this is all too much for him. He pumps his finger inside me slowly like he's relishing the sensation, muttering against my inner thigh so quietly the words are barely more than desperate exhalations.

He removes his finger, leaving me empty, but only for a second. Hot breath warms the space between my legs, and then his tongue is there, swiping along through my pussy lips. *Oh, God.* I clench my fists to restrain the wave of pleasure that assaults me. I didn't know what this would be like, but it's better than I could ever have imagined. He's like velvet, tending me so carefully, caressing my most delicate parts like he treasures them, and a burst of heat surges through me. I never imagined it would feel this good.

He flicks my clit with the tip of his tongue, circling it back and forth. Sparks ricochet through my core. My back arches and my hips rise, seeking more. That rough scrape of his scruff against my sex.

And then he's not gentle anymore. He's *devouring* me, tongue spearing my entrance, laving my juices. He moans against me, his large hands dimpling my arse, hauling me closer so he can feast. He nips at my clit, sucking and flicking it, while the fingers of one hand thrust deep inside me again. Stars flash in my vision. I bite back another moan, but holding it in makes me feel like I'm going to explode.

A wave of pleasure crests and crashes, bringing with it traces of doubt and regret; the unwelcome flotsam and jetsam of my ecstasy. *What the fuck am I doing?* I've held Seb Hawkston at arm's length for years, and to break now... here... like this? To ruin our friendship when there's a woman waiting for him downstairs?

I can't do it.

My body and mind go to war. My body wants him, *all of him*, right here on the gallery floor. I'd give him *everything*. But my reputation, my standards, my mother's rules and the brand I've built my career on... Can I destroy all that for one moment of pleasure in Seb Hawkston's arms? Can I do it knowing he came here tonight with someone else? Knowing I'm not even his first choice?

What I've done—*what I've allowed to happen*—is so out of character I can't reconcile it with who I thought I was. My heart thunders in my chest as dizziness hits like an attack of vertigo.

We're not even alone. There are other people in the room. If they were to see us, to realise who I am...

I jerk away from Seb's mouth, wrenching my hips from his hands. I shunt backwards across the floor, closing my legs and sitting up. My heart races, each breath a struggle.

Seb's mouth and chin, covered in my juices, glisten in the moonlight streaming in the window, but his wide, confused gaze is where I focus.

"What? What's wrong?" he hisses.

I shake my head, unable to put into words what's going on inside it. I need to get out of here. I need to get away from Seb.

What have I done?

I pull down my dress and stand, no longer caring that there are other people in the room. My movement disturbs their rhythm, and the man shouts, but I barely hear him.

The last thing I see is Seb's shocked expression before I run from the room.

10
SEB

"**M**ate, was that Erica Lefroy?"

I ignore the prick who's shouting after me, pausing his fucking to ask if the woman who ran away from me when I was in the middle of eating her goddammed pussy is *the* Erica Lefroy. The same woman whose ten-foot-tall image is plastered all over the walls of this room. I scoop up her thong and shove it into my pocket.

My cock is still hard; aching with need. *Talk about left hanging.* I don't know if I'm angry or confused or both, but I'm propelled by the force of whatever-the-fuck-emotion it is out of the gallery and into the empty first floor corridor. The hum of chatter from the party in the atrium below drift upwards, echoing around me.

I can still taste her. She's in my mouth, and at the same time, she's slipping through my fingers. I've waited for a chance with Erica for years, and for a second, I thought I had it. But now she's running—*fucking running*—away from me. You'd think I was some kind of assailant the way she's moving so fast.

I begin to jog, and in a few seconds, I've caught up with her. I grab her hand, but she yanks out of my hold, her face a vision of panic.

"Shit, Erica. What the fuck is going on? What happened back there?"

Her eyes are frantic as she takes me in. Her chest heaves with each breath, and the motion makes the silk of her gown ripple. "I can't do this. I'm not like you." She lifts a shaking hand. "I can't—"

"Can't what? What are you talking about?"

She presses her fingertips over her eyes, letting out a wavering breath before looking back at me. "I can't be *easy*. I can't hook up like this." Her voice sharpens, and then next three words out of her mouth are vicious. "Not with *you*."

My insides hollow out and a prickling heat spreads over my skin. "What?" I ask carefully.

A lumpy red rash spreads up her neck as she taps frantically at her temple. "You got inside my head with all your talk of being turned on when people fuck in the same room." There's an unhinged look in her eye that wasn't there before, as though what's happened has caused chaos beneath the surface. With a wild arc of her arm, she points back to where we came from. "What happened in there wasn't real. It was a mistake. It was madness."

"Erica..." Quiet shock reverberates through my tone. "You *asked* me to touch you."

"And I wish I hadn't." Tension lines her jaw. "I'd wipe every second of that encounter with you from my memory if I could. *Erica Lefroy* does not hook up on gallery floors with men like *you*."

My first instinct is to laugh. She's talking about herself in the third fucking person, for Christ's sake. But the look on her face—her lip curled in what looks like disgust—has me fixing her with a hard glare. "What the fuck does that mean?"

Emotion flickers over her face, a shifting landscape that I can't pin down, but there's a hardness that I don't like. "You want the truth?" She tosses the question out like it's a dirty thing she doesn't want to touch but is keen to share.

"I can see you want to give it to me," I throw back.

She squares her shoulders, but her breathing remains erratic. "No one takes you seriously. Everyone knows your brothers run the business while you're out fucking a different woman every other night. You don't even care who they are or know their names. You're a joke, Seb."

My chest burns like her words are acid dripped directly on my heart. I hold my features in neutral so it doesn't show. Nico and Matt might be the backbone of our business in the UK, but that doesn't make me fucking useless. I have never, until this moment, felt like an insignificant piece of the Hawkston Hotels Global Empire. In the last five years, I've completely turned the company's marketing and PR around.

"What the fuck? What's with the character assassination?"

"It's the truth. I've stood by and watched you do it for years." Her voice breaks, a mixture of anger and distress evident in the rupture. "A string of meaningless liaisons."

"That has no bearing whatsoever on my ability to do my job."

She presses a hand to her heart and pins her bottom lip with her teeth to stop it quivering. "I can't be one of those women."

"Fine," I quip, biting the word out so aggressively that the delivery undermines the meaning. *None of this is fine.* In fact, this whole scenario is a fucking car crash. I can't get my head around it. *How the fuck did we get here?* "But there's no need to attack me."

"I'm not attacking you." Her voice is calmer, but not enough for her words to ring true. *This is a fucking homicide.* "It hurts me to see it. I care about you. I care about our friendship."

I can't hold back my eye roll. "Seems like it."

"I do. *Deeply*. I wouldn't say this unless I did. No one takes you seriously because you don't take anything or anyone seriously. Not even the people you date."

"That's not true. I'm always respectful."

She gapes, gesturing to the atrium far below us, the pitch of her voice escalating. "You have a date waiting for you downstairs right now."

"Harriet? I ended it with her before I came up here with you," I blurt.

Erica's eyes widen. "Why? Why would you do that? God, did you… did you plan this?" She bends forward a little, her hand still splayed against her chest. The pitch of her voice escalates as she speaks. "Is that why you brought me up here? Did you want to start the evening with her and end it with me?"

"Shit. No." I slam a hand to my forehead. "That's not it. Harriet and I aren't a thing. It was never exclusive."

A dry laugh rasps in her throat. "Of course it wasn't. When have you ever cared enough about anyone to be exclusive? You can't even do it for one evening. You move from woman to woman like none of us matter." She gestures at me with rigid hands. "Wake up, Seb. Maybe no one has said this to you because of who you are, or how much money you have in your bank account, or because nobody cares enough to be honest with you, but your sex life is a mess." Erica nods her head as though she's agreeing with her own arguments. "You're a total manwhore."

There's every chance that Erica Lefroy might be the love of my life, but this is too fucking much.

"Who the hell do you think you are to talk to me like that?" Anger burns through the words, and the colour drains from Erica's cheeks.

She takes a small breath. "I'm Erica—"

I raise a hand to stop her. "If you tell me you're *Erica Fucking Lefroy* like she's not you and you want to hide behind your fucking brand again, I swear I will—"

"What?" She bites out. "What will you do?"

Tension crackles.

"I'll bend you over and fuck the brat out of you."

An outraged squeal pops out of her mouth. "Is that what you wanted to do tonight?"

Yes. No. I don't fucking know. "Don't pretend this is about my behaviour," I grit out. "This is your shit. Not mine."

"My shit?"

"Yeah. This isn't about my sex life, or you trying to put me back on the straight and narrow out of the goodness of your heart. This isn't even about our friendship. This is about you and your business. Your career. Your precious reputation. Your *brand*." My tone is scathing. "Don't pretend it's anything other than that. I know that's what you care about the most."

Rage flickers intensely over Erica's beautiful face. "I do care about it. I don't have the luxury of *not* caring. I didn't grow up with a silver spoon in my mouth like you did."

I scoff. "A silver spoon? Make it gold at least. Platinum, even better."

"Don't mock me," she spits. "Those spoons are so far down your throat you're probably shitting them out. No one put a spoon in my mouth. I grafted for it. Every day. I showed up every *fucking* day to achieve my goals. I took it *seriously*. I did everything I was told to do..." She falters, and something like pain flickers across her face. If she hadn't already irritated the hell out of me, I'd acknowledge it. But she has, so I stay quiet. "And now I'm here—"

"Right at the top," I sneer.

Her hand slashes through the air. "I will not slide back down. And you... your reputation would *destroy* mine. What we've built."

"We?"

"My mother and I. *We*. She sacrificed her whole life to make mine count. I can't destroy that. It would—"

"Jesus, Erica. This isn't the 1950s. You don't need your mother's permission. You can date who you want to date. You can fuck who you want to fuck. You can screw around—"

"I can't! One misstep and the whole thing falls apart. Years of work." She clenches both fists and whines through gritted teeth. "You have no idea what it takes to build a brand. You put on your suit and march into Daddy's company without a care in the world. You don't *know*, Seb. You don't fucking know what it took me to get here." Her finger jabs towards the floor, as if this particular spot in the gallery hall is where she's been aiming her entire life. "You couldn't do what I've done. You couldn't sacrifice everything I've sacrificed to get here. You think you can turn up to my shows with your bouquets of flowers, not taking a single thing seriously, all while I'm working my arse off to—"

"If you were with me, you'd never have to work your arse off. You wouldn't have to lift a finger another day in your life. You could forget all of this." My arm swipes through the air, up and down her body so violently it's as if I'm intending her to become a different person entirely.

Her mouth falls open and her eyes glisten with unshed tears. "You want me to forget everything I've worked for?" Her voice is quiet but full of heartbreak that messes me up inside.

I close my eyes, pinching the bridge of my nose so hard it hurts even after I release it. "All I meant is that I'd look after you. I'd take care of everything. You could let the whole fucking act drop."

She gasps like I've stuck a knife into her. "This isn't an act." She pokes her sternum. "This is me. This is all I have. *Erica Lefroy*. And you... you could *never* understand that." She holds up a hand to stay any movement I might make. "I'm leaving. Do not come after me."

She juts her chin and paces towards the lift. I try not to run after her, but my resolve lasts two seconds.

"Don't walk away from me when I can still taste you on my tongue."

She rears back, spinning to face me, a look of utter disdain crossing her face. "If the way I taste is bothering you, go home and brush your teeth." She almost turns away before rethinking it. "Or better yet, go and find someone else to stick your tongue in. Isn't that what you're good at? Why not go for a fucking hattrick tonight?"

I can't take another second of this shit. I thrust my hand into my pocket and scrunch the scrap of lace I grabbed from the gallery floor. Erica's thong. I pull it out and offer it to her on a flat palm. "I was going to keep this, but as you so rightly pointed out, I'm a manwhore. I have a whole fucking collection of women's underwear, and I sure as shit don't need to add yours." I thrust my hand a little closer. "Especially not when you're just as meaningless as all the others."

Her breath hitches as she stares at the thong. Fine lines appear at the corners of her eyes and she screws them shut, almost as though she's bracing through a wave of pain.

Neither of us moves, but the air between our bodies has a charge that burns my skin. I can't look at her, because if I do the sight of her suffering will break me. The thong sits in my hand like a grenade I've yet to throw.

"Take it," I insist.

Her eyes flick to mine, dark and full of a stormy defiance. "Fuck you, Seb. *Fuck. You.*" She snatches it and marches towards the lift.

Confusion and anger thrum in my blood as the doors open and Erica steps inside without a backward glance. The lift whisks her away and I stride to the nearest wall, fisting a hand and thumping the pad of it against the plaster. A groan scrapes up my throat, and I let out a fury-filled, "Fuck!"

I hit the wall one more time, then lay both palms against it and let my head hang as I wait for my breathing to return to normal.

If there's one good thing that's come from all this, it's that I finally understand I never stood a chance with Erica Lefroy. She thinks I'm a *joke*, and, despite what happened between us tonight, I know I'll never be good enough for her.

I contemplate going straight home, then reason that I'm not going to let Erica ruin my evening. I make my way down to the reception, but her perfume lingers in the air, triggering an onslaught of memories; her skin, her mouth, her tongue... her goddamn pussy. *Fuck's sake.*

Entering the main hall again, I grab a champagne flute from a nearby tray. The server's eyebrows rise as I swallow the contents in one fluid motion and return the empty glass to his tray.

Even though I try not to, I can't help scanning the crowd for Erica. *Is she still here? Did she leave?*

I refuse to think about her, but I cannot shed the bad mood that's clinging to me. And I am *never* ill-tempered.

This is unprecedented.

I grab another champagne flute, then search the room for some-one—*anyone*—to take my mind off Erica. It should probably be Harriet, but I can't see her either. She probably left. I spot an attractive blonde standing in front of a huge abstract nude. She'll do.

I force a smile and head in her direction. If Erica's still here and sees me flirting, so much the better.

But before I reach the blonde, my brother, Nico, strides into view, making a direct beeline for me. The haunted expression on his face, the near horror in his eyes, has me halting. I know, as if he's communicated it to me through some means other than words, that someone is dead, or soon will be.

"It's our father," Nico says, laying a hand on my forearm, and without giving me any time to prepare myself, he adds, "A heart attack."

"Shit." Even though I guessed something like this was coming, the reality is a punch to the gut. "Is the old man dead?"

"Worse." Nico gives a grim nod. "He's asking for you."

11

SEB

A few days after the party at the gallery, I find myself waiting outside my father's private suite in his London home. I don't know what state he's in, but given he's no longer in hospital and he only wanted to see me, not Matt or Nico, neither of whom had any interest in accompanying me to check on the cold bastard, he can't be that bad.

Ordinarily, I'd have told Erica about Dad nearly dying, even though we're under instruction not to mention his health outside the family. She's the first call I would have made. But we haven't been in contact since we fought, and I'm not about to open a message thread with, 'My dad nearly died and I'm not sure I give a fuck'.

Erica's vicious words at the gallery have plagued my dreams. But as much as I want to hate her for them, I can't. A lot of what she said was true, and whenever I allow myself to reflect on what happened between us, my mind fills with recriminations. I pushed her too far. I shouldn't have done it. Shouldn't have kissed her, tasted her... shouldn't have given in to temptation, because I've ruined everything we had.

I've fucked it all up.

Sighing, I lean against the designer wallpaper and stare up at the crystal chandelier overhead. I hate this house. Huge, stuffy, incredible views, prime real estate. But full of miserable memories. When we weren't at boarding school, we'd stay here for the holidays and Dad would fuck the nanny, the housekeeper... anyone who was available. Mum would sit in her room crying, and Nico would pass notes under her door. *Are you okay, Mummy? We love you.* Then he'd sign them from all of us. *Nico, Matt, and Seb.*

She never answered a single one.

Matt would punch walls and refuse to talk to anyone and I'd be left making jokes, trying to break the tension. As a kid, it was the only thing I could offer to lighten the mood. Maybe if I could make someone smile, we wouldn't all feel like we were dying. It was idealistic and naive, but I really thought there was a chance I could do it. Heal the whole fucking family with laughter. I failed, miserably.

I lean against the wall, trying to ignore the unpleasant memories about the years I spent here as a kid.

I pull out my phone and begin to scroll. It's two seconds before the algorithm brings me a video of Erica falling on the runway, and me jumping up to help her. She looks so beautiful, and simultaneously so helpless, that something—my heart?—physically hurts inside my chest. I'd rewind time to get to that point if I could. Before the naked photos arrived on my phone when I was sitting next to her. Before the gallery. Before I knew what her pussy tastes like.

Hmm. Maybe I wouldn't rewind that far, actually. I like that I know what she tastes like. That she hasn't a scrap of hair down there. I like that I can remember how soft and wet her pussy felt when I had my fingers in it. That I could smell her on them, even after she ran away from me.

I don't think I could give those memories up. But they're fading anyway. I can't hold them perfectly in my mind, can't catch her scent on me anymore.

I must stop thinking about her because, even after our fight, the thought of her still turns me on. My dick is thickening, and the last thing I need is a hard-on when my father finally calls me into his room.

I haul my attention back to the video on my phone. It's been liked thousands of times and saved almost as many. Erica's been tagged but hasn't responded.

The comments are in the thousands too. I scroll through. Some of them are inane. Others make my chest tighten, but one in particular has my attention.

5.5 seconds. Pause and look at the way she's looking at him.

Beneath it, more people chipping in.

OMG she loves him.

Who is this guy?

That is love, dude.

This is like a fairytale. I'm watching a fairytale.

I can't stop replaying this moment.

I've watched it 52 times already.

I replay the video, pausing it at exactly 5.5 seconds. And there it is. The moment she raises her head and looks up at me.

I stare, trying to see what they see. She does look relieved to see me. Maybe even pleased. In fact, the more I stare at her face, the more I *can* see it. The longing. The adoration in her expression.

Is it really there, or am I seeing this image through the filter of some online comments? If there's any truth to it, perhaps we can survive the argument we had last time we met. I keep scrolling.

She's lying on the runway. No wonder she looks pleased to see him.

You're all imagining it. I don't see it.

That bloke just wants to get in her panties.

Everyone wants to get in Erica Lefroy's panties.

I hit like on the last comment because the truth of it makes me snort. I add a response. '*But no one's allowed in. She's mine. All mine.*'

Satisfied that I've done my bit to claim Erica (using the online alias, *SeblovesBJs,* which I created when I was sixteen for just this sort of stupid commenting) I put my phone away.

But I can't stop thinking about her, and suddenly those comments don't seem funny anymore. My stomach roils at the thought that all those people out there really do want to '*get in her panties*'. That they want to do what I did... they want to put their mouths on her, between her legs, their fingers inside her... a sudden coil of red hot rage blisters inside me. The heat rises through my chest, my arms, and finally my fingers, which begin to pulse.

Christ, this thing with Erica has got right under my skin. If I can't have her, I don't want anyone else touching her. She might think I'm a joke, but this fucking isn't one.

The door to my father's suite opens and his PA steps out. She looks a little dishevelled. *Has he been fucking her while I've been waiting?* I wouldn't put it past him, even sick. Bile hits the back of my throat and I swallow it down, letting it mingle with the remnants of my rage about the online commentary.

"You can see him now," she says, propping the door open for me.

I slip my phone back into my pocket and enter my father's room.

He's sitting in a chair by the window, a blanket covering his knees. He looks older; withered, almost. I'm shocked at the difference since I last saw him, but I make sure not to show it.

"Dad," I say.

He looks at me, disappointment lining his eyes as he wordlessly directs me to take a seat. I settle in the chair opposite him and wait for him to speak.

"We have a problem, Sebastian."

"Seb," I correct.

He shakes his head dismissively. He's always ignored my preference for the short version of my name. "Sebastian," he repeats. "We have a problem."

A burst of laughter pops out. "Your spaceship lost its way to the moon?" My father stares at me blankly. "Houston," I offer. "We have—"

A shutter of fury descends over his face. "Your jokes aren't appreciated. This is a serious matter, and you ought to take it so."

I lean back. Dad never did like my jokes. "You haven't told me what it is yet, so how can I take it seriously?"

His grunt conveys his irritation, then his energy shifts, and he becomes hyper-focused. "Your brothers are settled."

"Okay..." I begin when he says nothing more.

"Your reputation needs to be tamed."

Oh, fuck. Not this again. "My reputation—"

My father holds up a hand to silence me, then picks up a remote from his side table and clicks it. The large TV on the other side of the room turns on, and he presses more buttons. Images of me with a stream of women flick across the screen. Paparazzi photos. "These are only this year. There are more, in case you need reminding."

As I look at the images of the women, and me, all of us drunk, stumbling out of bars and clubs, climbing into chauffeur-driven limos, an unpleasant sensation bubbles in my stomach. But this is what he wants. To catch me on the back foot. I refuse to let him know I'm unnerved. I grin at the photos as if I'm entertained. Perhaps even pleased with what I see, even though being confronted with evidence of those meaningless encounters lands like a dead weight in my gut.

"Wipe that smile off your face," my father snaps, and the succession of images pause. "This is not a joke. You are making the family look bad."

I turn my focus to him. "As if you're a paradigm of morality." His eyes pin me like twin missiles. As a kid, I'd have cowered from this expression, but now I steel myself to meet his gaze. "You fucked every woman on the payroll."

"All of whom had signed NDAs. My dealings were quiet. Yours are despicable. Childish. You need to stop this and dedicate yourself to one woman."

Erica pops into my mind, and I clench my jaw so hard it hurts. No matter what I might or might not feel for her, she's made it clear she's not interested. Probably for a lot of the same reasons I'm standing here in front of my father like a naughty fucking school kid. Well, he can't reprimand me like one. I'm not doing anything to please him. God knows I spent enough time trying to do that in my youth. "If I want to do that, I'll do it. My relationship status is my business. Not yours."

He switches off the TV, lays the remote aside and places his palms on his thighs, sitting a little straighter. "Our family name is recognised the world over. The name is the business. You fuck around, you're messing with the business. The two cannot be disentangled. Why do you think I was so careful over the years? Did you ever read an article about my love life? My affairs? No."

"You're seventy-five. Things were different then. People didn't have iPhones, for one. Everyone has a camera in their pocket now."

"A man who makes excuses is no man at all, Sebastian."

I draw in a breath that puffs my chest. The old fucker might have a point there. I tip my chin to acknowledge it.

He clears his throat. "I won't last forever. I'm unwell. This time, my heart nearly killed me."

I keep my face still. I've never felt much emotion towards my father, but to hear him speak so plainly about dying causes an unpleasant sensation to sweep through my body, as if everything beneath my ribs is being scooped out. *Emptied.* A reminder that one day, we're all going to die.

"You're like me, Sebastian. We're made of the same cloth—"

"I'm nothing like you," I spit, thinking of all the women he fucked when we were young, a parade of them through the house, all while Mum turned a blind eye. I might have had my fair share of casual sex, but it was all consensual and I have never cheated on anyone.

He coughs and clears his throat. "Oh, you are. You love to fuck, but you can't love. You don't really care about the women you've been with."

"How would you know that?"

He reaches across to the side table and grabs a folder, which he throws at me. "They're all in there. Every woman you've ever been seen with. I have statements from most of them."

"What the fuck?"

"Open it."

I do as he asks. Each entry includes multiple photos and a typed statement with the woman's details. Address, birth date, fucking zodiac sign. The lot. Anger rises like a red flood. This isn't a montage of publicly available images. This is something else. "You've had me under surveillance? You approached these women? You—"

"Your time is up. I hope you've enjoyed sowing all those wild oats because it ends now."

I clench my fists to curb my fury. "What are you talking about?"

He picks up a large manilla envelope from the side table. "This." He holds it out to me, and for a second I stare at it. He jerks his chin. "Take a look."

I snatch it and open it, taking out a sheaf of large photographs. They're all of a beautiful young woman. She can't be much more than twenty. A decade younger than me. I vaguely recognise her face.

"Diana Marchetti," my father fills in. "Your future wife."

A chill runs through me like someone filled my veins with ice. *The girl sitting next to Antonio Marchetti at London Fashion Week.* "Wife?"

"Yes. I've arranged it with her father. A business deal, as such. I stand to make tens of millions from it. Maybe a hundred. Antonio owns the land I want our next hotel to be built on. He wants our family name for his daughter. Make her a Hawkston. One of the world's great families. This marriage"—he reaches across and taps the picture of the girl, right on the nose—"secures it."

The ground drops out beneath my feet and it takes a second to orient myself before the full force of my anger roars to the fore. "Absolutely not."

He tilts his head to the side and a cracked tongue slips out to lick his dry bottom lip. Like he's a fucking lizard. It repulses me. "Isn't it about time you did something of use? Made this family proud, instead of disgracing us constantly and publicly? You're not a child anymore. Can't hide behind your older brothers. It's time to be a man, Sebastian."

"Seb. And the answer is no, no matter how many times you insult me. And as for doing something of use, revenue is up ten per cent since I took over the marketing and PR department. I turned that shit around. Me." Dad gives me one resentful nod to acknowledge what I've done for the company. "So no. I will not do it."

"You can't say no."

"I bloody well can. I don't need anything from you. I can walk out that door and slam it, and never see your face again. It would give me pleasure to do it."

In each hand, he grips a fistful of the blanket covering his knees. "If I have to die—and death is the one thing I can't cheat, Sebastian—I want to make sure this deal is sealed before I do. Nico's on board as CEO."

"On board with this marriage?" The words explode as a sense of betrayal floods me. Surely Nico wouldn't sign off on this, not without talking to me.

Dad chuckles, seemingly amused by my alarm. "No. He doesn't know about that part. He's on board with the idea of the hotel, and unofficially, all the board members are in agreement too. I'm this fucking close." He raises one hand, creating a tiny gap between his thumb and index finger. "I will go to whatever lengths necessary to ensure it happens. If you stand in the way of that, I'll have your accounts drained. Your trust funds emptied. You'll have nothing but the suit you're standing in. We'll call it an unfortunate fraud. Poor, idiotic Seb Hawkston, duped in a scam that emptied every bank account he has. I'll take everything from you and don't think I won't do it. Don't think I can't do it, because I can. And you know it."

He wants a new hotel this fucking much? To screw me over this badly? I don't know why I'm surprised. He's always been a shitty parent and a ruthless businessman. The most dreadful of combinations. Having a heart attack was never going to change that. "I don't give a fuck. I don't need money. I won't let you control my life like this."

Dad's ripe laughter fills the room. "You'd lose everything just to stay single? I know you hate me, but please tell me you aren't a complete fool. Your behaviour is obtuse. It's not as if you'd be leaving anyone behind. I know you don't give a shit about any of those women, and

I doubt they care about you either. Not really. Not on any level that counts." He indicates the folder containing my sexual history. "Trust me, I know what that's like. The hollow, empty feeling inside. Never really caring and wondering why not. At least this way, you'll have a woman who'll stick around for longer than a couple of weeks."

His barbs are well aimed, and I have to exert control over my features not to show he's hit the target. No one *has* stuck around. Not for long, anyway. "I am not like you. We are not the same."

His lips thin, mouth tightening as though he's stifling a knowing smile. *Bastard*. "I'm not asking too much," he continues. "Say a few words, wear the ring, fuck the girl, have a couple of kids, and live happily ever after. Fuck it, you can get divorced after the hotel is built. Mr Marchetti will be happy with a few Hawkston grandsons. Give them your name and your DNA and have done with it."

Enough. I leap to my feet, sending the photographs flying to the floor. Pointing a finger in his face, I growl, "You cannot fucking pimp me out like that."

He laughs. "No. You do that well enough yourself. Besides, you didn't seem to mind when you were sixteen."

I glare at him, recalling the brothel he took me to on my sixteenth birthday. The woman he bought me as a 'coming-of-age present.' The way he patted me on the back and said, "It's time to be a man, Sebastian. You can't sit at home with your mother forever. She doesn't want you there." And then he gave me a look that demanded gratitude. As if he expected me to run and tell my friends, so they'd think he was a great dad. The only acceptable response was to get on my knees and thank him for even thinking of me, when really, on some unspeakable energetic level, we both knew that wasn't it at all. None of it was for me. It was deep, and dark, and cloaked in shame that settled in my fucking bones.

At the time, I tried to convince myself it was a good thing. That it meant he finally saw me as a man, and that maybe, if I did this for him, then he'd treat me the way he did my brothers. But really, it was terrifying. The woman barely spoke to me for the few minutes it lasted. She did her job and asked for her cash, which I didn't have, so we had to traipse out into the corridor together to find Dad. He stood there with his wallet out, counting out the notes like he was giving me pocket money. He was the boss, and I was just another kid on the payroll. And then he looked me up and down, checked his watch with a disdainful sneer on his face, said, '*You'll have to do better than that if you want to call yourself a man*', which made it feel like the whole fucking world crumbled beneath my feet.

Everything changed from that moment. My whole fucking trajectory.

I've been trying to '*do better*', whatever the fuck that really means, every single time I've taken a woman to bed.

Silence sinks between us, raw and full of anger on my side. Full of an unbearable indifference on his.

"All this, for a hotel?" I ask, bitter resentment rumbling through my words.

"More than a hotel. A legacy. Like I said, I could die at any moment. I want to leave the biggest mark on this planet I can."

"And fuck your family in the process."

He quirks a brow. "I'm not fucking you, Sebastian. I'm edging you."

I drag a hand over my eyes, but I can't shut him out because his filthy chuckle penetrates the temporary darkness. I let my hand fall, straining to keep the emotion out of my voice. "You're sacrificing my life to your agenda. For this so-called legacy."

"Nothing so-called about it. Our name is one of the most famous in the world, and I've sacrificed a hell of a lot to make it happen. You have no idea what it takes to build this sort of business." His words stab right into the wound Erica created at the gallery. To be reminded of her now, when my father is tearing strips off me, is an agony I never could have anticipated. "None of you do. Nico might be CEO, but this will always be *my* company. It took sweat and blood to build this business, to give you all the life you've become accustomed to. The women. The boats. The jets. The fast cars. Could any of you boys have done what I did? Nico? Maybe. Matt? Possibly. But you? Never. Not in a million years. You're the joker in the pack. The little cunt who does nothing but smile and fuck, and crack a joke that's occasionally funny, but most of the time is just fucking stupid."

His comments land like blows across my back, designed to make me fall. Inside, I'm buckling, but I don't move. I refuse to offer him any confirmation that it hurts. "That pep talk supposed to get me to do what you want? Because it didn't work. I won't do it. Fuck you, and fuck your legacy."

I take steps to leave the room when he calls me back. "I'm expecting you at dinner with Diana. My PA will contact you with the details."

"And if I don't show?"

"I will make your life hell. And those flames will burn, Sebastian. I'll take every penny you have, and there's no way you could earn it back." He laughs again. "You don't have the balls to make that kind of fortune."

I stare at him. "How the fuck does a man without a heart have a heart attack?"

I don't give him the chance to reply before I leave, slamming the door on my way out.

12

ERICA

I've done a lot of things in my life. Ridiculous photo shoots. Pranced about on stage in my underwear. Swarmed half-naked in an artfully constructed pile of other models for a photo shoot. I'm not a stranger to putting myself outside my comfort zone. But letting Seb Hawkston put his tongue inside me has to be one of the stupidest things I've ever done.

Unfortunately, it's also the only thing I've been able to think about since it happened. How do we go back to being friends after the way I treated him? If letting him go down on me didn't ruin our friendship, the way we fought afterwards finished the job. I've never behaved like that before. I don't lose my mind and yell at people. But recently Seb's been pushing my buttons like never before.

Maybe I am losing my mind. Maybe I've already lost it.

But worse than that, maybe I've lost *him*. I can't think about that because it might break my heart.

I force myself to concentrate on what I'm doing. My kickboxing sessions with Amy are one of the highlights of my month. If she's not on tour and I'm not on a shoot, we meet in an exclusive gym, training with one of London's best instructors or sparring on our own.

Today, we're alone, and the whole time we've been here, I've been wanting to talk to her about Seb, but am unsure what to say. He watched her have sex, after all. Can I even have this conversation with her?

I bounce on my toes, sweat dripping from my forehead. Amy kicks at me and I block her with the pad, but I stumble anyway. The woman is pure muscle; she always wins, but today I'm an even worse opponent than normal.

Amy drops her fists. "What is wrong with you?"

I sigh, slinging the pads to the floor and spitting my gum shield out into my hand. "It's Seb."

"What about him?"

In a bid for time, I take my gum shield box from my pocket and put the shield in there. I snap it closed and slip it back in my pocket. "He told me he watched you have sex," I say finally, keeping my gaze trained on the floor.

"Oh."

I glance up when she says nothing else, mild panic racing through me. "I'm sorry," I blurt. "I would have asked you myself, but I felt awkward about it."

Amy's eyebrow piercing glints as it rises on an arched brow. "Why?"

I'm wishing I hadn't started this conversation now, but I did, so I might as well keep going. "Do you have... feelings for Seb?"

A slow smile spreads over Amy's face. "Are you jealous?"

"No!" *That came out way too fast.*

"You needn't be. I was so high, I didn't know he was there until the following morning. It's not like we did anything *together*. I have no claim on Seb if that's what you're worried about. He's a friend. Honestly, I'm not interested. Never have been. He's gorgeous, sure, but he's way too clean cut for me. Very straight-down-the-line. I prefer a bit of grit. A few tattoos. Someone who's lived a little rough. If you want to date him, you have my blessing." She bites down on the Velcro strap of her boxing glove and removes it, then tugs the other off before dropping both to the floor and kicking them towards the wall. "Plus, everyone knows he's been hopelessly in love with you for years."

My heart twists. "What? Who knows that?"

"Everyone." She drags out the word. "He flies all over the world to see your shows. He doesn't come to see mine."

"You have more. Yours are longer." I sound like I'm desperately trying to prove that what she's saying isn't true, and I'm not even sure why. "He'd have to quit his job to come and see you."

She kicks my discarded pads and they fly across the gym, bang against the wall, and fall next to her gloves. "He brings you flowers every single time. He adores you."

I rub a hand over my forehead, feeling even worse for the things I said to him at the gallery. "No. That can't be true. He's never... he's always... he..." *Damn it, why can't I stop stammering?* "He's always hooking up with other women. If that were true, why would he do that?"

Amy picks up her water bottle, takes a swig, and gestures emphatically with it as though the answer is painfully obvious. "Because you're Erica Lefroy. Ice Queen. Completely unattainable. He knows you'd shoot him down. I bet you've never once even flirted with him, have you?"

I might not have flirted with Seb before the gallery, but then I went and invited his tongue inside me. Whether or not I flirted with him before that feels like a redundant issue—we leapfrogged straight to oral sex in a public place. "No. I suppose not," I say, trying to ignore the uneasy swell of anxiety that accompanies the recollection. I should never have let it happen. *Ever.* A mistake. That's what it was. *A mistake that left me craving more...*

"So, what's the issue?" Amy says, her voice crashing through my thoughts.

"I let him go down on me at the gallery night." I spit the words so fast they're almost incomprehensible, and it takes a moment before understanding blossoms across Amy's face.

"Why, you dirty little slut," she says with glee. "Did you like it? Did you like having him"—Her gaze dips to my tiny boxing shorts—"down there?"

Heat bursts low in my belly. "I don't know. No. Maybe. Yes." I let out another groan as the memories flash back at me. "Afterwards—"

"Did you come?"

I huff. "Right to the crux of the matter, eh?"

"Yup," she says with glee. "Did you?"

My body feels like it contains an ocean of swirling emotion. "No. I stopped it before that." I rub my fingers over my forehead and let out a whimper that's doused in regret. "I completely freaked out. I ran away, and he ran after me, and then we had this horrendous fight." I press my hands to my cheeks, which are flaming at the memory. "I completely lost it. Went crazy. Told him he shits silver spoons." I drag my hands down my face. "I was so mean to him. Said everyone thinks he's a joke."

Amy crosses her arms over her chest. "What idiots think that? I certainly don't."

My throat constricts. "My mother?" I offer, realising it sounds pathetic. Amy rolls her eyes and I press my fingers to my lips, pausing before I add, "I called him a manwhore."

"Shit," Amy breathes. "That's harsh." She appears to mentally withdraw from me before she opens her arms wide, beckoning me with her fingers like she wants to fight. "You wanna do me too? I mean, come on. I can take it. Call me a whore."

I cover my eyes with my hands and whine before letting them drop. "God, no. I'm sorry. It's none of my business what he does, or what you do, but it felt like it at the time." I shudder at the memory. "I don't want to fight with anyone like that again. It was so intense. He said I only care about my brand and my business. My career." I grimace. "I think we might be over. Broken. I threw up afterwards."

Amy relaxes her stance. "You were *actually* sick?"

The memory of clinging to the toilet bowl and vomiting up my insides makes me want to retch again. "Yeah. It was either that or bawl like a baby."

"Oh, hun." She steps towards me, puts her hands on my shoulders, and pulls me into a hug. "You fought like you love each other."

Her words stun me and it's a second or two before I can speak. "No." I push out of her hold, shaking my head. "No, that's not what it was. He said hooking up with me was as meaningless as everyone else."

"Pfft." She flaps a hand. "That's definitely not true."

My shoulders slump, and there's a crushing sensation in my chest, like my heart really might be breaking. I stare at the floor. "It felt true."

Amy says nothing, but when I glance at her again, she's smiling. "What?"

She raises a brow and nods suggestively. "You like him."

"No," I snap back.

She beams wider, and irritation slips like grease through my insides. "Can you stop that demonic grin?"

She bounces on her toes, throwing a few shadow punches as she does it. "Do you want to fuck him? Because he'd be a great person to finally lose your V-card to. You've known him for years, and he cares about you. And he's *very* experienced."

I press my fingers against my temples. "How have you leapt to this?"

Amy stops bouncing. "Does he know you're a virgin?"

Her question stabs into me and I can't help glancing around the room to make sure no one's listening, even though I already know it's completely empty. "I don't tell people that." I wave a hand at her. "Except you."

Amy nods solemnly. "He might forgive you for your craziness if he knew. If I were a virgin and Seb Hawkston put his head between my legs, I'd go crazy too." Her eyes light up and she points two emphatic fingers at me. "You should tell him, and then fuck him."

"Argh. No." I lightly slap her arm. "Don't say that. Do not encourage me. I don't want to mess up this friendship forever." I groan. "I don't know if we even have a friendship anymore. He hasn't sent me a GIF for weeks."

"A GIF?"

I march to the side of the gym and pick up my bag from where I dumped it on the floor. Amy crosses to join me, swigging on her water bottle.

I pull my phone out, open up my chat with Seb, and pass it to her. She scrolls, a slight smile ghosting her mouth. "Aw, this is cute. His love language is GIFs." She scrolls more. "He sends them almost every day, even when you don't reply."

I love getting messages from Seb. Every time my phone buzzes, my heart leaps like the damn handset is a defibrillator pad as I wonder if it's from him. I try to sound casual when I say, "He doesn't send them to you?"

"Nope." She hands me back my phone, and I put it away. "I'm not that special. Whereas you—"

"Stop it. You cannot categorically know how he feels about me. He'd sleep with anyone. He brought a date with him *that night*, at the gallery. He's *always* with someone else. If I hooked up with him, it wouldn't mean anything to him, and he'd move on to the next woman in five seconds flat. I doubt he'd even glance over his shoulder to check I was okay. Onto the next hotel room. The next naked woman who sends a picture to his phone." Amy arches a brow and I explain about the photos he received the day I fell on the runway. "I don't think he knows how to have a sexual relationship that *actually* means something," I continue. "And I'm not willing to risk everything to find out. I can't do that. I *won't* do that. I mean… my *virginity*." *My heart.* "That's a big deal."

Amy props one hand on her hip, staring like she's trying to unearth the truth I'm not sharing. My heart does a funny palpitation, and I press a hand over it. Her eyes dart to my hand, her brow creasing. "You're frightened."

No shit. I flop down on the bench by the wall and start shoving the pads into my bag. "Yeah. I don't want to be tossed aside when he gets bored. I'd lose my friend and gain nothing but heartache." Amy rests a hand on my shoulder, which I shrug off as I zip up my bag and sit up. "And I don't want to lose his friendship, if I haven't already. *And* my mother hates him."

"So what? Who cares what your mum thinks?" Amy's question sounds casual, as though Mum's opinion should be irrelevant. And I guess it should be, but it's not. Amy wouldn't really understand that… her parents are the ultimate support team to her career. Not overbearing, but supportive. Whereas my mother is involved in every facet of my life, and I have no idea how to unravel that shit. "Has she ever met Seb?"

"I don't think they've ever spoken. She has no interest in talking to him."

"Your Mum is weird as fuck. Who's not interested in Seb Hawkston?"

I raise a shoulder. "Bad for the brand."

"Ah. You don't really believe that, do you?"

Do I? I know Mum does, and I've absorbed so many of her opinions over the years that sometimes it's hard to tell what's hers and what's mine.

The memory of Seb telling me he'd bend me over and fuck the brat out of me if I mentioned my brand again causes a searing heat to ignite in my chest. It feels like arousal and heartbreak all at once.

Our friendship is definitely fucked beyond repair, whatever Amy thinks about the matter.

"Just rebrand," Amy offers. "I do it all the time. Seb could totally be part of your rebranding."

I sigh. *I wish.* I can't keep talking about Seb because I might start crying, so I redirect the conversation. "Speaking of rebranding, I want to move into movies and I've got this huge audition coming up... I haven't told anyone, but it's for *Taming the Beast.*"

Amy's eyes widen, and her mouth puckers into a tiny O shape. "The film based on that post-apocalyptic Beauty and the Beast story?"

"Yes. They're filming most of it in the UK with a British cast."

Amy squeals. "Really? Because I'm reading it right now. It's in my bag." She whistles. "That's the biggest book in the market at the moment. It's *filthy.*"

I wipe the sweat off my forehead with my forearm. "It's a romance."

Amy lets out a wicked cackle. "It's page-porn. Survivalist *Fifty Shades.* Fifty-shades-of-fuck-me-up-the-arse meets *The Hunger Games.*"

"The Hunger Games is dystopian. Not post-apocalyptic."

Amy waves her hand at me like she doesn't give a fuck about the difference between the two. "Don't get me wrong. I loved it. Millions of people loved it. But some of the things he does to her..." She fades off, a smile on her face as she shakes her head. "I had to take a rest break. Several times." She winks.

"I wouldn't know."

Amy swallows another gulp of water from her bottle and wipes her mouth on the back of her hand before she speaks. "Woah. Hold up. You want to audition, but you haven't read the book? You have to go read it right away." She moves quickly towards her bag and pulls out the book, thrusting it towards me. "Read it. Get inside the character's head. Get yourself a hand mirror and have a wank."

I rear back. "Jesus, Amy. A wank? A mirror?"

"Yeah," she deadpans. "Just pop it between your legs so you can see yourself when you masturbate. I promise you, this shit works. It'll loosen up your sexual energy in no time. You'll start loving your pussy as much as the world loves your face."

"You are so crass." I snatch the book from her, then reconsider, pinning the book between finger and thumb and holding it away from me. "Did you wank over this book?"

She shrugs, amusement sparking in her eyes at my obvious discomfort. "Yeah, but I washed my hands."

"Ew." I push it back at her.

She laughs and accepts it. "Fine. Go buy a new copy. That's an order." I rest my elbows on my knees and hang my head, but Amy crouches in front of me, pushing my head back up with a fingertip. "Wait, you do masturbate, don't you? Flick the bean? Get yourself off? Tell me you give yourself an orgasm from time to time?"

I shake her off, wishing I hadn't raised this whole issue in the first place. But then again, if I can't raise it with Amy, who can I talk to about it? Whatever I say, I know it's not going any further. She's not going to judge me, even if her tone is vibrating with shock at the possibility that I might tell her I've never touched myself. "Yeah. Sometimes."

She pins her lips. "Do it more. You look like you need *more*." She cocks her head as if reconsidering. "What you really need is to get laid. Finally. What are you waiting for? Prince Charming?"

The words are like an electric wire that runs right through me. *If she knew how unfortunate that choice of title was...* It has Seb frolicking through my mind like he lives there. Like he's dancing naked in the fucking rain. "No. It's just... the brand, and Mum, and—"

"You've got to kick your mother out the bedroom. Energetically. Throw her the fuck out, lock the door, and go have sex." She nods emphatically at the book. "That Vanessa bitch is the horniest woman to survive the end of the world. If you want the role, you have to be prepared."

I give a helpless laugh. "They won't put all that on screen. It's not a porno." I've been avoiding thinking about this particular aspect of the story. About how sexual this character is, and how I'm *not*. It's not the camera thing that I'm worried about. I've done a lot of sexual photo shoots. They're always pairing me up with male models and having me pretend to swoon. I can do it for the photos... but the idea of doing it in an audition kinda freaks me out. But I really, *really* want to get this job, not least because it's the kind of role that Mum would absolutely loathe.

"*Taming the Beast* is not on brand." Amy cackles like she's read my mind. "It's worse than Seb Hawkston. Your Mum will really hate it."

"I know. But I *really* want it."

If I'm going to do this acting thing, I am going big. Every other dream I've had, I've made come true. *Or Mum has,* a little voice whispers.

Well, this one is for me. If there's one thing I am manifesting, it's this role. *My freedom.*

Amy rises to sit next to me and slaps her hand on my thigh. "You can do anything. You're Erica Lefroy." She says the name as everyone does: like it doesn't belong to a person, but a commodity. "And you know what else?"

"What else, Amy Moritz?" I reply, throwing her famous name right back at her, but she doesn't rise to the jibe.

"You can totally fuck Seb Hawkston too, and there's bugger all your mum can do about it. Call him up and tell him you're sorry. And then go have hot, sweaty make-up sex with him."

13
SEB

I didn't like the sound of Dad making my life hell, so here I am, walking in to one of Antonio Marchetti's restaurants. He owns a string of high-end Italians across the West End. Black and white tiled floors, well-placed wall lights, red velvet banquettes, and green velvet stools at the long marble bar. It smells like hot olive oil and garlic.

Dad is tucked into a booth at the back. He looks remarkably well, considering it's only been a few weeks since his heart attack. I feel a tiny pinch of something that feels disconcertingly like disappointment, and it makes me feel like I deserve to go straight to hell.

I'm late, so Antonio Marchetti and his daughter Diana are already seated.

Dad and Antonio stand when I reach the table. Diana stays seated, hands clasped on the table. She doesn't even look up. *Guess she wants to be here about as much as I do.*

"We were worried you weren't coming, Sebastian," Dad says.

"Wouldn't miss it," I say, taking Antonio's hand and giving it a firm shake. "This is a great space." I gesture around the room.

"Diana did the interiors," he says with pride.

On cue, Diana looks up to acknowledge that we're talking about her. She's pretty, her cheeks a little rosy, her eyes a honey brown colour. She gives me a cute smile that looks almost like a smirk. Something about this scenario amuses her, that's for sure, but I can't fathom what it is.

"Great job," I tell her.

"Glad you like it," she says, her voice smooth and her vowels rounded with an unmistakable public school accent. There's something feline about her. Maybe the almond shaped eyes or her straightened blonde hair that clings to the sides of her head.

"Diana," Antonio says to his daughter. "This is Mr Hawkston Junior."

Junior, my arse. We're not in America. I'm junior to nothing.

Diana rises from her seat, but when I offer her my hand, she doesn't take it. Antonio watches the interaction with a narrowed gaze, and Diana deliberately averts her eyes, as if she's reluctant to catch her father's stare. "Hi," she says to me. "I've been saving myself for marriage. I hope you're ready to pop my cherry because it's going to go off like a bomb."

My mouth drops open, a surprised laugh caught in my throat. Dad jerks back in his seat so hard his spine slams against the leather. Beside him, Antonio splutters and springs to his feet. The glasses on the table shake and dad touches the base of his wine glass to steady it.

"Diana!" Antonio growls, his cheeks shaking.

Her mouth forms a neat O and she touches her fingers to her lips, displaying perfectly manicured pink nails. "Goodness. I don't know what came over me. Sorry." Her voice is so sickly sweet that the apology rings false, leading me to suspect that she knew exactly what she was doing. She can't be fully on board with this arrangement either. Antonio lowers himself to sitting, both hands flat on the table as he glowers at her. Flashing a tight smile, she holds her hand out to me. "Hi, Mr Hawkston Junior."

I grip her hand, stifling my grin. "Good to meet you." I release her and flick my jacket out of the way as I sit next to her.

Well, this is fucking awkward. Or hilarious. Or both.

Our fathers continue the meeting like nothing unusual has occurred. Dad outlines the basics of the land and hotel deal. The Marchettis want to keep a long leasehold of the land, which I can tell fucks Dad off. He wants the freehold, but Antonio won't let it go.

"I also want to ensure that Arthur Knatchbull gets his luxury goods stores on the ground floor," Antonio says.

Dad has no issue with this because Hawkston Hotels has been dealing with Knatchbull Luxury Goods from the start. They're in all our hotels, as well as every luxury shopping street in the world. Clearly, the Knatchbulls and Marchettis are acquainted.

"And you're an interior designer, Diana?" I ask by way of making conversation while Dad and Antonio thrash out the details. This meeting really does feel like we're the kids and they're the men, and the whole thing makes me fucking angry, but seeing as Diana is sitting beside me, it would feel wrong to ignore her.

"No. This was my first project. I'm a social media influencer, but Dad doesn't think it counts, so he gave me the restaurants to design. With supervision." I glance at her father, who's paying us no attention. "I thought you might know what I did," Diana adds. "I thought you'd have looked me up. I looked you up."

"Ah. No. I didn't." *Because the only woman I'm stalking on social media is Erica Lefroy.* "What do you... influence?"

"Books. Romance, actually. I've just read that *Taming the Beast* book and I would love Erica Lefroy to get cast in the movie. She's so great." She lets out a sigh that sounds lovesick, and I try to hide the fact that Erica's name hit me like a shockwave. "You got a lot of publicity after you picked her up off the runway. I read all about it online. They're calling you Prince Charming."

"They are?"

"Yeah. You know... the whole lost shoe thing. You scooping her up and saving her. It's kind of adorable. She was like Cinderella, which makes you Prince Charming."

I should definitely change the subject, but if Erica isn't talking *to* me, then talking *about* her is the next best thing. I can't fucking resist it. It's the hit I've needed.

"She's so beautiful. You must know her really well. Do you?" She sounds starstruck. "I'd love to have a guy who'd be willing to do that for me. You know, if I fell over in public. Maybe I'm not pretty enough though..." She looks away awkwardly, probably remembering why we're here. If we get married, the guy who's supposed to scoop her up and save her is me.

"You're plenty pretty," I say.

The little smirk makes a reappearance, and the awkward girl of a moment ago is gone. "Oh, you're smooth." She leans back a little, showing all her teeth as she grins at me.

"Excuse me?"

"I wanted to see what you'd say if I played it coy."

I frown. "You were fishing for compliments?"

"No." She flicks her hair off her shoulder. "I wanted to see what kind of man you are. My followers tell me I'm pretty a lot in the comments, but I'm not like Erica Lefroy. I'm relying on all the makeup and the filters and—"

"There are no filters here. You're all good. I promise."

Her eyelids flutter like she's holding back an eye roll. "There you go again, trying to reassure me. I might not be a world famous beauty, but I'm happy with my face. It does what I need it to do."

I take a sip of my wine, unsettled by the attention she's paying to me already. Normally, I'm the one observing and taking notes. "Which is what?"

"Get people to stop scrolling. Then I can capture their attention with my witty book commentary." I press my lips together to stop from smiling and raise my wine glass. "How many followers do you have?"

"Half a million," she responds just as I go to take a sip of my wine.

I splutter into the glass. "Half a million? And your dad doesn't think that counts?"

She shrugs, but it's a kind of happy shrug that dismisses her dad's opinion, and like she's thrown off a spark, warmth hits my chest. "I'm a bit of a big deal." Her smile is so bright that I know she's not taking herself too seriously. "Really, though, it's just something I'm passionate about. And I think when we love something, we go after it differently. We don't stop, you know? That's why my follower count grew so fast."

My mind goes to Erica, like an elastic band pinging back to its resting place. I wrestle my attention back to Diana. "Consider me impressed."

"Thanks." She tips her head, eyebrows pinching. "You seem nice. I don't want to mislead you."

"About what?"

She leans in close and whispers, "I'm not actually a virgin, but don't tell my dad."

I pull back and wink. "You're secret's safe with me."

"We'll sort out the details of the deal." My father's voice shatters the fragile intimacy of our conversation. "And when it's all lined up, we'll announce the engagement."

"Four months. I think that's how long it'll take to sort it all out," Antonio says.

Four months.

This is surreal. I've woken up inside a nightmare. I must have. Some fucked up lucid dream where my father is marrying me off to a woman ten years my junior so he can build a mega hotel and take over the world.

There is no fucking way I am agreeing to this. As amusing as Diana is, she will not be my wife.

"You two will make such a beautiful couple. Diana deserves a good man," Antonio adds, and I force my face into stillness. I don't want to reveal *anything*.

We eat and drink, and there's even laughter. I don't dislike Antonio Marchetti, and I suspect he's been a marginally better father to Diana than Dad was to us. At least he's talking about her and what she deserves in a positive light, which suggests he cares about her at least as much as he cares about the deal. Unlike Dad, who doesn't give a fuck about me.

At the end of the meal, Diana and her father depart, leaving me and Dad at the table. We sit in awkward silence for a few moments, Dad dabbing his lips, which are dry and stained with red wine he certainly shouldn't be drinking, with a white linen napkin.

"She's lovely," Dad announces, even though I'm not sure he paid her much attention, and it wouldn't make any difference to him if she were a monster.

"She's fine. But I'm not doing it. This is my life and I'm sorry, but no. You can take all my money. I don't give a fuck."

Dad lays his napkin on the table and strokes it with a wrinkled hand. "I thought you might say that, so I have a little... *incentive*." The sound of his voice, all cunning and slimy, makes me shudder. I know him well enough to know that whatever this incentive is, it's not one I can escape. He opens his jacket and pulls out an envelope, which he places on the table and pushes towards me. I don't want to know what the fuck is in there—judging by the smug, self-satisfied look on his face, it's the piece that will royally fuck me up the arse and play the checkmate—but I can't leave without knowing what the old bastard has planned.

I pick up the envelope and open it. Inside, there are photos of a man fucking a girl from behind. Gripping onto her as she's bent over a desk. She's young. Probably underage. Illegal. But it's not *her* that draws my attention. It's the man in the images.

It's me.

Horror seeps into every cell of my body. I flick through a couple more images of the same from slightly different angles. I don't recognise the venue. The woman. How do I not remember this? Wouldn't I remember it? I don't recognise her, or the room, or any of it, but it's the most incriminating set of images I've ever seen. I glance up at my father, who still looks delighted, like his final play has won the game and he knows it, and it all clicks into place.

I turn them over and slam them on the table, pushing them back at him. "These aren't real."

He sits back, amused. He picks up an unused steak knife and twists it in his hand. The blade glints and catches the light, making me blink. "No. But they look real, don't they?"

Fuck. They *do* look real. And if it's *me* in the photos and it took me a second to realise they weren't real, they'll fool everyone else for sure.

"The girl is real," Dad says. "A living, breathing woman. Very compliant, especially for a fee. A talented actress too. *Very convincing.*" He draws out the final phrase, and my stomach turns over. "She's eighteen, but she'll testify to say she was underage when this took place. I have witnesses who will testify to it too. Say they saw you with her."

"Witnesses?"

"Yes. You're careless like that, aren't you? Lounging in rooms where people are doing things you shouldn't see."

I grimace, thinking of Amy Moritz and her backup dancer.

"Maybe this time, it was you. Doing the things you shouldn't have been doing, rather than just watching. That sounds pretty believable to me. You're that much of a fool, you'd get your dick out when other people are in the room with their cameras out." He laughs, and a memory rushes me like I've been doused with a bucket of ice water: me, as a little kid, cowering in the corner from a man I knew was insane.

But today, I don't cower.

"You can't do this."

"I can. It's all arranged." He pokes the tip of the steak knife into the wood, marking the table. "All I need to do is press the button, and they'll string you up."

Tension wraps around my chest. "What the fuck did I ever do to you to deserve this?"

He strokes his chin, assessing me. "I won't use any of it if you agree to the marriage. Say yes, and I'll torch the lot right now."

My shoulders tense. This could not be more fucked up. Half of me—maybe more than half—wants to leap over the table, snatch the steak knife, and slit the old man's throat, letting the blood spill out. The other half—the more reasonable part—has me saying, "I won't do that."

He folds his lips, shaking his head as though I'm the disappointment. The stupid kid who doesn't know a good business deal when it slaps him in the face. "Then you'll go to jail. For a long, long time.

Maybe you won't make it out. Despicable man like you. Your behaviour has paved the way for this. Everyone will believe it. Dug your own grave, if you will." He chuckles. "Is it really worth your freedom? Your money? Your entire life?"

Is it?

I grip the edge of the table and hold my tongue, not wanting to expose my true feelings to him. But I know he sees the weakness in me. I know he's interpreting my hesitation as contemplation. Knows that I'm considering this. And I fucking hate that I am.

How hard would it be to marry Diana? And why am I so against it, aside from the rebel in me not wanting to bow to my father's bullying?

Erica.

Why does she have to pop into my head at the most inconvenient moments? Would she even give a fuck if I got married to someone else? She'd probably kick me down the aisle herself. If she's the reason I'm saying no, then I need to get my head examined.

"You have four months of freedom," Dad oozes. "Do whatever you want with it, but keep it discreet. Then you marry Diana. Pop that cherry." A lecherous chuckle slips through his dry lips. "Pump her full of pretty little Hawkston babies to secure this fucking hotel deal. After that, you can walk away. Give her a nice divorce settlement. And as a kicker, I'll leave you the hotel in my will."

"Fuck you. No. I won't do it." I thump my fist on the table. "You will not control me like this."

He leans back, chin propped in one hand, his elbow resting on the armrest of his seat. He doesn't look remotely troubled by my refusal, like he knows it's only a matter of time before I bend to his will. "You were always so eager to please as a child. Desperately trying to make us all laugh. To make us happy. What happened to that little boy, Sebastian?" He croaks out a laugh that has me convinced my father is truly evil. "Tell him I miss him, won't you? He would have done this for me."

"You killed him." I push up from my seat, intending to leave before the urge to physically maim him takes over. I'm drawing the attention of other diners but I hardly see them. The world is a fucking blur.

He snorts. "Four months, Sebastian. Then we'll announce the engagement."

"The fuck we will," I spit over my shoulder.

I stride through the restaurant, hoping I never have to see that fucker's face again. There isn't even a trickle of love in me for that man. I hope he dies a slow and painful death—preferably before Nico gets married in three months, so I won't have to see him at the wedding—and that damn hotel never gets built.

But, as good as it feels to walk out on him, he's the one with all the power. If he wanted to, he could rip me a new one and leave me to bleed out in the street. He'd do it too. No doubt about that. So while it might feel like I've achieved something as the door crashes shut behind me—my own little rebellion—I can still hear him laughing out here in the corridor, and it feels like shit.

No one wins against William fucking Hawkston. *No one.*

14
ERICA

I am a glutton for punishment. Either that or I'm completely spineless, because I'm in the waiting room of the Harley Street plastic surgeon's room sitting next to my mother. Sometimes it feels like her influence is a vine wrapping its tendrils around me. *Inescapable.*

Where would I be if I truly cut myself loose? The thought raises the hairs on the back of my neck. We're energetically enmeshed, and as much as I'd like to sever our connection, I don't know where I would be—*who I would be*—without her.

A glance around the waiting room tells me I'm not alone in this codependence; there are an alarming number of young girls in here, sitting with their mothers.

Am I really going to let her force surgery on me? Isn't that a step too far?

Nerves crawl in my stomach like insects disturbed from under a dark log. I remind myself that Mum is doing this to help me. She only wants to help. *Doesn't she?*

People keep looking at me. *Sometimes, I really wish I wasn't famous.* I'm wearing a short summer dress, but my hair is tucked up in a baseball cap. A huge pair of sunglasses are perched on the bridge of my nose, even though we're indoors. I must look crazy, but Mum insisted.

Because how awful would it be if someone recognised me and told people I was considering surgery?

"Miss Thomas?" calls a nurse.

I don't react, but Mum grabs me. "That's us. I had to use a fake name."

Us.

My body revolts over that one word, but when Mum hauls me out of my chair, I don't resist. We follow the nurse, who leads us to a fancy consultation room on the first floor with a wide bay window that looks down over Harley Street. The surgeon, a man in his fifties with salt and pepper hair, sits behind a desk.

He stands and gestures to the seats opposite his desk. "Miss Thomas?"

Mum shakes his hand, and I sit. I remove my cap and my glasses, and let my hair fall. The surgeon does a double-take, blinks, and clears his throat.

"Erm..."

I stand and grab his hand. "Erica." He still looks confused. "Lefroy," I clarify.

"Oh. Yes," he stammers. "I thought I recognised you. I'm Mr Williams."

"You understand," Mum purrs from her seat. "We have to be discreet."

"Quite." He sits and checks his notes, then looks up at me. "Breast enhancement?" I say nothing. *I don't want this.*

"Yes," Mum replies. "Maybe a couple of cup sizes bigger? Erica's always been rather modest in that department. Unwomanly. Extremely unfeminine, actually."

What the fuck?

The surgeon looks awkwardly down at his papers. "I wouldn't say that. Any kind of surgery requires careful consideration and psychological preparation. Do you want this, Miss Lefroy?"

He stares me right in the eye. I'm pretty sure he can tell that I don't want this. It might as well be scrawled over my forehead that I'm here under duress.

"Of course she does," Mum replies.

The surgeon's eyes flicker. "Miss Lefroy?"

Mum's intention pulses against my left side like her thoughts are creating a force field. There is only one answer here.

"Yes," I say, but the self-betrayal makes me want to scream.

Beside me, Mum lets out a relieved sigh. "Yes, and while we're here, can we ask about that bump on her nose?"

I flinch.

The surgeon frowns. "Rhinoplasties are not my specialty—"

"But could we get it shaved off? Can't you do it with laser now, so her nose wouldn't need to be broken? She wouldn't get black eyes and have to miss work? Reduced swelling?" Mum leans across and grabs my chin, tilting my head to a certain angle so the surgeon can see what she means. "Right here." She taps a spot on the bridge of my nose. "If we could get rid of it, she'd be absolutely perfect from every angle, and I could stop having to remind her to keep her head tilted west-southwest in public. That would lighten my mental load tremendously."

I trace the bridge of my nose with my index finger. There's nothing wrong with the shape of it. Intellectually, I know that. But Mum is fixated on ironing out perceived imperfections, and apparently, I have a lot of them. It feels like shit to have my features dissected this way, as though I'm not even here, and by the person who's supposed to love and protect me.

"Perhaps you have a colleague who could deal with it?" Mum says.

The surgeon's face hardens. "I wouldn't recommend anyone touch Miss Lefroy's nose. We have plenty of clients who come in requesting the Lefroy nose. This is what people aspire to—"

"Ha! They can't have seen her close up," Mum barks.

I stare at the floor, a lump rising in my throat. For years, I've accepted everything Mum has said as though it was the gospel truth. I've done what she wanted. Obeyed all the rules. I have no idea who I am without the framework she's erected for my life, but listening to her talk to the surgeon really brings it home that she doesn't actually care about *me* at all. She's not on my team, and whatever I want to do from this point on, I have to do it alone.

The surgeon's jaw flexes. "Surgery is not a matter to be taken lightly. There are no guarantees—"

"We know all that," Mum says. "But where there's no pain, there's no gain. Isn't that right, Erica?"

Resentment simmers in my blood. *Where is Mum's pain? Who's going under the knife here? Me or her? Or maybe it's that 'us' she keeps talking about.*

Fuck. This.

I stand and lean across the desk, holding out my hand. "Thank you for you time, Mr Williams. I won't be taking this any further."

He grips my hand, a slight smile warming his face. "Miss Lefroy. I wish you all the best."

I thank him again as I stuff my hat and sunglasses into my bag and turn to leave, striding across the room and letting myself out.

"Erica," Mum yelps. "Where are you going? Put your hat on! Someone will see you." I keep moving and she calls, "We're not finished."

"I'm finished," I respond as I trot down the wide staircase of what must have once been a glamorous London townhouse.

"Why you ungrateful little..." Mum's footsteps rattle down the stairs behind me. "You do realise that without me, you wouldn't be who you are now?"

"Yes. You've told me." I open the door to the street and pass outside. The breeze is a welcome change from the stifling heat of the consulting rooms.

I keep walking, not knowing where I'm going, Mum running along behind me. The urge to turn and scream at her builds in my chest, bolstered by a fog of anger. I need to get away from her before I lose it.

"You should be grateful I'm taking such an interest in you," she calls out.

I spin to her. "*I* should be grateful that *you* took an interest in me? In your only child?" It comes out louder and harsher than I intend, with years of resentment and repressed rage bubbling up behind it. But I no longer care that people might recognise me or hear what I'm saying. Mum's expression turns brittle, and an unpleasant tingling heat spreads out from my heart, but I force myself to speak despite how fast my pulse is racing. "Do you even like me? Because it doesn't feel like you do."

"Of course I *like* you." Each word is simultaneously clipped and over-exaggerated, the implication that I'm being ridiculous all too clear. "I love you. I want the best for you."

"Then why do you keep trying to change me?"

Mum rests a hand on her hip, stepping a little closer to me and glancing around like she's checking who's watching. *She's still thinking about the fucking brand.* "You know what I'm seeing here, Erica?" Her voice is cool and level. "I'm seeing judgment. Millions of women have breast implants. Why do you think you're better than they are?"

"I don't. You're not listening. I don't have a problem with breast implants. If you want them, have at it. Get them as big as you want. What I do have a problem with is not being able to choose. It's my body." My voice breaks. "*My body*," I repeat, and it sounds pathetic. I loathe that she's reduced me to this. "I want to choose. For once, I want to choose. Why is that not enough?"

"Settling is not a life choice. I want *perfection* for you. No one can hurt you if you're perfect, Erica. *No one.* The more beautiful you are, the safer you are. I'm protecting you."

This is so warped. Those creepers wind around me, dragging me under where I can't understand what's real or right, but I fight against it. "I'm fine. I'm fine as I am." I try to sound confident, but I don't feel it. *Maybe I'm not fine.* Maybe I need all the diets, the exercise, the salon appointments, the physical trainers. Maybe I need plastic surgery too.

"Fine isn't good enough," Mum says. "You didn't get to be *Erica Lefroy* because I settled for 'fine'."

I can't make myself heard. Nothing will get through. I shouldn't have come to this stupid appointment because I was never going to go through with it, but I was too afraid to say no. Nothing I think or feel matters, because to the outside world, it looks like I have everything, and to my mother, I'll *never* be good enough.

A cruel longing rises in me as I stand in the street, staring at the woman who raised me. Why couldn't I have had a mother who loved me for *me*? Instead, I have one who critiques me and changes me and makes me into what she thinks the world wants to see, rejecting every aspect of me that doesn't meet her exacting standards.

I don't know who I am without all of that. I am so lost. And now I'm yelling at her in the street. *In public.* People are looking. People are looking because she turned me into *Erica Lefroy* and now I can't walk outside without being recognised.

"You need to take a long, hard look at yourself, young lady," Mum hisses. "You owe me everything. Your fame. Your fortune. Your career. I got you that big break, dragging your portfolio to Arthur Knatchbull and making him see you. That's what got you here. My grit and determination. Without me, you'd be nothing. How do you have the nerve to walk out of an appointment like that and tell me I did the wrong thing? When I'm the one who built you up? I *made* you. I *own* you."

The urge to cry rises up my throat. I'm choking on it. She *owns* me? It's always felt that way, but hearing her say it aloud is new. To know that she *actually* sees me that way changes my reality in an instant. The awful thing is, that while I hate it, I know Mum has a point. I wouldn't be where I am without her. She drove me to this high. Always pushing, pushing, pushing. Greedy for more. And it got us a really long way.

Us.

"I hate you. I really fucking hate you." I put out my hand, curling my fingers. "The keys to my apartment. Give them back."

"Erica—"

"I'm serious. You can't let yourself into my life whenever you want anymore."

"This is pathetic. I'm surprised at you, stooping this low." She digs into her bag as though she's trying to find my keys. "I wasn't going to do this, but now I will." She pulls out a newspaper, flashing it at me. "I always know best. I knew those tiny breasts would hold you back." She flaps a hand at my chest, which feels as though it cracks in half at the dismissive way she gestures towards it.

"What are you talking about?"

She thrusts the article at me, and I glimpse the headline. *'Erica Lefroy, the world's least sexy supermodel'* before she pulls it back.

"They saw you buying a copy of that *Taming the Beast* book, so now it's all the gossip that you're trying out for the movie. And to make it worse, one of your old audition tapes has been leaked. It breaks my heart to say it, but you are a terrible actress, Erica. Completely wooden."

I take a step back from her. People are passing us by on either side, staring in that way people do when they think they recognise you. A hard stare. The '*Where do I know you from?*' stare. It's difficult to concentrate on Mum, knowing people are watching.

Mum flaps the newspaper again and starts quoting from the article. "'*Breasts so small they might as well be inverted*'." She smiles as though this insult delights her. I freeze, my throat growing so choked up I can hardly breathe. *I'm going to cry.*

"How on earth do you expect to become a movie star when the papers are talking about you like this?" Her eyes dip back to the paper. "'*Completely devoid of sex appeal*'. They call you an *Ice Queen*. I could have protected you from this if you'd only shared your aspirations with me. If you hadn't hidden this desire to shift into the movies. We could have sorted out your breasts long ago. I only want the best for you, Erica. I want to give you everything so that you can fly. And look at you now." She wafts the paper up and down my form. "So near the top. So close to being a superstar, and you'll fall at the final hurdle because you won't go through with that surgery." She raises a shoulder in a tiny shrug. "It's just a little cut here and there."

I raise a trembling hand, my voice quavering just as much. "It's not just a little cut. It's you saying, yet again, that I'm not good enough. That there's something wrong with me. What kind of mother does that? What kind of mother says—"

"Well." She cuts me off with a disgruntled breath. "I'm glad you've got all that off your chest. Making your poor mother feel guilty. No one else will look out for you the way I do. No one cares as much as I do. How you can be so cruel to me, I don't understand."

My mind feels sluggish. How has she flipped this around so fast? "Me? You think I'm being cruel?"

"I do. And you'll pay for this cruelty. You'll never get what you want, and all because you won't get your boobs done. You think you're good enough as you are? You're not. You never will be. You'll never get to Hollywood, not with a reputation like yours. Frosty, virginal little bitch with no breasts."

I cup both hands over my mouth, stifling the cry that escapes beneath them. Confusion settles like mist in my brain; my psyche torn in two by the inconsistency. *I can't keep up.* I stutter like a toddler trying to form a sentence. Finally, I gather myself enough to drop my hands and speak. "You were the one who wanted purity. Innocence. Chastity." I sound like I'm shattering into pieces, and I hate it. "That was the whole thing. The whole *Erica Lefroy* deal. *Untouchable.*"

"Yes, but then you went and wanted the movies. Very selfish of you to want something different when we're about to launch the fragrance and cosmetics. Only thinking of yourself."

As much as I want to stand up for myself, there is a truth to this I can't deny. I have been secretly trying to move away. *Maybe it's me. Maybe I really am a selfish little bitch.*

"On the plus side," Mum continues, "everything that article says about you shows what a wonderful job I did with the *Erica Lefroy* brand, doesn't it? You can't be sexy in a way that isn't wrapped up in virginal purity. You can't get a lead role in a film like *Taming the Beast* because I perfected this version of you." She violently jabs a finger towards me. "And it worked. You're worth millions. One of the most famous women in the world. You know what this shows?"

"What?"

"That your mother always knows best." She holds out her hand to me, her face a mask of compassion that doesn't fool me for a second. "So stop being a silly little girl and come back inside so the doctor can fix you up."

15
SEB

"Yeah, I'll be there asap," I bark into the phone. "I'm in midtown. Wimpole Street. I'll be in the office in twenty minutes."

"Hurry the fuck up," Nico replies.

Arse. I am never late to work. I hang up without responding and stare out the car window as we cruise through town. I should have been in the office half an hour ago, but after meeting Dad for lunch, I didn't fucking feel like it. On top of that, the moment I walked out of that restaurant, everything that's happened with Erica hit me like a shit ton of bricks. Since the night she kicked me out of her flat, I've seen her once. *Once.* Where she let me go down on her and then screamed at me and ran away.

Maybe this time, it's over.

Maybe I've lost her.

I should never have tasted her.

Fuck it. Having my head between Erica's legs, her clit on my tongue, her taste in my mouth, is the highlight of my life. I don't regret it for a second. Besides, I'll likely lose her anyway, given how all this stuff with Dad and Diana is playing out. As much as I'd like to say I'm confident that I can outplay my father, I don't know if I can.

I miss her. I miss Erica *fucking* Lefroy with an ache that gnaws at my heart.

After lunch, I decided enough was enough, and instead of going to the office, I got my driver to take me to Vauxhall, where we sat outside her building for forty-five minutes while I wondered whether or not to get out of the car.

She could have contacted me. She could have called and apologised. But she never did. Maybe it doesn't bother her that we're not talking. *Maybe she doesn't care.*

I clench a fist and press it to my lips, closing my eyes as a blistering pain spreads through me.

In the end, I got out of the car, strode into the lobby, and asked for her, only to be told that Miss Lefroy wasn't there. So here I am, on my way to the office.

"Sir, there's a jam ahead. I'm going to take a turn down Harley Street," comes the driver's voice, bringing me back to the present.

"Sure." I stare out the window, watching the passersby going about their day. But then I catch sight of a disturbance on the pavement outside one of the Harley Street surgeries. People appear to be arguing. I twist in my seat as we drive by, trying to get a better look. Is that... *Erica?*

She's yelling at someone. An older woman who looks a lot like her. That's got to be her mother. I recognise her from the fashion shows. Erica is flapping a piece of paper in her direction. *Is she... crying?* The older woman yells something, leaving a distressed-looking Erica in the middle of the pavement.

"Pull over," I instruct the driver.

"Sir, I can't park here."

"I don't give a shit. Fucking pull over. Now."

The driver nods at me in the rearview mirror and the car cruises to the side of the road. It's an obnoxious place to park, but I don't give a fuck.

I leap out of the car, rushing back down the pavement to where I'm sure I saw Erica. I dodge through passersby, weaving my way towards her. There are tears streaming down her face. I've never seen her look like this. Harassed. Distraught. Out of her fucking mind, worse than when we fought in the gallery. That she'd let it happen in public is even more concerning. *What the hell just happened?*

People are slowing down to stare at her, not only because she's clearly in distress, but because it's *Erica Lefroy* in distress.

Through the crowd, her eyes latch onto mine.

Her footing stumbles as recognition, panic, and relief flood over her features. But then she stiffens, half turning away like she means to run from me.

A few strides takes me to her, and I grip her shoulder. She turns, her wide, dark eyes meeting mine, sharing the depth of her desperation in an instant. I don't need her to tell me she needs me. I can read it on her face. I pull her towards me and she collapses against my chest, shaking fingers gripping my shirt.

"Shit, Erica," I mutter against her hair. "What happened?"

People are calling out her name, staring at us. Erica pulls away, but her fingers remain twisted in my shirt, eyes flashing panic as she realises the crowd is closing in.

"I have the car." I nod where the vehicle is still idling, hazard lights flashing. "Come with me."

She gives my shirt a gentle tug. "Who... who's in the car?" Her voice breaks.

What? "No one. The driver."

"No other women?"

Shit. If it were anyone else, the question would be a joke, and I'd crack a joke in response. But this isn't a joke, not least because it's *Erica* and the last time I saw her she was screaming at me in the gallery, and now she's standing here in the street with tears running down her face, looking at me like I caused them. Nothing about this is funny, and the tension is so thick and cold that you could crack it like ice. At the sight of her, something topples inside me, pieces scattering like a house of cards.

She might have hurt me, but I hurt her too. *Badly.*

Before I can answer, someone yells her name and we both look up to find multiple mobile phones pointed in our direction. A Vespa draws up alongside us, and the guy on the back hops off, equipped with a great big fuck off camera. I didn't even know they did that anymore. Proper 90s-style paparazzi.

"Erica! Give us a smile," he calls. Wrenching out of my arms, she turns to him, mascara streaking down her face as he points the camera and clicks. She stalks towards him, looking like she's going to murder him. And if she does, the whole thing will be caught on camera. *I can't let her do this.*

I catch up to her in a couple of steps, tucking her behind me in one swift move.

"Mate, you're blocking Lefroy," the photographer says, lowering the camera. I step closer and put my hand over the lens. "Oi!" he yells, trying to snatch it away, but I wrap my other hand around the body of the camera. He's a little guy, and he won't be able to fight me for it.

"Delete the photos and get back on your fucking bike right now, and you can keep the camera," I growl.

"Fuck off, mate. This camera's worth thousands, and the photographs—"

I yank the camera from his grasp and smash it to the ground. "Wrong choice." I offer him a compensatory mock grimace.

He squeaks like a mouse having its entrails ripped out, whimpering over the shattered camera as he sinks to the ground to pick up the pieces. I scoop it up before he can, flipping it around until I find the memory card, which I slide out and put in my pocket. I hand him back the ruined camera and he cradles it like treasure. I'm about to walk away, but because I don't want to be a total dick about it, and the guy looks like he's about to weep, I undo my watch and slip it off my wrist, holding it out to him. "Here."

He stares up at me, confused, and I shake the watch at him, but he still doesn't take it, so I bend down and tuck it into the pocket on the front of his shirt, and tap it. "It's Cartier. This is your best work day this year. Now, fuck off."

I straighten to find people staring and filming me, while Erica still stands behind me. I can't very well smash every phone on Harley Street, so I put my arm around her, using my body to shield her from everyone.

I pull her close and whisper, "Get in the car. I'll take you wherever you need to go. There are no other women in there, I swear."

She relaxes and allows me to usher her to the waiting Bentley. I open the back door, waiting for her to get in before closing it and moving around to the other side to get in myself.

Inside the car, the sound of people calling Erica's name is muted, and the air is cool.

"Go," I instruct the driver.

"Where to?" he asks.

I look at Erica. "Where do you want to go?"

She glances at me through thick lashes, and her chin trembles like she's on the cusp of breaking down. *Fuck*. She shakes her head like she has no idea.

People are crowding the car, leaning in at the darkened windows. I've never been so glad for the safety glass in my life. Muffled calls of '*Erica, Erica*,' meet my ears.

We can't fucking sit here while she works out what she needs.

"Just keep moving." At my command, the driver shifts into the lane and I click the partition to separate us from him.

When we're alone, I turn to her. "What happened?"

She closes her eyes, pressing the knuckles of one hand to her lips as if to stop them quivering. She says nothing, but I sense that it's not that she doesn't want to tell me, but rather that she doesn't trust herself to speak without breaking.

She passes me the tabloid paper she's clutching, folded open to an article entitled, *Is Erica Lefroy the world's least sexy supermodel?*

I glance over it.

Rumour has it that Erica Lefroy, Britain's top model and reputed Ice Queen, is looking to audition for the role of Vanessa Darkmoore along-side Hollywood heartthrob Michael Drayton in the upcoming block-buster, Taming the Beast, based on the multi-million-copy bestselling book by Abigail Enwright.

It remains to be seen whether Lefroy can hold her own alongside Michael, who was nominated for an Oscar last year for his performance in Downtown Meat Market. Lefroy might have a perfect face that fits on the Golden Ratio mask, but can we really imagine the woman who never smiles, with a figure like an overgrown adolescent boy and breasts so tiny they might as well be inverted, playing the role of the tortured sex bomb Vanessa, who captured the hearts of millions of readers worldwide?

If her recently leaked audition tapes are anything to go by, I very much doubt it. Never have I seen a more awkward screen performance. I hate to break it to you, Erica, but you don't have my vote, and I'm not sure you've got the sex appeal to captivate a man like Michael Dray-ton, let alone the worldwide cinema-going audience. If I were Abigail Enwright, I would have serious questions about Miss Lefroy, if she does indeed attempt to go for this role.

As ever, we're interested in public opinion. What do you think? Erica Lefroy, hot or not?

Beneath it there's a website address for readers to cast their vote online.

When I look back at Erica, she's leaning forward, her head in her hands as tears drip between her fingers and onto her knees.

This reaction cannot just be about the article. She's well-versed in shitty publicity. It's part and parcel of being in the public eye. Hell, we've sat on her sofa and laughed at some of the outrageous comments on her social media posts. Those trolls can be vicious, but I've never seen her like this.

I fold up the paper and put it aside. "Where the fuck is my phone?" Erica glances my way, frowning, but I keep theatrically searching my jacket pockets for it even though I know full well it's in my trouser pocket. "I've got to submit my vote. Hot. The answer is fucking hot. Erica Lefroy is hot."

She lowers her head, rubbing her thumb and forefinger over her eyes, but there's a hint of a smile on her face, even though she's refusing to look at me.

I abort my fake search for my phone. "Michael Drayton's very good looking, but really, he's not worth all these tears."

She glances at me sideways, the tiniest curve to her lips. "You couldn't not make a joke."

I take her shift in demeanor as permission to move closer. I want to touch her so badly. Comfort her. I might have guided her to the car just now, but that felt necessary. Protective. I had to shield her from that shit out there. But now, in the car, virtually alone aside from the driver, I don't know if I can touch her again. Not after our last encounter.

She leans into me, her weight settling against my side. *She must want to be held.* My heart aches at the thought and I slide my arm around her back, not knowing what the fuck to say next.

"Your breasts are definitely not inverted."

Good one, Seb.

She leans forward, spurts of pitiful laughter breaking through her tears. "Are you not done yet?"

"I'm taking a stand against fake news." She snorts like a pig, but at least it sounds like one who's having a good time. Or a moderate time. Maybe one who was wailing about being turned into bacon and has discovered they're being upgraded to a hog roast. "I'll run down Oxford Street in my boxers yelling, 'Erica Lefroy has perfect tits', if it'll make you feel better." I stroke my chin, striking a thoughtful pose, and Erica peers up at me. "I mean, you'd have to let me see them first. I don't want to inadvertently add to the fake news."

She sighs and leans back against me. "I really hate you sometimes." I can tell by the resigned and yet relaxed way she says it that she doesn't mean it. "But thank you."

We sit in silence for a few minutes until her fingers find my wrist. Heat leaks through me from the point of contact, my awareness narrowing as if her delicate touch on my skin is the only thing of importance in the entire universe. She slides the sleeve of my shirt upwards, her thumb resting on the pulse point. "You gave him your watch?" she whispers.

I shift my hand so my sleeve slips down. "I'd have given him more than that to leave you alone."

"Thank you," she whispers again.

An awkwardness I can't make sense of descends. Erica glances out of the window, but I'm not ready to lose her attention.

"Michael Drayton, eh?" I say, referencing the actor from the article. "He's the one Nico hit that night at Martini Gems. Do you remember? Kate was drunk, and he was dancing with her and Nico didn't like it."

"I remember."

"Did he have his nose straightened in the end? He tried to send Nico a bill for plastic surgery to fix it."

Erica's energy turns frosty, and I don't know what I said to cause it.

"You want to tell me what's really wrong?" I ask gently. "What happened back there?"

She slumps into the seat. "Mum wants me to get a boob job. And I said no, and then she gave me that article as evidence that she's right and I'm wrong and I'll never make it in the movies."

"Ah." I rub a hand over my jaw. "So the inverted boobs comment hit hard."

"Today, yeah."

"Unless your boobs are fantastic actresses, I'm not sure it matters."

She huffs. "Yeah. That's more or less what I said. But she also wants me to get my ears pinned back, and the lump shaved off my nose. And there was something else..."

Her nose? Her ears? "What does your mother see when she looks at you?"

Erica clasps her hands in her lap and stares down at them. "Imperfection."

I have so many questions, because, in my mind, Erica Lefroy is the most perfect woman I've ever met. I don't push for her to say more because I can tell she doesn't want to elaborate, so I merely say, "I'd never want to change a single thing about you."

She bites her bottom lip and stares into her lap, and for a while, we sit in silence as the car drives through the streets of midtown. I know we can't continue to ignore what happened last time we met, or why we haven't spoken. It's sitting here with us, the great big unspoken elephant in the back of the car, and finally, I can't bear it any longer.

"So... are we okay now?"

She turns slowly to look at me. "Feels like you're asking that a lot recently."

"Feels like I need to," I say solemnly, easing my arm out from behind her. "So... are we?"

Erica glances out of the window, and her response comes a beat too slow. "Because you made a few shitty jokes, or because you smashed a camera and forced me into your car in the middle of Harley Street?" The tilt of her mouth tells me she's teasing, or trying to, but I sense discomfort beneath her pretense.

"Neither. Because last time I saw you, I had my head between your legs, and then you called me names and ran away."

She emits a pained sounding sigh, tips her head against the headrest and closes her eyes. "Oh. Yeah," she murmurs. "That."

"That," I repeat quietly, a slow sense of dread filling me. Maybe bringing this up is a bad idea.

Silence fills the car for a few tense moments until Erica opens her eyes and glances at me. "Amy said I should call you to apologise."

"You told her what happened?"

"Yes." She glances away. "Sorry. I had to talk to someone about it."

"But you didn't take her advice?" Erica shakes her head, and I sigh. "You could have talked to me. You know that, right?"

She rubs her thumb into her opposite palm, over and over again. "You didn't call me either. And you said what happened between us was meaningless."

That's the biggest goddamn lie I've ever told. Tension throbs between us, dragging the beat of my heart into its rhythm. "You said you'd wipe every second of the encounter from your memory if you could."

She side-eyes me. "You said you'd bend me over and fuck the brat out of me."

I cough, spluttering into my hand. Never did I think I'd hear Erica say those words. In fact, I never expected her to mention them again. "I did. I meant it too. You were really fucking mean."

"I'm sorry," she whispers with what sounds like genuine regret.

"Me too. I wanted to call you, but I wasn't sure you'd want to hear from me." I wait for a moment in case she wants to tell me she did want to. Or maybe she missed me. But I get none of that, and although her lack of response causes a pinch in my chest, I keep talking. "Anyway, we can pretend nothing happened, if you want. I've brushed my teeth many times since then. Twice a day, at least. So what's that? Like 100 times. Roughly. Safe to say, I have well and truly divested myself of your intoxicating bodily fluids, delicious as they were."

Dropping her head into her hands, she brings her palms together until only her nose and mouth are covered. "Ugh, Seb," she moans, lowering her hands to her thighs. "I think I went temporarily insane, letting you loose down there. That's never happening again."

Never? The word slides between my ribs like a well-honed blade, but I can't afford to indulge the pain it causes with her by my side. I don't want to scare her away again.

She looks so awkward that my own discomfort recedes to the back of my mind. I'd love to take her in my arms and tell her none of it matters. There's no reason to be embarrassed or regretful or whatever it is she's feeling. I'd never judge her.

"I think I went temporarily insane being allowed down there," I admit. "Like a starving man at an all you can eat buffet. You can't let him taste the food and then take it all away. That's enough to send a hungry man crazy." I keep my tone as light as possible. It's for the best if she thinks I'm emotionally detached enough to joke about what happened, especially after she said what happened between us can never be repeated.

"Good thing you're the most well-fed man I know then.." She keeps rubbing at her palm, and although it sounds like she's teasing, there's a bitterness there too. At least I think there is. Could she be... *jealous*? Not that I'd wish jealousy on anyone, but—*fuck it*—I'd love it if she were. More likely, she's judging me again and her words from that night ring loud in my head.

Go and find someone else to stick your tongue in. Isn't that what you're good at?

I want to tell her I haven't stuck my tongue in anyone since that night because now that I've tasted her, I never, *ever*, want to taste another woman in my life.

From this moment on, it's Erica or no one.

But I keep quiet, and lift one of her hands from where it's resting on her thigh. I half expect her to snatch it away, but she doesn't, so I just sit there holding it. "If you want me to remember, I will. If you want me to forget, I will." I reconsider this. "Actually, I'll never forget. But I'll push it right out of mind, if that's what you want. If that's what it takes to have you in my life."

She squeezes my hand, turning bloodshot eyes on me. "I'd like to have you in my life too. Please." My hand feels hot in hers, our pulses clashing as she takes a few sobering breaths. "Really, Seb. I'm so sorry. I was horrible to you. I didn't mean it."

Her apology slides into my bloodstream like a sedative, slowing my heartbeat and making me feel woozy, but rather than sink into the comfort of it, I force myself to stay present.

"Don't bullshit me," I say with a gentle firmness. "You meant it."

"Not all of it. Mostly it was me freaking out. Because... you know. It's you. And me." I'm not entirely sure exactly what she means by that, but before I can request clarification, regret fills her dark eyes. "Please don't hold onto it. What I think about your sex life is irrelevant. It's none of my business." I wince; her anger might be preferable to her indifference. "And you're not a joke. Not to me, at least."

Thank fuck for that last part. I want to lift her hand and kiss it, but I daren't. Not yet. Erica's might be the only opinion that really matters to me, but what she's offered isn't enough to know that I'm fully redeemed in her eyes. "That sounds like you think I'm a joke to everyone else."

"I can't speak for anyone else, but to me... you're important. Really important." The repetition squeezes my heart, and I'm so fucking thankful to hear her say it that I feel like a total loser. "I'm so sorry. Can we be friends?"

Friends. That word doesn't remotely encompass what I want to be to Erica. What I want to have with her. A dull ache spreads behind my sternum, and without thinking, I rub the heel of my free hand against it.

"Yeah. Always. You're important to me too." I raise a brow at her, maintaining levity in my tone despite the pain in my heart, as I say, "I was still your friend when I was eating you out. I'm definitely capable of both of those things. Just in case... you know... there's any wiggle room on that."

A smile cracks her face even as her eyes roll. "There is absolutely no wiggle room. That was a complete one off. Never to be repeated."

I thump a fist against my heart. "Hit me where it fucking hurts, Lefroy." The pain in my voice is so exaggerated that it could only be construed as false. *Little does she know, it really does fucking hurt, and I wish to God I could tell her the truth.*

She puffs out an exasperated sigh, but I can tell she's amused. "How can you be so sweet and such an arse all at once?"

"I'm uniquely talented. Now, tell me." I nod out the window, where the streets of London are flashing by. "Where am I taking you?"

"Weren't you on your way somewhere?"

"You're more important than anything I was going to do today. Where do you want to go?"

She's silent for a long while. "Anywhere, as long as it's with you."

16
ERICA

We pace in silence down the path across Hampstead Heath. Seb chose the location in an attempt to cheer me up, calling his brother, Nico, to tell him he wasn't coming into the office. I feel a bit guilty that he's missing work for me. But it's a beautiful day, and I can't think of a better way to spend it than with Seb. I'm so relieved that we've worked out our differences, and our friendship is once more on track, that I feel a bit heady. Maybe it's the heat. And it is *hot*. Thankfully, I'm appropriately attired in a short cotton dress and pumps, complete with baseball cap that doesn't match, and my oversized sunglasses, but Seb is in a full suit. Somehow, despite the sun beating down, he hasn't broken a sweat. The path is dusty, and it's ruining his highly polished shoes, but he doesn't seem to care.

He undoes his tie as we walk, rolling it up and putting it in his pocket, and then he removes his jacket, hooks it over one arm, and undoes the buttons at his neck and cuffs. He rolls up his shirt sleeves and throws the jacket, collar hooked on his index finger, over one shoulder.

He looks unbelievably good, and whenever anyone walks past us, they stare. At *him*. I'm not even sure he notices. He's got a natural swagger, a confident walk like he owns the place. It's a sort of grace, a power, that most people don't have. It's in his bones. There's probably nowhere in the whole world that Seb Hawkston wouldn't be totally at ease, flashing that gorgeous smile, inhabiting every inch of his body like he's happy to be there.

I can't imagine what that's like.

"This is a PR issue," he announces, sounding like he's been thinking of how to phrase it since we got out of the car.

"How so?" I ask.

"You're worried this article and others like it are going to ruin your chances of landing a role in *Taming the Beast*."

A stream of anxiety trickles through the centre of my body. "Yes."

"So... fix it."

"How do I do that?"

He doesn't look at me, but he smiles and his dimple pops. "You could start by smiling in photographs." The comment immediately makes me scowl, and Seb bumps his shoulder against mine. "You have a beautiful smile."

"Smiling isn't going to get me an acting career."

"It might. But yeah, you need a total overhaul." He grabs my hand, and the gesture is so casual that it seems to mean nothing to him, but my heart leaps at the unexpected contact. We veer off the path and onto the grass, where clusters of people are sunbathing. Seb dodges through them, me following behind, until he reaches a shady spot under a tree.

This is the first time we've ever hung out together, alone, beyond the walls of our apartments. If Seb has noticed that fact, he hasn't mentioned it. But with his hand in mine, everything I've missed hits me so fucking hard. The freedom of being here with him, defying my mother, risking a little piece of my heart. I feel more alive than I have for weeks. I always feel alive in Seb's presence, like he makes every cell in my body fizz. And now, in the light of day, in public, in the heat of this unusually warm spring, surrounded by the happy chatter of all these people, the sensation is magnified.

It feels a little like I imagine being in love feels. Not that I'd know. But if I had to guess, this moment, right here, his hand in mine and the sun on my skin... it's somewhere close.

Seb stops, throws his jacket on the grass and points to it. "Sit down."

The command has a little ripple of something hot cascading down my spine, and I sit on his jacket before I can think too hard about what it means. He stands over me, silhouetted against the sun. Broad shoulders tapering to lean hips. My heart does a strange, quivery beat as I imagine what I'd do if he lowered himself on top of me. I blink the thought away, adjusting my sunglasses so I can see him properly.

"I have a suggestion," he says. "You're going to want to say no, but I want you to think carefully about it before you answer. And remember that I do marketing and PR all day, every day. I know what I'm doing."

"Okay," I say cautiously. "What is it?"

He drops beside me and lies down. I take him in: the strong jaw, the dimple, the hair, light brown and gently mussed, that all but screams 'touch me'. He is outrageously gorgeous. I can see why women would want to jump into bed with him. Not me, though. *Definitely not me.*

He props his other hand behind his head, exposing the tanned, veined forearm closest to me, and an unmistakable pulse throbs between my thighs.

Oh, fuck it. Maybe me.

Still staring up into the branches overhead, and for no apparent reason, he smiles, and that dimple pops.

The throbbing between my legs bangs like a drum.

Fine. Definitely me.

Hypothetically, of course. Not in real life. Just in my head, locked away safely in my imagination. Because Erica Lefroy and Seb Hawkston are not a pairing that works long-term. And I don't do casual. I mean, really, I don't do any kind of dating at all, long or short term.

"Are you going to tell me what this idea of yours—"

"Date me." He deadpans the words as though they mean nothing, but the fact it took him so long to come out with it lends them a weight that undermines his tone.

"No," I reply on reflex.

"I don't mean for real," he says, rolling his eyes. "I mean... for show. For PR purposes. I might not have been the right guy for you before, but this is my fucking moment. Let me help you get this movie deal."

My skin is hot, and it's not just the sun. "I'm listening."

He blows out a breath, and if I didn't know him so well, I'd say he was nervous. But Seb doesn't get nervous, does he? "You need to look like you aren't so aloof, right? Like you might... enjoy sex." The corner of his mouth tips upwards. "I'm your man."

Oh, fuck. My body is trying to stage a coup against my brain. I press my thighs together to stop the pulsing sensation that's taken root there. "No."

"Come on, Lefroy." He pulls out his phone. "Did you even check the social media coverage of me helping you off the runway?"

"No. I didn't. I—"

"You need to look at it." He scrolls and passes his phone to me without another word.

I've deliberately avoided looking at any of this stuff. Most of the time, social media is nothing but a distraction. But when you're in the public eye, it can also be vicious. I've been in the game long enough not to let it get to me. But if I'm honest, it was the fact that it was me and Seb, together, in the public eye, that had me avoiding it.

The first comment I see reads, *'Who is the hottie? That man is absolute fire. He makes Erica Lefroy look ugly'.* And then the reply beneath, *'How do you not know who Seb Hawkston is? Only like the hottest billionaire in the WORLD'.*

"Is this an ego boost for you?" I hand him back the phone, and he stares down at what I've just read.

He scrolls away. "Ignore that one. Here, look." He forces the phone back into my hand.

May love like this find me ASAP.

Where do I find a man like this?

I wish someone would look at me like that.

I bet they're having amazing sex.

Something twangs in my chest, like the snap of a guitar string.

"You're tagged," Seb says. "They've tagged you so many times, and you never responded. You didn't acknowledge it *at all.*"

"Why should I? It was nothing. I can't go around acknowledging every insignificant little thing that pops up on social media."

A flash of *something* crosses his face; a slight tightening of the jaw, a pressing together of his full lips. *Did I just hurt his feelings?*

He tips his head, his tone almost bored as he says, "I get it, Lefroy. Trust me, you've made it very clear you're not *actually* interested in me. But I'm offering you a solution. As a *friend.*" Despite his casual tone, the word crackles with tension. He gestures to his phone. "People love this shit, and they would love you too if you'd acknowledge it."

"I don't think this is something I should engage in."

"It's already in motion. This train has left the fucking station and you don't need to be on it, because it'll take you with it either way." I pull a face, which he ignores. "They're desperate for this to be a thing. For you and me to confirm it."

There's a hint of longing in his words, and I know it's only because he sees this as a problem he can fix, and he wants to help, to be *useful*, but suddenly, I'm mentally back in the gallery, Seb's face between my legs, and an erotic pulse shoots through me. The ghost of his tongue is *right there* like it never left. I force myself to concentrate. "I don't see why I should volunteer details about my private life just to satisfy—"

"It wouldn't be *real*. That's the whole point. It would be completely fake. But people would eat it up. Look at the comments again, and tell me I'm wrong."

Something writhes in my stomach. Maybe I'm just hungry. Or maybe having Seb lying next to me while I'm reading comments written by strangers that say things like, '*She must love him because, otherwise, why would she be looking at him like that?*' is making me feel weird. My gaze snags on one comment.

Everyone wants to get into her panties.

Beneath it there's a response that reads, *No one's getting in Lefroy's panties, because she's mine. All mine.*

"Listen to this," I say to Seb, and I repeat the comments. I dare a glance at him, but he's not looking at me. His mouth, and that damn dimple, are a dead giveaway though. "And you know who the user is?" I taunt him.

Seb arches an eyebrow, inviting my response.

"SeblovesBJs."

His expression doesn't flicker. "Good username."

"Is it you?"

"Hmmm. I do love BJs."

I playfully slap his arm. "You are such a dick. So this isn't you?"

"Of course it's not me. SeblovesBJs, indeed. That sounds like a teenager. A horny one at that. I am a mature man of sophistication," he says with mock sincerity. "I only use the term *fellatio*."

Laughter honks out of me. "It sounds like you. SeblovesBJs even calls me 'Lefroy'." I fix him with a hard, truth-searching stare. "It's you, isn't it?"

He laughs. A glorious sound that starts small and cascades to a full belly laugh that has me laughing along with him. "Okay fine. It's me. I love BJs and I don't want these random people thinking they can get in your 'panties'." He makes quotation marks with his fingers like he thinks the word 'panties' is ridiculous. "I'm doing cyber-security. SeblovesBJs is my alias."

"Really gonna scare them off, SeblovesBJs. You sound terrifying."

He snatches the phone from me, still laughing. When he recovers, he says, "So, what do you say about this dating thing? You've got to admit it's a good idea."

"Hmmm. Is it really a good idea to date a man whose online alter-ego is SeblovesBJs? I don't think so."

He sighs. "That's a very old username. I'm not that kid anymore."

"Could have fooled me."

His expression turns serious. "If it will help, I'll do this for you."

Heat rises to my cheeks as I lie back and contemplate what he's offering. I'm a bundle of nerves at the mere idea, and knowing that he's watching me, scanning my reactions and deducing God knows what from the tiniest muscle flicker around my mouth or eyes, makes it worse.

I should tell him no. Fake dating Seb? That's a disaster waiting to happen.

But I'm not going to tell him no. I've already decided. The thrill at the mere idea of pretending to date him is so intense I can't ignore it.

Besides, he might be right. This could be the perfect way to adjust public perception of me. And then there's the added bonus that Mum would hate it.

Amy's words from the last time we met gatecrash my mind. *You can totally fuck Seb Hawkston too, and there's bugger all your mum can do about it.*

I shove them away as rapidly as they entered. This is not about fucking. This is about fake dating.

But it's risky, not least because we've already crossed the line between friendship and sex. For it to work, and not destroy our friendship, I'd need to put limits in place. Maybe if I only agree to do it until I hear back about the audition, I could handle that.

"The audition is in two and a half months. I should find out in three."

Seb nods as though he's calculating something in his head. "So, around the time of Nico and Kate's wedding?"

"Yeah. Exactly." I turn to face him. "If we do this, we end it after the wedding. I don't want to steal their thunder or ruin their celebrations, so we'll wait until we get home. I should have heard about the role by then, so we'll know if it's worked or not."

"So..." he says slowly. "Short and effective. All for show."

"Yes."

"And until then, I will worship you in public, without reserve, and when I'm finished, the whole world will know just how desirable you are."

Fuck me. Hearing him say those words makes my heart race, but I play it down. "So SeblovesBJs is gonna get on his knees for me?" I tease.

"I've been on my knees for you for years. Seriously, whatever you want me to do, I'll do it."

He sounds so earnest that my chest feels all tingly, and it's hard to breathe. We're dangerously close to pushing a boundary I really don't want to touch, and yet, even edging close to it is a high I can't resist.

For a few moments, I stay quiet, mentally coaching myself on how to breathe until the restriction lifts. *Could I really do this with Seb?*

"If we do this fake dating thing…" I begin, and he rolls to his side to face me as I speak, propping himself up on one elbow. *So attentive.* "We need rules."

"Sure."

"Number one. No sex."

He sits up. "None?"

"Of course, none. You can't fake date me *and* be seen falling out of a nightclub with another woman. Or climbing into a cab. Or taking someone to one of the hotels or… any of it. You can't embarrass me like that. You have to quit playing around."

A gentle smirk twists his lips. "I meant with you, Lefroy."

My mouth drops open, and at my evident shock his grin breaks wide.

I sit up too and cross my arms over my chest. "Stop it. Be serious."

He settles his features. "So, celibacy for the duration then?"

"Yes."

"Okay," he says without missing a beat.

I pull back, blinking at him. "Okay?

"That's what I said."

"So you'd give up sex to fake date me?"

"Yes." His expression mellows and he tilts closer as if about to share a secret. "If I were committed to you, fake or otherwise, I'd never look at anyone else."

My pulse quickens. Hearing those words, in that deep, serious tone, unsettles me more than if he'd made another crass joke. "Great," I say, hoping he didn't notice my reaction. "If we're going to do this, you need to devote yourself to me, and me alone."

He raises a lazy palm. "I get it—"

"Do you? Because you cannot fuck with my reputation. I do not mess about."

Lying back on the grass, he puts one hand behind his head again. "There is no issue here. I'm all yours for three months. I'll be very convincing." A hint of his mischievous smirk appears. "Plus, I already know what you taste like, so if anyone asks—"

I lunge at him, clapping a hand over his mouth, but it's so impulsive that I hadn't thought it through. I'm nearly lying on him, his breath hot and damp against my palm, his large hand sliding over my lower back. My thoughts scatter like dominoes, piecing themselves back together in a pattern I don't want, but can't resist. *This feels good. This is wrong. I'm excited.* Our eyes lock, igniting a fire beneath my skin. I must look horrified because Seb's blue eyes flash with amusement, cracking the energy that held us bound, and something wet and warm licks the palm I have smacked over his mouth.

His tongue.

I leap back, wiping my hand furiously on my dress, but unable to ignore the relief that he's given me an excuse to break free of his embrace. *If he hadn't licked my hand, what would I have done? What would have happened?* My heart crashes against my ribcage. "Gross. You are such a child. I can't believe I'm even contemplating trusting you with something this important."

His grin widens. "I promise I'll treat your reputation the way I'd treat your heart."

"Stomp all over it?" I waggle my head to let him know I'm joking. I don't really think he'd do that. Not on purpose, at any rate. In spite of all our ups and downs, he's always been a good friend to me, and I hope I've been one to him too.

He gives me a dismissive frown. "No. Treasure it and keep it close to mine." Pressing a hand over his heart, a teasing gleam appears in his eyes and he adds, "obviously."

His words raise a swirl of emotion and I blow out a quick breath to release the tension. He sounds like he's joking, but the conflict of wanting it to be real, and hating that it's all part of this pretense he's concocted, is too much to contain. I grab a fistful of grass and throw it in his face, making him splutter and spit out the blades that find their way into his mouth. Seeing him so discomposed makes me laugh, and when he laughs too as he wipes his mouth on the back of his hand, I feel giddy.

"So," he says when he's cleared the grass from his lips. "Is this happening or not?"

"Yes. But we need to make a real splash. Very public. Very showy." Seb winces, but he said he'd do anything, and I am taking him at his word. "And I have the perfect idea."

17
SEB

When I said I'd do anything for her, I hadn't anticipated what Erica might ask of me. But I'm nothing if not faithful to my word, so here I am, standing in the middle of a huge photographer's studio that feels more like a warehouse and is teaming with people, waiting for her to show up.

I've agreed to pose with her for the launch of her new fragrance. This is likely to be the biggest launch of a temporary fake relationship ever.

In all honesty, I'd hoped for simpler pleasures. To take her out to a restaurant. To hold her hand in public. To listen to her laugh as we walk along the river, just the two of us. To dance with her at parties. To do regular things that we might do if this relationship was real. Things I've longed to do with her for years and never been able to. Not pose for photographs that will be seen by millions of people.

It's a harsh reminder that this is all for show, and Erica has gripped matters the way she would any other business opportunity: with a calculating exactitude that lacks any romance.

My phone buzzes in my pocket and I pull it out and open the one word message.

Discretion.

It's from Dad. He's sent the same fucking word three times now and so far I've ignored them all. The first one came after the images of me smashing a camera on Harley Street appeared on social media. When I opened it, the message sent a chill through me. Only he could send a one word message that fills me with fear.

It's been a week since then, and although the word doesn't quite have the impact it did the first time, I can't shake the feeling of apprehension that settles over me when his name pops up on my phone. I reckon he's watching me. Sometimes, I suspect someone's following me, but I'm probably being paranoid. But either way, the words he spoke at our last meeting have been haunting me.

You have four months of freedom. Do whatever you want with it, but keep it discreet. Then you marry Diana.

Smashing a camera on Harley Street in front of dozens of people, and ushering one of the most famous women in the world into the back of my car, is far from discreet, and what I'm about to do is even worse.

I push Dad and his messages out of mind because if I think too hard on it, and the threats he made, I'll break out into a cold sweat.

Erica appears, looking beautiful, but casual, in a white t-shirt and jeans as she greets me and we exchange pleasantries. She hooks her arm in mine. "I've made all the calls, so we'll be able to redo all the marketing materials for the launch. The posters, billboards... all of it."

"Couldn't we have slid an article into the tabloids instead?" I ask.

"We'll do that too when we formally announce our relationship status," she says as though it's all been decided.

She waves me off to the changing rooms, where I strip off and put all my stuff in a locker, putting my birthday in as the code. A prickle runs up my spine as I do it, and although no one's here, I get that sensation of being watched again. It's creepy, so I sling on the robe I've been given and leave.

Outside, an assistant greets me and escorts me to sit with a makeup artist, who pads my face with powder and god knows what. A hair stylist applies something sticky to my hair, and then two more makeup artists appear, working in unison to paint tattoos on my forearms and chest, all the way up my neck. The image is a specific one; an infinity symbol, which is the symbol for Erica's brand, and also the name of the fragrance she's launching. It takes hours.

By the time they finish, my muscles are aching from trying to hold still. Two more people appear and help me change into an all-black outfit—boots, jeans and button-up shirt. They roll the sleeves up carefully to expose the tattoos, but it leaves me wondering why the fuck I have tattoos on my chest if I'm wearing a shirt.

Finally, the photographer tells me to take a seat before a huge white screen.

I'm not a self-conscious guy, but this is fucking weird, what with all the lights and the cameras and the people milling around. When Erica suggested this, I thought we'd be doing a quiet shoot. Me and her and the photographer. Not this spectacle. These clothes. The body paint.

"Which agency are you with?" the photographer asks me as he walks around me, testing out the lens of his camera, coming up close and taking pictures of my face.

I blink as the camera clicks in my face. "What?"

"Which modelling agency?" He gives a low whistle as he looks at the digital screen of his camera. "I know Erica picked you for this, but whose books are you on?"

"He's not a model," comes Erica's voice, and the photographer looks up from his camera, breaking into a smile as she approaches. "He's actually my boyfriend."

Boyfriend.

The word is a pinprick to my heart, sliding in like a needle that makes me wince. It's so fucking cruel that the first time I hear her say it, it's not real. But my reaction to the word is nothing compared to the insane twisting-flipping thing my stomach is doing at the sight of her. She's wearing only underwear and heels and looks every inch the model. Black lace skims over her breasts, thin strips of it gracing each hipbone. Her stomach is toned and flat and those legs really are the length of the fucking Nile. *So. Much. Skin.*

Fuck me.

The photographer greets her like an old friend, and Erica thanks him for doing this for us at late notice. I can't concentrate on what they're saying because this is the first time I've ever seen her wearing as little as this in real life, and with her hair and makeup done too... *it's a lot.* She's like a pinup from a magazine come to life.

She's a different woman from the eighteen-year-old I saw in the housekeeper's catalogue all those years ago, swamped in that cheap jumper and trousers. Then, she was beautiful but innocent. Now, she looks like sin, and I would follow her to hell without a second thought.

I'm not the only person who's noticed, because the general bustle around us has stopped. People have slowed down to watch her, and the other guys around the set are suddenly sitting upright like a load of dogs waiting for her to drop treats into their open mouths.

I have to grip the edge of my seat to stop myself from erupting and throwing them all out.

"This is great news. You two will be completely comfortable with each other," the photographer says. "What are we going for?" He pulls out his phone and scrolls as though he's checking some list. "*'Love that lasts forever. Passion across lifetimes. Desire that can never be exhausted'*."

"Yeah," Erica says. "I know we were going for purity and innocence, but we're making some last minute changes. This is all about sensuality. Sexuality. The infinite love that everyone wants to find."

"Perfect. Love it," the photographer says.

Erica turns her attention to me. "You look great. Suits you," she says, taking me in. "You're not so preppy anymore."

I pull back. "Preppy?"

"Yeah. You know. When you're not in a suit, you're always wearing polo shirts and chinos. You're a hair's breadth from tying a cashmere jumper around your neck and sailing down the Thames." She mimes vomiting, and my mouth drops open. I had no idea that's what she thought of my casual attire. "You do look great in a suit though," she says, reaching out and rubbing my knee like she thinks I need the reassurance. Her touch burns through the jeans.

"What I want is for Erica to straddle you where you're sitting," the photographer interrupts.

Oh, fuck. "Really?"

The word pops out like the bleep of an alarm clock, and the photographer and Erica share a look as though they'd expect nothing less from someone who doesn't do this for a living.

Be cool, Seb. Erica Lefroy is about to straddle you in underwear and heels in front of a shitload of people.

She steps right up to me, gives me a little smile, and proceeds to straddle me without a pause. Her familiar scent wraps around me, both floral and lightly spiced, and I have to rein in the urge to press my nose to her neck and inhale it. I don't know where to put my hands, so they're just hanging at my sides. Her thighs are warm and heavy on mine, and her breasts are right there, soft flesh exposed over the top of the cups. I could dip my head and lick them.

Fuck it, in this position I could motorboat them, and I really fucking want to. *This is a disaster.* As if to drive the point home, my dick, which I'm all too aware is right beneath her, gives an unwelcome throb.

The photographer's camera clicks a few times, then he stops and stares at me. "Sensuality," he barks. "You know what that word means, right?"

"Fuck's sake," I mutter under my breath.

"You need to loosen up," Erica whispers. "Pretend I'm one of those women you take back to the hotel." She lifts my hands and settles them on her bare hips. *Oh, Jesus.* I've dreamt of exactly this; the feel of her soft skin against my palms and the warmth of her body so close to mine. The neural pathways are fucking ingrained. If I close my eyes, I'll be thrown into a fantasy of her riding me just like this, bouncing on my dick and looking like she's having the time of her life. I'm aching with a need that has no place here.

"Put a hand on her throat," comes the photographer's order.

My heart skips a beat, and the longing in my veins starts to fucking vibrate. If I put a hand on her throat when she's sitting on my lap in her underwear, I'm *definitely* getting hard. There could be a hundred people watching and it would still happen.

"Come on," she whispers. "Studio time is expensive."

"I'm pretty sure I've got it covered," I hiss back, which makes her roll her eyes.

"Erica," the photographer says. "Lean in and undo two buttons on his shirt and slide your hand in. And Seb?"

"Yeah?"

"Try and look like you're enjoying it." I grimace. If he knew how much I was enjoying it, he'd throw me off the set. "Imagine this is the one woman in the world for you. You want her. She's *everything* to you. This isn't *just* sex. It's everlasting love that comes with a large side order of orgasms." My dick pulses and I hope to God Erica can't feel it. Why does he have to throw out words like 'orgasms' when I am trying my best to hold my shit together? "That's what we're selling here. Buy this fragrance and you'll be desired and desirable. We want people to look at this image and know the two of you had sex as soon as I put the camera down." My balls tighten like he's just ordered them to prepare for action. "Just relax and pretend you're in private. Be who you'd be if no one else was here."

I close my eyes, screwing up my face. *This is torture.* The fantasy of Erica riding my cock flashes through my mind and I snap my eyes open.

"Please try," Erica hisses. "This is a key part of our plan." She offers me a hesitant smile, holding my gaze as she undoes a button on my shirt. It pops free, and a frisson of sexual energy runs through me. I do my best to tamp it down by clenching my abs, but it doesn't fucking work. Erica bites her bottom lip, and all I want to do is suck it into my mouth and dig my teeth into it. Her eyes are hooded as she takes in the tattoos covering my pecs. "You don't have a single tattoo in real life?"

I swallow. "Nope. No tattoos."

"Shame. They suit you." Her hand slides beneath my shirt, and the touch is a gentle caress that raises every hair on my body. She leans back a little more, and her pussy presses right against my dick. I can't help but shift my hips beneath her, increasing the contact. She tips her head back, dark hair falling over her shoulders.

A pulse flutters in her neck, a delicate thrumming beneath the skin. If I could press a gentle kiss to the spot, I would. I'd swipe my tongue right up her throat. I'd—

She lets out the tiniest whimper, and the sound sets me on fire. I want her to make that noise for me over and over again, moaning my name with the same level of whimpered desperation. It takes all my restraint not to moan her name in response. Without thinking, my hand rises to that expanse of her throat, closing softly around it.

Click.

The shutter noise on the camera might as well be a bomb. I jerk and turn to the photographer, who lowers the lens.

"Ignore me. Keep going," he instructs.

Erica hasn't let up in her '*I'm so turned on*' act, and the photographer clicks away, moving around us. She's so convincing, thrusting her breasts in my face and arching her back, grinding on me like she can't wait to get my clothes off, that I am struggling to convince my body this isn't real. Heat rages through me, and my blood is a power fuel that rockets to my dick. *Prepare for fucking lift off.*

Erica rubs her crotch against mine, and my hand moves up her throat and round the back of her neck like I have no control over it, but it knows exactly what it wants. And it's this woman, just like this, under my control.

My dick starts to thicken in my jeans.

Fuck, fuck, fuck.

Her fingertips graze my nipple, teasing it beneath the shirt. Arousal builds in my core, my dick throbbing.

Any second now, she's going to feel my erection right between her legs.

Her thumb brushes over my nipple again. *Why the fuck is she doing that?* No one can see beneath my shirt.

"I didn't realise we were making porn here," I murmur.

Her breath is hot as it hits my cheek, and she's panting just a little. "Is that what this feels like to you?"

My stomach drops. *Backtrack, backtrack. You fucking idiot. Why would this feel like porn unless it was turning you on?*

"I just didn't expect... I wasn't ready..." I sound like I took my brain out when I removed my suit.

Erica slides her hand back out of my shirt and cups my face, pressing her forehead to mine, not dropping the act for a second. "I'm a model," she says, the sensuality in her tone rippling over my skin. "This is what I do. I'd be a pretty shit one if I didn't know how to use my body."

"Right," announces the photographer, looking delightedly at the screen on his camera. His gaze flicks up to me. "You. Seb. Lose the shirt. We'll do the same again but topless this time, and then we'll do the kiss, and then we're covered."

What the actual fuck?

18
ERICA

A look of grim determination fixes on Seb's face as I slide off his lap. He unbuttons his shirt and a couple of assistants come over to help him out of it so he doesn't damage the tattoos.

In all the years of our friendship, I've never seen Seb without a shirt on. And he's right, this whole situation feels weird. Not like porn *per se*, but watching Seb remove his clothes is *hot*.

The muscles in his shoulders and back ripple. I am *melting*. His bare chest is covered in my logo, the infinity symbol snaking its way over his pecs, his abs, all the way down to the v that tapers into his jeans. It's as though I've branded him all over. *Mine*.

"Let's change the jeans," says the photographer, and someone runs over with a pair of pale jeans. "Boots and socks off. Let's do bare feet and stonewash this time."

The flicker on Seb's face is minute as he bends to undo the boots, slides them off, and removes his socks. Another assistant grabs them and takes them away. Seb straightens and reaches for the buttons on his jeans. His gorgeous hands slide the metal button through the hole. *His dick is under there.* A guilty, shameful heat runs through me because this really does feel like watching porn. A slow and sensual kind made just for me. *Absolutely off-limits.*

"Eyes up, Lefroy," Seb chides.

My stomach flips, but I cover up the bizarre way I'm feeling about his barely concealed dick with a laugh. A pretty convincing one too. Check me out, so cool and amused in the face of my friend's penis. Feels like I'm winning at life.

But as he undoes the jeans and slides them down, my gaze goes straight to his crotch, where the fabric of his boxers is doing nothing to hide the size of his package. And it is *big*. My cheeks burn.

He grabs the fresh jeans from the assistant and pulls them on. "I prefer these. All that black made me feel like I was dressed to break into someone's house."

You can break into my house any time.

He sits back down and I take a steadying breath before I resume my position on his lap again.

His large, warm hands land on my bare hips. Heat unfurls from the points of contact, rippling out like ink in water. *Shit*. I wish my body wasn't reacting like this. It's incredibly inconvenient. I keep my head down, refusing to look at him because... he's Seb. He sees right through people. It's this uncanny ability he has to know what people are thinking.

Right on cue, he says, "Getting a bit hot and bothered there, Lefroy?"

I bite my bottom lip and Seb's blue gaze takes in the motion, a hint of a smile settling on his lips. His thumb strokes over my hip bone and my attempt to answer dies in my mouth. What should have been a firm *No* comes out as little more than a breath. Another whimper.

"Let's wind this up," says the photographer. "Do what you were doing before. Keep it moving, as natural as possible, and then move into the kiss."

My stomach dips. I hadn't really thought this through. I remind myself that Mum will hate it. That this will help reshape my image. I can be the sexy woman I need to—

Seb hauls me closer still, severing my thoughts. There are inches between his bare abs and my stomach. His hands run up my back. One slides over my shoulder and up my neck, and the pounding in my pussy is *unreal*.

"Kiss me," he whispers, and the raw command settles right between my legs, my pulse beating as though my heart has lodged down there too.

We edge closer, breaths mingling, tension fierce.

"This is fake," I say, almost breathless and so quiet that no one else but him could possibly hear it.

"Yeah." The word is deep and low, and I know, in this moment, he'd agree with whatever I said.

"Just for show," I repeat, but I'm dizzy with how close he is. The whisper of his breath as it fans my face. The gentle pressure his hands exert on my hips as he eases me towards him and positions me over his crotch. *His dick.*

"Fucking kiss me, Lefroy," he says, and before I can process the order, I'm already doing it. My hands are in his hair, palms rasping against the stubble on his jaw, lips pressed to his, soft, warm, and wet when his tongue slips inside my mouth.

I'm kissing Seb. We're kissing. He's kissing me.

I moan into him, grinding on his lap, kissing him with a fervor that I really shouldn't, my hand sliding over his chest, my thumb grazing his nipple.

And that's when I feel it. *Hard. Big. And pressing against my pussy.* Holy fuck, is that his dick? Is that Seb Hawkston's penis, separated from my clit by a couple of layers of clothing?

Excitement flashes through me, and my core throbs, aching with want. I tilt my hips until I'm at just the right angle to rub myself against it... That feels *good*. So good. *Too good.*

Maybe it's not his dick. It's probably the buttons. The thick fabric of the jeans rucked up because of how he's sitting.

But either way, if I tip forward the pressure is *perfect*...

"Oh," I moan, so quietly that only Seb can hear.

"Shit, Lefroy," he murmurs in response, frustration and desire squeezed in the sound. *This has gone too far.* It's supposed to be fake, but knowing I've reduced him to such desperation makes my stomach flutter and my heart race.

"Okay, and relax. We've got what we need," says the photographer.

Seb lets his arms slide down until his hands are on my hips again. He's definitely breathing a little heavy. I go to move off him, but his fingers clamp down.

"Not yet," he says, voice husky.

My heart thumps. "Are you..."

"Don't move. Give me a second."

Oh, my God. He is *hard.* This might be fake, but his erection is very real. Fire rushes through my bloodstream, a heady sensation of power and lust combined. *I made him hard.* I cling to him, aware there are at least a dozen pairs of eyes on us. Probably more. *Do they know? Do they all know that my clit is thumping and his dick is hard?* "Oh, but..." My sentence dangles like a hanged man.

He groans against my neck, breathing steam into my veins. His lips are *right there,* hovering like butterfly wings over my throat. "Fuck," he curses, and the strangled sound of his voice is almost enough to tip me over the edge. His hands tighten, fingers anchoring into my flesh, his quads tense beneath my thighs.

We cannot do this. I'm about to shift off him again when his head snaps up and his gaze locks onto the photographer. "Get out."

I gasp. "Wait, Seb—"

"I... uh..." begins the photographer.

Seb jerks his chin. "What's she paying you?"

The photographer's gaze flicks between us, but he must decide Seb is the one in charge because he says, "Five thousand."

"I'll pay you ten times that to get the fuck out of here and take everyone with you. Clear the room."

"But—"

"I need five minutes with my girl. Now."

My girl.

The photographer's eyes peel wide, and for a second he stares, gaze bouncing between us, but then he makes his decision. "Everyone. Out," he calls, spreading his arms and shooing them like an alarmed herd of sheep.

When they're gone, the studio falls deadly silent, me still straddling Seb's lap. The beat of my heart slows, but I'm hyper alert, aware of everything from the tension of my bra strap constricting my ribs on every inhalation, to the abrasive rub of his jeans against my bare thighs and the press of his erection still edging against the lace of my underwear. And his hands... *his hands* on my skin.

"You can't order everyone off a set like that," I reproach him.

"You tweaked my nipple." The words grind out like he's annoyed, but he's speaking quietly. "You kissed me *and* you tweaked my fucking nipple. At the same time. That was a dirty move, Lefroy."

He groans, and even though he's not looking at me, I know all his other senses are fixed on me. His attention dusts over my skin like the gentlest of strokes. "Tell me I'm not alone here."

I glance over his shoulder at the empty room. "There were a lot of people in here before you waved them out with a wedge of cash."

"No, I mean... are you..." He sucks in a breath, closing his eyes and rubbing his finger and thumb over his lids. "Fuck," he curses on an exhalation, unable to finish his sentence.

I know what he's getting at because I can still feel his erection. I'm sitting on it, pussy *throbbing* right over it. *Of course he's not alone in this.*

He's so beautiful, especially with this tormented emotion clear in his expression. And yes, I'm turned on... so far on, I don't know what *off* feels like anymore. My body and mind battling for supremacy. My mind says no, *don't be stupid*, but my body wants to fling off my remaining clothes and let him take me right here in the studio. Virgin or not, I *want* this. I want *him*.

Before I can think twice about it, I kiss him again, and he eats it up without question. My tongue sweeps against his, each movement of our mouths a wordless confession that spells out *wanting*. *Mutual wanting*. If this kiss were fire, it would scorch the earth, and every bone in my body liquefies under its heat.

Oh, God. I grind against him, the rough rub of my clit against his jeans barely enough to satisfy me.

A raw sound rumbles in his chest like I've unleashed a wild beast. It strikes me like a slap to the face. I break away, the air instantly cooling my wet lips. "No," I murmur. "We can't."

He pants, touching two fingers to his mouth, blue eyes feverishly scanning my face. "What the fuck was that, Lefroy?"

"I'm so sorry." I sound just as breathless as he does. "I was in the zone."

He rubs a hand over his face and lets out another low, grating noise. "What zone? The *'fuck me right now'* zone?"

"No," I say, even though it sounds pretty accurate, given that when I peel off my underwear, it'll be wet. *So wet.* "I got carried away. I'm so sorry. That was extremely unprofessional." My near-nakedness hits me all at once, and I have to resist the urge to cover myself. "When I'm working, I can lose myself in the role. It doesn't mean anything." *Complete denial. That's what I'm going for.*

I ease off him, and he sits for a moment, sighing as he hangs his head. Gone is the man who ordered everyone out of the room with such authority. He'd never let anyone else see this version. *This one's just for me.*

I want to reach out and tell him *I get it*. And I'm sorry. For the nipple. For the kiss. *I shouldn't have done any of it.* But instead, I pretend to be completely indifferent. It's better if he thinks this is me being a professional. *A professional nipple-tweaker.* Professional cocktease. *Ugh.* Tension bites at my stomach like I've downed a bottle of bleach, burning up my throat with the truth that wants to spill out on a chaser of guilt. *I'm attracted to you. For real.*

I can't tell him that I'm just as turned on as he is, or that having him beneath me like that sparked an explosive thrill like nothing else, because where would that leave us and this fake dating? And more importantly, he's Seb. We're *friends*. Anything more than that, and I'd ruin my most important relationship.

He ruffles a hand in his hair, glancing up at me while his head is still angled towards the floor. "You're a good actress. That felt pretty real to me." He blinks exaggeratedly like he's trying to wake up from a dream. "I'm sure you'll get that role in no time."

I cringe, and the guilt only gets worse. *I hate lying to him.*

He stands and adjusts himself, drawing my attention to his bare feet. All tendons and slim ankles. There's something intimate about it that appeals to me. *He'd walk around like this at home.* I've seen his bare feet before, sure, but when he's also half naked and his torso and arms marked up with *my* logo…

I want to keep him, just like this. Mine, mine, mine.

I am so far from indifferent, it's getting to be a problem. And Seb… maybe he *was* moved by that kiss, by the pretense of the whole thing… the proximity, the skin, the underwear. But he would be that way with any woman, wouldn't he? It means *nothing*. I've known him long enough to know that much. If he gets hard for a woman whose name he can't remember the next day, then this was both an inevitability and completely meaningless.

There is absolutely no way I can ever admit to him that I might have felt a little something unprofessional too.

"What happens now?" he asks.

I blow out a breath, hoping it'll take the distracting thoughts of Seb with it. "Now, you go wash all this off…" I trace a fingertip over the infinity symbols marking his forearm, and his eyes track the movement. "And go back to the office." I sigh, lamenting the disappearance of all that ink.

"You really like the tattoos."

"Nah. I like my mark on your skin," I admit in a moment of crippling honesty that has Seb taking in the slightest of inhalations and my chest tightening in response. A series of other marks I might make on his skin pass through my mind… teeth marks, bite marks, scratches…

Ugh.

Fake. This is all fake.

I'd better not forget that or I'll be in real trouble, because Seb Hawkston is not mine *at all*.

19
SEB

*S*he likes her mark on my skin? *What the fuck does that mean?*

I'm pretty sure she knew I had a hard-on, but I have no fucking clue how she felt about it. If we had been in private, I would have had no doubt that she was into it. *Into me.* But this is her job. She could probably pretend to look any way whatsoever at the drop of a hat.

She saunters to the door, opening it to allow everyone back into the room and they file in like unruly school children returning from detention, shooting glances my way.

"Let's put one of the photos on social media now," Erica says when she returns to me, grabbing my hand and tugging me over to the photographer, who's already loading images up onto a laptop.

"Now?" I ask, confusion wrecking my voice. I can't fucking focus after what just happened, and Erica is already back to business. We're definitely not on the same fucking page here.

"Yeah. We're an item, so let's tease it."

Sensing us approaching, the photographer glances over his shoulder. "Erica, these are fantastic. You two have intense chemistry. It's sparking off the screen."

Erica peers over his shoulder at a load of photos of us looking as though we're about to strip each other naked and fuck like bunnies.

Bunnies. No. I don't fuck like a bunny. I fuck like... a dog? No. Scratch that. A...

Erica nudges my arm, saving me from the peril of my own thoughts. "Wow, look at you," she muses, pointing at the screen. "You're a natural. Thank you so much for doing this for me." She catches my eye as I lean over the screen next to her, and there's what appears to be genuine gratitude scrawled across her face. I feel a flush of pride at having been able to help her pull this off. "Truly, I appreciate it. I know this is not your thing at all."

My chest tightens. Having Erica straddle me in her underwear? That's always going to be my thing. "Anytime," I say casually.

She focuses again on the screen, leaning over the photographer to take control and scroll through the images, humming with what sounds like appreciation as she peruses them. She stops abruptly. "This one. Don't you think?"

I look at the photo she's chosen. Her head is thrown back, and the expression on her face is one of ecstasy as my hand closes around her throat. I look a little like I'm either about to kill her or ravage her. It's a brilliant photo. I want it blown up and stuck on my bedroom ceiling. *Is that weird?*

But putting it on social media? That seems... *provocative*. It's going to mess with Dad and any ideas he has about marrying me off to Diana Marchetti. Anxiety churns in my gut, but I'm too far in to pull back, and I want to do it for Erica. I give a nonchalant shrug. "It's okay."

"Great." Erica calls over the assistant I recognise from the fashion show and instructs her to upload it on her social media accounts with a filter to hide the fact it's unedited and a caption about us being a couple and the launch of her new fragrance.

The assistant agrees and moves into action.

"I'm going to shower," I say, moving off towards the changing room. I've half a mind to have a quick wank just to rid myself of the sexual tension, but Erica follows me, walking right behind me in her underwear. I'm so aware of her presence, she may as well have jumped on my back and clung there. I spin. "What are you doing?"

She recoils a little at the sharp edge to my voice. "Unisex changing rooms."

"Right." I stifle a groan. I can't catch a break today; all I need is a moment alone, or at least without Erica, to calm down.

I push into the locker room, grab a fresh towel and head for the shower. I let myself into a cubicle, strip off the jeans and my boxers and stand under the running water, lathering myself up to get the stubborn marks off my skin and the shit out of my hair.

And Erica out of my head.

I'm almost finished when a squeal comes from the changing room, jarring my heart. I slam off the water, grab my towel, and dash back out. "Erica?"

"Oh, my God. Seb." She's standing in the middle of the room, fully dressed, staring into an empty locker. "My stuff is gone."

"What stuff?"

"My wallet. My bag."

"Really?" I glance where she's pointing and then my gaze flits to the locker next to it, where I put all my stuff. My stomach sinks. It's open too.

That prickling feeling that trickled down my spine earlier comes back to me. *This is no coincidence.*

I step towards it and pull the door fully open. *I locked this. I know I did.* I pull my suit off the hanger, checking the pockets, but a nasty certainty is already filling my gut.

Nothing.

No phone. No wallet.

Erica's watching me, waiting for some kind of signal from me as to what we should do.

"Who is gonna steal our stuff here?" I ask. "Aren't you employing everyone?"

"No. There are loads of other photo shoots and filming going on. This place is huge. I have no idea who comes in and out."

Fucking brilliant. But who cares? "Let's go have lunch."

Erica blinks at me like I've gone mad. "Lunch? We just got robbed. I need to cancel my cards—"

"Relax. We can report them stolen later."

"We have to go to the police. I have £200,000 in my current account."

"I have £28 million in mine," I deadpan.

Her jaw drops, eyes widening. "Then we should definitely cancel the cards."

"Sure." I hurriedly dry myself and start dressing. Erica averts her eyes as I pull on my shirt, but I still have the towel around my hips, and when I grab my boxers, she fully turns around to let me dress. I haul them on beneath the towel and in moments I'm decent, tie and jacket and all. "I'll deal with it."

I stride out into the corridor, Erica at my heels again. "You'll deal with it? What does that mean?"

I stop the next person walking towards us, a young woman, and I explain the situation to her, telling her I need to use her phone. She blushes, flutters her lashes at me, tucks her hair behind her ear and lends me her phone. I thank her and step away to call my PA, instructing her to cancel all my cards and sort out my phone. When I'm done, I pass the phone to Erica, who's hovering nearby.

"What?" she asks.

"Give her your details. She'll sort you out."

Erica takes the phone and speaks to my PA for a few minutes, hangs up then hands the phone back to me. "Is that it?"

"Yeah. She'll fix it."

"Wow. That's amazing. Thank you." Erica beams at me, but then her delight flickers like a dying candle before snuffing out entirely, and something dark and unpleasant rushes in to take its place, seemingly out of nowhere. "Have you slept with her?"

I recoil. I've just been rock solid underneath this woman, unable to think of anything else but the way her body moves over mine, and she's asking if I'm screwing my assistant? A dull mist of annoyance fogs my mind, but beneath it is something subtler and more appealing. Is it possible Erica cares who I sleep with? I want her to care. *I do*. But she said everything that happened between us during that photo shoot, and afterwards, meant nothing. So why the fuck does she sound like she cares?

"She's not helping us out because I fucked her," I say, my confusion making me sound more aggressive than I mean to. "She's doing it because it's her job."

Erica crosses her arms over her chest. "But did you fuck her?"

"No. She's my PA. I don't mix business and pleasure. You said my sex life was none of your business, so why are you asking?"

A confused expression passing over her beautiful face, almost as though she doesn't know the answer. Or perhaps doesn't like whatever response springs to mind.

I step a little closer, keeping my voice low. "Make up your mind, Lefroy."

My words hang heavy in the air, and Erica seems to choke on them, her thick eyelashes fluttering against her cheeks as she coughs.

Leaving her standing in the middle of the corridor clearing her throat as she frowns at the floor, I pace back towards the young woman and hand the phone back to her. Thankfully, she's been waiting too far away to have heard a word of Erica's accusations.

"Thanks so much," I say to her. "You're a lifesaver."

Her blush deepens as she takes the phone, our fingers brushing. I feel nothing, but she flinches slightly at the touch. "Erm, that's okay." She composes herself and locks eyes with me. "Could I..."

Well, damn. I know what she's going to ask because it happens all the time. Her gaze drops away, taking my stomach with it. I really don't need this, what with Erica already convinced I'm always jumping in and out of a new woman's bed.

"Could you what?" I ask gently.

Erica paces to join us, looking composed and beautiful once more.

"Could I get your number?" the girl asks.

And there it is. Bold of her to ask me out when I'm standing with *The Erica Lefroy*. Then again, she hasn't really looked at Erica properly, so perhaps she hasn't seen her or doesn't know who she is.

Erica shoulders me aside, one territorial hand clamping around my arm. "You can't. Because we're together. Exclusively. He's not giving his number to anyone."

The vehemence with which Erica is fending this woman off has warmth stirring in my chest. She was so adamant after the photo shoot that she felt nothing, that I could never have imagined this scenario arising. And fuck, it feels good to be claimed by her, even if it is completely fake.

"Oh. *Oh.* I'm so, so sorry. I didn't mean..." the woman trails off and walks away so fast she's almost running.

"The cheek of her," Erica says when she's out of earshot. "So rude. Couldn't she see I was with you? I was standing right—"

"You can put the claws away." I keep walking, heading for the exit, and Erica has to increase her pace to keep abreast of me.

"Claws? I am not—"

I stop and face her. "It's all pretend, isn't it? There's no need to be annoyed."

Her eyes dart away and she huffs. "Yes, but that was rude. Obviously, we're together."

"She didn't know. You were the one asking me if I was sleeping with my PA a second ago." My comment is the gentlest of reprimands, but Erica's gaze falls to the ground and she tilts her weight to one foot, then the other. "You don't have to fight anyone off. You'd never have to fight anyone off if you didn't want to."

She stills and her shoulders fall, but she doesn't look up. Satisfied that she's heard me, I continue my walk to the exit. I need to get back to the office before Nico castrates me for playing truant.

"What does that mean?" she calls after me.

I spin to face her, continuing to walk backwards. "It means, I'm all yours." I spread my arms wide. "I told you, SeblovesBJs has been on his knees for you for years."

I kiss the fingers of one hand and hold them up to her, and the grin that breaks across her face sets my heart alight.

20
SEB

"The account is empty." The voice of my banker booms from my desk phone, which I've put on speaker. I'm too agitated to sit down, so I'm pacing my office. Normally, this large, airy room with its vast glass windows and epic views over London's skyline, is a place of refuge for me. A sanctuary of sorts. I know what the fuck to do when I'm behind my desk, and this small corner of the world is mine to control.

But now, standing here being told that £28 million has gone fucking missing without a trace, I am wishing I could wind back time. I'd rather be posing for photographs with Erica grinding on my lap than here facing this shit show.

"What the fuck?" I run my hands through my freshly washed hair. It's a mess, but thank God it doesn't have any of that awful product left in it.

"It's all gone, sir."

"Where? Where the fuck has it gone? Whoever took my wallet can't have spent 28 million quid in the supermarket."

"The card hasn't been used."

That uneasy prickle works its way up my spine. "What do you mean?"

"Whoever took your card, can't use it. Didn't use it. It was cancelled before they had a chance to use it."

"You're telling me everything's gone, but it has nothing to do with the fact that someone nicked my shit at a photo shoot earlier today?"

"Yes, sir. That's what I'm saying." His voice trembles and he clears his throat. The poor prick sounds nervous. "When did you last check your balance?"

There's a hint of accusation in his voice that I can't ignore. "Are you implying I lost 28 million quid? I just didn't notice?" A lead weight sinks through my gut, tugging me down into the darkness of shame. That could have happened. I don't look at my accounts that often. I have so many that I mostly trust that whatever I left in them is still going to be there when I come back I have people monitoring my money. Our family's financial advisors. My father's—

Fuck.

A numbness works its way up my legs. *I need to fucking sit down.* "Is there any trace of it?"

"Excuse me?"

I lean against the desk, both palms flat on it, head hanging down between my shoulders. I lift one hand and tug on my tie, yanking it loose. "The money. Surely it leaves a trace. A path. A fucking exit route from my account."

"No, sir. None of that. This is... inexplicable. It appears to have..."

"To have what?" I snap.

"Vanished, sir."

I cover my face with my hands, press my fingertips into my eye sockets, and let out a rumbling groan.

"Sir? Is everything— "

I fucking knew it. I hang up before he can say anything else. My heart hammers. This is seriously fucked, and I know exactly who's to blame. And I know I will never, *ever*, see that money again.

A knock on the door followed by my brother's voice calling my name has me rushing to compose myself. If he finds me like this, he's going to think I'm fucking messy. *Useless*. Especially after I didn't show up to work this morning, which is a first. Actually, a second, given I skipped work to spend the afternoon with Erica. *She's leading me astray…*

"Yeah. Come in," I say as I sit behind my desk, trying to steady my breathing. *It's only money. It's okay.*

It's not only money. It's Dad's first move on the fucking chessboard.

Nico enters, striding right up to me and dropping a brand new iPhone in its box on my desk. He stares at me for a second, and I wonder what he knows. "How was Dad when you had lunch?" he asks, and I breathe a sigh of relief. If he's asking about Dad, then he's not going to lay into me about playing truant earlier.

"He's okay. Same old prick, really. Seems to be recovering well."

A not-insignificant part of me wants to tell Nico everything. That Dad is gonna fuck me over. Drain my accounts if I don't do what he wants. That I have to marry some young woman I hardly know right when Erica has finally agreed to date me.

Fake date me.

Whatever. It's close enough. I don't want to ruin it by having to get married to someone else.

But I can't tell him. The idea of sharing this with Nico, letting them see that, yet again, Dad is playing me in a way he'd never do to him or Matt… using me for his own gain… the shame of it is too much. I can't tell anyone. This is between me and Dad, and I will fucking sort it out myself if it kills me.

Nico nods, sliding his hands into his pockets, but still eyeing me with suspicion. "What were you doing in east London earlier? At the Wakefield studio?"

I rest my elbow on the desk and drop my forehead to my hand. I could lie to him. Or I could tell him the truth. "Who told you?"

"Your PA told me after you called and asked her to cancel all your cards."

I heave a sigh. "I really need to talk to her about keeping my shit confidential." Nico's harsh gaze doesn't leave my face, and I know he's waiting for more of an explanation, so I offer it up. "I was doing Erica a favour. She had a fight with her mum last week and she's been upset. So—"

"So you got half naked and let her paint you?" He says it with such disdain—as if I must be a class-A moron to have participated in such frivolity—that I want to punch him. He flashes his phone at me, and sure enough, there's the picture of me and Erica. I know Erica said it wasn't porn, but it's definitely sensual. Suggestive. Fuck it, she looks like a goddess climaxing on my lap.

Maybe Nico has a point.

"This is not a good look for business," he says. "And she's named you. '*My boyfriend, Seb Hawkston, agreed to pose with me. Isn't he gorgeous? I couldn't think of anyone better to launch my new fragrance—Infinity—with than him*'."

A noise in the doorway draws both our attention, and I glance up to find Matt standing there, phone in hand. My stomach drops.

"When did you get tattoos?" he asks.

Resting my elbow on my desk, I drop my forehead into my hand. "Do you have nothing better to do than stalk me on social media?"

"The receptionists are all out there gossiping about it," Matt says, gesturing with his thumb over his shoulder. He approaches my desk, looming over me before dropping into a chair opposite. "What's the deal with Lefroy?"

"What do you mean?"

"You've never had a proper girlfriend and suddenly you're dating your best friend?"

I bristle. "You had a wife and now you're engaged to your nanny. What's the actual question?"

Matt grunts and shifts in the chair. "I'm just saying, you're the guy who never takes a woman to his house. One night stands in the hotel. Keep it casual, make it meaningless. It's practically a mantra you live by."

I hold in the groan that wants to spill from my mouth. My past behaviour has done me no favours here. I wish I could wipe it all away, especially if it means my brothers would take this relationship between me and Erica seriously. *I'm truly a lost cause if the first relationship I need them to take seriously isn't even real.*

"And she's never shown an interest in you before either. You know... romantically," Matt continues. "It makes me wonder what changed."

Nico paces to the window, hands in his pockets. "What he means is, why now? Why would Erica Lefroy decide you're good enough now?"

We're all quiet a touch too long. Every muscle in my body strains with tension. "I really don't like what you're implying," I say, finally.

"I'm not implying anything," Nico says. "I'm just interpreting Matt's inability to ask a direct question."

"Fuck's sake," Matt mutters, staring at me. "Don't be an idiot about this. I get why *you'd* do it. You've worshipped that woman forever—"

"Have not—"

"Stop," Nico cuts in. "Matt's about to use multiple words in a row. Don't disturb him. It might never happen again."

A smile threatens to break across my face even though I'm already pissed off at the direction this conversation is taking.

Matt scowls in Nico's direction, then focuses back on me. "Are you really dating her?"

There is no fucking way I am telling them this is fake. *No way.* "Yes."

Matt weighs this up. "It seems to have come out of nowhere. She's never spent time with you in public and suddenly you're the guy in the perfume campaign? I mean… no disrespect, but what the actual fuck?"

"We've spent loads of time together," I counter, but it sounds weak, even to my ear.

Matt lets out a sigh that softens his shoulders. "You've spent time together at home, on the sofa. Watching movies. But not out in public."

"We've been at plenty of parties together."

"Yeah, but you didn't arrive or leave together, did you?"

A chill rolls over my skin. I've always known how Erica liked to do things, micromanaging our friendship to suit herself. And I was really, truly, okay with it. I'd give her anything she wanted and do whatever she wanted. If it weren't for the way Matt is questioning me on it, I wouldn't give it a second thought. "She's Erica. She likes to do things on her terms."

"Exactly," Matt quips. "Why do you think she always asked Nico when she needed a public date? Why didn't she ask you?"

I mentally run over the past events she attended with Nico before he was officially with Kate. Charity galas, fashion show after parties. The whole fucking lot. He was always the one on her arm, not me. In the past, I chalked it up to Nico being boring and responsible, and Erica assuming I wouldn't enjoy the events. But now, with Matt staring at me like he feels sorry for me, I realise I've been deep in denial, and a truth that has hovered at the edges of my consciousness is suddenly flashing before me in fucking Technicolor. Erica chose Nico because she didn't want *me*. Her words from the gallery batter through my mind on repeat like an endless round of gunfire.

You're a joke.

Manwhore.

A wave of pain crashes through me, bringing with it the thought that, even if I do everything for her, there's still a possibility that she'll never think I'm good enough. Not for anything *real*, at any rate.

"Because Nico's a boring old sod who likes those kinds of parties," I say, but even I can hear the defensiveness in my tone.

"Thanks for that," Nico says on a laugh.

Matt presses his lips together and nods, as though my comment proves him correct, even though he still hasn't fucking said exactly what he thinks.

"Hold on, what exactly are you implying?" I ask him.

"He thinks she's using you," Nico states.

That wave of pain crashes back like the incoming tide, wearing me down. She *is* using me, and I fucking offered. That's the whole point of this fake dating scenario, but knowing that Matt and Nico think that's what's going on when they have no idea the relationship is fake is so uncomfortable that all I can do is mutter, "What?"

"Whenever I went out with Erica, I always knew it was for show," Nico says. "That's her thing. Maintaining the public image."

I clench my fists, wishing I had a bottle of scotch on hand so I could down the whole fucking thing. "Yeah, maybe with you it was for show. But that's not what this is," I say, lying through my teeth. "Why would you think that?"

"There was that sudden flurry of press about her leaked audition tapes. How unsexy she is"—Matt winces and throws me an apologetic glance before he continues—"and that she'd never be able to pull off a role in a film like *Taming the Beast*. Then, out of the blue, she's all over you on social media, announcing that you're dating... She's not a woman who does anything by accident."

"That's true," Nico adds. "She's one hell of a business woman."

I want to step in and say it's really her mother driving the entire business, but Matt chimes in before I can.

"Exactly. Did she trip and hit her head or something? Or go on an Ayahuasca retreat and not come down from the high? Her being with you... It's completely out of character."

All I can hear in my head is Erica's constant refrain of *'this is all fake'*. And I can already see the expressions on Matt and Nico's faces if I admit it. "What is this, an intervention? You didn't hear me telling either of you that Kate and Aries would never take you seriously. Why can't you do me the same favour?"

"That's not what we're saying—" Nico begins, but I cut him off.

"Really? Because that's what I'm hearing. That Erica would have to have sustained brain damage or be under the influence of some mind-altering substance to be dating me. It's exactly what you're saying." I stand, my temples pounding with the onset of a headache. I can't take much more today. My balls are blue, my bank balance has taken a hit, and Nico and Matt still treating me like the joker in the fucking pack is the final straw. "You know what? This is really none of your fucking business. Get out of my office."

They share a look and retreat together from the room. When the door closes, paranoia hits me. *They're talking about me.* Actually, fuck it, they're probably not even doing that. That's probably the whole bloody conversation over and they'll go back to more important things.

I take a deep breath, trying to push all of it out of my mind. Does it matter if Erica's using me? I offered. Does it matter that she'd never date me *for real*?

I can't think about it now. By way of distraction, I grab the box containing the phone Nico dropped off. It's already been set up. Ready to go.

There's already a message on it, but my stomach drops when I see who it's from. *Dad.*

I open it to find a series of images, screenshots from social media or tabloid websites, showing me smashing the photographer's camera last week. Tucking my watch into his front pocket. There's even one of Erica leaning over me on the grass on Hampstead Heath when I licked the hand she cupped over my mouth. Seeing it brings back the memory of the salty taste of her skin, and heat rushes me. I flick through more images. They're not from social media. They've been taken on a professional camera. He has people watching me. *I fucking knew it.*

One final image comes through. This one *is* from social media: the one from the photo shoot, where Erica's on my lap, head thrown back, looking as though she's having an epic, life-altering orgasm.

After the photos is one single message.

Dad: I said discreet.

I type a quick response, sending it before I can hold back.

Me: Fuck you.

Instantly, one of the fake images of me with the underage girl comes through. I nearly drop my phone at the shock of seeing it again. I delete it and call my father, holding the phone to my ear as it rings.

"Sebastian," Dad croons when he answers.

"Did you have someone steal my wallet? Erica's stuff too?"

He clears his throat. "I thought you needed a reminder that I can take you down in person and online. Anywhere, anytime."

A hot ball of rage simmers in my chest. "What the fuck do you want?"

"You know what I want. I want you to behave. I want you to agree to this marriage. I want you to get down on one fucking knee and propose to Diana Marchetti."

"No. I don't care if you take every fucking penny I have—"

"I'll take more than money, Sebastian." My phone buzzes and more of those incriminating images come through, each one worse than the last. I feel sick looking at them, the taste of bile hitting the back of my throat.

"You're the worst father in the world."

Silence. "I'm a businessman first, a father last."

I drop my head into my hand, the pounding in my temples ratcheting up tenfold. *That heartless fucking bastard.*

"You have four months," Dad confirms. "Give me your word that you will marry Diana. If you don't agree, I will release these photos. Tonight."

Tonight?

I've seen charges like this take men down. Destroy lives. And I know he'd do it to get his way. *Ruthless.*

My mind spins, Erica's name racing through it over and over. I can't hold on to logic as the panic whirls in my system. Dad's words from our meeting rush in, booming through my thoughts, crushing everything else, washing her name away, eroding it like the flow of a rampaging river over rock.

It's not as if you'd be leaving anyone behind; I know you don't give a shit about any of those women, and I doubt they care about you either. Not really. Not on any level that counts. Trust me, I know what that's like. The hollow, empty feeling inside. Never really caring and wondering why not. At least this way, you'll have a woman who'll stick around for longer than a couple of weeks.

Maybe it's true. Maybe no one will ever give a fuck about me. Not really. Not on any deep level. But Erica has just announced us as a couple on social media. If I say no to Dad, and he does release these images, Erica gets taken down by association. This will hurt her chances of achieving what she wants, and there's no way that can happen.

If we stick to her time frame and end things by Nico and Kate's wedding, then I'll be clear for a month before this marriage to Diana is announced and Erica will be fine. She'll have moved on. Not that there's anything to move from. Ours will just be another flash in the pan celebrity relationship. *Yesterday's news.* Searing pain rips through me at the thought, but I suppress the fuck out of that sensation.

"Fine. Fucking fine. I'll do it. But back the fuck off and let me do whatever the hell I want for these final months."

"And then you'll marry Diana?"

"Yes. I'll do whatever you need me to do."

"Good boy. I knew you'd see sense."

"You sick bastar—"

"Are you involved with that woman? In the photos? Erica Lefroy?" The interruption cuts off my flow. *Erica has no place in this conversation.*

"That's none of your business."

Dad's slow breathing gusts down the line for a few rounds. "Fine. But don't fall for her at the last hurdle. I'd hate to see you go down the aisle with a broken heart."

21
ERICA

I've been screening Mum's calls since our fight on Harley Street, but tonight, at the launch party for my cosmetics line and the Infinity fragrance, I'll have to face her.

I take a seat at my dressing table and open up my phone—a brand new handset that Seb sent over as a gift, all set up and ready to use by his PA—and reread Mum's last message. She sent it in response to my social media post of me and Seb at the photo shoot.

What were you thinking? You look like a whore.

When I didn't reply, she sent another that said, ***He will destroy you.***

That last one lingered in my mind, latching onto all my insecurities.

I can't deny that Mum is partly right, but her focus is wrong. She thinks Seb will destroy my brand, but I know it's my heart that's at risk.

Maybe it's always been my heart.

I hit delete on both her messages and force myself to take a few deep breaths to settle my nerves. The cosmetics launch is a huge event taking place at a venue just off Leicester Square. Mum wanted it floral and pretty and innocent, but I've completely sabotaged her arrangements and revamped the entire thing. It was intense, and I wasn't the only one pulling all-nighters to get it done, but it was worth it to take control. She's going to go nuts. Now, we're using the images of me in my underwear, and Seb beneath me, looking like it's the only place in the world he ever wants to be.

Heat pools between my legs at the recollection. Those photos are *hot,* and since I last saw Seb, I've spent almost all my time analysing them, choosing the best ones, and having all the publicity posters for the launch remade and distributed at short notice. I have been obsessing over Seb Hawkston, and every time I looked at those pictures, I felt all warm and bubbly inside. *Giddy* might be the word for it, if that also encompassed the feeling of low-key arousal that hummed in my veins at the same time.

If I'm a whore, I'm only a whore for Seb.

The problem is, he's a fire that will burn me to ash if I get too close.

I can't let that happen, so I've made a list of rules to keep our fake dating on track. He'll probably think I'm crazy for suggesting them, and instigating them at this late stage is as good as admitting that I'm the liability. I need the rules because I don't trust myself around him, and if I want to have a friendship with him when this arrangement is over, which I do, then I can't allow the lines between us to get any more blurred.

My body is already confused.

I will not let him break my heart.

My phone buzzes again and I glance at it to see a message from him come in.

I'm downstairs. Ready for our first official date?

My heart flutters. I shouldn't be feeling like this in response to a text, but the way he kissed me during the photo shoot has been playing on a loop in my head. The feel of his tongue on mine, the scrape of his stubble against my skin... and the agonized look on his face when it was over. When he was *hard.*

Was he, though? He didn't explicitly confirm it. Maybe I got it wrong. It's not as though I have much experience in that arena.

Blowing out a quick breath, I hit the call button and he answers instantly.

"Hi," I say, standing from my seat at the dressing table and brushing down my dress with my free hand. It's a navy silk evening gown with a scooped back so low it only just covers my bum. It's pretty special, if I do say so myself. And—*bonus*—it's another thing Mum will hate; she picked out a pastel coloured floral dress, all chiffon and reeking of innocence and purity. This dress is, dare I say it, sexy. *Provocative.* I'm also not wearing any underwear because the fabric wouldn't allow it.

"Hey." Seb's deep voice sends another ripple of desire through me, and going without underwear suddenly feels like a bigger risk than I thought.

I tuck the list of fake dating rules into my purse. "Are you still in your car?"

"No. I'm in the lobby."

Heat rushes up my neck and I fan myself, glad he can't see me. "Okay. I'll be down in a sec. Can you look like you're pleased to see me, in case anyone's watching?"

"I'm always pleased to see you."

A few minutes later, we're buckled into the back of his car. Before I lose my nerve, I pull the list out of my clutch and pass it to him. It's lengthy because I wanted to think of everything.

"What's this?" he says, taking it from me and unfolding the piece of paper.

"I've been thinking about our arrangement, and I think we need boundaries."

He doesn't lift his gaze from the list, eyes moving back and forth over my script. I try to keep my cool, knowing he's reading the section entitled 'Physical Contact'.

All physical contact must be initiated by Miss Lefroy.

Physical contact permitted: Hand-holding, a kiss on the cheek, an arm around the shoulder or waist (no lower). You may take Miss Lefroy's arm or she may take yours.

You will not pay undue attention to any other women for the duration of this arrangement.

You must at all times appear delighted with Miss Lefroy and take great pleasure in her company. Under no circumstances are you to display annoyance or frustration in public with or directed at Miss Lefroy.

There will be no nudity of any kind, nor will there be any sort of sexual relations between you and Miss Lefroy.

Any deviation from the above is entirely at Miss Lefroy's discretion and must be discussed in advance.

"You came up with all these yourself?" he asks, mirth dancing in his eyes.

"Yes. Can you take it seriously, please? If we don't outline things properly, we might get confused."

"Confused?" He leans in, his lips tipping up at the corners. "Confused how?"

His flirtatious tone, paired with the gleam in his eyes, is a blatant flouting of the rules. "Don't do that. You're making it sexual." I sound snippy, but Seb only smiles.

"I'm not. But I don't date people I don't want to get sexual with. What would be the point?"

"It's pretend. We—"

"Yes. Pretend. But it has to *look* real." He stares at me, a challenge in his eyes. "If you want to convince people that we're together, you can't stiffen when I touch you."

"I don't stiffen."

"You did. In the lobby just now. I was doing my best to look pleased to see you, but when I put my hand on your lower back, you shot up like a rocket. I thought you were going to take off."

My mind flits back to the moment I glimpsed him casually leaning against the wall. So handsome in his tux. When he touched me to lead me to the car, the flush of attraction I felt for him was so intense that I couldn't handle it. I totally stiffened. "I did n—"

He blasts out a sigh. "At the photo shoot, you were all over me, and now I can't touch you? Your inconsistency is what's confusing, not the lack of boundaries"

My pulse races that little bit faster. He's right, of course. I wish I could tell him the truth, but to admit that I'm worried I might fall for him for real feels like something I could never say. "That was work. That was my job. The physical contact we had then was absolutely necessary."

"I'd argue that they're the same."

"No. There were limits at the shoot. Boundaries. Instructions for exactly what we had to do."

He raises an eyebrow. "If you need instructions, I can give you instructions." He tries to pass me the list, but I push it back at him.

"Keep that. It's yours. I know what's on it."

He sighs. "No one is going to think we're a real couple if I adhere to these rules. The point is—"

"The point is, you're helping me. And I really appreciate it, and I will owe you. Big time. Especially if I get this movie role. But please, let's do this my way." I lay my hand over his. "I need you to do it my way. Please."

My voice cracks on the last word, and something like understanding fills Seb's eyes. His voice is gentle when he says, "Where's the line? Where can I touch you?"

Electricity fizzes through me, and the answer booms in my mind. *You can touch me everywhere.* I lift my hand from his. "You can't. Not unless I say so."

Disbelief fills his eyes. "Really?"

"Yes." I lean over and tap the physical contact section of the list.

Seb peruses it again, then slowly raises his head. "Lefroy." He says my name as though he expects the mere sound of it to inject some sense into me, but I am not letting him touch me. *I can't.*

"Please," I say again, sounding so pathetic I can hardly stand it.

His shoulders fall, and the sound of his next exhalation fills the car. "Fine." He, puts the list inside his jacket pocket. "Let's try it your way. Let's see how convincing we are without touching." He chuckles to himself, but it's a dark and disapproving noise, as though he's indulging me while simultaneously knowing I'll fail. "Just so you know, I'm ready to worship you any way you want if you change your mind about how you want to run this fake dating gig."

I take him in, in all his cocky glory, looking so handsome, so sure of himself, that the flush of attraction I felt earlier repeats itself, settling deep in my core. *Damn you, Seb Hawkston, for being so irresistible and knowing it.*

22
SEB

There is a red carpet when we arrive, and a crowd of people screaming Erica's name, as well as a host of paparazzi.

The noise is insane, and the flashing of the cameras is blinding. People crush towards us, held back only by the security lining the rope that separates the carpet from the public. *Jesus fucking Christ.* What did I sign up for here? I should have brought a bodyguard. I've had my fair share of press—good and bad—but this is next level.

Erica is composed and stately the entire time, gliding down the carpet like a couture angel. She couldn't look more beautiful if she tried. But the papers aren't wrong; there's an iciness to her glamour that isn't inviting. She rarely smiles, and there's an edge to her beauty that suggests she'd never let you fully in.

"Who's the date, Erica?" someone yells.

So *this* is what it's like to be with Erica in public. Most of the time, people don't know who I am. Just another bloke in a corporate suit, but in Erica's company, I'm of interest. A burst of pride at being associated with her, at being her date, inflates my chest.

Erica reaches for my hand, and as she touches me, sparks jolt right up my arm. She pulls me closer to her and then lets go. I stand next to her, but not touching, and it looks ridiculous. Two kids who don't like each other standing side by side and waiting for the school photographer to snap our picture.

I don't know what the fuck she's playing at, or why she's suddenly so adamant that I can't touch her, but it's not going to work. The press will be writing articles about our impending and inevitable breakup before the night is over if we keep this up.

I remain at her side for a few moments longer. It could be less than a minute, but it feels like an absolute age, and with each second that passes, I feel more and more like a spare part. What the hell am I doing here if we aren't putting on a show? This is *insane*. I have three months with Erica before I lose her, and just under four before I have to commit myself to someone else. I'm on a ticking fucking clock here, and I don't want to waste any more time. Ignoring her damn rules, I slide my arm around her waist, pulling her close, but as I do she stiffens. She fucking stiffens. *Again*.

I plaster a smile on my face. "Loosen up," I whisper, amused at how the tables have turned since the photo shoot. "You're not convincing anyone." She scowls at me, but I only raise a teasing brow and whisper, "You want to be an actress? You're gonna have to do better than that. Come on Lefroy, I know you can do it."

She tilts her face slightly in my direction, and that's when I see it. That hint of competitiveness in her gaze. That fire I know so well.

She shimmies a little, the silk of her dress pressed right against me, her hip nestling into mine. There's heat radiating off her, and I wish she'd stay like this all night. Fuck it, I wish she could stay like this forever, and knowing she can't has pain hovering in my periphery like an optic migraine. "This is my boyfriend. Seb Hawkston," she calls.

Someone wolf-whistles.

"Seb fucking Hawkston," someone else yells, and I can tell they know exactly who I am. I can't decide if I'm relieved or unnerved. Somewhere between the two. "You gonna give her a night in the hotel, Seb?"

"More than one," I yell back with a wave, and all Erica's softness evaporates. *Was that the wrong thing to say?* The cameras flash like crazy, and I keep my arm around her, despite the fact that annoyance is seeping out of her skin.

She breaks away and goes inside, and I follow her at pace, my heart thumping. The doors swing closed behind us, leaving us cocooned in an entrance hall that feels unnaturally quiet, the thick doors muffling the screams from outside.

Erica glances around, and seeing that we're alone, she snaps, "A night in the hotel?"

"More than one," I clarify. "You're special. You get more than one."

"Fuck's sake, Seb. You're talking about me like I'm a hookup."

I tilt my head. "What? Not at all. You told them I was your boyfriend. If you're my woman, I'm taking you to my fucking hotel. In every city in the world. Every fucking night if I could. Why would I pretend any different?"

"I don't want to be another woman in your hotels." She waves her hand between us. "It's not going to work if you're treating me the same way you've treated everyone else."

She's upset. *Fuck.* And no wonder. I think of Emerald and those naked photos, and Erica throwing me out of her apartment to go back to the hotel. She probably thinks I actually went through with it. That I left her apartment and went to the Hawkston Mayfair and fucked that woman's brains out. Maybe I should tell her I didn't, but this point I'm not sure it would be enough to convince her that she could never be just another woman to me.

"What do you want me to do?"

"Argh, I don't know." She turns on the spot, one way then the other, like she wants to move but doesn't know where to go. "But it won't help me to be seen as another one of your many women. You need... You need to look at me like I'm the most beautiful woman you've ever seen, the most amazing human being you've ever met. You need to look like you want to be with me forever, that you think you're lucky to be—"

"I do think all that." The silence crackles, and the annoyance splinters and falls from Erica's beautiful face like broken glass from a frame. "I do. I do feel that way—"

"What way?"

Oh, Christ. My chest is hot and tight. *Did I just say I wanted to be with her forever? Do I want that? Fuck, even if I do, I can't.* "You are beautiful. It's not even an opinion. It's just a fact. Most of the world agrees with me. And the fact that we're even friends, that you've ever given me the time of day in any capacity, blows my mind."

She falls silent, absorbing what I've just said. Probably trying to work out what the fuck it actually means. I'm not even sure I know what it means.

"Tell me what you want me to do, and I'll do it," I say softly.

Her shoulders sink, the fire in her eyes dying out. "I know this is all pretend, but I want..." Her breath hitches, eyes darting to mine and away again. "I want to be the reason you'd give everyone else up. I want to be... the one." Her voice cracks a little, and I see just how important this is to her. "It needs to look like I'm the one for you."

The one? That's not just fake dating. That's fake love. It's way too fucking close to my reality, and to tell her as much when there's a list in my jacket pocket of things I *cannot do,* feels like a mistake I can't afford to make. "Lefroy—"

She holds a hand up to cut me off. "Before you say it, I know this is all fake, and I'm not the person that you're going to feel like that about, and this is only going to last a few months, but I need you to make me feel like it's true. And I know it's asking a lot for someone like you to imagine what it's like to choose one person. And especially for it to be me, when we've been friends so long, and this"—her hand flits rapidly between us—"would never go anywhere. I know you aren't *really* interested. Not to the degree I need to convince the world you are." She sighs. "And I'm not into you, either." A sharp sting whips across my chest and I clench a fist, gripping it hard enough to distract from the discomfort her words cause. "We're friends, that's all. So it's a lot. To make this play out like love."

The air feels loaded with invisible energy, and for a few precious seconds we're frozen in a moment that belongs only to us.

"Have you ever been in love?" I ask, and the way she jolts reveals that she wasn't expecting the question. I don't even know why I asked.

Her gaze collides with mine, and the impact makes me realise she hardly looked at me during her outburst. "No. Have you?"

Numbness spreads through me, and when I drag my answer from the depths of my being it feels like a lie. "No."

She inhales, and when she exhales, the sound trembles. "I know what a big ask this is, and I'm sorry. But you offered, and now we're here and we're on the posters and we're on social media and we've committed to this, and when I open that door"—she points to the door to the main ballroom beyond—"everyone will be there, including my mother." She shakes out her hands, and I want to grab them and hold her still. I want her to see that I'm here for her even when she's spinning out and desperate, but I hold back. I still don't know if she wants me to touch her or not. "We have to pull this off. They have to think this is real. Everyone has to. No one can *ever* find out that this isn't real."

"That you're not the one?" I whisper.

She swallows and licks her lips, and I follow the motion. Her mouth is so beautiful, so wide, her lips so full, that any other time I'd be thinking about kissing her again, but her expression is so insecure, so *afraid*, that a hollow ache sets up in my ribcage instead. "Exactly."

I want to ask her what the fuck she's frightened of. *What does she think I'm going to do?* I step closer, taking her hands in mine. "Do you trust me?"

My heart thumps while she weighs up the question, eyes flitting over my face as though it might help her decide. "Yes."

"Then let me take the reins. Forget your rules. Scrap the list. Let me show you what it would be like if you were the one. Can you do that?"

She hesitates, her eyes wide and dark and fixed on me like I might be able to save her, although from what I'm fucked if I know. I can't even save myself. My father is blackmailing me, stealing my money, and coercing me to commit to someone else. Doing this for Erica will only make it worse.

But I would endure anything to help her get what she wants.

"You need to give me permission to touch you," I continue. "To initiate it." I release her hands and hold mine up. "I swear, I won't do anything inappropriate. But you can't expect this to look realistic if I can't touch you. If I'm dating someone, and I like them, I'm going to touch them. That's part of the joy of being with someone you like. Being able to hold them. Kiss them—"

"There'll be no kissing." Erica takes a tiny step back, and the movement causes the silk strap of her dress to fall down her arm on one side.

I reach out, easing the strap of her dress back up with the tip of my finger. I do it slowly, *so fucking slowly*, stroking the velvet of her bare skin. Erica doesn't move. She barely breathes. The moment is charged like a thundercloud, at least on my side.

I want to run my hands over the rest of her body, kissing every inch of her skin. *Fuck.* I should never have suggested this fake dating thing because it's going to be painful. I know it already. It's the worst temptation ever. The one woman in the world who would never agree to go out with me, asking me to convince the world she's the one.

This is fucked, and we've only just begun.

I raise my eyes to find she's watching me as I break the contact between our bodies and lower my arm to my side again. She gives a shaky breath, a small, erotic-sounding gasp slipping out, and I swear it tugs right on my cock. I rub a palm over my eyes and scrape it down my face, letting out a groan to distract from the heavy thump of arousal beating through my body. "Okay. No kissing."

"And no hotels," she adds.

Before I have a chance to reply, the door to the ballroom swings open, and we're exposed to the room. There are people gathered drinking champagne, and like a scene from a movie, they all turn to where we're standing.

The MC for the evening catches sight of us and calls out, "The woman we've all been waiting for! Miss Erica Lefroy, ladies and gentlemen."

23
ERICA

A roar of applause explodes from the ballroom. With one last look at Seb, I turn to the noise and force a smile onto my face. It's habitual to avoid smiling for the cameras because Mum banned me from doing it, telling me it didn't look good, but tonight, I'm grinning as I step into the limelight.

The room looks incredible, with black and rose gold decorations everywhere, balloons in both colours interspersed with monochrome images of me and Seb hanging from the walls. Towers of champagne glasses are nestled on tables next to our makeup products, which is packaged in black boxes with *ERICA LEFROY* and the infinity symbol embossed in rose gold. There's a table with gift bags for everyone, and I can spot a few of my model friends over in the corner already digging in. *I can't believe I pulled this off.*

It takes me approximately five seconds to sense Mum in the crowd. She's tall, so it's easy to spot her, and her dark hair is blow dried and glamorous, falling around her shoulders in waves. She's gorgeous, but the scowl on her face makes her totally unapproachable. I wonder if it's deliberate. Does she choose to scowl because she looks hotter that way? Tonight, I suspect she's actually mad.

But I don't care. I am flouting the rules, and a perverse delight stirs in my chest at the thought of her turning up tonight to discover the branding completely revamped, and the room covered in images of me and Seb all over each other.

Fuck it. I hope it kills her to see me with someone she deems so off-brand and inappropriate. He dips to my ear, his breath hot and his voice alluring as he whispers, "Your mother is glaring at us."

"She hates you." I pull a false conciliatory expression. "She thinks you're the opposite of the Erica Lefroy brand." Seb's eyes widen and I lean in, whispering, "She expressly banned me from having a public friendship with you. But I don't care anymore. Now, you are my extremely public boyfriend. So yes, you have my permission to make it look real."

His expression brightens as a delighted smirk drifts over his lips. "Right now?"

I glance over at Mum, who is sipping on champagne, but her glare is still fixed on us. When I look back at Seb, his gaze is so hot it's like someone turned on a heater right behind his eyes. I manage to catch the 'Wow' that wants to trip off my tongue, because having Seb Hawkston look at you like that, even if it's only fake, is a full body sensation of deliciousness.

"Erica?" he repeats. "Now?"

I glance at Mum again, who is making her way deliberately across the room towards us.

"Yes. Now," I confirm, and Seb lowers his mouth to my neck, his breath brushing my skin with a warmth that makes heat pool between my legs. I tip my head back and let out a whimper, so low that no one but Seb can hear it, and I feel him smile against my skin.

"Very convincing," he murmurs as his hand slides around to my lower back, palm pressed flat to the bare skin as he tugs me against him. This time I don't stiffen, I *soften*. His lips are against my ear when he adds, "Good girl."

I turn molten. Nothing about this moment feels fake. My body is having a very real reaction to his voice, his hands, the feel of his hips against mine, his breath on my neck. I should probably have worn underwear because I can already feel the slickness gathering between my thighs. I'm either going to faint or start rubbing myself against him like the horny woman I am.

"Erica!" My mother's screech is sharp, all decorum thrown to the wind as she clamps a hand about my forearm and wrenches me out of Seb's arms. She's so furious, she's not even pretending to give a shit who can see us. "We need to talk."

She drags me through the ballroom, pulling me out a side door and into the corridor. Heaving frustrated breaths, she places her hands on her hips as she stares me down. "What are you doing? The decorations? The photos? You've ruined everything. And now... Sebastian Hawkston? I told you he was not right for this brand. I told you he was—"

"I don't care."

Mum puffs. "What?"

"I do not give a fuck what you say anymore."

Her mouth opens and closes, breasts shuddering beneath the cowl neck of her velvet dress. "Tonight is not the night to have a quarter-life crisis, Erica."

"I'm not having a crisis," I reply, sounding far calmer than I feel.

"Teenage rebellion, then. It might be a decade late, but your behaviour is starting to feel like that. Walking out of the consultation rooms and screaming at me in the middle of Harley Street. Prancing about in your underwear to launch this fragrance. And now this? Showing up in a dress that looks like midnight sex and letting Seb Hawkston feast on your neck in public, like the two of you walked out of an erotic vampire movie. This is the launch of your cosmetics line. It's

supposed to be flowers and purity out there. The theme is innocence."
She yells the last word, spittle blasting all over my face. I blink and
rear back, but Mum continues undeterred. "It's not Sebastian fucking
Hawkston sucking on your throat."

I set my shoulders. "If he wants to suck on my throat, then I will let
him. If he wants—"

"He definitely wants," Seb drawls, his voice all deep and sexy.

Together, Mum and I turn to find him leaning in the doorway, a
gentle upward tilt to his lips.

"Good evening, Mrs Lefroy." He strides towards her, holding
out his hand. "We've never formally met, but I'm your daughter's
boyfriend. Seb Hawk—"

"I know who you are." She casts a disgusted look at Seb's hand.
"You're the one who takes every woman he fancies to his hotel. A
revolving door you've got in those Hawkston Hotels, is it?"

I cover my mouth with my hand, horrified at Mum's words.
Whether it's true or not, to say it to his face strikes me as unforgivably
rude. But I've said things to him that are almost exactly the same, and
the truth hits me with a devastating clarity: I've been walking around
parroting my mother's opinions without even realising. I've been as
much of a bitch to Seb as Mum is being now. My chest crumples as
regret fills me, and I wish I could undo all of it.

There isn't a flicker on Seb's face to reveal how he feels about what
she's just said, whereas Mum is panting, as though her words have
exhausted her.

She turns to me. "Don't do this. A man like him will destroy you. I
guarantee it. And you'll bring everything down with you. The company, the brand. The whole thing." She points at me, her finger jabbing
the air in my direction. "Don't be a fool. He can't commit. He's a
shallow, vain man who just wants to tick the famous Erica Lefroy off

his bucket list of women. We've worked too long and hard on this to allow—"

"Stop." Seb steps between me and Mum, sliding an arm around my shoulders as he holds up a palm in her direction. "You will not speak to Erica like that. And you will not speak to me that way either. You don't know me, and you don't know how I feel about your daughter, so rather than allow you to make assumptions, I'm going to tell you. Erica is so much more to me than a famous name, and to be quite honest, the fact you'd even suggest it has me questioning *your* feelings about her. She's the most wonderful woman I've ever met, and every moment she spends with me, I'm grateful to be in her presence. I would do anything for her. I've never met anyone more driven and focused, and I admire the tenacity with which she goes after her goals. She's a force of nature, and I'm honoured to play even the smallest part in her life. I know how lucky I am, and I treasure every second that she's by my side. I always have."

"Well... that was..." Mum flinches and pulls herself up tall. "What a load of nonsense. Quite unbelievable. All of it."

Seb clenches his jaw and his arm tightens around me. "I was going to say it was a shame we'd never properly met before," he says to Mum. "But now I suspect that not knowing you has been a blessing I didn't know I had. I'm going to walk away. And I'm taking Erica with me." He bows his head a little. "Have a good evening, Mrs Lefroy."

My heart is crashing against my sternum as I allow him to turn me in the other direction, and as we walk away the power of her stare sinks deep into my flesh, like she's branding me with her ill will.

As he ushers me back towards the ballroom, Seb rests his hand on my lower back, and then it sinks lower, his fingers teasing the edge of the silk. My breath catches in my throat as his hand slides beneath my dress.

Oh, holy fuck. Seb's hand is resting on my arse, and I have no underwear on. This is a step too far—a few inches lower and he could have his fingers inside me. Panic races through me at the possibility, but Mum is watching and I don't want to let her know that this isn't absolutely fine by me.

"Hmm," he muses, squeezing my bare arse and glancing back over his shoulder. "You were right about one thing," he says, raising his voice to speak to Mum. "I am going to destroy your daughter. Many, many times. And you know what else?"

Mum puffs, unable to form a response.

A wicked grin cascades over Seb's mouth. "She's going to scream my name while I do it."

24
SEB

As soon as we re-enter the main party, I slide my hand out of Erica's dress. But fuck me, if her arse wasn't the softest, smoothest thing I've ever felt. My dick is definitely raising its head. This woman can get me hard like no one else.

I need to do something, or I'll have an obvious boner in my black tie trousers. "Come on, let's get a drink."

"I don't drink."

"Yes, you do." I say, and she raises a brow. "Sparkling water at drinks parties, tap water at home. Never with ice. Tea. Coffee, but only decaf. Never a mocktail, because they're too full of sugar. And you have been known to succumb to the odd elderflower cordial when it's particularly hot." She achieves the feat of smiling and frowning simultaneously, and I add, "But no alcohol, because the perfect Erica Lefroy never does anything naughty." She elbows me and a chortle pops out of me like a bubble. "Let's get you that sparkling water."

I escort her to a secluded corner of the bar, where I take a champagne for me and water for her. She takes a sip, full lips pressed to the edge of the glass, eyes wide as she stares at me.

I'm having a hard time concentrating because now I know she's got no underwear on. I force myself to keep my eyes up, but in my periphery, I can see the outline of her nipples through the silk, and it's a cruel temptation.

She sets down her glass and, without warning, throws her arms around my neck and kisses my cheek, pressing her nearly naked breasts against my chest. "You're the best fake boyfriend ever," she whispers in my ear. "Thank you so, so much. I'm going to be in your debt forever for that display."

Her enthusiasm draws a laugh from me, and she squeezes me tight before letting go and stepping back.

"Mum's face was priceless," Erica continues. "I thought she was going to pass out when you said all that stuff. How on earth did you come up with it? Maybe you're the one who should be auditioning for the movies."

I flinch the tiniest bit, surprised she thought I made any of it up. Every word of it was true. "Maybe," I admit.

"And when you said that thing about me screaming your name…" she fades off, and a blush creeps up her cheeks even as a giggle spills from her beautiful mouth, sounding like a cascade of starlight.

I clench my jaw to hold back the surge of emotion flooding my body, but my hands prickle with it. I want to reach out and pull her against me again. I don't ever want to let her go. I want to hear her scream my name over and over again. I might want it more than I've ever wanted anything.

"She'll probably have nightmares about that," I say, forcing a rough laugh.

"Probably." Erica lays a gentle hand on my arm. "I'm sorry for how she spoke to you." I keep quiet and she adds, "About the…" She wafts her hand.

"Revolving door?"

Erica grimaces. "Yeah. It's not personal. Not really. She doesn't like men, but you're the worst type. Because…"

She fades off again, but I know what she's not saying, and she knows I know. Her father ran off with another woman before she was born, and because I haven't committed myself to anyone before, I could be just as bad as him. "It's okay. I don't care what your mother thinks of me."

"You don't?"

"No. I only care what you think."

Erica studies me and the moment crackles; if I were to touch her, static would spark between us.

"Well, I think you're great," she says with a levity that undermines the tension and, I hope, whatever she really feels. She pops a hip and rests a hand on it, pushing her lips into a theatrical pout. "But are we going to talk about how you just had your hand down my dress?"

The sight of her pretending to be riled up for confrontation draws a snort from me, and I'm thankful she's redirected the conversation.

"Are we going to talk about how you're not wearing any under-wear?"

"No. But I admit you were right, and I was wrong. We need to have the physical contact to make this convincing." She taps her chin. "I don't want to scrap the rules entirely though. I want to tweak them."

"Let's hear it."

Her tongue slides over her bottom lip, leaving it glistening and moist. I try not to look. "Your hand on my bum is fine, but only in public, and only over my clothes."

I hold back the grin that wants to work its way over my mouth. "So we're not getting naked together anytime soon?"

She affects a coy smile, eyes gleaming. If I didn't know better, I'd think she was flirting with me. "No." She pauses. "Unless my mother can see."

I chuckle. "That's some kinky shit you're into, Lefroy."

She gasps and lands a playful thwack on my arm. It's definitely a flirtatious move, and if she were anyone else, I'd think she wanted something to happen between us. But with Erica, I have no fucking clue what she wants aside from the role in *Taming the* fucking *Beast*.

"Not what I meant and you know it," she reprimands, but I don't reply because over her shoulder I catch sight of Mrs Lefroy re-entering the ballroom. Setting my glass aside, I loosen my bow tie and rapidly unbutton my shirt.

Erica's jaw drops wide and she reaches out to stop me. "What are you doing?"

"Mummy's here." I nod at where Mrs Lefroy is standing on the other side of the room, throwing daggers our way.

Erica glances over, then turns back to me with a cheeky glimmer in her eye. I arch a brow, asking wordless permission, and Erica grants it with a nod. With my shirt half undone, I haul her into me, sliding my hand right back down the low scoop back of her dress, but not inside it this time.

"Do your shirt up, you idiot," she mutters against my shoulder.

"In a minute." I hug her tighter. "I'm busy right now."

She laughs, and the sound brings another smile to my lips. *Can she feel how hard my heart is racing?* I catch the scent of her perfume in her hair. It's the new one. *Infinity.* I lean my head against hers, inhaling deeply, recalling how she smelled like this at the photo shoot. When this fake relationship ends, this scent will fucking haunt me.

But if this is all I get with Erica—a fake relationship for three months—then I am taking every fucking scrap of it. I will devour it like a man starved. And then I'll feast on the memory when it's over.

We hold eye contact, heat rolling through me in waves as an idea forms. It's crazy, but she might just agree to it.

"You need this to look different, right?" I ask, and she nods cautiously. "You need it to look like I've changed for you. You—Erica Lefroy—are so sexy, so irresistible, that I'm putting aside all my old habits because you've altered my life. No one else is coming through that revolving door again. Ever."

A flinch skitters over her face that I can't make sense of. "Mmm-hmm. Ideally, yes."

I can hardly believe what I'm about to suggest, because it's a wild idea, and I've never done anything like it before. It'll piss Dad off, and who knows what that might lead to. But all my concerns are outweighed by two undeniable facts: it feels like the right thing to do, and I want it to the core of my being.

"Move in with me."

A small jolt runs through her. "What?"

"You want me to show the world that it's different this time?"

Her chin quivers the slightest bit. "Yes."

"Come and live with me. In my house. I've never done that with anyone before."

"Live with you? Like... roommates?"

I can't help smiling. "No, like my girlfriend."

"Fake girlfriend," she corrects.

"Yeah. Until Nico and Kate's wedding. The full three months."

"Because you can't last longer than that without sex?" She teases, probably hoping I'll laugh along with her, but I'm too busy ignoring the twinge in my chest as I recall that she called me a *manwhore*. A derogatory title, but one I've earned, I suppose, even if I did it bathed deep in shame. And I can't change it now.

"Hey, I'm joking," she purrs, recalling my attention, but there's something in her gaze that has me wondering if this isn't all a joke to her either. If something about what she's just said bothers her the same way it bothers me. But I can't think about that now. There's so much I haven't told her. Can't tell her. If this were a real relationship, keeping the kind of secrets I'm keeping would be a shitty foundation. But it's not real, as she keeps reminding me. "Terrible joke. Sorry," she adds.

I give her a squeeze to let her know I'm not offended. "Move in with me tomorrow and stay until we leave for Nico and Kate's wedding."

"And what happens after the wedding? Do I just move out?"

"Does that mean you're moving in?"

"Yeah." She flashes me an unguarded smile. "It's a good idea."

Excitement fizzes through me. *Erica Lefroy is going to live with me, in my home, under my roof.* I'm not stupid enough to believe she's agreeing because she genuinely wants to live with me. This is about her career, and getting back at her mum, just like the photo shoot and this launch party. I *know* all that, but it doesn't stop me feeling like I might explode at the idea of living with her.

"But how does it end?" she continues. "We should have discussed this before. If I'm living with you, how does it end? *Why* does it end?"

It's right on the tip of my tongue to explain. To tell her everything so we can work out how the fuck it ends *together*. But my mouth refuses to form the words, '*I have to get engaged to someone else*', so I say, "We'll work it out. You can break up with me. Make it big and showy and that'll be the end of that."

She looks unsure, and guilt skitters down my spine. "And... are we still friends after such a big public breakup?"

"Always." I pull her closer, and the soft music of the slow dance wraps around us. To me, there might as well be no one else here because I am consumed by the woman in my arms. "I'll always be here for you."

Even if it tears me apart.

25
ERICA

The GIF I received from Seb this morning was a cartoon polar bear that said, 'Hey Roomie!' in pink capital letters. They're so silly, but I love getting them. Sometimes, though, I find it hard to reconcile the stupid cartoon images with the sophisticated man who sends them.

Now is one of those times. He's standing in the grand hallway of his Knightsbridge apartment, fully suited up and ready for work. *Gorgeous.* I'm sure half the office must be in love with him. *How could they not be?* The thought stirs up a bilious sensation in my stomach.

I let my gaze drift, taking in his broad chest and the sleeves of his shirt, which—*thank God*—are down, cufflinks in place. Tie secured at his neck. He looks every inch the businessman. Every inch...

My gaze sinks to his crotch, hovering there for the briefest of seconds, but even that is too long because when my gaze flicks up again, Seb's there to catch it like a butterfly in a net. His lips part, dry amusement flitting through his gaze, but whatever he's thinking of saying, he doesn't.

"I've contacted the editor at the Daily Mail," he says, glancing at all the bags and boxes I've had delivered to his apartment.

He's running me through the steps he's taken to announce our relationship and spread the word. With each item he recounts, I breathe a sigh of relief. He's got this in hand; with any luck, public opinion about me is already shifting, but with everything he's doing, it should change quickly. His list of contacts must be huge.

"They're running a story on us moving in together," he continues. "A shitty gossip piece, but we'll have some element of creative control over it. He owes me a favour. Tatler is running a story too."

"Tatler?"

He ruffles a hand in his hair, looking bashful for a second. "Yeah. It's not insignificant society news."

It's endearing how low-key he's trying to play it. I know Tatler would be more interested in him than me. He's been on their list of eligible bachelors since he had his first shave. Seb Hawkston settling down is going to break a few society mothers' hearts. It's funny that it hadn't occurred to me before. I've been so preoccupied with myself and my career, and how this—*how he*—could help me, that I hadn't stopped to think of him. He's giving up a lot to do this for me, not least regular sex.

"Thank you," I say.

"You're welcome."

He picks up one of my bags and guides me to a room further down the hall. It's large, with a huge bed, and a view over Hyde Park. "This is your room," he announces.

I've been in his apartment many times, but I've never wandered into the rooms. I've always stuck to the main living areas. Maybe that's why I feel so awkward now, as he holds the door open so I can pass into the bedroom. Being allowed into the other rooms feels like he's offering me something intimate.

"My own room?"

He shifts his chin an inch. "Yes?"

It sounds like a question, just like mine did. I walk to the window and look out, ignoring the dangerous thrumming of my heart. *I didn't really think I'd be sharing his room, did I?*

I spin to face him, and all my self-preservation skills desert me. "Won't the staff think it's weird if we're sleeping separately?"

"They'll think what I tell them to think."

"Oh. Okay."

His eyes narrow, a smirk pulling at his lips. "You want into my bedroom, Lefroy?"

An unexpected burst of laughter leaves my mouth. "Ha. No. I mean... I don't know. I hadn't really thought it through. But this room is great."

"I'm glad you think so. Make yourself at home." He drops my bag to the floor and turns to leave, but pauses and looks back. "About my bedroom... it's off-limits."

"Oh. Right. Roger that. No one goes into the bedroom."

"Exactly."

"Hence all the women in the hotels?"

The words leave my mouth before I can stop them, and although I meant to sound like I was teasing, Seb's smile vanishes. *Crap.* I wish I could let go of the idea that he's been with so many women, but it's hard when I haven't been with anyone.

"Sorry." I tug on the loose thread on my sleeve, winding it around my finger. Seb observes the motion, brows flexing as he does. It shouldn't surprise me that he'd want privacy in his home, but for some reason, it stings. "I wouldn't have gone into your room. I—"

"Everywhere else is fair game. What's mine is yours." He smiles, and at first, it looks like he's holding back, but then it warms and I relax in its heat.

"I got you something," I say, keen to shift the conversation away from his bedroom and the awkwardness that just descended. I dig into my bag and pull out the slim rectangular gift I wrapped this morning. "As a thank you for doing this for me."

He takes it, shooting me a bemused glance. "You didn't have to do this. I didn't get you anything. Can I open it?"

"Yeah. Please," I say, but he's already tearing the paper, revealing a dark leather frame containing a black and white image of us from the photo shoot. Me, on his lap, my head tilted back, and him, gazing at me like... well, like he *wants* me. Seb's expression is unreadable as he stares at it, causing a swell of unease to rise in me.

Maybe it was a stupid gift.

"I thought you should have a copy, in case anyone comes to visit," I blurt. "You need at least one picture of me in your house to make this relationship more convincing. If you liked someone, you'd put up a photo of them, right? If you were in love with them, you'd probably have at least one photo of them in your house."

His eyebrows rise as he keeps staring at the picture. Warmth blossoms in my chest, rising up my neck. "I guess I would have one," he mutters, still not looking at me.

"You can get rid of it as soon as we end things. Think of it as a prop. You can keep the frame if you want and ditch the picture when all this is over. You could hardly bring another woman over with that sitting around. I wouldn't expect you to keep it."

He lowers it, meeting my gaze with his earnest one. "I'm not gonna get rid of this. Are you kidding? It's beautiful. I love it." He runs a hand through his hair and glances at it again, huffing to himself. Then he grins, eyes flashing at me with the promise of a taunt. "I look really hot here. Thanks, Lefroy."

My laugh takes me by surprise.

"Seriously," he says, his tone ringing with authenticity as he steps up to me and pulls me into a hug. "I can't remember the last time someone gave me a gift as thoughtful as this."

He presses a kiss to my hair, and the gentleness of his touch nearly overwhelms me. He's done so much for me. He's *still* doing so much for me. All these years, he's been here for me to lean on, sending his stupid GIFs. But have I *really* been a good friend in return? I've teased him, mocked him, called him a manwhore, and thrown him out of my apartment. Regret spirals through my chest, and I feel so unworthy that it makes me want to cry. I swallow the sensation down. I don't want to get weepy on my first day living with him, and in its place a heat rises through me that has me wanting to cling to him and beg forgiveness for any time I've ever said a hurtful word to him.

"You've been so good to me," I whisper, my voice almost breaking. "Thank you."

He pulls back to look at me, and his eyes—*so blue*—suck me in. I'm drowning in them. My body is hypersensitive, the places where he's touching me aching for more. His lips part, his tongue running over them as his gaze slips to my mouth.

In the back of my mind, a chorus starts up. *Kiss him. Kiss him. Kiss him.*

I sink into the present moment. Seb's holding me in it, and it's simultaneously terrifying and beautiful, and I don't want to ruin it. I don't want to move towards him or pull away, because whatever has us bound now is so fragile, it feels like if I took a breath, it would shatter into a million pieces.

A rough sound rumbles in his chest. An aching noise that means more than words. More than my name. It sounds like *want.*

My want. His want. His awareness of them both.

We're teetering on the edge of a precipice. His lips. My lips. And the bed, just over there. Two steps and he could have me on my back, deep in the sheets.

Stop it, Erica.

This is fake. He's your friend. You can't hop into bed with him like it means nothing, not when you've never done that with anyone before.

It would ruin everything.

He steps back and gives me a casual smile, and panic slices through me. Did I just imagine the tension? Was that sound in his chest just a rumble of... what? Appreciation? Contentment?

Was that all in my head?

"You don't need to pretend now," Seb says, and my stomach drops. *He knew exactly what happened, but he thinks I was faking it.* "There's no one here." He cups my shoulder. "Better than how you stiffened when we started out though. Good work."

I can't detect any mockery in his voice, and he raises the picture I gave him, moving on like nothing happened. "Thanks for this. I'm gonna keep it in my bedroom."

It's on the tip of my tongue to comment that if he takes it to his bedroom, which is *oh-so private*, no one is going to see it, and as a prop to convince visitors of our relationship, it'll be useless. But he's already waving me off, wishing me a good day, and leaving the room.

When the door closes and I'm left alone, the most acute sense of desertion I've ever experienced washes over me, and an unsettling ache takes hold in my heart.

Am I making a huge mistake?

26
SEB

After Erica's cosmetics launch, my father drained another one of my accounts. Seventeen million pounds, gone. After he took the £28 million, I spent a small fortune ringfencing the rest, splitting it up, hiding it, and moving it into other accounts, but it made no difference. I'd just moved that £17 million offshore and Dad still found it. When I realised it was gone, I didn't even call my accountant, because I knew exactly where it went.

Dad sent a message mocking my attempts to hide my cash from him. I deleted it and let the anger filter through my blood. A succession of thoughts followed, the loudest of which was whether I should find myself a gun and kill the bastard myself.

Previously, I'd have numbed out with alcohol and a nameless blonde in a hotel room. Maybe two of them.

But not anymore. Now, I focus on Erica. The way she makes me feel, and the fact that every fucking second of being in her presence is worth any shit my father wants to put me through.

We've been living together for weeks, and I guess you could say it's going well. I'm not getting laid, but she's in my house. Just down the corridor. I feel like a kid who's been granted their one wish, and while I'm delighted, I know I don't have long to enjoy it.

She's busy. I'm busy. We don't see each other that often, but when we do, it's like the apartment is having an electrical surge. I don't know if she can feel it too, but her essence sparks at my skin. It's a circuit running right through me the moment I walk in the door.

I don't want to fuck it up, so I've been putting a little distance between us. After that moment on the day she moved in, where I swear she wanted to kiss me, I haven't really touched her at all.

I don't know if it's making it better or worse. For me, it's amplifying the longing. But I'm an expert at playing it cool. Being casual. Making it all into a joke.

It's what I do best.

You ready to kiss me again, Lefroy? I've wanted to ask. Make light of it. But for some reason, I can't make light of *that*. It's a treasure of a question that I don't want to ask, in case her response confirms it's nothing more than fool's gold.

I'm fucking torturing myself and I'm enjoying the torment.

Tonight, I'm late home from work, and the flat is quiet. I don't know if Erica is here or not, but I settle myself at the island and start checking emails.

Another message comes in from Dad.

This time, the message is a link to Diana Marchetti's social media account. I've never looked her up, even after she told me she was an influencer. No inclination, to be honest. But now, I click the link and start to scroll. There are thousands of photos of her looking young, beautiful, and happy. Most of them are book-related, and she's wearing a selection of floaty dresses and heels, posing in tourist spots in London in each. She's cute. It's cute. I don't know why Dad sent it to me. Maybe he thinks pictures of Diana rubbing up against a red letter box or an old school phone booth full of second-hand books will win me over.

"Who's that?" Erica's voice pops in my ear and I nearly drop the phone. How did I not hear her come in?

"Erm... I don't—"

"She's wearing my shoes."

"What?"

Erica leans over, pointing at the shoes Diana is wearing in the photo. "Those silver heels. The *Erica Lefroys*. They're limited edition."

"I knew that," I say, scrabbling for an explanation as to why I'm looking at photos of another woman.

Erica frowns. "You did?"

"Yeah." Thankfully, the word rings true, because it is. Now that she's mentioned it, I do recognise the shoes. "That's why I'm looking at it." *And that's the lie.*

Her features soften. "That's so sweet." She ruffles my hair and moves off to grab food from the fridge. "I'm making a salad. You want some?"

Thank God we've moved off the topic of Diana Marchetti. If guilt doesn't tear through my stomach lining by the time our arrangement is over, I'll have to start going to church because it will be a fucking miracle, and I'll be a believer.

Erica grabs a chopping board and a knife and starts taking cherry tomatoes from a paper bag.

"You don't need to do that," I say. "I can get the chef to prepare it, or we can get something delivered."

"But then I can't count them."

I frown. "Count what?"

"The tomatoes. I'm allowed twelve half cherry tomatoes."

What the fuck? "You're allowed six full cherry tomatoes?" She nods, continuing to cut without meeting my eye. "Per day or per meal?"

"Per meal." She gestures to the chopping board, where she's made two piles of halved cherry tomatoes. "These are yours, and these are mine."

I wait for her to laugh because she surely can't be fucking serious. I start filtering my memories for times I've eaten with her and come up short. Never in a restaurant. But at drinks parties... did she eat the canapes? Surely when we had snacks on the sofa, she ate them. *Wait... was it just me that ate them? Did she actually eat them?* I rifle through more memories, sure I've seen her lick her fingers. My dick twitches. *Definitely seen her lick her fingers.*

"Who said you're allowed that many?" I ask.

"My mother."

"She makes the rules?"

"All the rules."

Now, that's some fucked up shit I didn't know. "What else is on the list?"

She lays down the knife and places both hands flat on the counter, defiance glimmering in her gaze. "No chocolate. No dairy. No milk in my tea. No artificial sugar. No sugar at all really. No crisps. No snacks. No alcohol." Her chest puffs up with a lengthy inhalation. "And no Seb Hawkston."

"Ah. So I'm the seventh tomato?"

Her response comes late and quiet. "Something like that." She picks up the knife again and continues to cut, this time counting out slices of cucumber.

"I've seen you put milk in your tea," I say.

She pauses to push a strand of hair off her forehead with the back of her wrist. "I'm rebelling."

"Oh, yeah?"

She nods at me, but it's a lengthy nod, all the way up and down, as if to say, '*You, over there. You're my rebellion*'.

I really fucking wish I was.

My heart bangs against my ribs. Sometimes, it feels like she's giving me an opening, offering me something more, and I don't know whether I'm imagining it or if it's really there and she's waiting for me to grab it with both hands.

I've done a good job of ignoring it, siphoning off those lingering looks and the sparks that I'm starting to suspect aren't one-sided. But when it comes down to it, I have no idea if Erica feels anywhere near what I feel. Maybe this is just business for her. The PR. The movie. The career. And so far, it's working. The articles in the press and on social media are shifting. And the fans want her to play Vanessa in *Taming the Beast*. They're clamoring for it.

She keeps chopping, and something inside me snaps. I *need* to push this. I need something from her that's more than pleasantries. I shift off the bar stool, coming to stand next to her. I pick a cherry tomato from the paper bag, plucking it right off the vine.

She watches me do it, not moving as I do, the knife hovering over the board. I'm standing far too close. She knows it. I know it. Heat prickles all over me as she turns to me. "What?"

I lean my hip against the counter and raise the tomato so it's at her eye-line, rolling it between my thumb and index finger. Dark eyes focus on the tomato, then me, and back again like she's calculating something. "What?" she says again, although I know she knows exactly *what*.

I nod at her mouth. "The seventh tomato."

"What about it?"

The prickling sensation in my body intensifies in my groin. My *dick*. "I want to see you eat it."

She stares at the tomato for a little too long before she says, "You want to put that in my mouth?"

"Yes. And then I want you to swallow."

Tension ignites, sending the whole place up in burning flames. Erica's throat bobs as though she's actually swallowing.

"Nuh-uh." It comes out all breathy.

"Come on, Lefroy." The command is a deep rasp. "This is what rebellion tastes like."

Her breaths come in gentle pants that I can hear over my own breathing. "I'm not hungry," she whispers, but everything else tells me she is; her body tilting towards me; her pupils blown wide; her pink lips slightly parted.

"Scared?" I ask.

"No."

"Eat it, then." I roll it between my fingers, and she follows the movement. "It's just a tomato."

She leans even closer. "Is it?"

Her voice wavers, and there's a desperation in her eyes, as though she doesn't know what I want, what I mean, or what she's supposed to do.

It hits me like a ton of bricks. I'm being an arsehole, taunting her this way. Maybe eating one last tomato is going to send her toppling over the edge, tumbling into the abyss of the unknown. Maybe she really *can't* eat it. Maybe her mother fucked her up *that* much. I snatch it in a full fist and shove it in my own mouth, crunching down on it, letting it pop against my teeth. I chew and swallow. "Yeah," I say, so casual that the tension recedes to the shadows. "It's just a tomato."

Her body slumps against the island and I feel like the biggest wanker on the planet. I need to get away from her, clear my head before I make even more of a prick of myself. I push off the counter and head towards my room.

"I'm going to have a shower," I call over my shoulder.

I'm about to turn into the hallway when she calls my name, and I spin to find her pointing the knife at me. "I'll eat it because I *want* to eat it," she says. "*When* I want to eat it. Not because you want to shove it down my throat." She lowers the knife and picks a tomato quite deliberately from the paper bag and sucks it into her mouth, chewing it slowly. Her eyes glimmer with the taunt, the double entendre, acknowledging that we're playing a game, but still skirting the edge of the board. She swallows, then flashes me a smile so beautiful that it sets my own free. I rub a hand over my jaw to conceal it, shaking my head at her.

"Fuck. I'm an arse," I say, my hand sliding round to rub the back of my neck. "Sorry."

"It's okay. You're not the first guy who's asked me to suck his dick."

I nearly choke on my next breath. "What?"

"You are the first to try it with a tomato metaphor though. A plus for effort. Gold star." She bites her lip to hold back her grin. "The celibacy getting to you that bad, huh? It's been a few weeks of fake dating and you're ready to crack."

I splutter a laugh. "I'm not—"

"You are." She rests a hand on her hip. "I know you." The intimacy of the phrase and the softness of her tone, utterly devoid of judgment, snakes its way around my heart and squeezes. *I'm a total prick.* "Go wash that one-track mind down the drain. Dinner in fifteen minutes. I'm expecting my friend to join me, not the guy who wants me to suck his dick under the table."

I roll my eyes, pretending to dismiss her as though she's talking shit, although she's absolutely bang on. I want her mouth on me. I'd love her lips around my dick, but to be honest, I'd take them anywhere she wanted to put them. And it's not the celibacy. *It's her.* Seven years of *her*. Seven years of wanting and pretending I don't. Pretending every woman I've ever fucked is her.

No wonder I don't remember their names, because there's only one name that's ever fucking mattered to me.

Erica Lefroy.

Christ. I'm sick in the head. I must be.

I blow out a breath as I turn away from her, determined to be a better friend. To cool the fuck down, thankful she's got so low an opinion of me, that she's chalking this episode up to nothing more than me being *me*.

But even as I walk away, her words replay in my mind. *Under the table.*

What a fucking dream that would be.

27

ERICA

I wanted to suck that tomato from between his fingers. Wanted to press my lips to it, dig my teeth into it, and suck it inside my mouth, holding it there while I kissed him so I could pass it back to him with my tongue. *I wanted, I wanted, I wanted.* Internally, I was hemorrhaging with want.

When he returned from his shower, hair wet and scraped back, he was a total gentleman. It was as though the tomato episode never happened, and when it was happening, I was so blown away by the whole thing that it's hazy in my memory. *Did he really ask me to swallow it? Or did I make that bit up?*

Since that night, time has flown. We've had a series of public dates. Restaurants and bars mostly, but a couple of walks along the river too. Anywhere we can be seen publicly. He hasn't kissed me again, but he's held my hand over the table, pulled me into him as we've walked. Outside of the apartment, we've performed. But inside, there's an immovable awkwardness that's taken up residence like another flatmate. A great big burly presence that we have to tiptoe around, not daring to look at it in case it does... *something.* We're both ignoring it, hardly communicating, him working long hours and me the same, just so we don't have to be here together, enduring whatever the fuck this has turned into. It sucks the joy out of living together, that's for sure, and yet there's still that buzz of temptation, like the roar of a river beneath its frozen surface.

I don't know how much longer I can go on like this. Luckily, the audition for *Taming the Beast* has come and gone, and I'm pretty sure I nailed it. Even the press is backing me, and I checked with the bookies online, and I'm odds on to get the role, and if it were up to the fans on social media, I'd already have it.

I don't want to get excited too soon, and I haven't mentioned it to Seb because I know he'd be as excited as me, and if two of us get excited together... it's not worth the risk. I can't let that energy explode in these four walls. He'd smile, his dimple would pop, he'd throw his arms around me, and then...

I shake the thought away. Then... *nothing*. Whatever I feel for Seb has to be a secret. Locked down. Our arrangement is so close to over. We're leaving for Kate and Nico's wedding *tomorrow*.

And then we'll have to break up.

And then we can go back to normal. But what is normal now?

Maybe we've fucked our friendship already. Maybe it died that day in the gallery...

I'll put it out of my mind. Put him out of mind, at least for now. I've got the day off so I can pack up all my belongings, ready to return to my own home when we get back from the wedding in the Caribbean. I'm trying to ignore the unsettled—*sad?*—feelings that are coming up, so I'm focusing on other things. I've had a long bath and now I'm sitting at the kitchen island plucking my eyebrows with a hand-held mirror. It's not sanitary, but I'll wipe the surface down later and Seb will never know.

Beside me is the issue of Tatler that covered our relationship. Seb must have powerful contacts because they whipped the story up fast and shunted other pieces to fit it in.

I flick through the pages, staring at the pictures of us. Of *him*.

I can hardly catch my breath looking at them. I am abso-fuck-ing-lutely doomed when it comes to this man. He's so handsome, and that *smile*... it's enough to knock you sideways.

So much for putting him out of mind. A pulse sets up between my legs as I stare at him, and I have to acknowledge the slutty version of me, the one I've locked up tight—or perhaps my mother locked her up and threw away the key—is getting louder. Harder to ignore. And the cage I put her in is wearing thin.

By every measure that counts, I'm a virgin. But I don't feel like one. I feel like a needy little whore, wrapped in a virgin's body. Pretending I don't have needs. Urges. Pretending I wouldn't love it if Seb threw me down on the floor, the bed, shoved me against the wall with his hand around my throat, and fucked me as I screamed his name.

Oh, God.

I want him. But not like this. Not fake. Not pretend. And not because his balls are so blue he doesn't know what to do with himself. He's so used to getting women to do whatever he wants that this situation is probably fucking with his head. It's fucking with mine.

Ugh. All those women. It makes me feel nauseous.

Would it have been so bad to let him kiss me on one of our dates? To let people see? To let his tongue slide between my lips? That night in the gallery feels like so long ago, I'm beginning to forget what it first felt like to have his mouth on me. How my blood turned molten as soon as he touched his lips to mine. And when his mouth went south...

Oh, fuck. I must be ovulating because here I am sitting at his kitchen table, horny as anything. I squirm on the stool, creating pressure between my legs, which only makes it worse.

I'm definitely not going to be able to ignore this. Maybe I can go sort myself out in the shower. Or the bedroom. Or... right here in the kitchen. I glance at the time. Seb won't be home from work for hours.

My body is hot and tight and the need to touch myself is oppressive. I can't think straight. I don't masturbate often, and when I do, self-loathing clings to me. *No one wants a whore.* That's what Mum always said. I've repressed the urge for so fucking long. Behaved myself. Stuck to the rules and been such a good girl. But bit by bit, I'm breaking those rules. The milk in my tea. The seventh tomato. *And Seb. Seb. Seb.*

I can't sit here anymore, staring at his face on the page, the harsh pound of blood between my legs making everything down there feel swollen...

It feels dirty. Naughty. But I can't ignore it. *I'm a new woman and this is my rebellion.* I stand, pushing the magazine away. But then I pull it back and tear out the page with the biggest picture of Seb on it. He's in a suit, buttoning the jacket with one hand, holding mine with the other. And he is *beautiful*...

I tuck the picture into the pocket of my robe, intending to head to my bedroom where I can touch myself in private. But then I stop, an idea crossing my mind.

Our arrangement is nearly over, and I've never been into his bedroom.

What if I went there instead?

28
SEB

"We'd love to run a joint marketing campaign," says Arthur Knatchbull. "Luxury goods and Hawkston Hotels. It's a perfect union."

An alert pings on my phone, and I glance at it under the table. I'm in the boardroom with Matt and our leasing agents, meeting with the marketing team from Knatchbull Luxe about leveraging both our brands.

I swipe on the phone. Motion detected in my bedroom. *What the hell?* No one should be in there.

I click into the CCTV system and bring up the live footage. Erica's standing in my room wearing a dressing gown, like she's just got out of the bath or something. *What is she doing?*

A chill runs down the back of my neck, trickling down my spine. *Fuck.* What if she goes into the bathroom? She cannot go in there.

"Seb?" Matt asks, calling my attention back to the meeting. "Thoughts?"

I have no fucking clue what they just said. "Sounds good."

Matt frowns. Fuck, I hope that made sense.

My gaze ping-pongs between Matt, Arthur, and the phone screen, but it's the phone that captures my attention. I watch, hardly breathing, as Erica pads about my room. She lifts the photo she brought me, which I placed on the bedside table, stares for a few seconds before replacing it, and starts opening cupboards, peering inside. She pulls out a suit jacket and puts it to her nose, holding it there like she's inhaling it.

Wait a fucking second. *Is she sniffing my suits?* Her eyes flutter closed and when she tips her head back, her mouth slightly open, I imagine the sound of the sigh she releases.

And that's when I know it for sure. She's turned on.

I nearly leap to my feet, wanting to pump a fist in the air, but panic quickly suffuses my elation.

My bedroom is the one place I've carved out as absolutely mine. When I have parties, I lock the door. It's *my* fucking space, and no one gets in. *No one.* Not even Erica Lefroy. *Especially not Erica Lefroy.*

I can't take my eyes off the screen. It's clear she has no idea that I can see her. If she knew, she wouldn't be in there. *Please, don't go into the bathroom.* She edges up to the bed, stroking the sheets with one finger.

"Seb? Are you with us?" Matt asks.

"Yeah. Absolutely." *That didn't sound in the least convincing.*

I glance back at the phone just in time to see Erica fling off her robe and toss it on the floor.

I can't breathe. My heart feels like it's exploding.

She's naked. Completely fucking naked.

Oh, fuck.

Blood rushes to my dick. I rocket from my seat before anyone notices that I'm already half-hard. This is so wrong. I should have told her there are cameras in my room.

"Sorry. I have to go. Excuse me." I gesture with my phone, then panic that they can see the screen, and shove it deep in my pocket, which serves the dual purpose of disguising my semi.

"Seb," Matt says, his voice sharp. "This is—"

"Can't. Sorry."

I leave the room before anyone can say anything else and unmute the phone screen.

"Okay," comes Erica's voice as she talks to herself. "Let's do this."

Do what?

I start running to my office, dialling her number, but she doesn't answer. I push open the office door and call her again.

No answer.

I dial again, with the same result.

I pull the phone from my ear and glance at the screen. Erica bends over, touching her toes like she's limbering up.

Oh, sweet Jesus.

I should look away. I should put my phone in a drawer and lock it. Pretend this never happened.

But... I don't. *I can't.* Call me a weak man, but the woman I've fantasised about for years is bending over, naked, in my bedroom, when I expressly told her never to go in there. Instead of doing the right thing, I click on my computer, loading up the live feed to the big screen as fast as I can, and take a seat.

She arches her back, hands behind her head, just like she did when she was sitting on my lap during the photo shoot. Except now she's *naked.*

Erica Lefroy is naked in my bedroom. The only fucking problem is, I'm not there.

I drag my free hand down my face as I stare at the screen. *Holy mother-fucking-fuck-fuck-fuck.*

She's doing some kind of yoga stretching at the foot of the bed, tits jiggling. *Holy shit.* My dick gives an angry throb beneath the desk, and heat rushes my entire body.

If only she'd answered the phone before. Maybe I should try again, but what would I say? "Hey, get out of my room. I know you're in there because I can see you." I can't do that because she's taken all her clothes off—

She flops back on the bed, gets comfortable, spreads her legs and raises her knees, pulls a tiny mirror from the pocket of her robe and positions it between her legs.

She slides her hand down and—

Oh, fuck. I cannot watch this. I can't let her do this, not knowing I'm here seeing it all when she thinks she's alone.

I jerk up from my seat, dick rock hard in my trousers, and lock my office door. I grab my phone from the desk and dial her number, daring only the slightest glances at the computer screen between ring tones. Yup, Erica is writhing, naked, on my bed, with a fucking mirror between her legs. She tweaks a nipple and lets out a groan. I'm already so turned on, I'm probably leaking pre-cum.

Fuck, fuck, fuck.

I dash over to the computer and mute the sound.

The ringing on my end of the line stops, and in the half-second of silence I expect the answer machine message to click in, but it doesn't.

"Seb?"

Oh, my God. She answered. She answered the fucking phone. I pace to the window, away from the computer screen.

"Hey. Erica." My voice sounds shaky. "Are you at home?"

Are you at home? What a fucking stupid question to open with. Now I definitely can't admit that I can see her.

"Yeah," she says, a little breathy. "Where are you?"

"In the office. What are you doing?"

"Making lunch."

I have never heard a woman sound more turned on when telling me she's making lunch. All the blood in my body surges straight to my dick, if it wasn't there already.

"Do you need something?" she asks, still breathless.

"No. Sorry." *What the fuck am I doing?* I'll turn off the screens. Pretend I never saw any of this. "I'll see you late—"

"Wait. Do you have a moment?"

What the fuck? "Erm—"

"Can you stay on the line?"

My skin prickles, and I glance back over at the screen where Erica is quite clearly still lying naked on my bed, touching herself. Looks like she's got the phone next to her. Must be on speaker. "Huh?"

"Just... talk to me. It's quiet here. I'd like to hear your voice."

My whole body is one great electric fucking current. I'm about to short circuit. My brain might fucking explode. "You want me to talk to you?"

"Mmm. Yeah. Just for a bit. You can go in five minutes."

Five minutes?

I pull out my desk chair and sit down. *Tell her. Tell her you can see her.* "Phone sex?"

She laughs. "Yeah. Something like that. Just talk to me while I make the food."

Christ, she thinks I'm joking. And she's still lying to me.

Fuck it. I start talking about my day, the meetings I went to, who I've spoken to on the phone...

But I'm not engaged with my own words because I'm watching Erica. Her perfect body sprawled out on my sheets, dark hair spread over the pillows. She's propped up on them so she can watch herself in the mirror.

I stifle a groan at the sight.

"What have you been up to?" I ask, straining to keep my voice neutral.

She moans a little. Very quietly, so that if I couldn't see her, I wouldn't know what she was doing. "I had the day off. I was looking at that Tatler spread about us moving in together."

"Oh."

"Yeah. I was reading it. You look so handsome in those pictures."

My stomach turns over so violently that I might need emergency surgery to fix it, and when she pulls out the picture of me, which she's obviously torn from the magazine, I think it drops right out of my fucking body.

She's been sitting at home, flicking through a magazine article about us, looking at a picture *of me*, and getting all riled up. And she's let herself into my bedroom to get it out of her system. On my bed. While listening to me talk shit.

Her back arches as her hand moves faster. Energy buzzes through me like it's me she's touching. This is the most mind-blowing fucked-up scenario I've encountered, and I've done a lot. Seen a lot. But nothing has turned me on like this before...

I can't take it. I will definitely explode if I don't do something about it.

I put my phone on speaker, placing it on the desk, and undo my trousers, releasing my dick, which is already thick and hard. *This is so bad. I'm a bad man.*

I grip the shaft, easing my hand up and down, and the relief is visceral. I have to bite my lip not to groan.

"Are you still there?" she says, one of her hands playing with her nipple, the other rubbing at her clit.

"Yeah." I'm so hard I won't last a moment. I tug on my dick, matching my speed to hers, hoping to fuck she can't hear what I'm doing. "I'm here."

"Ahh," she moans, and it sounds like a lusty sex noise. She doesn't even try to hide it. Fire whips through me. "Don't go anywhere."

"You okay?" *Like I don't fucking know.*

"Uh-huh." She places one hand behind her, levering herself up even more, getting a better view of her own fingers teasing her clit in that mirror. "Hang on. Something's boiling over—"

Something's boiling over? Erica Lefroy, you dirty little minx. I nearly laugh, but I'm too fucking turned on. My hips thrust forward, like my dick wants to leap right through the screen. *I wish.* My muscles tense, my quads like rock as the sparking, electric pleasure of an impending orgasm shoots from the base of my spine, zapping up my shaft. My balls tighten.

"Seb!" Erica slams a hand over her mouth, her body going rigid, nipples swollen, as she orgasms right where I can see her. Quietly shuddering.

My orgasm shoots through me, thick ropes of cum decorating my fist, my other hand gripping the desk.

"Erica," I gasp.

I wince as my orgasm tails off. That definitely sounded climactic... I lean back in my chair, breathing heavily and surveying the mess I've made. Erica, on the screen, has collapsed like a ragdoll, still naked, her perfect body spread across the white sheets. *My sheets.*

This is the hottest thing that's ever happened to me. And she doesn't even know.

"Thank you," she whispers.

My heart thumps. "What for?"

"It was nice not to have lunch alone again." She stands and puts on the robe before remaking my bed.

"Oh, right. Yeah. Lunch. Well, if I didn't have to work, I'd have lunch with you every day." I cringe. *I fucking would as well.*

She inspects the bed, and, apparently pleased she's left no trace of her activities, pulls the cord on her robe tighter. "I could call you." She laughs. "Lunchtime phone chat every day. Like a real couple."

I can't bring myself to laugh. This is so messed up. *What does she even mean?* And, more importantly, how will I ever tell her what I've done? "You know where I am. Next time something's boiling over." *Good God, this is fucked.* She frowns, but I add, "See you tonight," and hang up before she can say anything else.

29
ERICA

A few hours after I left Seb's bedroom, I invited Amy over. I was itchy with guilt, and I needed someone to talk to about it.

I let myself into his room when not going in there was the only rule he gave me. I disobeyed it so flagrantly, giving in completely to my untamed desire. I let him talk me through it, and hearing his voice, even with the corporate shit he was murmuring about, made it so much more delicious. I've never had an orgasm like that before. It wrecked my body. I felt it in every cell, buzzing and tingling, lingering in my system for minutes after it was over.

I deceived him. I used him. I'm the worst friend in the world.

But I can't regret it.

Once I've told Amy all the sordid details, she leans across the table towards me, eyes alight with glee, and says, "You slut. On his bed too."

"Okay, yes. That was naughty. I feel really bad. He told me not to go in there."

Amy performs an exaggerated eye roll. "When I told you to do mirror work, I did not tell you to go lie down on your fake boyfriend's bed and do it." She pauses, as if reconsidering her words. "Not that Seb would mind. If he knew, he'd probably come in his tailor-made pants."

I point at her. "Do not. I repeat *do not* tell him. *Ever.*" She nods and I pin my lips, contemplating not sharing for a second, but then I blurt, "He rang. When I was... you know."

Her eyes go so wide that I tilt away in case her eyeballs actually pop. "And you answered?"

"Yeah. I made him stay on the line while I..."

Amy slams her hands on the kitchen counter and leaps from her seat. "You did not! Did he know? I mean... did he know what you were doing?"

I shake my head. "No. I was very quiet. Told him I was cooking."

"You are bad." She cups both hands over her mouth and squeaks. "That's so bad. Without his consent? That's like... oh, you little devil!" She laughs, muffled at first, until she lets her hands fall and releases a sound so loud it fills the room. "I've half a mind to tell him myself, just so he knows what he's got himself into. You pretty much violated the man." She waves a hand in the air like she's casting a spell. "He ought to know what his 'girlfriend' gets up to when he's at wor—"

"Stop." I cover my face and groan. Amy knows this is all fake; she's the only one I've told, not just because I trust her, but because I have so much dirt on her, I could take her down forever. Actually, I probably couldn't. Amy doesn't give a shit about that stuff. She's all free sex, wild music, and hanging out with Seb Hawkston in public. She'd bounce right back up again like one of those weighted inflatable dolls. "It was bad. I feel terrible. But..."

Amy cocks her head. "What?"

"You need to see what's in his bathroom."

I get up from my seat, beckoning her to come with me, heart thumping as I prepare to disobey Seb's rules for the second time in one day. But I have to show someone what's in his ensuite. *Have to.* I was so surprised when I saw it, I nearly fainted.

Amy follows me through his bedroom, which is so neat, there's no way he'll ever know I came in here. I push open the bathroom door, and there it is.

Me.

"Holy shit!" Amy squeals, her mouth dropping wide. "You're on the wall. You're fucking huge."

"I know."

We stare at the image of me on Seb's bathroom wall. It's a sultry black and white one from the Claudia Kirchwood shoot. Even I have to admit, as objectively as possible, it's beautiful. I'm in a white silk dress, gazing up at the sky, my shoulders resting against a marble column. As I stare at it, my conversation with Seb when I gave him the framed photo the day I moved in, drifts through my mind.

"If you were in love with someone, you'd probably have at least one photo of them in your house."

"I guess I would have one."

Does this photo mean what I think it means? My breathing shallows and my thoughts scatter. I feel like I'm going crazy, not knowing what it means or what I want it to mean. I need Amy to say something to anchor me in place before I fall apart.

She steps up to it. "This is proper art. Wow." She taps it. "Water-resistant. This bad boy is bathroom-ready. Must have cost a fortune." She turns to me, eyes wide. "I think he had this made. Commissioned it for his bathroom." She jerks a pointing finger at it. "This is why he locks his bedroom when he hosts parties. This is why he takes women to the hotels." Waving both hands at me, she bounces on the spot. "He never brings them back here. It's some weird thing he has. No one gets into Seb Hawkston's *actual* bedroom. Fuck me, it's because *you're already in here.*" She laughs. "It's ironic that you're the one person he probably should have locked out, given what you got up to today."

I'm hardly listening because my stomach is in knots. "Is that *really* true? He doesn't take women here?"

"Haven't you heard that rumour? Always in the hotel."

Ah, shit. I feel even worse now. This place is his sanctuary, and I violated it. "Yeah, I've heard it. But I didn't know for sure." Guilt squirms in my gut. "We should get out of here. He'll be home soon."

Ignoring me, Amy steps back from the picture, eyes glinting as she looks around the large bathroom, all marble surfaces and chrome fittings. She paces towards the shower and walks into the huge glass chamber until she's standing beneath the shower head. "Knew it," she says, gazing straight at the enormous photo of me. "How many times has he jerked off in the shower staring at you? Fucking millions, I bet."

It hadn't occurred to me, but the image is placed in perfect view of the shower. *Has he done that? Would I like it if he had done that?* A coil of heat smoulders in my core, and I begrudgingly admit that part of me definitely likes the idea.

Amy steps back out. "It's a bit weird. Is it weird?"

I shrug. "Kinda. But I masturbated on his bed earlier, so... maybe not *that* weird?"

Amy guffaws. "You two are so fucked up." She stares again at the picture. "This is from your big breakout shoot, isn't it? How old is this photo?"

"Seven years."

"Reckon it's been here all that time?"

Goosebumps rush over my forearms. "We hadn't met seven years ago."

Amy tips her head to one side, still staring at the picture. "Doesn't mean he didn't know who you were." She rests one hand on her hip. "It's like a giant vision board. Manifestation 101. He wanted you in this room, and today, he got it. Shame he wasn't here for it." She glances at me, an amused reprimand in her tone. "You really did him dirty."

I cup a hand over my eyes, wishing Amy wasn't enjoying this quite as much as she is. Letting my hand fall, I check the time. Seb will be home any minute. I grab Amy's hand, insisting we leave, and lead her back to the kitchen.

We only just make it before the clink of the front door unlocking has nerves spiralling through me. *He's home. Oh, dear Lord.* My legs are shaking. Everything is different now. He's had me on his bathroom wall for God knows how long and never fucking mentioned it. I masturbated on his bed, and he has no idea.

Unsteady on my feet, I drop onto a stool at the kitchen island.

It's okay. He doesn't know. He never needs to know what I did. *Ever.*

"Erica?" he calls.

My body boils like I've been dipped in molten lava. Guilt and arousal rage through my system; a toxic mix that makes me dizzy. *I did a bad thing to a good man.*

"In the kitchen," I screech. Amy pulls a face at the sound and mouths, 'calm down.'

Fuck, fuck, fuck. If I don't keep my shit together, he's going to know something up.

"Is it safe? Nothing boiling over in there?" he calls, and I can hear a hint of amusement in his tone.

I can't imagine what's funny. I want to sink through the floor and plunge into the downstairs neighbour's flat rather than sit here and face him, pretending I didn't orgasm while looking at a picture of him, hearing his voice, and watching my own fingers slide in and out of my wet pussy.

It was all such a turn on.

Amy is fanning her face, pretending to swoon, struggling to hold in her laughter.

"Don't say a word," I whisper.

Seb appears in the doorway, looking like a model from a Tom Ford shoot. *I can't breathe.* He pauses, glances between us, and his gaze fills with suspicion. For a second, neither of us says anything, and he leans against the doorframe, so sexy that I have to look away before my pussy walks over there herself and attacks his face.

"Ladies," he greets us, his voice deep.

I'm going to melt.

Amy rises from her seat. "Look at you, doing that sexy door lean." She pretends to faint, swiping the back of her hand over her forehead. "I did like the tattoos though. Such a shame they washed off."

"Sorry," he says with an adorable smirk. "Come here, you." Pushing off the frame, he paces towards her and gives her a kiss on both cheeks, but she loops her hands about his neck and hugs him fully.

Normally, he'd make eyes at me over her shoulder in gentle mockery of Amy's enthusiasm, but today he doesn't look at me. A chill works its way down my spine. *Something's off.* The way he's avoiding eye contact feels deliberate.

After a moment of polite chitchat, Amy excuses herself, grabs her bag and her gigantic faux fur coat, and bustles out.

In her absence, the silence stings. Seb stares at me, and in his gaze I read something unnervingly serious. *Why do I feel like I'm choking?*

He watches me carefully, as if he's reading *everything* on my face. And then, rather than question me on it as he'd normally do, his expression hardens as he breaks eye contact.

He approaches the table and takes a seat opposite me, rubbing a hand over his forehead and up into his hair. "I've got to tell you something."

My heart hammers an uneven beat. "Are you fake breaking up with me?"

"No." He puts his hands on the table, fingers splayed, and stares at them. I stare too, because damn, he has perfect man hands. But—*ugh*—I hate this anxious feeling that's bubbling up while I wait for him to tell me whatever is on his mind. "I'm really sorry, but..." He closes his eyes and time drips, slow and thick.

"Oh, God. What is it? How bad?"

He winces, opening his eyes to stare at me while his face is still angled towards his hands. "That depends."

"On what?" He sits, quiet. *I can't take it.* "What? You're making me nervous. What's wrong?"

"Nothing's wrong." He frowns, reassessing. "Not really."

"Why are you being so weird then?"

He looks up at the ceiling. "Fuck," he mutters, as if he's praying to some god stuck between the downlights. Then he looks back at me and it all sprays out like a round of bullets. "My bedroom. There are cameras in there."

I don't move.

"I asked you not to go in there," he adds, and my stomach plunges right to the marble floor. "I saw... *everything*."

My body flushes hot, panic roaring through me. "Oh, God. Oh, my God. You saw?"

"Yeah. I saw."

I cover my face with my hands. "Oh, my God. I'm so sorry. So sorry." I can't look at him. I completely abused his rules. His space. I'm a *terrible* human being. I invaded his privacy and masturbated on his bed, and he *knows*. He *watched*. But...

Hold on.

A single thought jerks at the chaos rampaging through my head. *He watched.*

More thoughts tumble like a house of cards now that I've picked up the first one.

He was on the phone. He was *talking* to me. My head snaps up, hands falling from my eyes. "Wait, you watched? You *watched*?"

He lowers his chin.

I cup one hand over my mouth and point at him with the other. "You were on the phone and you said *nothing*? You let me... *fuck*, you just watched? You sat there in your office and watched me and said *nothing*? How could you do that? You... you—"

"You asked me to keep talking. What the fuck was I supposed to do?"

"Not keep talking," I shriek. "Not... let me... to the sound of your voice. Oh, God. *Your voice.* Jesus." I cover my face with my hands again, but they're trembling. "You... you could have said something. A friend would have said something. A friend would—"

"You went into my bedroom after I specifically told you—"

"This is a total betrayal of trust." My voice sounds gritty; hard and somehow broken all at once. "How could you... how could you? You should have hung up. You should have—"

"Should have what? Politely asked you to stop masturbating on my bed? Don't make out I'm the bad guy. You're guilty here too. Yes, I could've stopped you. I probably should have. But I've sat on the sofa beside you for years and done nothing. Not touched you. Not held you. Not really. Not the way I've wanted to." He clenches one fist on the table. "And I've fucking wanted to. So much. So if you're asking me to stay on the phone when you're lying naked on my fucking bed, then I'm staying on the fucking phone. I'm not going *anywhere*. Because

I've never seen anything as beautiful as you coming undone on my sheets."

Heat burns through me at his words, and despite the humiliation raging through me, a throbbing begins between my thighs. I leap out of my chair. I can't sit still and keep staring at him across the table like we're having a casual supper together.

"No. No. Don't say that. Don't say any of that. I don't want to hear it." I bite my knuckles, hoping the pain might wake me from this nightmare. It doesn't, and I let my hand drop. "All this time? *All this time*? I thought we were friends. I thought... That's not friendship... that's... that's—"

"You know what isn't friendship?" His harsh tone cuts across me. "Letting yourself into someone's bedroom"—he points violently in the direction of his bedroom—"while they're at work and giving yourself an earth-shattering orgasm on their bed. That's not fucking friendship."

He's right. This isn't friendship. This is a mess. A fuck-up. A giant, enormous fuck-up, all because of that article and the film and the PR... and the stupid fake dating that feels like maybe it wasn't entirely fake after all.

"You're right," I admit. "This hasn't been a friendship since the night at the gallery. When we argued. I should probably never have spoken to you again. It was over."

"Over? What the fuck are you talking about?" he growls, frustration thrumming in his voice. "Friendships don't end because you have one argument."

I tear at my hair, barely able to think straight. "It wasn't the argument. It was you... you... your tongue... *inside* me. It broke us. It was... it was—"

"It was what?"

"Wrong. It was wrong."

Fury flashes over his face, and he gets out of his chair and rounds the table towards me. I back away, but he follows, and the full force of him crossing the room, so much power in every step, steals my breath. My arms flail, trying to wave him off, keep him at a distance, but he grips my wrists, one in each hand, in a movement so precise it's like he's been trained to do exactly that. To pin me down. Restrain me. My back arches, my breasts press towards him, our mouths dangerously close. He's never touched me like this, not once. He's been gentle, sweet, considerate, *always*. But the man before me now looks none of those things. He's every inch the predator, and in the back of my mind, I know I've pushed him somewhere new. *Somewhere dangerous.* As his grip tightens on my wrists, the anger in my blood turns hotter, and beneath it, there's something fierce I don't want to name. The same thing that drove me to his bedroom in the first place...

His chest heaves, the warmth of his breath gusting against my cheeks. "Admit it," he whispers, almost panting.

Arousal coils through me, my pussy swelling between my thighs. *Pulsing.* "Admit what?" I say, barely a whisper.

"That this isn't fake."

"It is. It *is* fake."

"I never took you for a liar, Erica Lefroy." The way he says my full name chills my blood, and yet it turns me on even more. "Admit that you want me to lay you down on those sheets and fuck you until you scream my name. That you thought about it earlier today. That when I was talking to you over the phone, you were imagining me being there with you. Touching you. My hands. My tongue. All over you. My mouth on your clit. My cock inside you." A potent ball of heat burns *down there*, like I've shoved a hot coal inside my pussy. I'm going to burn from the inside out. He's hit a bulls-eye, and whatever he glimpses in my reaction confirms it, because he leans a little closer and whispers, "Do you want me to fill your needy little cunt, Erica?"

"No. No," I murmur, my voice so weak there's no chance of convincing anyone. I collect myself, and when I say, "No," a final time, it sounds strong. It sounds like it really means *no*.

But it doesn't fool Seb. Not for a second. "Stop lying. There's no point. You've already given yourself away."

Arrogant arsehole. The heat of arousal that was licking my insides transforms to a rageful blaze. It's no longer just my pussy that's burning, but my entire body, and I'm pinned to a stake in the middle of a bonfire of Seb's making. It's violent, but I'm powerless against him. He's so much stronger than I am. *He could do anything with me. To me.* And part of me wants him to do it; wants him to push this until I break. "Don't you dare assume you know what I want. Don't be this guy," I spit. "Not with me."

He raises a brow, stiffening ever so slightly. "What guy?"

"The one who says a few dirty words and expects a woman to get naked. This isn't you."

His voice is low and soft like velvet when he says, "How do you know?"

I shake my head. *I don't know.* This isn't the version of him that's mine. This one belongs to someone else, and *God,* that voice makes me want it, want him, *every version of him*, but I won't allow it. This isn't what I do. This isn't *Erica Lefroy*. But why I am clinging to a version of myself I've been trying to shed? I don't know what's going on here; all I know is that who we're being in this moment isn't who we've always been and the abruptness of the change is terrifying. "This isn't *us*."

"Us? What us? I'm confused, because you already got naked, and I didn't have to say a word. I'm just asking to be there in person next time."

The sincerity in his expression makes my heart thrum even faster as something close to panic squirms beneath my skin. I snatch my wrists from him, and he lets go but holds me captive with his gaze. I want to break eye contact, but I force myself not to. "You'd happily ruin this friendship just so you could get your dick wet? That is just so *you*." My voice drips with disgust, concealing the panic that I'm going to lose my friend. Already lost him, probably.

A muscle pops in his jaw like he's clenching his teeth, holding back a tidal wave of frustration that snuffs out the sincerity. His voice is a low, unforgiving rumble. "I know what you're doing, and I'm going to call you on your bullshit, Lefroy."

Unable to help myself, I snarl at him. "What? What am I doing?"

"You're giving me Ice Queen because you're frightened."

"I am not *frightened*. You don't scare me."

"I don't mean me. I mean you. That for whatever reason, you're scared of what you want. Scared of your own desire. Every time something happens between us, you run away. You're—"

"Don't psychoanalyse me. If I want that, I'll pay for it."

"Maybe you should."

I gasp. *That fucking bastard.* I'm so shocked that I don't respond, standing mute as we stare at one another, heaving breaths that reveal just how much this means to both of us.

"You have me in your bathroom. On the wall." The words snap out like an accusation.

He rakes a hand through his hair until he's cupping the back of his neck and bitterness laces his words. "The bedroom wasn't enough? You had to go in there too?"

"Why am I on the wall?"

"Because you're beautiful."

Beautiful. The word is infused with such vitriol that it doesn't feel like a compliment. It feels like he's stabbed me with an icicle. *Right to the heart.* He knows me well enough to hit where it hurts, and he chose to strike the blow. He's the one person who I always thought saw me as more than a pretty face, and I wanted him to own it. But he didn't.

I press a hand against my chest to soothe the pain. I don't want to be on the wall because I'm beautiful.

I want to be there because he loves me.

The thing is, I have no clue how to communicate that in a way that won't make everything worse, and I'm angry and hurt enough that I won't even try.

He's still waiting for a response, but when it's clear I have none, he turns away and stalks to the living area, pulling the stopper from a bottle of Macallan.

Don't turn away from me. Not now.

"Did you masturbate to that picture?" I yell.

His expression is stony as he pours himself a glass. I expect him to throw the whole thing down in one, but he doesn't. He takes a slow sip, closing his eyes as though he's trying to regain his self-control. When he opens them, his gaze is hard and unforgiving. "Yes."

"When we were friends?"

Another cool sip. "Yes."

"How many times?"

This time, he swallows the remaining liquid in one. "I didn't keep count."

He pours another glass, and I watch him. *Wanting him. Hating him.* He must feel my glare, but he ignores me as he takes his glass, steps towards the full height windows that look over the park, and pushes a button on the wall. The glass slides back, allowing him to proceed out onto the balcony. He turns to me. "Goodnight, Erica. Sweet dreams." He steps outside and closes the glass behind him.

30
SEB

I've officially killed our friendship stone dead by telling her about the camera. Maybe I should've kept my mouth shut. *Maybe I should've told her I came too.* Told her that seeing her try to stifle her noises—*God, how I'd love to hear them again*—as her body quivered on my bed was enough to have me shooting my load all over my trousers.

Maybe I should have told her that she's on the wall because I'm obsessed with her. Because I have been for years. Because she's the only woman I ever want to come home to, the only one I want to share my life with, and the only way I could ever make it happen was to hang her on the fucking wall. Maybe I should have told her that I've never taken another woman in there because it would sully a space that was only meant for her, even if she never darkened the fucking doorway. And I know how pathetic that is—I've always known. It's why I normally lock the door and why I had the cameras installed. No one but me and my housekeeper ever go in there.

I swallow a gulp of whisky, letting it slide down my throat, warm and blurring my mind. Taking the edge off. I shouldn't have spoken to her the way I did. But damn it, I can't live with what I saw, what happened today, and not address it. I couldn't have ignored it; the guilt would have eaten me up. Whatever I thought she would do when I told her, denying the feelings that drove her to do it wasn't it. I should march into her room and make her face the fact that there is something real here, however much she wants to call it fake.

Behind me, the glass slides open. *She's coming out?* I don't turn, but everything in me strains like a flower leaning towards the sun as she paces towards me until she stands beside me. She leans on the railing and stares out at the park beyond. The hum of black cabs racing through Hyde Park rises through the darkness.

"I deleted the footage," I grind out. "If that's what you want to know. You're safe. No one is ever going to see it."

"No one except you," she says quietly.

My body pulses as images of her flick through my mind; her hair, her legs, the smooth expanse of her stomach, the way her back arched and her tits shook when she came. The memory is so vivid that I can't shut it down. I'll remember it for the rest of my life, whether I want to or not. I can't put any of this into words, nor do I think it would be appropriate to try, so I say nothing.

"You think I need therapy?" Her voice is small, and the question makes my heart ache. *Fuck. I can be a real arsehole sometimes.*

I take a sip of my drink. "I shouldn't have said that."

She steps closer, and her shoulder rests against mine in a touch so slight I'm not sure it's deliberate. "I'm sorry," she whispers.

I finish my scotch and turn to face this beautiful woman, who's been my friend for years. The fading summer light shimmers across her cheekbones, and a dull ache spreads through my chest. I don't know if it's guilt or regret, or something deeper still. But her long dark hair is all glossy and draped over one shoulder, and I have to bite my cheek to stop the impulse to twist it round my fist and drag her closer. "For what?"

"All of it." Her gaze drifts from mine, and for a moment, the composed Erica Lefroy looks vulnerable. "You're right. Obviously." She waves her hand above her shoulder, gesturing towards my bedroom as if to say everything that happened in there proves it. "I'm attracted to you."

The words light a fire in my gut, spreading through my entire body, and I wish I had another scotch I could down. I've longed for her to say something like this for years, and now that she's here, confessing it, I'm so overwhelmed that I can't think of a single thing to say.

The silence feels like it lasts an eternity.

"Are you going to say anything?" There's a hint of worry in her voice that has my whole body aching to take her in my arms, hug her, make all of her worries disappear. But I also feel like I'm walking a tightrope... one wrong step and every good moment we've ever shared is going to plunge into oblivion. *How the fuck do I handle this so she doesn't fly off the handle and run away again?*

"Are you sure?" I regret the words as soon as they're out—I don't want to give her the opportunity to change her mind, but I do need her to be sure. I want her to walk into whatever this is with complete certainty. I want her by my side, not behind me, pulled along by the insatiable desire I feel for her. This has to be her choice. Whatever *this* is.

"I don't make a habit of breaking into other men's bedrooms and..." She waves her hand in the air like she's too embarrassed to say 'masturbate' out loud. "You know. So, yeah. I'm sure. I'd have thought it went without saying, to be honest."

I chuckle, but it sounds more like a cough because I kill it. I don't want to make her uncomfortable. "It does, but, *fuck*, it feels good to hear you say it."

She looks up at me through hooded eyes that are full of apology, as though she's worried that I'll never forgive her. She needn't be.

I'd forgive her for anything. *Everything*. "I'm sorry I went into your room."

"I'm sorry I watched." I shrug like it's no big deal. "If it makes you feel better, I came too."

Her beautiful mouth pulls up at one side. "You did?"

"Fuck, yes. Hard. At my desk."

She hangs her head, but the apples of her cheeks grow round for a second as she smiles to herself. "So... what now?" Her voice is breathy and full of need. The silence that follows is brittle, the sexual tension like glass on the cusp of shattering. She didn't just come out here to talk. I can feel it in my bones. I set my glass down on the table and turn to face her, taking in the eager tilt of her body towards me, the unhinged edge to her gaze, as though she's both frightened and aroused at once.

"Tell me what you want."

She inhales. "I... I don't know..."

I step a little closer, and her energy prickles all over my skin. *Take it slow, Seb. Take it fucking slow.* "Do you want me to touch you?"

She takes a few uneven breaths, not breaking eye contact, and then she nods, very slightly. I reach out, my fingertip grazing her shoulder, following the soft curve of it. The skin to skin sends a lighting strike right to my dick. I've touched Erica before, but never as intentionally as this. Never when the future of our relationship hinges on it, and each brush of skin is charged with both of our want.

She lets out a small whimper as though she could come if I did it one more time. To be honest, I think I might come if I touch her again.

"Here?" I ask.

She nods.

I run my index and middle finger across her collarbone, resting them in the divot at the base of her throat. "Here?" I whisper.

She nods again, swaying a little on the spot, her eyes fluttering closed.

I raise my open hand up her throat, my touch light, but I squeeze it just a little, and she moans at the pressure. "Do you know what you want yet?"

Her nod of the head is infinitesimally small. "Everything."

"In that case…" I slide my hand to the back of her neck, fingers tangling the hair at her nape, tilting her head up to look at me. I pull her so close that my breath ricochets off her cheek when I whisper, "You're going to let me do everything I've ever wanted to do to you."

She swallows. "All at once?"

"No." I stifle a smile. "Unless you want me to break you."

"Seb." There's a desperate edge to her voice when she moans my name, and she pulls back, her grip tightening on the balcony as she stares out at the darkened park. It would be cold out here if it weren't for the heaters on either side of us. She leans over the railing. "I think I might have a heart attack. I might be sick. I might—"

I step closer and put a hand on her waist, easing her gently round to face me again. I wait until she calms. "Please don't do that." I lean closer to her ear. "I have a much better idea."

"What?"

"I'll make you come so hard you'll pass out."

She shudders, a whimper sliding between her perfect lips. "Oh, fuck me." It's not a command, it's a helpless and vulnerable whisper, and the need in her tone turns me on like nothing else. I groan against her neck, pulling her flush against me, and she tips her head back, breathing rapidly. "This is going to mess everything up."

"It won't. I promise. It's going to make everything better." She lowers her head and I press my forehead against hers, our breaths mingling. "Really," I add with a slight shrug, "We're fucked now anyway. So we might as well."

In the look she gives me, I see all sides of her. Fear, trust, humour, and even the desire that drove her to sneak into my room earlier today and brought her back out here to find me now. All of it is fucking precious, and I wish I could catch it and hold it in my hands. But I can't, and I'm painfully aware that this moment is pivotal and with every second that passes, it's slipping through my fingers. My body rails against the transience of it. I want to keep it... keep her, keep *us*, right in this version of the present, where everything is a possibility, and the future is unwritten. Where everything I've ever wanted is right here for the taking. I want to live in this sweet moment of tension forever.

"Okay," she murmurs. "Yes. Okay."

Her words are a pistol fired at the beginning of a race, and our mouths move at the same time. She's soft, and at first the kiss is gentle, her tongue caressing mine, but it torches me like a flame. I want to devour her—*all of her at once*—leaving no piece of her available for anyone else.

Our kiss turns ravenous, teeth and tongue and lips shifting against one another. Her hands move over my shoulders, tugging at my shirt, warm fingers sliding against my skin like she doesn't know where to stop or what to touch. *Like she wants all of it. All of me.* Desire I've kept locked down for so long rages through me with such force that I don't know how I'll contain it. I want to strip off right here on the balcony and fuck her until I can't see straight.

But I have to keep a handle on this. Savour every moment before it's gone. I grab her wandering hand to stay its nervous motion. "It's okay," I soothe. "We're okay." She breathes a few breaths and I slide my hand over her stomach, teasing up the hem of her top. "Let me?"

She nods and I ease my hand under the waistband of her trousers, and it feels so good to do it. Like the culmination of every desire I've ever had. As my fingers slip beneath the fabric, I'm pretty sure it's the zenith of my sexual experience. Out of anything I've ever done, with *anyone*, this right here, sliding my hand into Erica Lefroy's waistband, is the hottest, most sensual, most exciting moment I have *ever* experienced.

I hold my breath as my fingers dip lower, and her answering gasp is a desperate exhalation that I inhale as though it will give me life. "Keep making those noises," I murmur against her mouth, "and I'll come before you do."

"Oh, fuck," she whines. "This is... you are... oh, *fuck*. I... I don't know what we're doing. Maybe we shouldn't..."

We shouldn't. "Tell me to stop, and we won't." The seconds pass in silence as I wait for her response. Her body tenses beneath my fingers, and in the tips of them, I feel a pulse. Hers or mine, I don't fucking know. "Lefroy?"

She gives another gasping little inhale, as though the sound of her name revived her from near death. "Don't stop." My own need is mirrored in the sound of those two words. I edge my hand inside her underwear, sliding right down, and it's me who lets out a groan this time. Her skin is soft as silk and I slip lower, passing over her clit. She jolts in my arms, her grip on my shoulders tightening. As tempting as it is to stop and play there, I go deeper, teasing her lips and then her entrance. She's completely, deliciously, slick.

"Oh, fuuuck," I moan. "You're soaked." I slide a finger in and out, just a touch, and her hips buck towards me. "Is this pretty pussy all wet for me?"

She doesn't answer, but her hands tug the hair at my nape as I slide two fingers inside, finding her walls slick and soft. I work her, in and out, building in tempo. "You're so tight. *So tight.*"

"Mmm," she moans in response, rolling back against the balcony railing, and I move with her. She spreads her arms, hands clinging to the metal, and I lean over her, holding her up, working her with one hand. She's so wet that the noise of my fingers thrusting in and out is fucking glorious. I'm rock solid, grinding against her, more turned on than ever. I can't get enough of this woman. The way she throws her head back, her eyes shut, letting me have my way with her body, finally. *Fucking finally.* I've waited *so long* for this.

I thrust my fingers deeper, imagining it's my cock sliding in and out. She lets out a gasp of arousal. "You like that?" I ask. "You like that it's me, sliding my fingers in and out of your wet cunt?"

The guttural "uh-huh" that forms her response might be the sexiest fucking sound I've ever heard. Her breathing turns to pants, and I'm so turned on I can't think of anything but this woman, her body, her breath, the soft feel of her, inside and out. The way her body reacts to each stroke of my fingers is a high I've never known.

"I loved watching you today," I mutter, sliding my fingers out and use my thumb to tease at her clit. "Touching yourself. You worked it so fast." I add pressure to her clit, rubbing my fingers over it. "So hot, Erica. So greedy for that orgasm." I swipe over her clit again and again, increasing the speed. "Is this how you like it? Fast? Right here?"

She moans, sending the sound up to the stars. "Yes. *Please.*"

"Hold on—" I stop what I'm doing to slide her trousers and thong down, and she lets me, kicking them aside when they reach the floor. *Erica Lefroy, half naked on my balcony.* I can't fucking believe it. There's a tiny strip of hair that wasn't there last time. It's so neat it's like a track I want to speed down. *Fuck me.*

I nod at her legs. "Spread them." She obeys, and like a reflex I drop to my knees, placing a hand on each of her soft thighs and staring up at her perfect pink pussy—her clit, swollen and poking out. I glance up at her. "I always knew you had a beautiful face, but now I know you've got a beautiful pussy too." I want nothing more than to take the whole thing in my mouth, but I refrain, trailing a finger up the inside of her leg instead, relishing the way it makes her shudder as I get closer to the apex. "You're perfect."

Her hand reaches into my hair and grips it, tilting my head up to face her with such force that my fingers dig into her thigh to steady myself. Her dark eyes fix on me.

"Don't call me perfect. I don't want to hear that word."

"You don't want to be perfect?"

She shakes her head. "Not anymore."

A slow grin creeps over my face. "Does this good girl want to be bad?"

She closes her eyes, her lips forming a small, private smile, her breaths huffing in shallow pants. "Yes, please."

I stand, leaning against her, putting my hand back where it was before, teasing her gently, letting my fingers edge into her entrance so I can drag her wetness up to her clit before working it with my fingers, fast and furious, exactly how she did it to herself.

"Oh, God," she mutters, clinging to me once again, rocking against my hand. "Seb, shit. Oh, oh, oh—"

"That's it, baby," I growl. "Fuck my fingers. Ride my hand." She grinds harder and faster, her juices covering my fingers. "Come for me. Let that pretty pussy have exactly what she wants."

"Yes," she mutters. "Yes. Oh, God, yes."

My dick, painfully hard, rubs against her hip. A dangerous pressure builds, low and deep, but I don't stop. This is all I've ever wanted.

Everything, right here, in one moment: Erica, my hand on her bare pussy, her body writhing against my balcony wall. This is a dream come true. Every drop of blood in my body rushes to my dick, making it swell until it aches.

Her hands tighten around my neck, hips bucking, back arching, greedy for everything I'm giving her. And I can't give it to her fast enough. "Ohhhh," she moans, going rigid in my arms before she shudders, body shaking, limbs trembling... And it's perfect—she's perfect—I don't care what she says. I'm pressed right against her, thrusting the thick length of my dick against her hip. I'm all but fucking her with my clothes on.

Pleasure swirls at the base of my spine, my balls tighten, and *fuck*, I'm not going to last.

"I'm coming. I'm coming," Erica squeals into the night air, and it fucking undoes me.

I let out a deep, low groan as violent jerks wrack my body. "Me too. Me too." My back bows, my jaw tenses and I let out another bellowing groan as my dick unloads right into my fucking boxers, hot and wet. *Shit.*

Erica goes limp in my arms, moaning nonsensically, muttering words I can't understand, the sound heavy with arousal.

I hold her up as she shakes, and it takes a second for me to realise she's laughing. "Why are you laughing?"

"I didn't pass out. You said I was going to pass out."

I start to laugh too. "Fuck. Let me try again." I reach for her, but a wave of dizziness takes over. "Actually, I think *I* might pass out. I just unloaded seven years' worth of cum."

Erica is so still it's like she's not breathing. "Seven years?" she whispers.

Fuck, fuck, fuck. "A lot. It was a lot," I say, trying to sound as casual as possible despite the fact my heart is pounding. "My balls are sticky."

She laughs again—*thank God*—and a teasing smirk forms on her lips when she says, "You really came in your trousers?"

"Yes, I fucking did," I say, affecting a casual bravado as I give thanks that she isn't querying the seven years comment any further. Although she's already seen the photo in the bathroom, so maybe it doesn't matter anymore. "Haven't done that since I was a teenager."

She clings to me, pressing her face into my shoulder, muffling the breathy sound of her laughter. "That was beautiful." I don't know if she means the orgasm or me dry-humping her leg like a dog, or the fact that I just admitted my balls are sticky, but I'm not about to question her. If she says it's beautiful, then it fucking well is. "I've never... no one has ever... No one's ever made me come like that."

I tense. "Like what? Outside? On a balcony? Or with their hand?"

"No. Ever. I mean... no one's ever made me come, except me."

I tilt my head, trying to restrain the shock that wants to burst across my face. *No one has ever made her come?* No one's felt her body quiver, no one's heard those little sounds she makes. *Just me.* How is that even possible? Fuck it, I can't say I'm not delighted to hear it though. "You've been dating the wrong men."

She smiles, but it's small and there's a peculiar sadness in her eyes that I don't understand. "Maybe."

I want to wipe that sadness away. I want to love this woman so fucking hard that I never see that look in her eyes again. I want to get on my knees and *feast* until she screams with joy. "Come to bed with me."

Even before she pulls away, I know I've lost her. *Fuck, Seb. You idiot. Too much, too soon, too fast.*

"We need to get some sleep," she says. "We've got a long journey tomorrow."

I'd almost forgotten about Nico's wedding. "So? We can sleep on the plane."

She rolls her eyes. "If I have to spend a week with your entire family, pretending to be your girlfriend—"

"Pretending?"

"Yes. Pretending." She sighs. "One orgasm doesn't make it real."

"It was more like two orgasms, if we count the almost-phone-sex. And it felt pretty fucking real to me." I can't help the bite in my words, but Erica doesn't take the bait.

She places her hand on my arm. "Let's not fight anymore. I'm tired of arguing with you. I like you. More than a friend. Isn't that enough for now?" She leans in and kisses me on the cheek. *On the fucking cheek.* "I need to sleep well tonight. I can't do that if you're... there. Being you."

"Being me?"

"Being all... fuckable."

The biggest grin works its way across my face. *Erica Lefroy thinks I'm fuckable.* "I have never had to try this hard to get a woman into bed."

A bray of laughter fills the night air. "You barely tried. You just said, 'come to bed with me'." She cocks a hip, her brow rising in disapproval, but she's still half naked and completely irresistible. As though she means to take every good thing from me tonight, she bends to pick up her trousers, pulling them up and fastening them. *Hiding everything away.*

"Normally that's all it takes," I deadpan.

She breaks out into a full smile and edges up on her tiptoes, even though she's so tall she doesn't really need to, and pecks me on the lips. "Not this time." She slips her thong into my hand and whispers, "But you can keep these. For your collection."

I fist my hand around the still-damp fabric. "There is no collection."

Her mouth falls open. "You lied?"

"I did." She reaches for the thong, which I tuck into my pocket. "But I'm keeping yours forever." I pull her close and kiss her again, deeper this time, sliding my tongue into her mouth and sinking into her softness. We kiss like that for endless minutes, savouring the sweet roll of one another's tongues. When we break apart, our foreheads rest together, breaths hot against each other's mouths.

"Promise me you're not running away," I say.

"I'm not." She steps back until only the tips of her fingers are hooked onto mine. "I'm just... taking it slow."

Slow. Fucking slow. As if I haven't been taking this slow for seven fucking years.

31
ERICA

So far today, Seb has given me space. Not polite space, but actual space where I feel like he's deliberately ignoring me even though he's sitting right beside me on the private jet. It's like the silent treatment, but if the silence were stuffed full of unspeakable sexual tension.

We're on the way to the Caribbean, to the private island owned by Seb's father, where Nico and Kate's exclusive wedding is being held. I was always coming as a guest in my own right, given my long-standing friendship with Nico, but now I'm here as Seb's official date, which means I'm travelling with the family. Nico and Kate are already out there, but the rest of the guests won't arrive for a few days. For now, it's me, Seb's brother, Matt Hawkston, his two kids and his fiancée, Aries. Then there's also Jack Lansen, Kate's brother and Nico's best man. Amy's coming too, but not until the day of the wedding. I feel a little out of my depth, plunged into the inner Hawkston circle like this, but even when Amy arrives, I'm not sure how much I'll get to see of her. She's flying in briefly to perform with Jack's girlfriend, Elly, who's already out there as the maid of honour.

"What the fuck are you doing with those Smarties?" Seb says, glancing over the aisle at Jack, who's got ten tubes of Smarties on the table. He's sorting them out into colours, seemingly putting certain ones back in their own tube.

"Elly only likes the orange ones," Jack says without looking up from his task.

"You know you can buy tubes of orange only Smarties?" Aries says.

Jack jerks his head up from his task. "Fuck, really?"

Everyone laughs.

"You're so cute," Matt says, reaching over and ruffling Jack's hair.

"Fuck off," Jack mutters, waving him off with one hand.

"Hey, Abigail," Seb calls, beckoning the stewardess with one hand. She offers him a smile and comes down the aisle towards us, but something about the eager way she's looking at him sets me on edge.

"Yes, sir. How can I help?" She bats her eyelashes, and Seb gives her a panty-melting smile. Anger flares right beneath my breastbone at the way a tiny blush creeps over her cheeks.

"Can you sort the Smarties out?" Seb says, all endearing charm. "Jack here wants all the orange ones in a separate tube. For his lady love." He grins, and Jack scowls at him.

The stewardess bows her head. "Of course, sir."

She reaches over to Jack's table and starts taking the tubes.

"Woah, hold up." Jack tries to shield the Smarties. "I want to do this—"

"If I have to watch you fiddle with Smarties all the way to the Caribbean," Seb interrupts, "I'll eat every single one of them before you can say, 'Seb Hawkston is the fucking bomb'."

Jack rolls his eyes and leans back in his chair, allowing the stewardess to scoop them up and take them away. "I want to check them," he calls after her, rushing up the aisle to follow her wherever she's taking them.

Matt and Seb chuckle about Jack and how he's a completely different man since he got with Elly. Aries, however, doesn't seem to be listening. She keeps staring at me, and it's weirding me out a bit, so I wipe a hand over one cheek and then the other. "Do I have something on my face?"

"Sorry. Shit. I'm staring, aren't I?" Aries gushes.

"A bit."

"Sorry. I just can't believe you're the *real* Erica Lefroy. And you're dating Seb. *Actually* dating him. I mean, if it works out, you could end up being my sister-in-law."

"Oh," I say, completely taken aback by the idea of becoming a member of the Hawkston family.

Matt, sitting across the aisle reading a broadsheet, snaps his paper down and looks over. "Aries," he reprimands, but she keeps going.

"I'm completely starstruck. I've been trying to act cool and normal, but I can't fake it. Please don't mind me if I just stare at you. It's just… you're so pretty. It's crazy." Aries, all green eyes and long red hair, and completely gorgeous in her own way, leans across the table and examines me like I'm some sort of exhibit. If she weren't so friendly and cute, I'd be appalled, but there's something endearing about her. Her energy is inviting and I don't mind at all. "You're perfect. Even more beautiful in real life." She reaches forward and, thinking she means to touch me, I back away a bit, which seems to bring her to her senses. She blinks, dropping her hand and pulling her neck in. "I'm so sorry. I'm terribly uncool."

"That's really okay. It's—"

"You must be pretty special," Matt tells me. "Aries doesn't know who anyone is. Doesn't read the news. Doesn't scroll on a phone. Hardly uses Google." He huffs.

"Matt's still annoyed because Aries didn't know who he was when she turned up as the new nanny," Seb interjects. "She thought he was the gardener."

"He was mowing the lawn," Aries nearly yells. "What was I supposed to think? Also"—She leans across and rubs Matt's knee, which brings a faint smile to his otherwise grumpy face—"No offense, but you're no Erica Lefroy. This woman is the face of a generation. You can't walk down the street without seeing a picture of this *perfection*." She waves at my face, and Seb catches my eye, amusement flashing in his gaze. "Buses, posters. Every makeup counter in the UK. You're a complete nobody by comparison."

"So charming, Aries, dear." Matt flaps his newspaper back up and continues reading, like he's the parent and we're a rowdy bunch of kids.

Aries rolls her eyes at Seb, who answers with a half-smile that makes his dimple pop. She reaches out and pinches his cheek, grinning as she nods her head at me and says to him, "She's out of your league, handsome."

A twinge of discomfort hits me at her teasing him this way, as though they have a chummy kind of friendship that Seb and I can't have now that he's made me come. Not that our friendship was ever quite like the dynamic he and Aries have going on, but seeing them interact makes me uncomfortable. I want *every* type of friendship with him. All of it. All of him, and every facet of his personality, just for me.

Seb's gaze darts away, and if I'm not mistaken the tiniest hint of red tinges his cheeks. Or maybe that's just where she pinched him.

Something twists unpleasantly in my stomach. *Jealousy?* She's beautiful, no doubt about it. And so open and friendly. A flirtatious tease. She's a lot like Seb in that way, and nothing like me. And they do seem to get on well. *Better than me and Seb?*

Aries, forgetting the entire interaction, which seemingly meant much less to her than it did to me, sits back in her seat and says, "Let's play strip poker."

Matt's newspaper snaps again, but this time he folds it away and stands up. "Absolutely not. Honestly." He looks at me while gesturing at Aries and Seb. "These two are a nightmare together. I think I preferred it before they were friends."

Maybe I would prefer it if they weren't friends too. I frown and Aries explains, "Seb was a dick to me at first. Said I was just the 'hot nanny'." She does finger quotes for emphasis. "Who Matt was fucking because he was having a mid-life crisis." A disapproving sound rumbles in the back of Matt's throat, but Aries tosses a red braid over her shoulder, looking so carefree that I can tell she doesn't give a hoot what Seb said back then or what Matt thinks about her telling the story now. "But after that, it was love."

Love? She blows Seb a kiss, and he hangs his head for a moment, and this time I'm certain he's blushing. "I'm really sorry," he mutters.

"I forgive you." Aries nudges him so forcefully with her elbow that his arm jolts off the table.

"Fuuuck," Seb blurts as his chin nearly hits the surface.

Matt puts his hand out to Aries. "Let's check on the kids," he says, nodding his head at a further compartment of the jet, where I know his son and daughter are watching a movie. Aries gets up and follows him, and I'm ashamed to admit I feel a pang of relief when she's gone, which I know is ridiculous. She's engaged to Seb's brother, for crying out loud. She's not about to make a move on Seb. She's not a threat to me, but it feels like she is.

But why do I care? A threat to what? This whole relationship is *fake.*

But last night's orgasm was *very* real.

Now that Seb and I are alone, the tension is stifling. We haven't touched one another all day. I've barely looked at him. And yet I'm more turned on than ever just being in his vicinity. Last night, on the balcony, was completely reckless. So unlike me. So out of character.

Or was it? Maybe this is my character now. I mentally count up the incidents. The gallery, masturbating on his bed, the balcony last night. It's like I'm morphing into a new person. *Letting that needy little slut out of the box...*

I've done things in the past twenty-four hours that I would never have done before. And I loved all of it. I want more of it. In fact, what I really want is to straddle the gorgeous man next to me and see where it leads... I need to know he's mine and only mine. Fake or not.

"Sorry about Aries. She can be a bit much." He leans back in his chair, scrolling on his phone, giving me the barest of glances as he adds, "She certainly likes your face."

"I like hers."

Seb raises a brow. "Now, there's an image—"

"One that shouldn't even be crossing your mind. You're my boyfriend."

He turns in his seat. "Fake boyfriend." I scowl at him and amusement flashes in his eyes. He leans closer, whispering in my ear. "Are you jealous?"

"No."

"There's no need to be. Aries only has eyes for Matt. She's besotted. God knows why. The man's a beast."

Disappointment sinks like a stone in my gut. I wanted him to say there was no need to be jealous because he only has eyes for me. Not because Aries only has eyes for Matt. The omission leaves a bad taste in my mouth. But I can't expect him to start professing his undying love after a couple of heavy make-out sessions, can I?

I feel secure about most things in my life. My modelling career, for one. I know I'm good, and I've made great contacts in the industry, and the work has always been consistent ever since the Claudia Kirch-wood photo shoot. But now that I'm not talking to Mum, and I'm trying to rebrand and shift into film, everything in my life feels like it's up in the air. I'm at sea in a new world and it's thrown me for a loop, and trying to navigate it all with Seb in tow is almost more than I can take. I'm sending myself mad. I am not a jealous type. But then, I never really cared enough about anyone to even consider being jealous. Didn't have time or energy to waste on that particular emotion.

But Seb... I wanted him right from the very start and I wouldn't let myself have him because it went against everything Mum and I were working for. He was forbidden. Off-limits. Now that we've crossed the line, everything's unravelling.

I twist away from him and look out the window. Nothing but clouds, but I pretend it's more interesting than it is. Seb scrolls on his phone. Maybe last night wasn't a big deal for him. Of course it wasn't. He's probably brought hundreds of women to orgasm with his hands. Probably even on that very balcony.

"You okay?" he asks.

"Didn't sleep very well."

"There's a bed back there. You can take a nap." He gestures over his shoulder. There isn't a hint of suggestion or flirtation in his tone, and his nonchalance pisses me off. How can he be so cool after what we did last night? Is this what he's always like with women the morning after? *What a nightmare.*

"Are you going to ignore me all the way there?" I ask, sounding far too bitter to be casual.

He puts his phone down. "I'm not ignoring you."

"You are. I just said I didn't sleep very well, and you didn't even ask why not."

"I think you need to look up the definition of ignoring. I answered you. I even offered you a solution." When I don't reply, he frowns, and then his eyebrow arches, a tiny smile gracing his lips. "You want me to pay you more attention?"

I pout dramatically. "Yes."

He huffs a laugh and goes back to his phone.

"What's funny?"

This time he puts the phone back into his pocket, and his attention is all on me. "I'm over here trying desperately to block you out because after last night, having you come all over my hand and moan in my ear, being near you is really... challenging. All I can think about is stripping you naked and tasting you again, and you said you wanted to take it slow. So... this is me trying to take it slow. Sorry if I'm not as responsive as—"

"It's hard for me too." He makes no effort to finish the sentence I interrupted. "That's why I couldn't sleep."

He cocks his head, taking me in. "Was I on your mind?" The suggestion in his tone is unavoidable, and my heart lights up at the sound of it.

I suppress the smile that curves my lips. "Maybe."

"Are you reneging on that 'take it slow' thing?"

"Maybe."

His dimple pops, and I want to lean over and tease it with my tongue. "Glad to hear it."

He goes back to his phone, an amused look on his handsome face. I slap my hand over the phone screen and push it down. "Don't ignore me."

He puts his phone on the table. "I'm more aware of you than anyone else. I couldn't ignore you if I tried. I'm fucking *attuned* to you." He lifts my hand and kisses the back of it, and a rolling heat spreads through my body from that point.

More. More of that. More of his touch. His lips.

"Don't pretend you're a gentleman. We both know you're not."

The deep rumbling laugh that follows my words fills me with a buoyant hope. *I love it when he laughs.*

He raises both hands. "Guilty. So, seeing as we're both clear on that…" He slowly lowers his hand and passes it beneath the table. "Is it okay if I do this?" His fingers trail over my knee and my entire body clenches.

"Yes," I say, all breathy. "That's okay. More than okay."

"What about this?" His hand slides up my inner thigh, and I grow slick in response.

"Yes."

His hand teases at my underwear, and he leans in close. "Have you ever had sex in a private jet?"

I stiffen. "No." *I've never had sex at all, let alone in a plane.*

"Do you want to?"

It's suddenly difficult to draw a full breath. "In general?"

"No, not in general. Now." His index finger slides under the elastic of my underwear. "Right now."

Oh, Lord. "Your family is on the other side of that door," I hiss.

"I'll lock it."

I hesitate, and it's all he needs as encouragement. He slips out of his seat and locks the door that separates the rooms. *Oh, crap.* I have to tell him that I've never had sex. I have to tell him that this is all new. That what happened last night was the most I've ever done with anyone, and that if he wants me to return the favour, I'll have no idea what I'm meant to do. *What if he gets his dick out? Fuck, fuck, fuck.* But what with the way he's looking at me, like he wants to strip me and ravage me here on my chair, I can't move, let alone start explaining everything to him.

"I don't want to have sex here," I mutter.

"No?" he asks, not sounding at all dejected. "Why don't you tell me what you *do* want?"

I close my eyes. "I don't know…" I let out a pained little moan, two parts shame, and one part desire. Or maybe the other way around.

Seb must only hear the desire, or he's choosing to ignore the shame, because he murmurs low in my ear, "What were you imagining yesterday when you were lying on my bed? Spread-eagled and naked, listening to my voice… what you were imagining?"

"I can't… I really can't…" *Say those words out loud.*

"You can. Try it."

I want your mouth between my legs. I want your tongue inside me. I want… "Nuh-uh."

His fingers find their way back to my knee, stroking gently as they trail all the way up my thigh. "I'll wait." My body is turning liquid as he teases at my underwear again. I've never felt this attracted to anyone, *ever.* There is no way Seb and I are ever going back to being friends; it would be impossible. "What was I doing?"

Here goes. "You were… doing what you did in the gallery. You were…"

"Eating you out?" I nod. My lungs feel so constricted that I can barely draw in the air to allow me to breathe, let alone speak. "Do you want me to do it now?"

Heat expands in my belly, spilling lower until everything feels like it's burning between my legs. "No… this is practically public."

"Door's locked. And I can be very quick. Just give me the word."

"Yes."

"Good girl."

A blast of arousal hits me when he calls me a good girl, and I know if he said it again, I'd do anything he wanted. I'd give it all up for him, right here in the middle of the jet. Thankfully, he doesn't repeat it. He folds the table out of the way and kneels at my feet, gently pushing my knees apart and sliding my skirt up, teasing my underwear down and throwing it to the side. "I've wanted to taste you again," he mutters. "I've dreamed about it."

He lifts each of my legs until they're on the edge of the seat and begins kissing his way up my inner thigh. He pauses, pressing a moan against my skin that sends a vibration right to my clit. "You have the prettiest pussy." His fingers slide against my entrance. "So wet." He moans again, and it sounds so carnal that whatever wetness is there increases instantly. He flicks my clit with his thumb. "This little beauty... perf—" He sucks on it, cutting off the word, and my fingers clench around the arms of my chair. I let out a guttural, lusty noise, which I immediately try to subdue. *His family is right next door.*

He laps at me with the flat of his tongue, spearing me with it, sweeping and licking and teasing. A fizzing sensation erupts in my core. He must be able to tell because he speeds up, two fingers teasing at my entrance as he works my clit with his tongue, his other hand gripping my hip, moving me exactly where he wants.

Someone bangs on the door, rattling the handle. *Fuck.* I try to shift, but Seb pins me in place and my orgasm rises like the inevitable swell of a wave, and I can't fucking believe it's him down there after all these years, devouring me with an expertise that would unsettle me if I wasn't on the brink of breaking apart.

I hike up my skirt, threading my fingers into his hair, gritting my teeth as I rock my pussy against his jaw, his chin. His mouth. I can't get enough.

The door handle rattles again.

I bite my lip to keep quiet, but I can't hold it all in. Seb's working some magic down there. I scrunch my eyes closed and let out a little squeal. His smile ripples against me.

"Mr Hawk—"

My lids fly open to find a stewardess standing in the doorway. The one facing me, opposite the door Seb locked. *Oh, no, no no.* We forgot the *other* door. Her eyes widen as she takes me in, her eyes dipping to where Seb threw my lace underwear, right in the aisle near her feet. I squeal for real, my thighs clamping around Seb's head, but he doesn't stop, he merely goes harder, forcing my orgasm while his hand thrusts out from beneath my skirt, his fingers glistening with my arousal as he flips the bird at the stewardess. She dips her head and retreats, maintaining a composure that makes me wonder if it's not the first time she's burst in and found one of the Hawkston brothers indisposed like this.

"Stop, fuck, stop," I plead, but he grips me tighter, holding me in place as his tongue works faster, fingers resuming their internal work, and I completely lose it, pleasure unravelling like a loose coil of ribbon, sprawling through my body. My thighs tremble and my feet kick off the seat, but Seb holds one up with a strong grip on my thigh, allowing him more access to push me right to the edge of what I can bear, until I'm screeching, "Stop, stop, stop!"

He removes himself from beneath my skirt and sits back, looking delighted, his mouth and chin glistening. I sit there, breaths heaving, legs trembling, letting the sparkles of my orgasm diminish.

"You didn't lock the other door," I say, reproach edging my voice. "She saw me."

"What happens in the jet stays in the jet. They've all signed NDAs."

"Yeah, but... fuck." I'm still breathless, my limbs tingling from the orgasm. "I'm not just some random woman you've dragged onto the flight for entertainment. I have a reputat—"

Seb propels himself upwards until he's leaning over my chair, his face next to mine. *His gorgeous face.* "I thought your reputation was why we were doing this in the first place?"

"Fake doing this."

"Fake relationship. Real orgasms. Works for me."

I put my foot against his chest and push him away. "Hand me my thong."

He moves back and grabs it from the floor. I snatch it from him and pull it on, standing when I'm done.

"Where are you going?" he asks, stepping aside as I move towards the aisle.

"I'm going to apologise to that poor woman. That was completely unacceptable. We can't—"

"Seb! Open the fucking door," comes Matt's booming voice. I'd totally forgotten someone was trying to get in from the other side.

Seb rolls his eyes but wipes his mouth on the back of his hand, and moves to open the door. "What the fuck are you doing in here?" Matt hisses.

Seb mumbles some response and I make my way down the aisle in the opposite direction, intending to apologise to the unsuspecting stewardess.

I pass through the far door to find her rearranging champagne glasses. I glance around for Jack, but I can't see him. Fuck knows where he is.

"Can I help you?" the stewardess says when she sees me. She's pretty, her makeup thick, but immaculate.

"I wanted to say that I'm sorry. You really shouldn't have seen that. And—"

"It's my job. Nothing I haven't seen before."

Her tone is kind, but the words sting nonetheless, the implication all too clear. I'm just another woman. I might think I'm something—*Erica Lefroy, after all*—but here, on the private jet, I don't count. Because it's just Seb, doing his thing, in his space. It's *normal*.

"Oh. Right. I didn't want you to feel uncomfortable."

"I don't."

"Okay. Because I'd hate to do that to you. Nobody deserves to walk in and see that, especially—"

She stops rearranging the glasses and turns to me, her face all compassion as she lays a gentle hand on my arm. "Miss Lefroy. Please, don't worry. I'm all right. It was only one time. It didn't mean anything to me. I'm not upset."

Wait. *What?*

My face must be doing things I can't control because the stewardess puts an arm around my shoulders to guide me back to my seat, her voice soothing as she says, "Why don't you sit down and I'll bring you some sparkling water?"

Numb, I let her escort me back down the aisle and I drop into my seat like a zombie next to Seb, but I can't shake the thought that, not only has he messed around with other women in here, but he's messed around with *that* stewardess.

I sit staring into space.

"What?" Seb whispers. Damn him, sensing that I'm out of sorts. He never misses a change like that. Matt and Aries are sitting across the aisle now, although they're not concentrating on us at all, and Jack still hasn't reappeared. Maybe he's still sorting out orange Smarties.

"Nothing."

"Bullshit. You've gone all frosty."

I heave a breath, wanting to tell him. To explain. But there are too many people around, and this revelation has thrown me. I don't know how to handle it; in fact, I feel like I can't. Panic is coiling through me like a serpent, cutting off my air supply. I feel dizzy. I get up from my seat so fast that Matt glances over his paper, eyebrows raised. I ignore him and pace back through the jet towards where the kids are watching TV. Neither of them acknowledges me, thankfully, because I feel as though I might burst into tears, or perhaps flames of rage, if anyone speaks to me.

"Hey," Seb calls behind me.

I don't turn. I keep walking until I reach the bathroom, and then I step inside and try to close the door, but before I can lock it, his hand slams against it and he pushes it open. "What's going on?"

I shove him back with a sharp, "Get out."

"Nope. Not until you tell me what's wrong." Beyond him, I can see Matt's teenage son peering down the aisle towards us, all gangly limbs and dark eyes pinned on me. In a split second, I make the decision. I'm not standing out here with an audience. I tug Seb into the bathroom and close the door behind him.

It's small. Not tiny like a toilet in a commercial jet—it's expensively kitted out with a sleek interior—but we're still pinned into a bathroom and he's far too close for my liking. For this conversation, anyway.

He crosses his arms, his normally smiling face fixed into an uncharacteristic frown. "What's wrong?"

I swallow, determined not to shy away from this. "You slept with that stewardess, didn't you?"

He frowns as though he's cycling through a mental folder of air stewardesses he's fucked. "Maybe." My eyes nearly pop out of my head. *How does he not know?* He tips his head towards the door, back the way we came. "Wait, Abigail? Yes. Maybe six months ago. It was a long flight."

"A long flight!" I explode. "Seriously? Is that what this is?" I wave between us. "In-flight entertainment?"

"It *was* entertaining."

"Oh, fuck you." Nausea cramps my stomach, and I rub a palm over my forehead. If it wasn't so tiny in here, I'd be pacing.

He catches my hand, teasing it away from my face. "Hey. Really? You're going to get mad about everyone I've ever been with when you're the one who keeps saying this thing between us is all for show?"

"Stop it."

"Stop what?"

"Stop turning this on me. Don't make me sound like I'm crazy for having an issue with this."

"I'm not. I'm just asking. I genuinely don't get it. I don't know what we're doing."

I thrust my chin at him. "What you're doing is fucking everything that moves."

He pinches the bridge of his nose, silent for a long moment. "That was before. What do you want me to do? Build a time machine and erase my sexual history?"

I let out an exasperated groan. "Yes, actually. That would be great. Because I can't do this. I can't go places with you and there be someone you've fucked everywhere we go. Even if this is all fake between us, you should have made sure the stewardess today wasn't someone you'd—"

"We only crossed the line from a relationship that you repeatedly said was completely-fucking-bullshit-fake into something not-entirely-fake last night. *Last night.* Excuse me if it slipped my mind to check who was on the staff today."

I heave a breath, annoyed that he—*maybe*—has a point. "You are the most infuriating arsehole in the world. It feels like I'm stuck in a tin can 35,000 ft in the sky with your ex. If we weren't in midair, I'd open the door and walk out. Better yet"—I shove him in the chest but he doesn't shift an inch—"I'd push you out and watch you fall."

His gaze roves my face, and we stand there glaring at one another. He curses under his breath. "She's not my ex. She's ju—"

"Do not finish that sentence. Whatever you say is going to torment me, so I'd rather you didn't say anything at all." I drag a hand down my face and turn away, muttering, "I feel like an idiot."

He pulls me back to face him. "Well, don't. This"—he gestures between us—"isn't the same as that." He points back to the other room as if we could see right through the locked door to where *Abigail* is serving drinks. He rests his hands on my shoulders, and although part of me wants to shrug him off, I don't, and the heat from his palms seeps through my top. I want to lean into him and let all of this go. To rest against him. But at the same time, I hate that I've allowed him to get this close. I hate that I've let him touch me, taste me, because now he can hurt me in a way he never could before. I've made myself vulnerable to him, and I loathe it. "This is different. We're different," he says gently.

I can't bear the sincerity in his tone. I step back from his hold, allowing my anger and resentment to take centre stage as I bite out, "Different how? Aren't we all just women to fuck?"

He freezes, and every ounce of his disapproval rises to meet my anger like a brick wall. "If you can't tell what the difference is, I'm not going to spell it out for you."

I rest a hand on my hip, tempted to say nothing. But standing here in this tiny bathroom, surrounded by the scent of his cologne and the warmth of his skin, the longing for this man that I've buried deep within me bubbles up. "I want you to spell it out. I *need* you to spell it out. I'm going to go insane if you don't."

He rubs a hand over his jaw; no sign of his dimple. "No."

"No?"

"I'm not going to give you the truth if you don't already know it."

Something flutters beneath my skin, like butterflies chasing a breeze that skips from my heart to my stomach. "Please. Talk to me."

His eyes dart away, but when he looks back at me, the longing in his gaze is so intense I almost can't hold it. "Erica..."

He says my name like a lament, and in it, I hear pain and desire and a million other things he doesn't want to tell me. Fear grips me by the throat, and I'm suddenly questioning why I'm pushing him on this. Why do I need to hear his confession? What changes if I do?

I'm going to drown in this silence because there's a riptide just beneath the surface.

"It's okay," I say. "You don't need to—"

"I'm already in love with you." A tiny gasp escapes me and my knees weaken. I reach for the wall to steady myself, but Seb keeps on talking as though I haven't reacted at all. "Ever since I first laid eyes on you, no one else stood a chance. I have obsessed over you for years. From the first time I saw your face in a high street catalogue my housekeeper accidentally left in the kitchen. That's why you're on my bathroom wall, and that's why I've never taken a woman in there. Because even though you didn't want me, I wanted you and that's how I could have you in my space, in my life, all the time.

"Every single woman I've ever been with since then has been a shadow compared to you. Fuck it, anyone I've been with I was imagining you. In my head, it's always been you. I've measured every single one of them against you, and they've always lost. It was you I wanted, every fucking time, but I knew you didn't feel the same. All they were to me was a toxic distraction, over and over again. A distraction from the pain of not being able to have you." He jerks his head, and that thick lock of hair that always falls over his forehead flips back a little before falling again. I want to brush it off his face. "If that makes me a fucking arsehole, then so be it."

My heart hammers as his confession sinks in. *He loves me.* There are a million things I want to ask, but I settle on, "All of them?"

He licks his lips, jaw tensing. "Since I saw you, yes. It might have looked like I was having a good time—and I won't lie and say I hated it. That wouldn't be entirely true—but no matter how good the sex, it was always edged with a hopelessness that was *painful*, because I knew it was never going to be you. That I'd never be able to be with you in the way I could with them, because it wasn't what you wanted. Because *I* wasn't what you wanted."

His face is etched with what looks like heartbreak, and I feel like a bitch for having forced this out of him.

"I'm sorry," I murmur.

He sighs. "Don't apologise. It's not your fault. I wasn't going to tell you. I was going to take it to my fucking grave because you're my best friend and this is the shit that fucks things up beyond repair." A groan of a laugh escapes him. "I was going to keep it to myself because it makes me sound like a stalker at best, pathetic at worst, but... it's true. Every fucking word. There's only ever been one woman for me. I have worshipped the ground you walked on for years, and I made my peace with being your friend because I never thought I had a chance of anything more. But then you were crying in the back of my car, and I thought, 'hey, maybe there's something I can do here. Maybe I can help'. And maybe I never should have suggested this fake dating nonsense, but I'd have taken any excuse to be close to you. To move you into my apartment. To be near you. Fuck, I'd do anything for you.

And I'm sorry about Abigail. I'm sorry I didn't think to have her taken off the flight. But really, my mind hasn't been clear since I saw you lying naked on my bed." He closes his eyes and takes a deep breath. "I can't concentrate on anything other than you. Can't think of anything else. I love you. I love you so fucking much, it hurts."

I swallow, and the sound of it is deafeningly loud in the silence that follows his confession. "Did you just admit that you love me... in a toilet?"

At my joke, the serious expression on his face melts away, and he looks more like himself, his eyes brightening and his dimple reappearing. "Yeah. It's a toilet in a multi-million dollar private jet, if that makes it any better."

"I'm not sure it does," I whisper, although my entire body is buzzing and I'm smiling.

Seb dips his head as he drags a hand through his hair, then glances back at me. "Sorry. But I'm completely fucked here. I really meant it when I said I can't think straight. The fact that you just let me go down on you mid-flight... I think my brain melted. I'm surprised my dick didn't explode and decorate the cabin walls with cum."

"Oh, my God," I say on a half-laugh.

He looks a little abashed. "Romantic, right?"

"Disgusting."

He chuckles, but then his gaze turns sincere and he takes my hands in his. "Erica. Seriously. You have nothing to worry about. When you're in the room, you're the only person I see. You're the only person I've ever seen, and when you're not there, I spend the whole time hoping you'll turn up. It's a fucking sickness. Every other woman was just a shitty attempt to cure it. And it didn't work. None of it meant anything. Turns out, it's incurable. I think I might be cursed to love you forever."

My throat swells and the embarrassing urge to cry burns behind my eyes. "That's awful," I croak out, trying my best to sound like I'm making a joke. Sounds more like I'm dying though.

"For whom?"

"Them. Those poor women."

He laughs, loud. "They had a good time. You'll see." *You'll see.* My stomach flips. He pulls me into him, holding me tightly, one large hand cupping the back of my head. My cheek rests against his chest, and his heart thumps in my ear. It's the way he used to hold me before we brought this sexual dynamic into our friendship. So comforting. So *safe*. It makes me long for the old Seb, just a little. No, not the old Seb. The old *me*. The me who wasn't so jealous and paranoid that I was picking fights every other minute.

Seb squeezes me a little tighter, drawing me from my thoughts, and his breath ruffles my hair when he speaks. "Reckon we can stop arguing every time you have an orgasm? It's becoming a thing, and I'm not sure I'm fully on board with it. I'd prefer to snuggle, to be honest."

I laugh at this, pulling back to look up at him, and he cups my cheek so tenderly that the emotional response that ripples through me feels a lot like bliss.

My Seb. My friend.

My love.

32
SEB

The first thing I do when we get to the room is take a pair of trunks to the bathroom and get changed. Our luggage arrived before we did, so it's all unpacked. Erica and I are in a cabin a little walk from the main complex, where Kate is staying with her bridesmaids Elly and Marie.

There's only one bed in the cabin.

I could have told Nico I wanted two. Two rooms. Two beds. Twin beds. Bunk beds, for fuck's sake.

But I didn't. I don't want them to know that *this*... whatever this is, now I've told her I love her and she hasn't said it back... started out fake, and now I have no clue if it's real or pretend anymore. I don't want them to know any of that because I'm the joker in the fucking pack, and they'd probably laugh at how I could never get a woman to be with me for real.

As soon as we walked inside and Erica saw the bed, unease poured off her skin like she'd rolled in lotion of the stuff. I couldn't stand beside her and stare at the bed, the echo of my confession in my ears.

She came all over my tongue. Unraveled in my arms. But the one bed? *That's too much.* I mentally roll my eyes. I have no clue what's happening here.

I'm bordering on feeling insulted, but it's balanced by worrying about what the hell is actually wrong. She let me bring her to orgasm twice… three times if you count the phone sex. But she hasn't tried to touch me. Undo my belt. Slide her hand inside my trousers.

She hasn't even got close.

Why the fuck not?

I wash my face and dry it and my hands on a towel before stepping back into the main room. Erica's sitting on the end of the bed in a white sundress and sandals. Her gaze is as sharp as nails scraping down my back.

"Bed's all yours," I say. "I can take the sofa in the other room." The cabin is huge. I could probably sleep in the bathtub and be perfectly comfortable.

I don't look at her as I grab a t-shirt and haul it over my head.

I'm halfway into it when she says, "Stop." I halt, arms in the air, t-shirt almost over my head. "Don't put it on."

The corner of her lips tweaks up and I finally notice how she's looking at me. Hesitant, but as though she likes what she sees and isn't afraid to let me know. Relief shoots to my brain like a hit of cocaine; she might not love me, but she wants me. *Thank fuck, she wants me.* Slowly, I remove the shirt again and toss it over the back of a nearby chair.

"You don't want to share the bed?" she says, voice husky, her gaze fully fixed on my chest.

"I do if you do."

She doesn't give me an answer, but she stands and crosses the room towards me, her dark hair falling free over her shoulders. She raises a hand, reaching out to touch my chest, but she stops, her palm hovering an inch from my skin.

She raises hooded eyes to mine, the flutter of her lashes mimicking the beat of my heart. "It turned me on to touch you at the photo shoot." Her fingers still hover above the skin. "I thought you should know that you weren't alone in it."

I say nothing because I sense she's not really talking to me at all; it's almost as though her quiet confession is a reminder to herself that it's okay. It's *allowed.* Her palm sinks onto my pec and it's all I can do not to let out a groan at the warmth of the deliberate touch. She teases my nipple with her thumb, then trails her hand over my abs. Heat rushes to my groin.

"I didn't know you had a body like this beneath your suit," she murmurs.

"Are you objectifying me, Lefroy?"

She glances up at me, her cheeks wearing the lightest flush. "No," she whispers. "Just admiring."

She gives me a meaningful look, and I know the word choice is deliberate; a throwback to the first time we met when I said the same to her. The fact that she also remembers that conversation brings up a swathe of emotion I can't even begin to understand. A rough chuckle works its way up my throat. "I've waited a long time for you to notice."

I expect her to laugh, but she doesn't. She slides a hand round to the back of my neck and pulls me into the softest kiss, her lips meeting mine in a moment that feels so tender it makes my heart hurt. No one has ever kissed me like this. Like I mean more to them than a good night's fuck. Like they might want something from me that goes beyond sex, that lasts longer than one night, and that doesn't end when we wake up in the morning.

And something about that scares the shit out of me.

I've never had sex with anyone I cared about, let alone a woman I've just laid my heart out for. My words on the jet surprised me. If she hadn't begged for them, I'd never have said anything. I'm a fucking idiot. We're about to end this fake relationship. What do I say when my time is up?

I love you, but I have to marry someone else.

Erica's hand is still drifting over my abs, her nails scratching lightly at the skin, but I can't get my head straight. I've waded right into the ultimate pit of shit with this fake dating scenario, and I don't know if I'm going to get out in one piece.

I need to bring this whole thing back to solid ground, where I know what the fuck is happening and what to do.

Sex, I can do. You want a meaningless good time, then I'm your man.

Anything else... I don't know how to do it. In all honestly, given the way panic is thrashing in my veins all of a sudden, I'm not sure I'm equipped to do anything other than have meaningless sex.

In a desperate attempt to slow my thoughts, the guilt, the panic, I grab her, pulling her closer. I kiss her, hard and rough, coaxing her back towards the bed. She goes willingly, flopping back onto the sheets when her knees hit it.

I grab her wrists, holding them both over her head, pinning her to the bed. She lets out a gasping whimper as her back arches, her hips rocking against mine, where my dick is hard as fuck. I grind into her, and she grinds back, panting in my ear.

Her needy moans are making me dizzy with lust. I don't need to worry about shit when I can draw those sorts of sounds from her.

I slide a hand up her thigh, hooking my fingers into her underwear and slipping my hand inside. She's wet. So fucking wet.

I know what I'm doing here.

I tease my fingers out, grabbing at the tie on my trunks. If I can get them off, release my dick, we can fuck. We can just get the whole thing out of the way. It doesn't have to be a big deal.

I can fuck Erica Lefroy like it's meaningless, same as anyone else.

"What are you doing?" Erica says, and the horror in her tone has me freezing.

I meet her worried gaze, realising I haven't looked at her once. Haven't made eye contact at all while I've had her pinned to the bed.

"What do you think I'm doing?" I say, nodding at the tented fabric over my erection. "Getting my dick out so we can fuck."

Her scowl crashes over her face like a storm and she wriggles out from underneath me, sitting up. "Just like that?"

"Just like what?" Agitation marks every line of her body, her face, but when she doesn't explain, I add, "You're soaked. It's not as though we'd need more lube."

I know I'm being an arse. *I know it.* But somehow, I can't be a better man right now. Vaguely, in the back of my mind, I know some part of me is losing their shit, but here I am, containing it, telling Erica we should *just have sex.* Like that's the solution to *everything.* Her scowl gets deeper, and she shuffles off the bed so she's standing.

I stand opposite her, the two of us positioned like we're ready to duel. *Pistols at fucking dawn.*

My dick is still hard. I have no clue what's happening here.

She shifts, tilting her weight from side to side. Nervous. Awkward. *Well, bollocks to this.* I'm addressing the elephant in the room.

"You don't want to have sex with me?"

"That's not it."

"Then what is it? What's the problem?"

"You weren't looking at me." Her hands move desperately, fingers splayed, palms upwards, as though she's begging me for something I don't know how to give. "It was like I wasn't even there. It was like someone gave you a job to do and you were gonna put your head down and do it even though you didn't want to."

Woah. "Of course I want to." But then it hits me. *She's right.* I did want to get through it. Because being with Erica that way feels fucking scary. Like it might split me apart in a way I'm not ready for, and even though she's clearly not on board, it still seems like a good idea to me and I can't stop. "Right now. We should just do it. Get it over with. It's not as though we haven't done things before. So, let's just... go for it. We're making this into something that's much bigger than it should be."

"Really? That's what you think we should do?" she says, her tone so sharp that it digs into my awareness, letting me know I've crossed another fucking line I shouldn't have. I need to retreat from the offensive, but I can't, because what's behind the lines is so dark I don't want to see it.

"It's just sex," I reply.

For a reason I can't quite fathom, she looks like she might cry. *I am royally fucking this up on multiple levels.* I start pacing agitatedly, one hand in my pocket, the other deep in my hair. I can't look at her. The judgment in her gaze is pricking my skin like I'm walking through a field of needles.

"Just sex?" she asks.

I stop, only now looking at her full in the face. "Yeah." But the confirmation strikes her like a blow, and she recoils.

"Jesus, Seb. What the fuck is wrong with you?"

"Wrong with me? What's wrong with you?"

It's the look of pity on her face, rather than the question itself that cracks through the barrier I've erected. "Sorry," I begin. "No, obviously it's not just sex, but I haven't—"

"Had sex that wasn't just sex?" She cuts in, the words so accurate it's as though she's shot a bullet at my heart and splintered my ribcage.

She tugs on her bottom lip, staring at the floor and not at me, so she doesn't register the way my shoulders sink, and even though I don't voice an answer, it's clear she already knows it because she continues, "So you want to reduce whatever this is between us to 'just sex', even though you've already told me you love me?"

"Fuck. Yeah. Sorry. I just… I don't know how to do it if it means something. If you mean something. Which you do. I need to stop thinkin—"

"You want to make this feel meaningless so you can handle it?"

I let out a groan. "No. Yes. Fuck, I don't know. I can't build it up in my head anymore, so let's just fuck and get it over with."

I am exposing all my shit here, and a small part of me knows that I need to shut this whole thing down. I need to back away because it's not working for Erica. Every word out of my mouth is pushing her away, and she's just standing there watching me, her expression nearing one of horror.

"No one has ever told me they love me the way you did on the jet. But this… fuck, Seb. This is messed up. You can't follow a confession like that with, 'let's just fuck to get it out of the way'."

"Why not? It'll be good. I swear. It'll be just as memorable if we go at it—"

"Stop. You're driving me crazy. I don't want my first time to be—"

My brain snags on the way she says '*my first time*', but I ignore it, figuring she must mean '*our first time*'. "There will be so many times."

Leveling a serious gaze in my direction, she says, "But only one first time." She enunciates the phrase 'first time', clipping the Ts.

I stop pacing. "Could you repeat that?"

Her breathing shallows, her voice quiet when she says, "Only one *first* time."

Her eyes, the way they narrow to almost a wince, the tremble of her bottom lip, and the shadows of shame flickering over her cheekbones tell me everything I need to know. But still, I have to check. I need to hear her say it. "First time with me? Or..."

"Or. I'm a virgin."

My stomach drops and silence engulfs us like we've been submerged underwater. Memories swarm like monsters released from a cage. Losing my virginity; that hooker, her heavy makeup and equally heavy perfume, the scent of which I thought I might choke on when I thrust my virgin dick inside her. And my dad, waiting outside, watching the time, ready to greet me with a casual, '*You'll have to do better than that if you want to call yourself a man*'. His words ring in my head like a siren, and it's no longer her shame that's the darkest force in the room, but mine.

I can't breathe. A clawing sense of panic rakes up my throat. I need air.

"I have to take a walk." I grab my t-shirt from where I flung it over the chair and move towards the door, aware I'm being an arse, leaving her like this, but the emotional crap swirling through me propels me to escape. I cannot stay and talk about this with her. I can't let her see this.

She follows, alarm clear on her features. "Wait, Seb. We need to talk—"

I hold up a hand to stop her. "Not now. I'll be back. I'm not deserting you. I want to talk about this." The words stick in my throat as I force them past my lips. *I don't want to fucking talk about this.* "I just need..."

I fade off as the panic swells, and before she can say another word, I let myself out onto the sand and head for the water.

33
ERICA

He leaves and I don't stop him. I know this isn't rejection. I know he cares... but it damn well feels like rejection.

For an hour, I sit in the hotel room on our shared bed. Or not shared, as the case may be. Maybe he won't come back. Maybe he'll find another room to sleep in.

Maybe I should have told him I was a virgin before things got hot and heavy, but in all honesty, it felt like some dirty, shameful secret. Something that Seb Hawkston could never have understood, and by the way he walked out of here, I suspect I was right.

I held it in until the last second. My body was humming for him, desperate for him to take me whatever way he wanted. If I'd waited a second longer, he'd have released his dick from those trunks and it would have been so much harder to stop him.

It's not as though we'd need more lube.

In some alternate reality, we're probably going at it without reserve.

In another, we're probably not talking to one another at all. Maybe never even knew each other. *Never met.* A dull pain gnaws at my lungs, a sense of horror seeping into my bloodstream. I don't want to live in a world where I don't know Seb; where I can't touch him, talk to him, hear his laugh or see his smile.

I can't sit here and wait any longer. I open the door, the heat of the evening air hitting me like a blast of redemption. My sandals flip on the sand, the grains rough where they slip between the soles and my bare feet. I don't know which way Seb went, but I'm pretty sure I'll find him.

I pace along the sand, the rhythmical roar of the waves on the beach doing its job to calm my racing heart. I see him, down by the water in the moonlight, staring out at the waves. Alone.

I don't know what's going through his head, but I know that whatever it is, we're going to have to talk about it at some point. It might as well be now.

He doesn't turn, but when I'm close enough, his deep voice says, "Lefroy."

My insides compress at the sound of my name on his lips, but I offer a cool, "Hey," in response.

He taps the sand next to him. "Take a seat."

I sit awkwardly by his side, watching the waves. He takes a breath and blows it out slowly. "Sex, huh?"

"Yeah," I say quietly.

The rhythmic wash of the waves fills the silence

"All these years, and I never knew this about you."

Deep sadness rolls through his words, bringing with it a sense of betrayal that I know will linger longer than I want it to. "I don't tell people."

His gaze doesn't shift from the water. "I guess I hoped I wasn't just 'people' to you." He lowers his head, running his hand over the back of it and down his neck. "You think we really know each other at all?"

"Bits of each other. Not the whole story. I don't think you can know someone's whole story. Most of the time, they don't even know it themselves."

"Do you know yours?"

"Maybe," I admit. "Do you?"

He emits a hollow laugh. "If I do, I wish I didn't."

We sit quietly after that, me not wanting to push him. I keep expecting him to make a joke of all of this. To ridicule himself or his reaction, and the fact that he doesn't makes me think this means more to him than I could ever have anticipated. It holds a weight that's keeping him beneath the surface, and I wish I could lessen the burden, but I don't know how. I don't even know what the burden is.

Seb draws an infinity symbol in the sand with his fingertip, over and over. The logo for my brand. *Is he conscious he's doing it?* Then again, maybe it's just the number eight.

"How?" he says after he's traced the shape at least ten times.

"How what?"

"How have you never slept with anyone?"

"Do you mean why? Because 'how' makes it sound like I've managed to avoid some inevitable accident. Like tripping as you get off the bus."

His exhalation sounds almost like a laugh. "I don't think I've ever been on a bus."

"Figures. Tripping as you step off the private jet then."

He smiles to himself as he wipes away the infinity symbol with one hand. "Sorry. I didn't handle that very well. I was... surprised."

The hiatus before his final word makes me wonder if *surprised* wasn't the first thing he meant to say, and whether he used it to replace a deeper sentiment. Has Seb had me fooled this whole time? The smiles, the jokes, the impression that he doesn't really care too much or think too hard about anything...

But is that even true? There's always been that watchful look in his eye, like he notices more than you want to show. He sees *everything*.

"I want to sleep with you," he says, interrupting my thoughts. "Don't for a second think that I don't. But it's... it's just different. I wasn't expecting it, and I'm out at sea here." He nods at the water and laughs, but it's a pitiful little chuckle. "I want to do right by you. I want..."

"You want to make it perfect."

One side of his lips tugs up, but his dimple doesn't appear. "Yeah." He scoops up a handful of sand and lets it filter through his fingers. "Thing is, I don't know if I can do that."

I want to reach out and touch him. To close the distance between us that feels much more than the physical space. "I don't need it to be perfect. I just need it to be with you."

He's quiet, and I imagine him rolling my words around in his mind, examining every possible meaning for them.

"I need you to look at me when you fuck me," I add, and Seb hangs his head. Both hands come up to cup the back of his skull and his biceps flex as he pulls his head down. It doesn't look comfortable.

He releases the position, picks up a fragment of shell nearby, and flings it towards the sea. It doesn't reach the water. "I'm not going to fuck you." He pauses, and my heart dips in the silence before he adds, "I'm going to make love to you."

For some reason, this makes my nose tingle and a lump rise in my throat, even though his tone suggests it was a mere statement of fact. "Oh."

"Can you tell me what you have done?"

"Nothing, really." I sense his body tighten, but I'm not going to make this more palatable for him. "No one had really touched me until you did that night in the gallery." He nods as though this explains something he doesn't share. "Apart from that, there's nothing to tell, really. I had a minor fumble when I was a teenager, but I was drunk and so was he, so his dick wasn't even... "

Seb glances sideways at me, and I can't force the word 'hard' from my mouth. "Hmm."

"I never even saw it. It was dark. He still had his clothes on. *Ugh*. It was stupid. I didn't even know his name." I shudder, but the memory is interrupted by the slight shift of Seb's body away from me. "Sorry. I know you've done it with loads of people whose names you don't know. But it wasn't for me. I woke up the next morning feeling like shit, and I vowed I wouldn't do it again, and that if I wanted to be with someone, I would choose them in sobriety. It would be a deliberate, considered decision. Not an impulse. Not something I'd regret. You know?"

He doesn't look at me, but I can sense the sadness coming off him, and I'm not sure how it relates to what I'm telling him, but he's not sharing, so I keep going.

"Mum was also watching me. Measuring up every potential boyfriend against some unknown set of criteria. No one met it. When I came back from that party, twigs in my hair and mud on my jeans, she called me a little whore. Demanded to know what had happened. And after that, she watched me even more closely. And then stuff with my career kicked off, and I was busy, and I suppose I was in the habit of not seeing anyone. So I didn't. And then I was famous and still a virgin, and I hadn't met anyone and there was no way I could have done it with someone I didn't really know because the story would have leaked to the tabloids, or there would have been photos of my bloodied sheets on social media, or..."

Heat spreads from my heart, spilling through my torso. I never imagined having this conversation with him.

Seb rubs a hand over his eyes. "Fuck."

I bump my shoulder against his in a transparent attempt to lighten the mood. "So, yeah. I haven't seen a... *penis*." I cringe at how hard it is for me to say the word out loud, but Seb gives no indication that he notices, even though I'm sure he does. "In real life, or touched one or…"

He offers me his hand without a word, without even glancing at it. I thread my fingers through his larger ones and just being held by him that way makes whatever we're working through feel more manageable.

He shifts to look at me, and I turn to face him too. The openness in his expression causes a dull, wary ache beneath my ribs. "Are you sure you want it to be me?"

The question lights up my skin. My heart. Every erogenous zone in my body. "Yes. I'm sure."

He pulses my hand in his once, twice, before he looks back out at the sea and lets go. Just as I worry that he's going to shut down on me again, his arm comes around my shoulders as he pulls me into him until I'm leaning against him. He kisses my temple, and for a brief second I think he's actually going to whisper some secret, share something to explain his behavior, but he merely *hmms* in the back of his throat and kisses the same spot again. "I love you," he murmurs, and I know that's all I'm going to get, and for now, it's enough.

34
SEB

I slept on the sofa. There was a strange, crackling energy in the room, and although we'd talked on the beach, it still felt too tense between us to jump into bed together. Maybe it was me. *It was probably me.*

But it didn't feel right to come back and sleep next to one another because... *fuck*, I don't even know. The weight of expectation was so huge, I didn't know what to do. Which is totally unlike me. Sex is... easy, normally. As long as I don't actually think about it too hard. *I've probably been dissociating every time I've done it.* Is that even possible? The thought fills me with horror, but I couldn't process it last night, and I can't now, not with my father's cruel words constantly booming in my mind.

Letting Erica have the bed to herself was less about being a gentleman and more about being fucking confused and weighed down by a blanket of shame I hadn't even realised was there. But now that I've acknowledged it, it's so fucking heavy I can hardly move beneath its weight.

I crept out of the cabin just after dawn without saying goodbye. Erica was asleep, and I didn't want to wake her, but I had to leave early for Nico's stag do.

He didn't want a traditional stag. Nothing overly fancy. No crazy Vegas nights. No strippers, drugs, or excessive amounts of alcohol. Just a morning's fishing, an elaborate lunch on a beach on a neighbouring island owned by one of our family friends, and a night at an exclusive restaurant in town. Then back to our island the following day.

The heat of the sun is glaring down on me as I lie out on the deck, lathered in suncream. Matt, sunglasses perched in his dark hair, sits on a chair to my left; Nico lounges to my right. *So much for fishing.*

"You didn't invite Dad on the stag?" Matt asks Nico.

"Fuck, no," he mutters, taking a swig from his beer. "He's been calling me to go over the prenup to make sure that Kate can't take a penny from us if we get divorced. He thinks everyone's out to fuck us over."

"You had a prenup?" I ask.

"Yeah. Dad had the lawyers draft up a watertight one." Nico kicks the heel of his shoe against the deck. "I burnt it. What's mine is Kate's. If one day she decides she doesn't want me, she can have the whole fucking lot. I wouldn't give a shit. She's the only thing worth anything to me anyway."

I half expect Matt to try to catch my eye and mock Nico for what might be the soppiest thing he's ever said, but Matt only nods.

"If I hadn't felt duty-bound to invite Dad to the wedding, I wouldn't have," Nico continues. "But... it's his island, and it's bloody nice, so..." He raises his beer bottle, leaving the comment open.

We're all quiet for a moment, breathing in the hot, salty sea air and listening to the splash of the water against the hull.

"Aries doesn't like him," Matt mutters. "Says when we get married, she won't have him at the ceremony."

"Why doesn't she like him?" I ask.

Matt tips his head back, pulling his sunglasses over his eyes. "I don't know. Bad vibes or some shit. She gets a horrid feeling from him."

Nico snorts.

"She's not wrong," I say. "He's not exactly a bundle of joy."

"Who is?" Nico replies.

"Aries," Matt says, a tiny smile curving his lips, his head gently nodding. "Aries is a bundle of joy."

Nico leans over and pokes him in the ribs. "You're adorable now that you're all loved up."

Matt swats him off and we all laugh, and when we settle, Matt says, "We're trying for a baby. We want to have kids together. And it would be nice to give Lucie and Charlie another sibling."

"I thought Aries was pregnant already," Nico says. "She wasn't drinking last time I saw her."

Matt shakes his head. "Nope. She wants to detox her body and energy system before she gets pregnant."

Nico smirks. "What does that involve? Celibacy?"

Matt side eyes him. "No. She's detoxing her womb space. Does it every night before bed."

"What the fuck?" I splutter, unable to help myself.

Matt doesn't laugh, but makes a small circle in the air with his beer bottle. "She imagines clearing out all the gunk from other guys she's had sex with. At least that's what she told me."

Nico lets out a laugh, leaning forward in his chair.

"Seriously," Matt says. "She's big into that energy healing stuff. She claims when we have sex with people, their energetic crap gets into our systems. We're sharing more than bodily fluids, and it's all happening on a vibrational level." He gestures at me. "You're probably carrying shit loads of it around."

I don't know what to say to that, so I grunt, and the sound is half dismissive, half amused. *Maybe I need to ask Aries to detox my dick.* I laugh aloud at the thought, and Matt and Nico glance at me like I might be mad.

Maybe it's not funny at all.

Matt presses his lips together. "How is it going with Erica?"

"Why are you asking? You gonna tell me that she's using me again?"

He takes a swing from his bottle of beer. "Is she?"

"No."

"Okay. So… it's serious, then? It's been…" He looks at his watch as if my relationship with Erica is measured in minutes and hours. "A few months."

My stomach tightens. The deadline for ending our fake relationship is coming up, and we haven't discussed how it ends. I don't want it to, but I need it to end soon, so Erica doesn't get the back-splash from this engagement announcement next month. I want her to be free and clear.

Fuck it, I'd rather not end it at all. Especially not after everything that has happened over the past few days. It feels like this relationship is just beginning, not coming to an end.

"It's serious," I say, loathing the idea that Matt still doesn't think it is, even after several months, which, for me, might as well be a thousand years. What would it take for him to take a relationship of mine seriously? What would it take for him to stop seeing me as a joke?

"I think it's great," Nico says, resting one hand behind his head. "You and Erica. Finally."

"It is great," I confirm, but my clipped tone is a wall I've just thrown up, which Matt leans back from, a puzzled expression settling over his face.

Nico glances out to sea, where Jack Lansen is roving about the waves on a jet ski like the speed demon he is, three of Nico's friends trailing in his wake.

"Do you love her?" Matt asks me.

"Of course he does," Nico replies for me. "It's Seb. He's like a fucking puppy around that woman."

Matt frowns. "Does she love you?"

Nico looks between us, but, to my disappointment, he says nothing this time.

"You'd have to ask her. I have no idea," I admit.

Matt clears a strangled laugh from his throat. "I'm not gonna do that, am I?"

When I don't laugh in response, he sits forward and clasps my knee with one hand, squeezing it lightly. "I'm sure she does. It's great. I'm happy for you."

Why does it feel so shit to hear him finally say that?

Because it's all bollocks. It's fake, and it has to end. Doomed. And even though it's terrible, I want to hear Erica say those three tiny words before this whole thing implodes. *I love you.* I've never heard them from anyone other than my mother, and she was either doped up on tranquilizers or soaked in vodka. When she was sober, she never said it. Loving us was a dirty sin she could only allow when she wasn't entirely in control of her senses. It cheapened the whole thing, and even as a child, I knew her professions of love were hollow and shameful, as if she didn't want to love us at all.

To hear those words from someone who meant them, someone who wasn't drunk or drugged... I can't even imagine it. The thought of it makes me ache with a longing I daren't touch. I want this to be as real for Erica as it is for me, even if it destroys us both.

I know I'll break Erica's heart. It's an inevitability. So to wish that upon her... it's cruel, and I am a fucking arsehole for even wanting to hear it. I should step away now. End the whole thing.

But I'm not that good a man.

35
ERICA

While the boys are away, Kate and her friends are having a pre-wedding hen do. This is the last chance for a bit of relaxation before all the guests arrive and things kick off for real. Supposedly, Kate took all her friends off on a weekend in Barcelona for her real hen do. So, although this isn't the real thing, it feels like it, and I definitely wouldn't have been invited. I've met Kate with Nico a few times, but we're not friends. I'm the random girl who's tagging along because she's dating the groom's brother, and now that Seb's off with the guys, no one knows what to do with me, so here I am in an air-conditioned therapy hut down by the beach. We're all getting treatments and drinking cocktails—mocktails for me, seeing as I'm sober, and Aries, who's refused every alcoholic drink.

The island is equipped like a high end resort with multiple cabins and properties. This particular one has wide glass doors that have been flung open so it feels like we're getting massaged on the beach without actually having to get sandy. Each of us is wrapped in a fluffy white robe, either having our feet soaked, scraped and rubbed, or some kind of facial or massage therapy.

A few cocktails in, and we're playing truth or dare as the treatments take place. Marie, one of Kate's closest friends from university, a doctor of some description, takes a sip on her margarita glass as she stares at me over the rim. Her dark hair is scraped back in a high ponytail like she's about to scrub up for work, and the fact that she looks so uptight, and is simultaneously tipsy, is confusing me. Then again, I don't know her. Maybe she's like this all the time, sober or not.

"Is Seb's dick pierced?" she asks me. "I read that he had it done to please some woman he met in Texas. And now he has loads of sex because he loves pleasuring women."

Maybe I should have chosen dare.

"You can't ask that," Kate says, but her voice is tight and constricted because she's wearing a face mask that will crack if she moves her mouth. She's got beautiful bone structure, even caked in green goo.

"She chose truth," Marie quips before turning back to me, an eager expression on her face. "So, does he? Does it feel good? Is it big? Oh, my god, I bet it's huge. He looks like he has a huge dick."

"That's way too many questions," says Aries, sending me a sympathetic glance, her red hair bright against the white robe around her shoulders. "You can't ask that many."

"Fine. Just the one," Marie concedes. "Is his dick pierced?"

Panic floods my body. *I don't know.* I've never seen Seb's dick. But everyone is looking at me apart from Kate, who's reclining on a treatment bed as her face mask dries.

"We're supposed to be relaxing," Kate murmurs. "Talking about whether my future brother-in-law's dick is pierced or not is not relaxing."

Marie leans in towards me. "Make it quick, then. Pierced or not? Yes or no?"

Come on Erica. Say you won't share. Say it's private. Say—"Yes. It's pierced."

Oh, for fuck's sake. Why? Why, why, why?

"Ooh. Juicy." Marie clenches a fist and pumps it the tiniest bit. "What kind?"

"That's too many questions," Aries says again.

I have no idea what Marie means. *What kind of pierced dicks can guys have?* Where do they even pierce them? Must be painful. Just the thought makes me wince.

"Oh, come on," Marie urges. "Prince Albert or Jacob's ladder?"

"You do not have to answer that," Elly squeals, flapping her hand at me. She's Kate's oldest friend from school, a music artist with wild blonde hair that cascades down her back. I know her a little better than the others because she's a singer and has done a couple of shows with Amy, but we're still not close. She's sweet though, and I like her. She's dating Jack Lansen, Kate's brother. She's the one he was picking all the orange Smarties out of the tubes for on the plane. She points a finger at Marie. "No more cocktails for you."

Marie snorts and repeats her question.

Jacob or Albert? What do either of those even mean? Anxiety has me scratching at the palm of my hand. I'm going to rub it raw. Marie is staring at me so intently, I think she can tell I'm lying, but she won't let up and is too tipsy to care that I'm uncomfortable. I'm going to kill Seb when he gets back. I shouldn't even be here, and because of this crazy fake dating scheme, here I am hanging out with all of them like I'm one of the inner circle. Well, Seb can deal with the consequences.

"Jacob or Albert," Marie whispers at me as though she's sharing the world's dirtiest secret.

Prince Albert, like Queen Victoria's husband? Did they get their dicks pierced back then? Jacob sounds like someone from the bible. That's probably a better option. A holy dick piercing that's a stairway right to heaven. *Sounds good to me.*

"Jacob's ladder," I confirm before I can think too hard about what I'm committing to.

There's a collective gasp.

Marie lets out a cackle that sounds like a bird's caw. "I knew it. The dirty fiend. You can see it on his face." She sighs. "God, I bet it feels amazing. Does it feel amazing? Vaginal orgasms all night long."

"Stop it," Elly interjects, sitting up from the treatment bed she's lying on and glaring at Marie before focusing on me. "You don't have to tell anyone anything."

"It's part of the game. Don't be such a killjoy," Marie hisses, swirling the dregs of her margarita in the glass.

Elly folds her arms over her chest, lying back like a vampire settling into a coffin so the beauty therapist can massage her eyebrows. "Jack would kill me if I started sharing stories about his dick."

This makes me feel incredibly guilty, but a retching sound from Kate distracts me. "If you start talking about my brother's penis, *I'll* kill you."

Everyone laughs at this and, thankfully, we move on to the next person's turn in truth or dare.

Soon there's a disturbance further down the beach, and I notice a yacht anchored further out at sea. Seb and the others aren't due back until tomorrow, so it can't be them, although at the idea of Seb returning, my heart does a little leap. I thought he might climb into bed with me last night, even if it was only to snuggle, but he didn't. I'm sure it wasn't intentional, but he seemed a little cold, and I don't like how we left it last night.

Out at sea, a smaller boat is making its way from the yacht to the jetty, where five members of staff are lined up in their uniform, ready to greet the newcomers. I squint, trying to make out who's arrived, but I can't see. It's Kate who suddenly curses and bolts upright. "Shit. It's Nico's dad."

Pinpricks assault my skin. I've never met old Mr Hawkston, but I still remember Seb's first comment about him the first night we properly met. *A raging narcissist.* Seb doesn't talk much about his parents, and I don't think it was a happy home to grow up in. Kate hops off the treatment table, roughly wiping at her face mask with a damp flannel she grabs from the therapist. "I gotta go greet him," she says, chucking the flannel aside and tying her damp hair up in a ponytail.

For some reason, we all follow her down to the beach.

As we approach, I can make out an elderly gentleman with white hair stepping off the boat. He must be Seb's dad. Behind him is a slightly younger blonde woman with expensive hair, who must be Mrs Hawkston. She's elegant, wearing a floor length white dress with long sleeves, which looks almost like a bridal gown. With them is another man, perhaps in his fifties, and a girl who is either his daughter or a young wife. She's blonde too, pretty, and emanating an appealing sort of confidence as she stands bolt upright and looks around.

The four of them proceed up the jetty surrounded by staff, two of whom are definitely bodyguards. Tall, well-built men in all black, who stand either side of the newcomers. I'd put money on it that there are guns strapped beneath their jackets.

"Who are those people with the Hawkstons?" Elly hisses.

Kate shrugs. "I have no idea. Must be Nico's side because I don't recognise them."

"You didn't invite them?" Marie asks.

"I don't think so," Kate says.

"You think Nico's dad brought someone you didn't invite to your wedding?" Marie snarls. "That's so rude. What an arsehole."

"He does own the island," Kate replies. "We have to allow him some leeway."

"Gosh, she's pretty," Elly says, squinting at the young blonde woman, who's wearing a short dress and heels. She looks vaguely familiar, but I can't place her.

"Maybe Nico's daddy has a new toy," Marie drawls.

"Gross." Kate elbows her and Marie rubs at the point of contact, grimacing as though it really hurt.

My heart is racing as the group reaches us. I want to linger out of the way, but I'm so much taller than most of the others that I stick out like a giraffe. Kate's the only one whose height nears mine. Sometimes I really wish I was short. I can't believe I'm meeting Seb's parents for the first time like this; my hair damp and tied off my face, no makeup, and wearing a robe. I really wanted to make a good impression.

"Do you know Erica?" Kate says, introducing me to Seb's father after she greets them all. The disdainful look he gives me grates against my spine, and all hope of making a good first impression disintegrates like a sandcastle against the wash of the waves. "She's Seb's—"

"Miss Lefroy." The low growl of my name cuts her off and makes me internally shudder. Despite the heat of the sun, I feel chilled to the bone. Kate recoils, her eyes darting to Elly as if to say, *what's going on?*

"Mr Hawkston," I reply. "It's a pleasure to—"

He turns away and introduces the newcomers to Kate. "This is Antonio Marchetti, and his daughter Diana. Last minute additions to the wedding party. I assume you'll be able to accommodate them?"

"Of course. Absolutely," Kate says, and if she's annoyed that these people are effectively crashing her wedding, she doesn't show it. "When Nico comes back tomorrow, we'll take a look at the table pl—"

"Good. It looks like we've caught you all at an inopportune moment," he says, casting a deliberate glance over our robes.

"Oh, no," Kate says. "We were just having some cocktails and treatments further down the beach."

"Ah. Don't let us disturb you. In fact, why not take Diana with you? We've had a long journey. I'm sure some spa treatments would be most welcome. Don't you think, Diana?"

"A cocktail would be good," Diana says cautiously, as if she knows you can't disagree with Mr Hawkston, but is simultaneously aware that it puts Kate in an awkward position.

"Wonderful," Mr Hawkston says. "You should get to know Kate and Aries. You'll soon have a lot in common."

Kate's brow ruffles and Aries pouts her lips, but the confusion on both their faces is wiped in an instant as they welcome Diana with friendly smiles.

Mr Hawkston glances up at the sky, where dark clouds are gathering on the horizon. "Storm's coming in. If the boys have any sense, they'll head for land." His voice is flat, devoid of any inflection that might suggest concern for his sons and their friends. Kate's alarmed gaze turns to the sky and her cheeks pale, but Mr Hawkston has already shifted his attention to the Marchettis and his wife. He makes no effort to introduce her. Instead, he ushers her and Antonio Marchetti up to the main house, passing the rest of our group like we're inconsequential.

"What a fucking arse," Marie murmurs, rolling her eyes and letting her gaze rest on Kate when she adds, "Don't envy you that for a father-in-law."

"I hope he's sitting next to your mother at the wedding," Elly says to Kate. "Then they can be awful to each other all night long."

Kate shoots Elly a disapproving look that melts away into a conspiratorial smile. There must be some history there I'm not aware of, reminding me again how I don't really fit in here.

Marie turns to Diana. "How was it travelling with old Mr Hawkston?"

"Oh, fine. He mostly kept to himself. What about all of you? What were you doing before we interrupted you?"

"Facial massage," Elly replies. "It's so relax—"

"Erica was telling us about Seb's pierced dick," Marie jumps in. "Best thing I've heard all week. Apparently, he's got a Jacob's Ladder."

Diana's eyebrows shoot up. "No way. I've never slept with someone who has a pierced dick. Unless you count all the times I've masturbated over fictional characters who have them."

An awkward silence descends.

Marie cackles. "What?"

"My many book boyfriends," Diana explains. "I have an entire shelf dedicated to men with piercings, and I spend time with each of them."

Marie's smile widens, her laughter barely restrained. "Oh, yeah?"

"Yeah." Diana nods eagerly. "I thought about putting out an ad for someone who had piercings in real life, just so I could find out if it was really that much better. I never took Seb for one of them. Do you think he'd let us see it?"

Kate presses the back of her hand to her forehead, eyes fluttering shut as she murmurs, "Oh, sweet Jesus."

Everyone stills, sharing awkward glances and studiously avoiding catching my eye.

A giggle spurts from Diana, wicked and childish all at once. "You should see the look on your faces. I'm kidding." Her smile vanishes, and she puts her hands in a prayer position and holds them against her lips. "Not about the bookshelf thing. I really do have one dedicated to men with piercings."

"Phew," Marie quips as the other stifle awkward laughs. "Don't get me wrong, I'm all for a male stripper at a hen do, but I was starting to worry that you were going to beg Seb to do it. And I didn't sign up to be a bridesmaid at that kind of wedding."

Kate makes a choking noise, and Aries snorts a giggle.

"I would never do that," Diana says, pressing a hand to her heart. "What if you all went feral over it?" She glances at Kate. "I mean, once you'd seen it, you probably wouldn't want Nico anymore. Move aside, man with no metal. I've found something better." She shakes her head in a parody of disapproval. "I wouldn't want you swapping brothers at the last minute."

Kate's jaw almost unhinges, and both Aries and Elly stand stock-still like they've been hit with a stun gun.

Marie's expression contorts, landing somewhere between shock and amusement. "How do you know Nico has no metal? He could have a bionic dick down there."

Kate drops her head into her palms and everyone laughs, including Diana who laughs the loudest and starts apologising profusely for her inappropriate jokes, and she and Marie appear to strike up an immediate friendship. The atmosphere is fun and lighthearted, as it should be before a wedding, but a strange pang hits my chest. Maybe it's because this young woman can make casual banter about penises in a way I never could. Or maybe it's because we're still talking about Seb's dick. And that dick, whether I've seen it or not, belongs to me.

———

The following day passes slowly, the girls mostly hungover and lying by the pool, despite the fact that the clouds are heavy overhead and the air is muggy. The storm never materialised last night, but it's definitely coming now, and the boys are supposed to be sailing home in it.

Anxiety stirs in my nervous system, and I try to distract myself by thinking about other things.

Diana hasn't appeared today at all, and I can only assume she's spending it with her father. But last night I pieced it together. She's the girl Seb was looking at on his phone in the apartment that day, when he tried to make me eat a tomato. The book influencer who wears my shoes. A strange coincidence, and one that doesn't sit well, but it's probably nothing, so I put it out of mind.

Elly and Kate keep glancing at the sky with concern, and by late afternoon, it's so dark that it feels like nighttime. The waves hit the beach with a distracting thump-thump, and the wind has picked up.

No one has voiced their worries, and as evening sets in for real, bottles of champagne are popped and they start getting drunk again. By 8 pm, we're all seated around the outdoor table, the staff serving us platters of marinated chicken and potatoes.

But I can't eat. My stomach is gnawing itself like an anxiety-ridden child biting a thumbnail. The guys haven't arrived and the waves are ferocious. No sign of the boat. They all locked their mobile phones up, at least Seb said they were going to, so there would be no pictures taken, and they'd all be forced to forget about work and focus on the present moment. But if they were in trouble, wouldn't they have unlocked the phones?

Unless the boat has capsized...

I don't know how everyone isn't panicking. Kate throws back another glass of champagne. But then her gaze floats out to sea and I know she's concerned and numbing it.

I can't sit here anymore. My sobriety is wearisome, and my palms are sweaty. *What if something has happened?* The sea, black and rough under a cloudy sky, is terrifying.

Thunder cracks overhead and the rain pours down, shredding the air with its streams. Elly, at the other end of the table, springs from her chair. "Where the fuck are they? They were supposed to be back by now."

"Relax," Marie says. "They're probably harboured somewhere around the bay. I bet they're all getting drunk in a bar right now."

"They should have messaged," Elly says urgently. "If they were okay, they would have messaged."

Aries steps up to Elly, drawing her into a hug and whispering in her ear, which seems to calm her a little. Kate gets up from her seat, stumbling over chairs to get to them, and joins the embrace.

Across the table, Marie rolls her eyes at me as if I'm as emotionally detached as she is from the potential peril of the guys on the boat. "I bet they're absolutely fine. They're probably watching a stripper's tits bounce like water balloons as we speak."

I hope so. But I can't sit here and weep with the others. They've been kind to me, but they aren't my friends. I don't have a group of friends here. *I only have Seb.*

He'd better be okay.

If he's okay, I'll murder him for not letting me know.

I get up, excusing myself and heading back to my cabin. But even after I take a shower and get ready for bed, I can't sleep. I pace for what feels like hours, until my feet ache, at which point I finally clamber into bed with one of Seb's t-shirts, which I cling to as though it's the last remaining piece of him. *The boat should have been back by now.*

When the door opens, letting in a blast of warm, sea-salted air, I have no idea what time it is. I bolt upright to see Seb's silhouette in the doorway, his backpack still slung over one shoulder. He doesn't turn on the lights, but closes the door quietly, lowers the bag to the floor and creeps into the room. He's barely taken another step before

I leap out of bed and launch myself at him, throwing my arms around his neck.

He backs up a little, but I totter with him.

"Woah," he mutters as his arms slide around my back.

"I thought you were dead!"

"What?" His voice is laced with amusement that ruffles my hair. "Why would you think that?"

"The storm. The weather." My heart flutters and I press kisses to his neck, tasting his skin like it's my last meal that's about to be wrenched from my lips. I wind my hands into the strands of his hair at his nape. "We didn't hear anything, and I thought for sure the boat had sunk and you'd all drowned. I thought I'd never see you again." I pepper his face with kisses, his lips, his jaw, his cheekbones. "And I kept thinking how you'd slept on the sofa the night before you left, and we could have been together and now you were dead and I'd never get over it."

"Oh, shit," he says, and then a low laugh rumbles in his chest. "You wanna fuck me before I die, huh?"

I abort my kiss-attack, letting my hands slide out of his hair as I step back, irritation broiling my veins. "This isn't funny. I thought you were out in that tiny boat—"

"In this weather? Are you crazy? Of course we weren't in the boat. We put to port yesterday and stayed on the neighbouring island. We waited until it was calm to come back this morning."

So Marie was right after all. I glance over at the window, and true enough, dawn light is spilling into the room.

"You didn't message," I repeat.

"Nico had the phones. No contact. He wanted it that way."

"I thought you were dead," I repeat.

"Well... I'm not." He rests his hands on my upper arms. "I'm really sorry you were worried."

I tip my head back, letting out a loud sigh before I meet his gaze again. "Okay. That's okay." I blow out another breath, forcing myself into calmness. I'm not sure it works. "I'm gonna tell Nico what an arsehole he is when I see him later though."

"Maybe wait until after the ceremony?" Seb says, lips tugging into the irresistible smirk.

I cross my arms over my chest. "Only because he's getting married."

Seb grants me an approving smirk before he changes the topic. "How was the hen do?"

"Everyone was drunk. I was the only one who wasn't drinking. Actually, Aries isn't drinking. Did you notice? She said they're trying to get pregnant."

"Oh, yeah. Matt said that too. He fucking loves kids. He's a totally different father since he's been with Aries. What else happened?"

Prince Albert or Jacob's ladder? I swallow, suddenly nervous after recalling Marie's question. Better just admit it. "I told them all you had a pierced dick."

Laughter splutters from his mouth, shifting to a full on chuckle. "What? Why would you do that?"

I screw up my face. "We were playing truth or dare and that was the question. Does Seb have a pierced dick? Marie said she'd read about—"

"Marie? Read about it?"

"Yeah, Kate's uni friend. She'd seen an article that claimed you got your dick pierced for some woman in Texas." I hesitate, fiddling awkwardly with the hem of my nightdress. "Is there a woman in Texas?"

Seb scoffs. "The only people I know in Texas are oil tycoons, and I sure as shit didn't pierce my dick for any of them."

I laugh at his appalled expression, and some of my tension eases off. "I didn't want to admit I didn't know so I just opted for pierced. I mean... maybe you do." I shrug, hoping it looks cute and he might forgive me for telling everyone. "I don't know."

He rubs a hand down his throat. "Wow. I leave for one night, and you tell everyone about my dick while I'm gone?"

"It was just that one question. She wanted to know what type of piercing. And I didn't really know what a Prince Albert or a Jacob's ladder was so I just picked one."

He covers his face with his hands, hanging his head as he laughs. "What did you say?"

"Jacob's ladder." Seb's head jerks up, his eyes wide. I try to maintain a certain level of dignity as I explain my crazy logic. "It sounded... religious. You know. Holy. Like a stairway to heaven. So I went for that."

With a look that's somewhere between astonishment and admiration, he pulls me into a hug, his laughter still rumbling against his ribs. Against mine. I let him hold me for a moment, then pull back to look at him.

"Is it true?"

There's a cheeky glimmer in his eyes and he raises a brow. "Why don't you take a look?"

36
ERICA

He says it so casually, but a sentence like that crash-lands, evaporating the mirth in the air and replacing it with tension so thick, it crushes me.

Why don't you look?

As he watches me, the amusement slides off his face, and flames lick my insides. *Why don't I look?*

I could look, couldn't I?

"Is there... you know..." I stammer.

"Is there what?"

"Some kind of ladder down there."

He smiles, wide, his expression warm. He's not laughing at me... I don't get that impression at all. Rather, it's as though he adores me, and me being me makes him smile. "No," he confirms. "No ladder."

I bite my bottom lip. "Shit, really? Because I'll have to tell everyone I made a—"

He cuts me off with a kiss that simmers in my core. "I'd prefer if you didn't tell anyone anything," he says when he breaks away. "No more gossiping about my dick."

He rests his hand on my hip, and he presses his forehead to mine. Intimacy caresses me like the softest kiss. We're barely touching, but the longing I feel for him touches my *soul*. "I'd have died if you hadn't come back," I whisper.

Sadness ghosts his smile. "No, you wouldn't. You'd have picked yourself up and gone on to have an amazing career. You're going to be huge. Even bigger than you are already. You don't need me."

My chest tightens. Maybe I don't need him, but I *want* him. And really, that amounts to the same thing. "I don't want to wait anymore," I whisper.

The comment doesn't follow our conversation, but the low groan that Seb emits tells me he knows *exactly* what I mean. "Me neither." His breath heats my cheek, and a breathless gasp leaves my lips as a shiver of need runs through me. He gently pushes me away. "Sit on the bed."

I stumble back at his command, dropping to the edge of the bed. From a few feet away, he caresses me slowly with his gaze, an appreciative flare widening his eyes.

I glance at his trunks, and the tented fabric betrays his hardness beneath. Scorching heat settles between my legs and my breaths turn shallow. *I'm going to see his dick.* My body rages between panic and arousal with uncontrollable uncertainty. He tears off his t-shirt and chucks it on the floor, reaching for the waistband of his trunks, but before he lowers them, he stops. Worrying that he's having second thoughts, I glance up at him.

"Tell me what you want," he says, his breathing heavy and his eyes darker than I've ever seen. The sparkle that's normally there is absent, replaced with a heat that blisters. "Tell me what you want," he repeats. "Let's hear you say it. Take control, Lefroy. I know you want it."

He's there in his trunks, surrounded by a halo of dawn light that peeks around the curtains. His tanned skin is golden, his hair flecked with lighter strands highlighted by the sun. His abs, perfectly sculpted. My mouth waters. I long to reach out and touch him, but from my position on the bed I can't reach.

"I... I..."

A glimmer of amusement sparks in his gaze. "Come on." He tips his chin to coax me into a response. "Tell me what you want me to do."

My stomach is in knots, but arousal steams in my blood, my clit pulsing as I watch him watching me. Waiting to take my orders.

"Take off the trunks," I say, voice quiet.

"That's my girl," he murmurs as he tugs at the waistband, lowering it slowly, keeping his eyes on me the whole time. He's bold. So confident, exposing his body like this. My breath catches as his cock, thick and hard, springs free, and his trunks fall to the floor, where he kicks them aside.

No piercings. And big. Really, really big. My mouth dries out at the sight of it. *I don't think my heart is beating at all anymore.* Maybe I've died and taken that stairway to heaven already.

"Now what?" he asks.

The dare in his gaze fuels me. There is no way his cocky attitude is going to get the better of me. Not now. If he wants a woman who's going to give the orders and make the rules, then he'll get it.

"Show me..." My voice fades. *Crap, this is harder than I thought it would be.* He arches a brow that prods me to continue. "Show me what you do when you're alone."

He grips his dick in one hand, fisting it at the base. "Alone and thinking about you?" He shifts his hand slowly up and down his hard length.

My heartbeat slows to match the motion, the heavy thump of it echoing between my legs. Knowing he's done this so many times while thinking of me that he's lost count has a restless need filling my limbs and a prickling heat crawling over my skin. *Holy shit.* I can't believe he's doing this for me. That I get to watch him. It's like someone made a porn movie just for me, and then allowed me to sit and watch a private viewing. The pulsing and tingling at the apex of my thighs is unlike anything I've ever felt. It's impossible to ignore and I squirm where I sit, and Seb's dimple pops as he observes me. "Yes," I confirm. "That. When you're alone, and thinking about me."

His hand moves faster, fisting his cock up and down. With a flick of his thumb, he rubs the bead of precum into the head, which is swollen and smooth.

I lick my bottom lip and pin it with my teeth. Having never seen a guy do this, and now having it be *Seb* is... crazy. All these years just being friends and suddenly he's jerking off in front of me... *for me*... under my instruction. My body is on fire, and wetness slides between my legs. I don't think I've ever seen anything that's turned me on this much, *ever*.

I want to give him something in return, so I lift my nightdress and tug it over my head, leaving me only in my underwear.

"Fuuuuck," he rasps, pupils dilating as his hand continues its rhythmic motion.

I reach back and undo my bra, letting the cups fall, exposing my breasts. I remove it and throw it aside. His gaze falls immediately, settling on my nipples, which tingle and tighten just as he tips his head back and groans. "Argh, Lefroy. I knew it was fake news. You're fucking gorgeous."

The reference to that day when he rescued me after I fought with Mum makes me smile, and my fingers find my nipple, teasing it, sending a pleasurable ripple through me. Heat pools in my core, and with Seb's eyes on me, it feels like I might explode.

"Does this turn you on?" I ask, my voice breathy, giving away just how much it turns *me* on.

"So much," he says.

"Me too," I admit, and liquid heat spreads through me. *I can't believe I just said that.* "I want you to come. I want to see you come." I am on a roll, doing and saying things I've never even come close to. But because it's Seb, I'm more comfortable than I would ever be with anyone else. I've repressed this desire so long, been a good girl for such a long, long time, that I'm desperate to shed that skin. All of it at once.

I trail my hand down my stomach, watching as his hungry gaze follows it down. He mutters under his breath, fisting faster. The repeated slap of his fist on his cock is an erotic beat made just for me.

I'm levering myself up with my other hand on the bed behind me, my free hand now teasing at my thong. I run my finger along the waistband and Seb groans. Having him so eager for me is a special kind of magic. I feel all powerful, sitting here on the bed, half naked, giving orders. I'm comfortable with my body, but this gives me a newfound sexual confidence that I'm keen to explore. "You want to see?" I purr.

"Fuck, yes," he says again, voice broken and shaking with the rhythm of his pumping. His abs tighten, the head of his cock engorged. I want to lick it and see if it's as smooth as it looks.

But I shake my head. "No."

"No?"

"Be a good boy and get on your knees first. Then I'll take them off." He doesn't move, but the arousal in his gaze feeds me, making me more confident. There isn't a speck of doubt in my mind that he wants me, maybe more than he's ever wanted anyone. He's going to do exactly as I ask. "You said you've been on your knees for me for years."

"I have."

"I want to see it. You, naked, on your knees for me."

A smirk tugs at his mouth, and what looks like pride lights his eyes. "That's it, Lefroy. Tell me what you really want."

"You. On the floor," I repeat, and without hesitation, he sinks to his knees. My heart thumps, seeing his powerful body like this, his dick heavy and hard between his legs. His heated stare burns me up as he looks at me from his position on the floor. *Wow.* He's done his part... I'd better keep my word. I slide off my thong, bringing my legs up on the bed and parting them, exposing it all to him.

I tease my wet entrance with my fingers. "Come here."

Seb's eyes flare and he makes to stand again.

"No. Stay on your knees." He lifts his chin and lowers himself. As his reward for obedience, I sink a finger inside. *So wet. I don't think I've ever been this wet.* His responding inhale is so loud it booms through the room. I slide my finger in and out. "I want you to crawl."

His blue eyes darken, but he doesn't move. I remove my finger, trailing my wetness over my thigh, casting him a warning look. He won't get anything more from me unless he crawls.

His palms hit the wooden floor. "You're the only woman in the world I'd do this for."

"Just me?" I thrust my fingers in and out, dragging wetness up to my clit, circling it. Tingles expand from that point, and I move my hand faster, feeling my clit swell.

Seb groans. "Just you." He keeps his gaze pinned between my legs as he makes his way across the floor, his broad, muscled shoulders shifting with each movement. I mewl as I take him in, watching me. "You're everything I've ever wanted."

He reaches the end of the bed and rises, but remains on his knees, his cock standing proud. He fists it at the base again.

"You do you, and I'll do me," I whisper.

"Race to the finish line?" he says.

I let out the smallest laugh, and as I do, Seb stands at the end of the bed between my legs. He's so close I can feel the heat of him, smell the scent on him. It sends arousal spiraling through my body.

"We're not touching each other?" he asks and I shake my head. "Fine. But I'm coming all over you."

He leans over me, propped up on one arm as he works himself with his other hand, his bicep bulging with the motion. His abs are tight, perfect. And his dick...

He's masculine perfection, hovering right above me.

He nods downwards, where my hand is between my legs. "Come for me." The instruction nestles deep inside me, like a secret I'll never give up. "I want to hear you moan."

"Yes, yes. *Yes.*" The words are helpless, dripping with desire. *I'm not in control anymore.*

I reach up and grip the back of his neck with one hand, pulling him down closer. He's fisting himself over me, and my other hand moves rapidly beneath his as I bring myself off.

"Give me more of those noises," he rasps. "Let's hear how much you want this."

I'm already moaning almost constantly—*whimpering*—but at his words I can't help but let the sounds spill louder from my lips, relishing in the warmth of Seb's body so close. The slick sounds of me touching myself, and the rough back and forth of him jerking off, mingle with our ragged breathing.

"Tell me you love it. Tell me you fucking love it," Seb growls. "Touching yourself for me."

"I love it," I say breathlessly, fire whipping through me, burning through my inhibitions.

"You're close," he says, and it's not a question.

My only response is to touch myself faster. *Harder.* So, so close.

He stops, tilting backwards and gripping my thighs, raising both and staring between my legs. The sight of him fixated like that on the most intimate part of me burns me up and I rub my swollen clit. My body buzzes and my back arches off the bed.

"Fuck, you're beautiful. Come. Come now. Give it to me."

The command slips into my bloodstream and rushes to my core, bringing with it a wave of arousal that carries me away on a delirious surf. My legs kick out and I roll my head back and forth against the pillow, whimpering incessantly. "Oh, oh, God. *Seb*."

He crouches, and as the tingles of my orgasm spread, he fixes his mouth on me, displacing my fingers, licking up my cum and sucking my clit, forcing another orgasm to crest right behind the first. I grab his hair, squealing as he relentlessly eats me out.

I press my hips up and into his mouth, grinding against his jaw, but it's not enough. The urge to have him inside me slams into me, a potent longing I can't ignore. "I want you... inside me."

He lifts his mouth from my pussy, his lips and chin wet. "Really?"

I nod, a little frantic. "I'm going to come again. I need you. Please."

"Don't ask if you don't mean it." There's a desperate edge to his voice. "I won't be able to say no."

"I mean it."

He doesn't give me a second to rethink the request, pushing up to standing. He holds my gaze as he lowers over me where I'm still lying with my hips near the edge of the bed. Fisting his dick, he swipes it up and down my entrance, and I shift my hips, following the motion like I can catch it and swallow it, and the tip—*just the tip*—slips inside me.

More, more, more.

"Fuck, you're tight. Really tight. I don't want to hurt you," he murmurs.

"Please," I say, hating that he's hesitating. There is no pain that wouldn't be worth it. "Please, fuck me. I need to feel you inside me."

He shakes his head, speaking through clenched teeth. "Fuck, you undo me, Lefroy." He kisses me softly. "Remember I love you, okay? Because this is going to hurt."

Before I can say anything else, he lets out an unhinged groan and thrusts in, causing an agony I didn't see coming.

A wrenching and tearing pain collides with the pleasure of having his body, hot and heavy and slick with sweat, so close to mine. I dig my fingernails into his shoulder blades. "Ow," I cry.

Seb holds himself still inside me, as though my exclamation turned him to stone, and a worried look crosses his face. "You okay?"

"Uh-huh." I fist my hands in the sheets, gripping them tight. *Ow.* "You're... big."

"Sorry."

"Don't be," I whisper. "And don't stop."

He scans my face, searching for a sign that I really want this, and when I nod again, he kisses me before he thrusts, slowly, building in tempo. The force of him sliding in and out shunts my body up the bed.

He slows, gently touching my clit with one hand, sliding it between us. "Let me," he says. "It'll feel better this way."

I do as he asks, and I'm so wet that although his thrusts are hard, they're almost frictionless, shaking me to my bones. He feels so strong, his arm so thick and tense with muscle as he holds himself over me, his nose pressed to my neck as he shifts his body in and out of mine, his thumb rubbing over my clit in perfect time.

He's taking my virginity, eking out every last piece of it. Crushing it. *Making it his, forever.* The idea that I'm gifting it to him, that *he's my choice,* turns me on even more, and my orgasm rises to meet his.

He removes his hand from between us, tilting his hips so that each thrust hits my clit instead, sending bolts of pleasure through me.

"You feel so good," he mutters. "So fucking good." He thrusts a few more times until his rhythm slips and he adds, "Ah, *shit*. I'm going to come. I'll pull out."

He shifts as though he means to withdraw, but I grab the tight muscle of his arse, a hand on each cheek, and hold him in place. "No, please. Don't."

He tenses. "Don't?"

I dig my nails into his skin, tilting my hips off the bed towards him. "I want to feel you come inside me."

He resists the pressure I'm exerting, his shaft not fully inside me. "Fuck, Lefroy. You sure?"

"Yes. Yes. *Yes.*"

Relenting, he sinks deep again. "*Fuck*. I can't hold it back with you."

"Me too, me too," I mutter desperately, pleasure blazing through me as his perfectly positioned thrusts regain their pace. I grip him hard around the back of his neck, pulling our faces closer together, nose-to-nose as we come.

He closes his eyes, but I slide my hand from the back of his neck round to his cheek and cup his face.

"Look at me. Please. Look at me," I say, and he does. The connection hits like a lightning strike. Intense. Intimate. Almost too much. A vulnerability that I've never experienced, and certainly never shared with another person, assails me. I'm offering him my soul, and I can see in his expression that he feels the same. I'm consumed by his eyes, pools of intense blue that are deep, and open, and raw, like I've glanced at the sun and it'll blind me forever. His eyelids shutter as though he needs to close it down.

"Please," I beg, still cupping his cheek, his stubble rough beneath my palm. "Please don't close your eyes." I grab his jaw, forcing his chin up so he has no choice but to look at me. "I need you," I whisper.

His gaze clicks onto mine, and the ferocity of the eye contact has my orgasm cresting, an expansive tingling that shoots right to the tips of my toes.

"I'm here, I'm with you," he says, breath ragged. His words thrill me and his hand slides back over my clit, teasing it perfectly. I come again, back arching, toes curling, pleasure winding through me like streamers shot from a cannon. I whimper and thrash. "Oh, God, oh, oh, *oh*."

He thrusts twice more as I'm breaking apart, and comes with a groan, every muscle in his body tensing.

"Fuck. Fuck, fuuuuuck." The tendons in his neck stand out, his jaw rigid as he spills into me. There's so much cum that I can feel it leaking out almost immediately.

Oh, shit. We were supposed to use a condom. That's what people do, isn't it?

Seb sighs, lowering himself against me and nuzzling into my neck. "Wow," he says, breaths heaving. "That was—"

"We didn't use a condom," I interrupt.

He pushes up on his forearms and peers down at me, fine lines forming at the edges of his eyes. "Are you on the pill?"

"No."

He takes a long inhalation, head tilting to one side as he bites down on his lower lip. "Shit. I thought you wanted it that way. Without a condom."

"I did. I *did*." I clutch at my forehead. "I'm sorry. I wasn't thinking. I didn't want you to stop. I wanted—"

"I know what you wanted. I wanted it too." He cups my cheek, stroking his thumb over my cheekbone, and kisses me on the mouth. It's so tender compared to the rough thrusting he was doing only moments before.

"I'm so sorry," I whisper against his lips.

"Don't be sorry." He brushes a strand of hair off my cheek and tucks it behind my ear. "This is on me too. I waited years to do this with you. I won't regret a second of how it played out. Whatever happens, we'll work it out. I've got you."

My racing heart slows at the deep calm of his voice, and his words imbue me with confidence. I could face any eventuality—even an unplanned pregnancy—if I had Seb at my side, so I choose not to worry about it right now. Later, if I have to, I will.

"Are you clean?" I ask, which strikes me as just as immediate a concern.

"Yes." His eyes twinkle. "I wasn't going to become your fake boyfriend without getting the all clear."

"For all that fake sex we were going to have?" I tease.

"Exactly." A cocky smirk settles on his mouth. "Fake sex we just had."

"You're such an arrogant—"

"I love you." He kisses me again. *His dick is still inside me.*

I love you too. Any doubts I ever had about him being the right man for me fall away, and I wrap my arms around his neck.

"I thought you didn't want to look at me," I admit. "I was worried that you were already regretting it and we hadn't even finished."

"Regret you? Not in a million years, Lefroy. This is the pinnacle of my sexual experience." He jerks his hips and his cock flexes inside me, making me laugh, but his expression turns serious, his voice even more so when he says, "Sorry. I haven't done that before."

"Done what before? The post sex cock jerk?"

He smiles, but only for a second. "No. I haven't looked someone in the eye."

I can't conceal my shock. "What? Really?"

"Yeah. I don't look. Easier not to. I don't want to give anyone the wrong idea."

"What idea?"

"That it means something when it doesn't. Eye contact during sex is... not my thing."

Shadows flutter in the back of my mind, but the memory of his words, *I'm here, I'm with you*, and the way he looked at me when we orgasmed together is enough to dazzle them into submission. That, and his professions of love. But I don't want to make assumptions. "And what about this? Me and you?"

"This means something. It means everything. I'm honoured that you'd do this with me." His focus descends to where our bodies are joined. "As much as I'd love to stay inside you forever, I gotta come out."

He stretches over me to grab some tissues from a box on the bedside table, then slides out slowly and catches the mess. He rolls onto his side, staring at the mix of cum and blood that covers his cock, the sheets, my thighs, the tissue in his hand.

"Shit," he says, his face blanching. "Condom wouldn't have gone amiss. Are you sore?"

"A bit."

He trails a finger up my thigh, the tip of it mixing in our bodily fluids. "I'm sorry it hurt."

"It's okay. I don't mind. It wasn't a bad kind of hurt."

He bows to kiss my inner thigh. "Good. Because I like you even more like this." He slides what I'm sure is his cum back up to my pussy, and I can hardly draw a breath as he does it. I'm raw and a little uncomfortable, but I'd let him fuck me again right now if he wanted to. "Dripping with my cum. It's like you belong to me."

As he stares in wonder between my legs, I recall my words from the photo shoot. *I like my mark on your skin.*

This is the same thing, and I couldn't be more grateful that the fucked up desire to claim him like he's a piece of my property is reciprocated.

He wipes me tenderly with fresh tissues, throws them in the bin across the room in a perfect drop shot, and sits up. "I'll run you a bath. I'll get housekeeping to change the sheets while we're in there."

"We?"

He gives me an unabashed smile. "Yeah, *we*. We're a thing now, Lefroy. I'm getting in the tub with you."

I laugh and his gorgeous smile breaks over his face before he kisses me again.

He pulls back. "Pinch me."

"What?"

"Pinch me. I need to know I'm not dreaming."

I pinch him hard on the arm, but rather than wince or yelp, he lets out a satisfied groan and says, "Oh, thank God. This is one dream I don't want to wake up from."

37
SEB

I am done for.

Absolutely right royally fucked. I love her, and I have to lose her.

I didn't think I could love Erica more than I did, but when I looked her in the eyes as she came, the orgasm that overtook me was so fucking intense, it felt as though I could have kept coming for days, pumping her full of cum until there was nothing left of me at all.

Sex has always been meaningless. I've kept it that way deliberately, and there was a moment when looking at Erica felt like standing on the edge of the abyss. I wasn't sure I wanted to go down there. I thought it might kill me, but it turns out that what's in the abyss is bliss, connection, completeness. *Love*. The whole fucking Hallmark card aisle shit.

I feel like a changed man. The only problem is that I have to marry someone else. Maybe I could tell my dad to go fuck himself. I could explain to Erica that any photos of me soliciting underage call girls are fake. Maybe she'd understand. Maybe she'd come and visit me in prison after they locked me up on trumped up charges.

A chill seeps through my flesh at the thought, but I push it aside. I can't think about that now. All that matters is Erica.

I'm waiting outside the bathroom to give her a moment alone in there, but when I hear the bath running I knock on the door, wait for her to give me the all clear, and enter. She's leaning over the tub, glorious in her nakedness. *I cannot believe this is happening.*

"I was gonna do that for you," I say, staring at the steaming water.

She shrugs. "I was already in here."

I stride to the loo and put the seat up.

"Woah." Erica stares at me. "You're going to pee?"

I frown, gaze bouncing from her to the loo. I've never pissed in front of a woman before. All those one night stands, and I never did this. I am way too comfortable already. "Do you mind? I always pee after sex. I normally have to wait a while so it doesn't shoot all over the place, but yeah. I was going to."

"But I'm standing right here."

She looks so appalled that I can't help myself when I say, totally calm, "You want me to pee on you instead?"

She gasps, then reads the joke on my face and starts to laugh. "Maybe."

I shake my head, a smile still on my lips. "I really need to go, so you can either watch, or you can step outside."

She eyes me up and down, pauses a moment, then sits on the edge of the bath. "I'll watch."

"You're so dirty, Lefroy."

I turn back to the loo, but I can't fucking pee. *Shit.* Is this stage fright? I need to perform. *She's waiting.*

If I can't pee, it's gonna feel like I can't ejaculate. And fuck, did I just ejaculate. I've never seen so much cum. The fact that she's not on the pill is worrying, but for now, all I want is to be able to urinate.

Erica crosses her arms over her chest and stretches out her long legs as her eyebrow rises. "You can't do it."

I glance over at her. "Of course I can."

"Go on then."

Take a piss, Seb. Take a fucking piss.

Erica waits just long enough for it to be all too fucking obvious that I cannot pee with her in the room before she walks towards me, slaps me on the bare arse, and says, "I'll give you a little privacy." She flashes me the cutest smile, complete with a hint of gentle mockery, and leaves the bathroom. I hang my head, shoulders shaking as I laugh to myself. The door clicks behind her and I let go, a healthy golden shower decorating the bowl. *Thank fuck for that.* I was worried I might need to get my prostate checked.

When I'm done, I add some bath salts to the bath water and check the temperature. Erica knocks on the door, and I let her in.

"I could get used to this," she says.

"What?"

"Hanging out with you, butt naked."

"I have absolutely no objections to that."

She stands beside me, resting her hand on my back where I'm leaning over the bath. "You have a gorgeous body. Can I keep it?"

Oh, fuck. The answer is yes, obviously. It's hers. Always has been, and always will be. But I have no idea how I can make that happen.

"How long do you want it for?" I ask as casually as I can, ignoring the guilty thump of my heart as I stand upright and turn to face her. I took her virginity, and I have to end it between us. I'm going to lose this beautiful, wonderful woman, and I've barely had her for a moment. The pain in my heart is so intense, it causes a blinding light to flash behind my eyes, and when I blink it away, all I see is Erica. Her cheeks are flushed, her dark hair falling free over her shoulders, those perfect breasts on display. I want to reach out and hold them. Hold *her*. Never, *ever* let her go. Erica pointedly clears her throat, and I shake my head and raise my guilty gaze to meet hers.

"Sorry. You being naked is really distracting," I murmur, hoping she takes the comment at face value.

Her smile is barely a flicker. "I want to be with you. Properly. Not fake. This isn't fake. Not anymore." She steps closer, places a hand flat against my heart, soothing the pain that just wrecked my chest, and kisses me. "I want this to be real. Can we make it real?"

The only thing I've ever wanted is to make it 'real' with Erica Lefroy, and if I didn't know it before, I know it now, standing here naked with her hand on my heart. There is no way I'm marrying anyone else. I don't know how the fuck I'm going to sort it out with Dad and Diana, but I will. And I'll do it before Erica ever finds out it was even a possibility. She's the only woman in the world for me, and to marry anyone else would kill me.

Before I can think twice, I say, "Yes."

"Really?" Her eyes sparkle. "You want that too?"

"Yes. Absolutely. You're the only person I want to be with, ever. So yes. I love you, and I'd love to be with you. For real, for as long as you want me."

A wide smile spreads over her face as she steps into the water and sinks into the tub. "You can get in," she says, and it feels like she's inviting me to spend my life with her, and I've never felt so elated.

She's half-submerged, pink nipples poking out above the water, tendrils of dark hair trailing on the surface. *So beautiful.* This woman, this *goddess*, is finally *mine*. Love swells in every cell of my body until it feels like more than I can contain. She is everything I've ever needed, and everything I ever will.

I slide into the hot water at the other end of the huge tub. My legs rub against hers, her skin so soft that it makes me ache for something I can't even determine.

I take her foot in my hands and glide my thumb over the arch as I massage her foot. She hums, smiling as I work over the sole. If I could do this for the rest of my life, I would die the happiest of men.

"Will you tell me why you never looked the other women in the eye?" she says gently.

I release her foot and reach for the other, massaging it the same way. "I told you. I don't want to mislead anyone."

"Okay." She sighs, relaxing as I tend to her foot. "Why don't you remember their names?"

I rub each of her toes individually, bidding for time. "Sometimes I forget. Or they don't tell me."

She pulls her foot out of my grip and it slips back beneath the water. Gone is the dreamy look in her eye. "Bullshit. I'm calling you on yours. You remember everyone's name and all the details about their lives. I've seen you do it at parties. Recalling the smallest details about people you've met once, years before. You pay attention. So why don't you remember those women's names if you take them to bed?"

I bite down on the pad of my thumb, but the pinch isn't enough of a punishment for all the wrongs I've done. "You want to make it make sense, huh?"

"I don't want *it* to make sense. I want *you* to make sense *to me*. I want to understand why you're the way you are."

"Why I sleep around?"

Her lips tighten, her cheeks reddening. It could be the heat of the bathwater, I can't be sure. "I told you I was a virgin. I told you why, more or less."

I arch my back, tipping my head so I don't have to look at her. No one has ever asked me this question. Not even my brothers. No one has ever given a fuck, and I can't help feeling a little ashamed that it's taken this long for anyone to care. I wish I could be grateful that Erica is the one to finally take an interest, but I can't handle the intimacy of it, so I change the tangent of the conversation. "Why is it so terrible to have casual sex?"

She squirms in the water. "I don't think it's terrible. But I wouldn't do it the way you do it. I'd rather be in a committed relationship."

"So it's not the sex bit you take issue with. It's the casual bit?"

"Yes. I'd want to know I was sharing my body with someone who cared about me."

My heart thumps a little harder. "I care about you."

"I know. I care about you too. That's why I'm here, like this, with you." She gently splashes a hand in the water as if to encompass everything we are and everything we've done. "So, will you tell me why you forget their names and won't look them in the eye, when, otherwise, you're one of the most thoughtful, attentive people I've ever met? You don't miss a thing." I'm about to thank her for the compliment when she adds, "Except when you're cracking shitty jokes to avoid an intense emotion, so don't do that now, please."

38
ERICA

Seb stares, so handsome, so contemplative. *Have I gone too far? Is he going to push me away?* That moment when I thought he wouldn't look at me during sex was harrowing. I want to understand it.

"Turn around." He taps his chest and adds, "Come here."

It's not the order that has me obeying, but the vulnerability in his eyes. The attempt at connection. I shift so my back is to him, and he pulls me against his chest, where I rest, skin-to-skin, feeling his lungs expand and deflate with every breath. He trails one hand down my arm, over my breast, teasing my nipple between his thumb and forefinger. The touch is almost absent-minded, but I'm so grateful for it. I've been holding tension at the thought that he wouldn't want me anymore.

I melt into him and his fingers glide over my wet skin. He's not doing it to make a move, but more as though he owns my body and can touch it as he likes. *I love him touching me like this.* Heat trickles through me.

Behind me, his dick thickens, the length of him pressing into me. "Are you hard again? I'm trying to have a serious conversation—"

He makes a low rumbling sound in his throat that tells me he's smiling. "You're the woman of my dreams, and your naked arse is nestled between my legs. I'm listening to you, I swear, but my dick is having the time of his life, so you should probably just ignore him because, if you're around, he's gonna be hard for the foreseeable future."

Ignoring his attempt at humour, I change tack. "Will you tell me how you lost your virginity?"

Tension runs through him like electricity through a cable; it jolts against my skin.

"It's not a good story," he says.

I peel myself off his chest, twisting in the water to face him, eddies spiraling around me. I take his face in both hands, staring into his beautiful blue eyes. "Please, Seb."

He closes them, sucking in air and letting it out in a groan. "You're killing me with all the questions, Lefroy."

I lie back against him, letting his fingers caress me again. We lie silently for what feels like an age before he says, "I lost my virginity to a prostitute when I was sixteen."

I don't move. Don't breathe. *It's not a good story.*

He keeps stroking my upper arm, but his dick softens until I can barely feel it. I ache for the loss of it.

"Dad paid for it. Took me to a seedy brothel and waited outside the door, which was paper-fucking-thin, while I tried to fuck a woman twice my age." He breathes slowly, chest rising and falling against my back. "She didn't look me in the eye. Not once. It was as though I wasn't even there. The whole thing was over in seconds." He stops again, but I still don't move, feeling the heavy thump of his heart against my back. "Is that enough?"

I shake my head without glancing back at him. There's a lump rising in my throat at the thought of him, so young, being taken to a place like that. But before I jump to conclusions, I ask, "Did you... enjoy it?"

He coughs—*chokes*—a spluttering, dry laugh. It jerks me in the water, my skin slipping against his.

"I came. If that's what you mean." He resettles himself, inhaling slowly and grinding the out-breath on a melancholy groan. A darkness settles over us, or perhaps it emanates from him. *He's ashamed of what happened. Deeply, deeply ashamed.*

My heartbeat slows, my pulse thumping in the tips of my fingers. Should I change the subject? Talk about something else? But wouldn't that look too obvious? He'd know exactly what I was doing, and that would only reinforce the idea that this is unspeakable. That some part of him is unacceptable and unloveable. I want to hold his pain if he's able to acknowledge it. "Did you know her name?"

"No. She didn't tell me and I didn't ask. She didn't want to know mine either. We didn't really talk."

"Could you have said no?"

A humourless crack of laughter sounds. "No one says no to my father."

There's something so familiar about what he's saying. Both our parents have been far too involved in our lives. My mother. His father. They've transgressed boundaries they shouldn't have, and had influential decision-making power over things that ought to have had nothing to do with them. If that isn't toxic, I don't know what is.

"No one else should decide what you do with your body."

I say the words so quietly that I suspect he doesn't hear them, but then he says, "I didn't think anything could kill my hard-on for you, but this conversation has done it."

"Sorry," I murmur, trying to hide the sadness I feel for him because nothing about his voice is inviting pity, and I know he doesn't want it. But I can't help feeling it.

He blows out a breath, but the sound rings with pain. Regret. Shame. I hear it all in that one exhalation, and without him having to confirm it, there are several things I know to be true all at once. This is why he's never looked a woman in the eye when he comes. This is why he gives himself away so easily. He never meant anything to anyone, even his father. How could he value a body that was treated like that? Sex has to be meaningless, because then what his father did to him stays meaningless too. It's manageable, but it's miserable.

Seb Hawkston might have fucked a lot of women, but he's never let himself be loved, and he's never loved any of them.

Sobs leak from my mouth even as I try to stifle them with a hand. All his smiles, all his jokes and teasing... and *this* is what was underneath. And to think, I called him a *manwhore*... The memory causes a stabbing pain in my chest, regret flowing like a poison in my blood. I dissolve into tears.

"Hey, hey," he says, turning me in the water, cupping my face, wiping away a tear with his thumb. "Don't cry. I didn't mean to make it sound as though any of this is your fault. I'm so grateful to have you in my life. I have no regrets. I would retrace every step I've ever taken, willingly, because it's the path that led me to you."

The way he's looking at me, his eyes full of love, only makes me cry more. Am I worthy of it? Is it real? It feels real, but I'm not the one who had a picture of him on my wall for years. Potentially even before we met in person. Does he feel the way he feels because I've kept him at arm's length all this time? Did it give space for an infatuation to grow where it otherwise wouldn't have? The need to know the answer consumes me.

I wipe my tears with the heel of my hand, voice breaking as I ask, "If we'd had sex that night five years ago when you slept on my sofa, would you have looked me in the eye back then?"

He kisses the side of my neck. "You? Yes."

"Why?"

"Because you're the other half of my soul, Lefroy."

My throat thickens, and the back of my nose stings, tears throbbing behind my eyes. The need to keep him forever surges through me and I link my arms around his neck, pressing my naked body to his, the water sliding between us as he tugs me close.

"And you're the other half of mine." The words are a desperate, broken whisper against his neck. *I love you.*

He squeezes me, his arms around my ribs, and in his touch, I sense a need that matches mine. "I love you too," he says, even though I didn't say it out loud. "God, I love you, Erica Lefroy."

39
SEB

By the time we're finished in the bathroom, the bedroom has been cleaned and tidied, with fresh sheets on the bed.

We spend the rest of the morning messing up the clean sheets, and I draw orgasm after orgasm from Erica's body. The look on her face as she comes, the whimpers she makes, the way her fingers fist into the sheets, are like gifts I've wished for and never thought I'd get. When her head rolls against the pillow, and her dark hair spills over the sheets, it's divine. I can't get enough.

Afterwards, when we've exhausted one another, we lie tangled up, our hands clasped and fingers interlinked.

"You really are perfect," Erica whispers, glancing at where she's holding my hand. "You even have perfect hands. Perfect man hands."

I let out a low laugh. "I thought you didn't like the word perfect."

"I don't like it when Mum says it about me. She wants perfection at all costs, hence taking me to see the surgeon. And like I said before, anyone who tells you what to do with your body... who doesn't give you the choice... that's fucking toxic."

She looks away, and I know it's not lost on either of us the parallels that run between us. My dad, my body. Her mum, her body. Both owned, controlled, albeit in different ways. A common toxicity, and for a fragment of a second, I wonder if it could be the thing that drew me to her in the first place. The sadness I saw in her eyes all those years ago, in that picture in the catalogue. Something shared, like an injection of the same poison. *Romeo and fucking Juliet.*

"That's why I need the movie thing to work," she continues. "It would be for me. Away from Mum. Out of her grasp. I'd never give anyone that level of control again."

"I get that." *Of course I fucking do.*

She's quiet for a moment before she squeezes my hand, focusing back on my fingers. "Your hands really are perfect though."

She twists our interlinked hands, examining them from every angle.

"You have lovely hands," I say because I can feel her judging herself. Maybe even comparing herself to me and finding something lacking, which is bullshit I can't allow to stand.

"No, I don't." She sighs. "And my feet... Did you know there was an article in the Daily Mail about how I had hobbit feet?"

I laugh aloud, ripping the covers off her. "Let me see these hairy toes of yours."

She squeals, grasping for the covers in a vain attempt to keep them in place. "My toes are not hairy. It was a bad angle."

A belly laugh overtakes me, and I abandon the search for her feet as I roll onto my back, laying my hands over my tightening abs. "Spoken like a true model."

"Hey!" She slaps playfully at me, and I raise a forearm to parry the blow. She flops down next to me on the bed, the two of us staring at the ceiling.

When my breathing calms, I flip around, propping myself on my elbows, and kiss her shoulder. "There is nothing you could tell me that would make me change my mind about you," I whisper.

"In what way?"

"That you're perfect." She starts to speak but I press a finger to her lips. "I won't listen to any objections. To me, you are perfect. You've always been perfect, and you always will be."

"That's sweet."

"I mean it. Those hairy toes are absolute perfection."

She smiles, but it fades as a sly expression creeps into her gaze. "Do you like my mouth too?"

I'm wary. *She's up to something.* "Yes."

"My lips?"

"Yup."

She arches a brow. "Would you like them on your cock?"

Boom. I'm rock solid. I gesture at my dick. "Is the Pope Catholic?"

I lie on my back, and she shifts onto all fours, kneeling between my legs, which I spread wide to give her access. "I don't know what I'm doing," she admits, dipping down to lick the tip of my dick, which jerks like it wants to high-five her tongue. "I've never done this."

"You could bite my dick off and I'd enjoy it."

This draws a smile to her face and, I hope, fills her with confidence. She could never do this wrong. Ever. It's a dream come true that she's anywhere near my dick, let alone offering to put it in her mouth.

"Mmm," she says, dark eyes flashing up at me. "It's big."

My dick jerks again as she tickles the slit with the tip of her tongue. *Holy fuck.* For a woman who claims she doesn't know what she's doing, it feels unbelievable.

"You taste like me," she whispers before running the flat of her tongue all the way up my shaft. I let out a groan that shakes the bed. "Like both of us."

I'd worry she didn't like that if it weren't for how her hips are swaying, her nipples forming tight buds on her breasts, and how she swallows my cock as far as she can and sucks on it like she's been doing this forever. Her hand fists at the base, and she pumps it up to meet her mouth on the upstroke.

"I fucking love that mine is the first cock you've ever put in your mouth. That's a fucking honour right there."

She moans, the vibration causing ripples of pleasure to shunt up my shaft, making the head tingle. I want to thrust past her lips, fuck her mouth until I hit the back of her throat and fill it with cum, but I hold back, letting her get used to it.

She pops off. "Is it good? Do you like it?"

"Love it." I let out an appreciative groan. "Don't stop."

She swallows me again, pumping with her hand at the same time. She slips to the tip, rolling her tongue over my dick like it's a lollipop. She pulls long and hard, over and over again, and my hands twist into her hair as her tongue slops over my tip between each drag. If she keeps this up, I'll lose it in record time.

As if sensing my approaching orgasm, she works me faster, and I jerk my hips towards her, fucking her mouth gently. "I'm gonna come," I murmur. "Stop."

She hums a '*nuh-uh*' and shakes her head.

I'm gonna fill her mouth any second and she's not quitting. "No, I can't come, or no, you won't stop?"

She pauses just long enough to say, "I want to taste you," before she resumes, moaning again on my dick, making a sound that's so heavy with desire that I know she's enjoying this just as much as I am.

Pleasure sparks low in my hips, gathering in intensity before blasting through me as the suction drags my orgasm from me. My back arches, white spots exploding in my vision. "Fuuuuuck," I groan, as I unload into her mouth.

She keeps sucking right to the very end; until my dick is jumping in her mouth from the intensity of feeling. Aftershocks spark through me with each sweep of her tongue as she licks up every last drop of cum and swallows it down.

"How was that?" she asks, sitting back on her knees and looking at me, although I can tell she knows it was good.

I'm still panting for breath as the last of the pleasure trickles through me. "The best. You're a natural." She kisses the head of my dick again and I moan.

She wipes at her mouth. "I don't know what I was expecting... but... it was okay." She taps a finger on her lips. "Sort of like... oysters."

Laughter bubbles up in me. "I like oysters."

"You would," she says. "All salty and slimy and raw."

I drag a hand down my face as I splutter on a laugh. "Way to make a man feel good, Lefroy."

She grins, kissing her way back up my chest, and whispers in my ear, "You're my favourite flavour," which might be the nicest fucking thing anyone has ever said to me. "I'd swallow your cum any time you want me to," she adds, which makes me laugh again.

She nestles back against me on the bed, fitting herself right beneath my arm. I play with strands of her hair, twisting them around my fingers. As good as the blow job was, having her here beside me in bed feels better. *The best.*

"I love you," I whisper.

She's quiet a moment, then her eyes flash with something akin to guilt and she says, "Your father's here. He arrived yesterday."

The comment smashes the bliss filtering through me. I knew he was coming, but I'm not prepared. Her mentioning him, especially in response to me telling her I love her, feels like he's still here, wriggling his way into my bed. *Again.* Resentment filters into my blood like a toxin. "You saw him?"

"Yeah. He was pretty rude to me, actually. He was rude to all of us. He had some people with him who weren't invited to the wedding. Made Kate promise to rearrange the seating plan."

"Who were they?"

"Diana Marchetti and her father."

"Diana?" I blurt the name before I can stop myself, and Erica pulls back, suspicion flitting in her gaze.

"Yeah. The woman you were looking at on your phone that time in the flat? Kate said her dad had something to do with the hotel business. Or development. Or... I can't remember."

Diana. Here? Now? This is no coincidence. My father's mind doesn't work like that. It's all calculated. Every move, a shift on the chessboard. He's trying to outplay me.

Well, fuck that. I'm going to find him and tell him I won't do what he wants. I won't marry her. I won't lose Erica; not now. I'm done doing what my father wants.

40
SEB

I bang on the door to my father's house. Once, twice. Three times. *Nothing.*

Fucker's probably still asleep.

I pace on the veranda, palm trees waving in the breeze. It would be idyllic if I were in any state to appreciate it. *What the hell was he thinking, bringing Diana here?*

I'm about to thump on the door again when it opens. A uniformed member of staff, the butler I assume, opens the door, but I don't give him a chance to speak before I shove past him.

"My father. Where is he?"

The butler trots behind me. "He's not to be disturbed, sir."

"Fuck that." I grab the banister and swing up onto the first step, racing up the stairs to where I know his bedroom is. "Dad?"

The butler follows me up, muttering about the fact I shouldn't be here.

On the first floor landing, a door creaks open. My mother steps out into the hallway, blonde hair in soft waves around her face, a silk gown wrapped around her.

She opens her arms wide, a weak smile quivering on her lips. "Sebastian. My blue-eyed boy. My baby."

Her eyes are glazed, and she can't read the emotional temperature. She can't tell that I'm furious. I want to shove past her too, but I remind myself it's not her I'm mad at. I let her embrace me, and she's frail as she wraps her arms around me. Each vertebrae on her spine stands out through her robe as I return her hug.

"Where's Dad?"

She cups my face in her hands. "You get more handsome every time I see you. Such a beautiful boy."

"Dad," I repeat. "Where is he?"

"He's busy." Her focus drifts off. "You know how he is. Always busy."

I extricate myself from her hold and pace down the hall towards Dad's suite. If he's in the house, he'll be there.

Mum follows me, the butler following her, both of them traipsing after me like lemmings. My mind is a blur, emotion rocking to the forefront as I approach his room. I don't know what I'll say or if this is the best way to handle the situation. It's almost certainly not, but I'm not in a state to think clearly.

I bang on the door. "Dad?"

Mum is right behind me, clinging to my shoulders, her fingers thin. Old. Beneath the rage, pity gathers like a stagnant, helpless pool. I can't save her, not when I need to do this for me. For Erica. I try to shrug her off. "Not now, Mum."

"You haven't said hello. My baby hasn't said—"

The door opens and Dad stands there, looking far healthier than when I saw him last. *Damn.* He looks me up and down. "Fuck do you want?"

"The Marchettis are here? Diana's here?"

Dad's eyes widen, shooting to Mum over my shoulder, then taking in the butler who's also lingering in the hall. "Take her away," he instructs, and the butler nods and ushers Mum away, her shoulders sloping as she trudges back down the corridor without another word.

"You invited the Marchettis here? To the wedding?" The words burst out unrestrained. *Angry.* "You said four months. You said I had—"

"You've been fucking about. Publicly cavorting with another woman. It was jeopardizing the deal. I had to bring it forward."

"I'm not doing it. You can fucking ruin me, destroy my reputation, but I won't do it."

His left eye twitches. "Is it the woman? The one who wants to be an actress?"

"Erica. Yes. I love her. I won't give her up."

He sneers. "Actresses are little more than prostitutes. Everyone knows that." A cruel laugh cracks from his lips. "But that's always been your type, hasn't it?"

A bomb goes off in my chest, radiating a toxic heat. I clench my fists, trying to hold it in. "You're lucky I don't carry a gun, because I'd blow your fucking brains out for that."

He gives me a pitying look. "No, you wouldn't. Not you, Sebastian. You couldn't pull the trigger."

My fingers flex. "I hope your next heart attack kills you."

"Always such a sweet boy," he says with false sincerity.

"Fuck you. I won't do it. I won't marry Diana, and I'll tell Erica everything. Whatever you put out in the press about me, whatever story you spin, she'll understand. I know she will."

A sly smile crosses his face. "No one loves you that much, Sebastian. Don't fool yourself. Although I can see why you think a glorified prostitute is all you deserve."

I shove him, not caring that he's older and weaker than I am. He staggers back into the room, hocking up little bursts of laughter like phlegm from the back of his throat as he goes. "Maybe if you killed me, you'd finally be a man."

I can't hold back any longer. I reach around his throat and force him back against the wall. We stumble awkwardly, knocking against a table. A lamp goes flying, shattering into pieces. I thump him against the wall. *Hope his spine breaks.* The wall shudders and his shoulder knocks a framed mirror to the floor. The crash is almighty. *Explosive.*

I barely notice, focusing on the way my fingers close around his throat, throttling him.

"Stop!" My mother's voice, more lucid than I've heard it in years, slices through the room. In my peripheral vision, she flaps towards us like an unruly bird.

"Mrs Hawkston," comes the shrill voice of the butler.

Dad's choking and spluttering in my hands. He's not the man he used to be. Physically, I'm stronger. If I wanted to, I could kill him with my bare hands. And I do fucking want to. But then he would win. I'd have his blood on my hands and his death on my conscience, and I'd end up in prison anyway.

I glance over my shoulder to where Mum is standing, her hands clutched to her mouth. "Please, let him go."

Understanding spreads like sickness in my body, attacking each and every cell. It doesn't matter how badly he treats her, she will always choose him over me. It doesn't matter that I'm her blue-eyed boy, her baby, the darling son she wanted to hold on to. In this family, she'll always choose Dad because there is no room for any other response. *No one says no to my father.* But she doesn't deserve this—to have to witness the near murder of the man she chose to marry by her own son—not on top of everything else she's endured over the years.

I release him, and he strokes his throat with one hand. "Good boy," he croaks, and I want to fucking kill him all over again.

In the silence that follows, Mum teeters up on her tiptoes, clasping her hands before her. "Your father says you're getting married. We're very excited," she says, although she sounds more terrified than excit-ed. The butler stares at the floor as if he can neither hear nor see any of us.

"I'm not getting married. Whatever you've heard, it's bullshit. Sor-ry to disappoint."

"But Diana is so lovely. So pretty. Such a charming girl. She'd be such a wonderful society wife."

Revulsion roars through me like a tidal wave. A *society wife.*

"If you don't obey me—" Dad begins, reminding me of the threat he wielded over me weeks ago.

"Fuck this. No." Rage has tremors running through me. "I'm not going to do what you want. I am fucking done with you, and if you want to come after me, go ahead. Publish whatever the fuck you want about me. I'll fight you on it. And I will fucking win. But please, for the love of God, wait until after the wedding. Don't be a selfish bastard. This is Kate and Nico's time. Don't ruin it."

I turn to leave, glancing at my mother as I pass, wondering how the fuck she stayed married to him all these years. Small wonder she numbed out completely with the nearest bottle of alcohol.

"Sebastian." I'm nearly at the door when my name yanks at me like a hand on my collar, and I halt, turning back to my father. "You'll regret this."

I stand tall, meeting his gaze head on. "I will *never* regret choosing Erica."

41
ERICA

Seb sits on the end of the lounger. I'm sunbathing at our pool. It's enclosed and private, surrounded by palm trees. Sunlight glistens on the water.

He drops his head in his hands, and I can tell from his posture that all is not well. He ran off like something was wrong when I mentioned his dad, saying he had to discuss something important, but he didn't tell me what it was.

I sit up, rubbing his back. "Hey. You okay?" He shifts under my hand, almost like he doesn't want to be touched, so I stop and lie back down on the lounger, waiting a moment before I ask, "How's your dad?"

He sighs. "He's all right. Same old bastard."

"I'm so sorry."

He leans his elbows on his knees and stares at the water. He's clearly not going to say anything else, so I raise what's been on my mind. "About this fake dating—"

He turns abruptly, shedding all signs of whatever was bothering him. "Fake?"

I smile at him to show I'm kidding, but he doesn't smile back, which unsettles me. "We were going to end it after the wedding. We're technically in our final twenty-four hours, and I want to be really clear on this." I glance down at my hands then back at him. "We're not doing that anymore. Right?"

He gives me a '*don't be stupid*' look. "Lefroy, if you think we're ending this, you're fucking insane."

A nervous giggle bursts from me. "Really?"

"I've had a picture of you in my bathroom for seven years. I'm obsessed with you. Have been since I first saw you. This relationship is not ending now. No fucking way. It's just beginning. If you think I'm going to let you go..." He smiles, shaking his head at me. "You're delusional."

Pulling back, he surveys me as I lie on the lounger in a tiny string bikini. "Wow," he mouths, and heat fires in his gaze, shifting from admiration to desire like the changing images on a slide-show.

He crawls up the lounger towards me, kissing my skin as he goes, and liquid heat pools between my legs. He presses tiny kisses up my legs, my thighs, my stomach, my chest, my throat, until he reaches my face. He cups my cheek in one hand, his touch so tender that it makes me ache.

"You are so wonderful," he whispers. "Are you mine?" He kisses the tip of my nose. "Say you'll be mine."

"Yes."

"All of you?" He strokes my cheekbone with one finger, sending a shiver down my spine.

"Mmm," I concur.

My phone buzzes, but I ignore it, letting it ring out.

His finger continues to my chin, trailing down the side of my neck. "Is this mine?" I nod, hardly able to breathe as he trails his fingertip over my skin, running down my shoulder until he reaches the strap of my bikini. "This?"

I swallow. "Yes. All yours."

The phone rings again, and Seb glances at it where it lies on the ground at the side of the lounger.

"Don't stop," I murmur, but he leans over and grabs it.

"I think you're gonna want to answer this one," he says, flashing the screen at me. The *Taming the Beast* casting director's name is on the display.

"Oh, fuck," I mutter, bolting upright and snatching the phone from Seb's hand. "Hi," I answer. "Erica Lefroy speaking."

"Erica," comes the casting director's excited greeting. "How are you?"

"Great. Good. I think." I give Seb a worried glance, and he gives my thigh a reassuring squeeze.

"Well, hopefully your day's about to get a little better. We'd love to offer you the role of Vannessa."

I squeal, slamming my free hand over my mouth. "Oh, wow. Thank you, thank you, thank you. I will give this my all. Oh, thank you. You have no idea what this means to me. I am so, so grateful that you're taking this chance on me. I will absolutely do this role justice. I'll be—"

Her laughter cuts me off. "You'll be wonderful. We were all in agreement that you're a perfect fit. Congratulations. We'll be in touch with more details soon."

We say our goodbyes, and when I hang up, I let the phone fall to my lap, hands trembling.

"I got it," I tell Seb.

"I know." His excitement mirrors mine, blue eyes bright and smile wide, dimple on full display. He leans across and hugs me, and I'm enveloped in his scent, his warmth. *Wonderful*. Better, even, than getting the news about the movie. Being held by Seb is the best thing in the world. "Well done. You deserve it." He kisses me and it's a kiss that is filled with love, making me feel worshiped and adored with the slightest touch of his lips to mine. "You're going to be a star. You know that, right?"

"Yes."

"My girlfriend is going to be a movie star," he says, puffing his chest. "I like the sound of that." He kisses me again. "You're amazing. I'm so happy for you. We can celebrate tonight, at the wedding. Champagne—sparkling water if you prefer—and canapes, and we can tell everyone about it." A devilish smile breaks over his face. "Now, where were we?"

"About... here," I say, reading his intention and pressing my finger to the strap of my bikini.

He slides a finger under it, shifting it over my shoulder so it falls down my arm, and he kisses the spot it was a moment before. "So this is all mine too?" I hum an agreement and his other hand teases the opposite strap from my other shoulder.

My stomach clenches as the bikini slips, the top half falling to my waist, and Seb's sharp intake of breath makes my nipples peak. He flutters his eyes closed like he can't take it all in at once. "I don't deserve you."

"You do. *You do.*"

He opens his eyes and strokes his finger from my shoulder down the slope of my breast, right to the tip of my nipple, which instantly hardens and peaks, and the trace of a smile pulls at his lips. "Is this mine?"

I sound breathless when I say, "All yours."

"In that case, I want you to sit on my face."

I glance around the pool area. It's secluded, but not secured. "Here?"

"Right here," he says, tapping the lounger.

"What if someone comes?"

"They won't, but if they do, scream my name to let them know whose face you're riding."

A flush of heat attacks me. "You're so bad."

"Yup." With an uncanny focus, he tugs the strings of my bikini on both my hips simultaneously. "And I'm hungry, and there is nothing I want to eat more than your pussy." He tugs and I shift, allowing him to pull my bikini bottoms off in one go. My heart dips as the air hits my bare pussy, which pulses like it wants to call out to his tongue. *Here. Now.*

He nudges me out of the way so he can lie back on the lounger. "So, sit. Let me fuck you with my tongue. Please."

His words have desire rolling through me, and, I can't clamber onto him fast enough.

Straddling him, I hover over his face. "Won't I be heavy? How will you breathe?"

"Don't worry about me." His darkened gaze fixes between my legs, before his eyes, filled with amusement, flick to meet mine. "If I die, you can run a story in the press. *Erica Lefroy smothers boyfriend with her perfect pussy.* That'll sort your reputation for good, and I'll be the envy of every man in the world."

"But—"

He grabs my hips and yanks me down onto his mouth, his tongue sweeping inside me, releasing a desperate wave of need that has me rocking my hips against his chin.

"Oh, *fuuuuuck*," I moan.

He feasts, and feasts, and *feasts*, like he's trying to win an Olympic gold with his mouth. *First prize to this man right here.* His tongue laps and teases and spears me until I can no longer hold back the orgasm that bursts like a firework, sending sparks shooting through my vision.

When I'm boneless and quivering in the aftermath, he shifts me so we can lie together, limbs entwined. He wipes his mouth with his hand, but we're lying so close I can smell myself on him. He strums my cheek with his thumb and I kiss him, tasting us both.

"I like you like this," I whisper.

"Like what?"

I kiss him once more. "Mine."

42
ERICA

The island has filled up while Seb and I were otherwise occupied, and it's almost shocking to see how many people have descended for the wedding. The place is teaming with well-dressed men and women in brightly coloured outfits, and there are a huge number of yachts anchored nearby. More luxury boats than I've ever seen in one place. And I've seen a fair few when I've been on photo shoots.

Seb and I had so much sex that I'm still aching when I sit down at the wedding ceremony, and when Kate walks down the aisle looking like an angel in the sinking light of the afternoon sun. I'm still aching when Nico tells everyone he loves her and will worship her for the rest of his life. Still aching when they kiss and everyone claps, and Elly and Marie, in their sleek bridesmaids' dresses, yelp and squeal, and Seb looks dashing in his suit. It's too hot for jackets, but the guys kept them on for the service. I don't envy them.

I'm still aching when Seb catches my eye after the service and winks at me as he walks back down the aisle. *Still aching.* But it's a good ache. It's an ache that belongs to me and Seb, to our kisses and sweat-slicked skin and breathless orgasms that he wrung from me over and over again. I didn't want to get out of bed, but we had to get up and showered and changed for the wedding service.

Now, I'm standing with a glass of sparkling mineral water at the reception drinks, talking to Elly, Aries and Marie, the latter of whom hasn't mentioned Seb's pierced dick, thank goodness. If she raises the topic, I'll probably melt. It might not be pierced, but it's *perfect*. I love it. I love him. I love every part of him. I don't know why I haven't told him yet; I've wanted to say it so many times, and yet I'm still holding back like I'm waiting for something. But what, I don't know.

I'm hardly listening to what Marie is saying as I glance over at Seb. After the service, everyone ditched the formal dress to a certain degree, and he's taken off his jacket. His linen shirt is loose at the collar, the sleeves rolled up, and navy trousers hang from lean hips. A pair of aviator sunglasses perches on the bridge of his nose.

He looks so good that it's hard to look away. He's talking to Nico and Matt, making them laugh as though he hasn't ever suffered anything out of the ordinary. As if he is, and always has been, the happiest guy alive. He looks like he's having the time of his life. So casual. So relaxed. Maybe he really can shrug off every unsavory experience like it was nothing. Or maybe it's an act. Maybe he's performing for them. For everyone. Maybe he's *always* been performing. The thought unnerves me. He might have shown me a piece of something real today, but how much is he still holding back?

We've barely spoken about the fact we didn't use a condom that first time. My period's due next week, and Google seems to suggest I'm not at the right time in my cycle to get pregnant, but to be honest, it's not something I've ever thought about before. I have a latent panic over it, humming in my blood like the background drone of a far-off aircraft.

I can't get pregnant. Can't have a baby. I'm about to make a movie. I've finally got the role of a lifetime, and the man of my dreams and... *nope*. I'm stuck on an island in the middle of nowhere. I'm not even gonna think about it. Not yet, at least.

A nudge to my elbow brings me back. "Reckon there's something going on there?" Marie whispers, and I look at where she's pointing with her champagne glass.

Diana Marchetti is standing beneath a palm tree, a little way away from the main party. She's leaning against the trunk, and her bodyguard stands nearby, a fraction too close, his hands behind his back. I'm not sure what Marie thinks she can see, because I can't see it.

"I think you're imagining it," I say.

"No, definitely not. Wait... wait..." She hovers her hand in the air, and when the bodyguard steps closer behind Diana to whisper in her ear, Marie says, "There."

He steps back as if nothing is amiss, eyes alert and checking out the crowd. His gaze flicks to me and Marie, at which Marie's eyes pop and she turns away.

"You're definitely imagining it," I say. "That was nothing. He's just doing his job."

She fans her face. "Maybe, but he's hot. I can totally see why she would. Ridiculous, of course. They can't actually end up together. Not with a man like Antonio Marchetti as a father."

"No?"

"God, no. I hear he's very controlling. He'll have some arranged marriage lined up for her."

I stare at Diana, remembering how quickly Seb had shut down his phone all those weeks ago when I'd found him looking at pictures of her. He'd been strange too when I mentioned that his father had brought the Marchettis to the wedding, rushing off to talk to his dad like his life was on the line. I have no idea what might be wrong, so I try my best not to worry about it.

Marie grips my arm, gesturing towards an older gentleman striding across the sand towards Diana and her bodyguard. "Forget the bodyguard," Marie says. "Who's that? He's gorgeous. Ooh, Diana. Choose him," she coos, as if she's Cupid and has some say in Diana's love life. "How old do you think he is? Mid-forties?" She lets out a little sigh. "The men really flock to her, eh? She's beautiful, that's for sure."

But I'm not looking at Diana, because the older man approaching her is Arthur Knatchbull, the man who picked me for the Claudia Kirchwood photo shoot, and with a single choice changed the trajectory of my career. My life. I haven't ever met him in person and I didn't know he was going to be here, or that he had a connection to the Hawkston family. My heart races a little faster knowing that the man who changed my life is here, and after all these years, I'll finally get to meet him.

"That she is," says a deep voice.

I turn to find Mr Hawkston standing at my elbow, and it takes me a second to realise he's talking about Diana being beautiful. Marie turns to him too, but he doesn't greet either of us; instead, he keeps his gaze fixed on Diana.

Marie catches my eye and frowns, but neither of us speaks. After a few seconds of awkward silence, Mr Hawkston turns to me. "You're an actress?"

"A model," I correct. I don't want to say anything else, but then I reconsider. Why should I hide my achievement from this man? It's mine, and I worked damn hard for it, and I am excited about the future. "But I am moving into movies. I've been cast as Vanessa in *Taming the Beast*."

"Oh, no shit," Marie jumps in. "I read that. Awesome book. Real page-turner." Mr Hawkston doesn't react to Marie's words at all. She mouths at me behind his back, "*Kinky as fuck*."

Mr Hawkston eyes me, and the sensation of having given away something important slithers in my gut like a snake. "Congratulations, Ms Lefroy."

"Thanks," I say, but there's no way I'm sticking about for more conversation with this creep.

Shaking off Mr Hawkston's oily congratulations, I excuse myself and pace across the sand towards Arthur Knatchbull and Diana Marchetti. Excitement filters through me as I approach the man who changed my life.

"Mr Knatchbull," I say, stepping towards him. He turns from his conversation with Diana. "I'm Erica Lefroy. We've never met, but I've always wanted to tell you how thankful I am that you chose me for the Claudia Kirchwood shoot."

He raises a brow, confusion dusting his handsome features as he tries to make sense of what I've allowed to explode from my mouth. Diana glances away, her lips tightly pressed together.

Come on, Erica. *Keep your cool.*

"Sorry to interrupt, I'm just so excited to meet you," I say, in a mangled attempt to make it better. "That shoot changed my life. If you hadn't chosen me, I wouldn't be where I am today."

"Miss Lefroy," he says, his voice all cool decorum and a deep upper class British accent. "An honour to meet you after all this time." He holds out his hand, which I shake. Diana watches us with a poise that belongs to an older woman. I notice she's wearing a pair of my shoes, and when my gaze darts back up from her feet, she gives me a warm smile, which I return without reserve.

I turn back to Arthur Knatchbull. "Thank you. But the honour is all mine. I've always wanted to tell you in person how grateful I am that you chose me."

He holds up a hand. "I have to stop you because I won't take credit where it's not due. I didn't choose you."

Oh, shit. My stomach falls. "You didn't?"

"No." Silence pricks the air as the three of us stand in an awkward horseshoe on the sand.

"So who did—"

"Seb."

Shock ricochets through me like shrapnel, and I have to stop my hand from slapping against my wounded chest. My thoughts scatter in a million different directions, and it's all I can do to gather them enough to say, "Seb? As in... Sebastian Hawkston?"

Arthur smiles at my repetition of the name. "Yes. He barged into my office one day, many years ago now, and threw a high street catalogue across my desk."

His words scoop the air from my lungs, leaving me dizzy and breathless, and struggling to make sense of anything. "Wait, so it wasn't my mother? She didn't bring you my portfolio?"

He frowns. "Your mother? No. I've never met your mother. It was Seb. He told me he'd found the next big thing. I laughed at how sure he was about it. He said he'd never seen a face like yours. Something about your eyes. He thought he could see a sadness in them, and he made me swear to put you in my next project."

"That's so lovely," says Diana, giving me a melancholy smile, but her expression makes no sense to me, so I make no comment.

"That she has sad eyes?" Arthur asks her, his tone teasing.

"No, it's lovely that he noticed, and that he cared enough to do something like that," Diana corrects him and focuses back on me. "How long ago was that?"

"Seven years," I say, but it's barely a whisper.

"It is rather romantic, isn't it?" Arthur says with a glance at Diana. "He also said he'd found the woman he was going to marry. Knew it in his bones. I remember laughing because I couldn't understand why anyone would choose a woman who looked like she had sad eyes. But he was adamant that there was something special about you. I've never seen someone so awestruck by a photograph. He was possessed by it. Turns out, he was right. You were—*you are*—something special."

I'm not sure how I'm still standing, because my world is spinning. "Thank you."

"It's not me you have to thank. It's Seb. He's been your biggest fan from before you were famous. It's lovely to see the two of you together after all this time."

"Oh," I say, but it's hollow, and I sound distracted. I don't know what else to say, because all of this has come as such a shock. All this time, I've felt indebted to this man, who's standing here telling me I was wrong. It was Seb, and he never said a thing about it.

"Thank you," I say to Arthur. I glance at Diana, whose sad smile has transformed to a perplexed frown. I have no idea what she's thinking. "I'm sorry I interrupted your conversation. I just really wanted to say thank you, and now... I'm a bit confused... I didn't know..."

"You didn't know he was responsible for your big break? That all this time he had your back in such a huge, momentous way?" Diana fills in, her frown fading away as she clasps my hand in both hers. "That's pretty amazing. You're very lucky, but I'm not surprised you're a bit confused, especially if he never told you." The full warmth of her personality filters into my blood with her touch and her words, and the gratitude that washes through me is nearly overwhelming. To be understood by a complete stranger is a delight I hadn't expected to experience. "I really hope you and Seb get your happy ending."

Before I can wonder exactly what she means, the MC's microphone-loud voice crashes through our conversation, calling us all to take our seats, which we obediently do after checking out the elaborate seating plan.

Seb is sitting up on the top table as part of the bridal party. With him are Nico and Kate as well as Matt and their parents. Kate's mother, who has what looks like an extremely phoney smile on her face, is chatting to Nico's mum. Jack, as Nico's best man, is also up there with Elly, the maid of honour.

I'm sitting at a circular table with Marie and Aries, and Matt's eldest son, Charlie, as well as a few other guests I haven't met before. Lucie, Matt's daughter, was running around dressed like an angel in her flower girl outfit, but she's disappeared now. Perhaps the nanny took her off for a nap.

Everyone around me seems happy after the reception drinks, their smiles and conversation well lubricated with champagne. *I feel so sober.* I wish Amy was here, but she's arriving at the last minute, in true Amy fashion. Straight off the boat and onto the stage. Hopefully, I'll see her after her performance.

I glance over at Seb. He's only a few seats down from his father. I have no idea how he can sit up there with such a monster. *This family is fucked.* Maybe more than mine. Seb catches my eye and winks, his little dimple gracing his cheek for a second.

I smile back, but I don't think he sees because his father passes him a note and Seb glances at the tiny piece of paper, unfolding it slowly. As he reads, the amusement on his face vanishes; the colour drains from his cheeks, and a cold sweat breaks out on the back of my neck. Beside him, Matt, who sits between his father and Seb, looks between the two of them, his brow pinched.

Seb raises his head again, looking as though someone has died. I want to jump up and go to him, but I can't move because old Mr Hawkston stands up, and one of the staff passes him the microphone.

He clears his throat and begins welcoming people, but I'm hardly listening because I am looking at Seb, who's sitting still, brows drawn together, head tilted towards the table. This is his brother's wedding, but he looks like he's just been given a death sentence.

"We're all here to celebrate Nico and Kate. But before we focus on them, I have some other news to share, which we as a family are all overjoyed about." A chill runs over my skin, and Nico and Matt share a subtle glance, but it's obvious they have no idea what he's about to say. Kate looks confused too. Seb's jaw flexes, and he refuses to look at any of them. "My youngest son, Sebastian, is engaged to be married."

The room spins, sickness rising in my stomach. I can't breathe. *Seb, engaged?* My mind races, searching for some key memory, some piece of information that would make this make sense.

Aries smiles, leaning across to rub the back of my hand. "Congratulations."

I pull my hand away. "No... no."

What the fuck is happening?

"Please raise a toast with me to Sebastian and Diana," Mr Hawkston says, directing the attention of the room to Diana and Seb with a sweeping hand gesture. "Antonio and I are greatly excited by this union of our two families, and we foresee great things for the future."

Aries catches her gasp with one hand.

"Oh, my God." Marie whispers, her mouth hanging open as she stares at me.

"Here, here," Antonio booms, raising his glass without standing from his chair. Behind him, his two bodyguards loom, dressed in black. Huge monoliths of men.

"To Sebastian and Diana," Mr Hawkston announces, and everyone is on their feet, champagne glasses raised.

My heart races, my limbs prickly and weak.

"What? Noooooo," Aries says. "Oh, holy hell, that can't be right."

I say nothing. I'm the only one still sitting down.

"Are you okay?" Aries hisses in my ear, her hand on my elbow as if urging me to stand. I'm making myself conspicuous. Humiliation drips through the numb fog of shock, like acid burning through everything in its path. They all know I came here with Seb, as his girlfriend. *They all know.* This is horrendous. I need to get out of here. How could Seb do this to me? There must be some mistake. I can't make it make sense. It feels like Mr Hawkston's speech removed half my brain. I can't process.

I rise to my feet, one hand on the back of my chair. I glance at Seb, willing him to look at me. To give me something to explain this. Some acknowledgment that this news affects me too. That I'm not some random person in the audience who can watch the family drama unfold and remain unmoved.

But Seb doesn't look up.

His father says a few more words about Nico and Kate, and then the servers arrive with the food, weaving between the tables.

Everyone else sits down, but I don't move. Can't move. Marie takes one look at me, tops up her empty wine glass from a bottle on the centre of the table, and pushes it in my direction. She knows I don't drink, but when I look at her in question, she gives me the smallest of nods and shoves the wine closer.

As if that would make it better.

"Drink," she orders.

"I don't dr—"

"Tonight, you do."

I reach for it, but she pulls it back towards her. "Wait. Are you an alcoholic? Is that why you don't drink?"

Aries and Elly share a glance, and Charlie leans back in his chair, watching this play out.

"No," I respond, and even that one word wavers. I can't focus, but somehow I catch sight of Mr Hawkston and, like he senses my weakness, a cruel slash of a smile carves his face as he raises his glass in my direction.

Marie nudges her wine glass closer to me, and, unwise as it may be, I take it and tip the entire thing down my throat in one. The tannin of the red wine hits my teeth, my tongue, drying out my mouth. The alcohol rushes straight into my bloodstream, warm and dizzying. A sensation I haven't felt since I was a teenager. Marie nods to herself, takes the empty glass, fills it up, and shoves it back towards me.

"Aren't you a doctor?" I mutter, although I'm not fully with it.

"Yeah. And this is my medical advice. Get drunk and forget about him. And then get on the first boat out of here tomorrow and never look back." She hands me a third glass she got from I don't know where and forces it on me. I swallow it quickly, even though I know it's a bad idea. "What an arsehole. Men are always more trouble than they're worth."

"Hey," Aries bleats. "That's not fair. Matt is—"

"Now is not the moment to start talking about how great your fiancé is," Marie snaps, and Aries mimes zipping her mouth shut.

The staff surround us, placing the starters down. There's an awkward silence as the food arrives. I can't eat. I can't stay here when I want to throw up. Or scream. Or better yet, run into the sea and drown.

Over at the bridal table, Mr Hawkston stands and puts an arm around Seb's shoulders. Even from here, I can see how rigid Seb's body becomes. He wants to shrug him off, but he can't do it publicly. Seb keeps his head down, but when the old man moves away, Seb closes his eyes, his jaw hardening as he clenches that tiny fragment of paper in his hand. His shoulders curl inwards like there's a pain in his chest he doesn't want anyone to know about, but he still doesn't search for me in the crowd. I can't stay here and wait. I need to leave.

My head spins. *I'm drunk.* "I can't do this."

Marie and Aries go very still.

"Do you want me to take you to your room?" Aries whispers.

"No." Leaning over the table, I fill the wine glass one last time and drink it all. I slam the glass down so hard that Aries winces. "I'm okay. I can get there alone."

43
SEB

My blood runs cold as Dad leans away from me, a smug grin on his face that I want to cut off with a knife. I scrunch in a tight fist the tiny piece of paper Dad passed to me. I don't need to read it again. I know what it fucking said.

Love is a great weakness, Sebastian. If you don't marry Diana Marchetti, it won't be you I ruin. It'll be her. Erica Lefroy. She'll never work again. I'll make it so no one will hire her. Her reputation will be so utterly destroyed that she'll never work as an actress. She can kiss the role in Taming the Beast goodbye. Hollywood will never open its doors to her.

He could do it too. And I don't doubt for a second that he would.

Matt nudges me, nodding towards Erica as she moves through the tables, looking slightly unsteady on her feet. *How many glasses of wine did she drink?*

"What was that about?" he whispers. "What was on that piece of paper?"

I side-eye him with a slight shake of the head. This is too big, too complicated, too much of an almighty fuck up, to share with him.

I half rise from my seat, but my father leans across Matt, who tilts back in his chair to make space. Dad grips my hand, his fingers pressing onto mine. "Don't even think about leaving this room." He glances over at the two bodyguards standing either side of Antonio Marchetti. Is this going to turn into some kind of wedding massacre if I get out of my chair and follow my fake-not-fake girlfriend out of the room? *Surely the fuck not.*

I lean towards him, growling, "You could have taken me down. That, I would have understood."

"I would never have done that. Destroy my child's reputation and risk damage to the company? The family name?" A cruel laugh spits from his mouth. "You're a fool if you ever believed I'd do that to you." He lifts his hand to gesture along the high table, where our family sit like kings. "I'd never do that to *us*. But that..." He nods at Erica, a disdainful curl distorting his lip. "*She* has no impact on my business. My family."

His words drain every positive emotion I've ever felt. *I'm a fool. The joker in the pack.*

When I went to him this afternoon, I handed him the keys to the fucking kingdom, and I didn't even know it. He might not have known how much I cared for Erica before that, but afterwards there would have been no room for doubt, and he would have known exactly how to control me.

I've been outplayed by the master of the fucking game.

"You made it so easy, Sebastian," he croons, as though he's read my thoughts.

I stand, throwing the napkin from my lap to the table. Given the fact he doesn't want a scandal attached to our family name, I'm calling his bluff. He's not going to set the fucking security on me if I leave the table. "Enjoy your celebration," I spit as I walk away.

Outside, the air is warm and windy, the scent of the sea in the breeze. The sun is low in the sky, casting a pinkish tinge across the rare clouds. Palm leaves rustle in the trees overhead. I can't see Erica, but the only place it makes sense for her to go is our cabin. I run, heart thumping and panic clawing at my throat. I have no idea what I'm going to say to her, or how I'll explain what just happened.

I see her up ahead, stumbling across the sand. She's taken off her shoes, and the dress she's wearing has a slit up one side, exposing her legs when the breeze steals the fabric. Long dark hair flows down her back. She's still elegant, but even from here, I can see how each step wobbles as the sand shifts beneath her bare feet. "Lefroy," I yell, running to close the distance.

She doesn't look back. I yell again, closer this time, and she halts like I've yanked her by force, heels digging into the sand as she turns.

Tears track her blotchy cheeks. The sight of her hits me like a blow to the solar plexus, and I slow my approach.

"You with all your talk of love... it's bullshit." Her voice is thin, as though she's already screamed into the wind so hard she's made herself hoarse, but it's her words that root me to the spot. "You don't love me. You never have. And you know how I know? Because you don't know what love is. You've never been loved. No one has *ever* loved you. Not your mother or your father. And certainly not me." Tears are streaming down her face, and although there's a truth to her words that hits like bullets, I know she's lying about that last part. She's *got* to be lying. *Hasn't she?* She swipes at her tears with one hand. "Thank God this was only business. This was only my career. It worked. I got what I needed. I got the film role. Thank God I didn't let you in." She strikes her chest, banging right against her heart. "Not really. Because you would have fucked it. Ruined it. You would have *destroyed me* with this."

"Erica—"

"Fuck you." She thrashes an arm at her side, releasing her heels, which fly out of her grip and land in the sand. "I'm alone in the middle of nowhere." She points out at the sea. "I didn't come here with my friends. I came here with *you*. What am I supposed to do now? You have to get me off this island. Send me home. I don't want to stay here."

"Let me explain."

"Explain what? Did you know? All this time, did you know this was coming?" Erica slaps her hands to her cheeks. "Is this why you were looking at those photos of her on your phone? Because even when we were living together, you knew you'd be marrying her?" She draws in a rough gasp. "Is this why she's here?"

I can't fucking deny it, and in the beat of silence, she reads it on my face.

"Oh, you bastard," she whimpers.

"You said you needed three months. You put this end date in. I agreed."

"You didn't tell me *why*!" She barrels towards me, her arms flapping like wings. I easily grip her wrists, holding her still. Her jaw is tight as she stares at me. "Why didn't you tell me? You had months to mention it. But you didn't. You just let the clock tick down, and you didn't explain." Every word sounds like a cry for help. She tears her hands from my grip and I let them go.

"You never asked. Not once did you ask what would happen after our time was up."

Helpless puffs of air slip out of her mouth. "Don't try and escape this on a fucking technicality. Never in a million years did I consider that you might be getting engaged to someone else when this arrangement was over. That never crossed my mind. I don't see how it could have. How could I have asked about something so unexpected?"

I rub a hand over my eyes, trying to stem the panic that's crawling up my throat and spreading beneath my skin. "God, I wish you had. I longed for you to ask. Do you think I wasn't desperate for you to say,

'Hey, Seb. I like you. I like being with you. You mean something to me too. I'd like this to last longer than three months'. But did you say it? Did you say any of that? Not once. Not once did you suggest you might want this to be more than it was. Before the last few days, you never came close to saying any of that."

"I did ask. *I did*. Back when this began, I asked if we'd still be friends when it was over, because your friendship was, and always has been, important to me." She presses her hands together in what looks like a desperate prayer. "And you said yes. You promised me *yes*. And the whole time you knew it was going to end this way." Through gritted teeth she lets out a scream. "And when I asked today—*today*—you said I was insane to think this would ever end. You lied. You fucking lied to me." Her hand finds its way into her hair and she tightens her grip on the roots. "You looked me in the eye and told me you loved me. And I believed you because I didn't think you could possibly still intend for this to end on schedule... not after..."

Her voice breaks, taking with it my heart, shattering it into pieces. "I'm sorry. I should never have slept with you."

Her chest shudders with shaking breaths, tears falling as she raises her red-rimmed eyes to me. "Please don't say that. I don't want this to be something we regret. Don't make me hate you any more than I already do."

All I want is to hold her. I want to be the one to comfort her, to ask her what bastard piece of shit would do this to her. *Who the fuck would treat her this badly?*

Me. I would.

"I never knew if you cared," I say. "Not really. Not the way I did."

She screws up her face like I've struck a blow. "It was implicit. You knew. You didn't need me to say anything. You *knew*. You always know everything. I said I was yours. *All of me*. Don't pretend you didn't fucking know."

"Know what?"

Her nostrils flare on every breath. "Don't make me say it. Not now."

The warm breeze tugs at her dress and teases loose strands of her hair as we stare at one another, each a mirror of the other's agony.

"I didn't *know*. I hoped." I close my eyes as pain like I've never known tears through my chest. "I still hope."

The silence is heavy with those three unspoken words. I wish she'd say them. Admit that she loves me too. I don't know why I'd wish such a fate on her, to love a man like me when I'm abandoning her, but part of my soul aches to hear her say it. To know I'm not the only one losing my mind. *Losing more than my mind...*

"Is it your father?" she says. "Are you doing this for him?"

I'm doing it for you. "I have no choice." It comes out low and hopeless.

"You always have a choice," she pleads. "What does he have on you? What shit does he have on you that you would agree to this?"

Tension crushes my heart in a painful squeeze. "Erica—"

"If you don't want to marry her, say no. Don't let him do this to you. Don't let him control your life. Be a man. Choose me." She thumps her chest. "Choose me," she says, quieter this time, voice breaking through the tears. "I chose you. My mother hates us together, and I. Chose. You. I—"

"No, you didn't."

She tilts back, blinking at me. "What?"

"You didn't choose me. You never chose me. You chose *you*. Your career. The next move. I was a means to an end. I was a piece in your game. I'm always a piece in someone's fucking game. We were never the same... never on equal footing in this relationship, fake or otherwise. I would choose you every day, and I'll still choose you, even when I have someone else's ring on my finger and another woman in my bed. I choose *you*. Every fucking time. I'll fall asleep thinking of you, and wake up thinking of you. I'll dream of you at night. You will fucking haunt me because I choose you in every single way I can. I have no choice but to choose you. You don't feel like that. I know you don't. Because I was never good enough for you before, and I'm not now either."

She covers her mouth with wavering fingers, bending nearly double and letting out a pained groan that sounds like she's suffered a fatal blow. She breathes shaking breaths into her cupped hand, and when she straightens her eyes are shimmering and wet. "That's not true."

"Lefroy." I say her name gently, but there's a reprimand in the sound. *Don't treat me like a fool.* "This arrangement wasn't about *my* career. My reputation. My fucking PR. It was yours. It was always about that for you. But for me, it was only ever about one thing, and that was you. Being with *you*. It's always been about you."

For a second, she looks like she could break, but she wipes it away with bitterness, and I see the transformation in slow motion as she turns the Ice Queen on me, forcing the words out when she speaks. "Well, congratulations." Tears hang on her lower lashes. "You finally fucked Erica Lefroy. You destroyed her. Many times."

"It was never like that. You know it wasn't. Not with you." My hair flops over my forehead and I rake it back. "I wanted to be with you. I always wanted to be with you. And I was going to take whatever chance I had, real or otherwise. Three months or forever. Would you have agreed to it in the first place if I'd told you the truth? If I'd said, right from the start, that I had to get married to someone else?"

"I wouldn't have let you anywhere near me. I wouldn't have let myself..." She fades off, shaking her head like she's denying whatever might have followed. "I gave you my virginity." She chokes on the words, but repeats them, even though it clearly pains her. "My *virginity*. I gave you so much. And you took it. You took it knowing..." She sucks in a shuddering breath and closes her eyes, composing herself before she adds, "Knowing we had no future."

I want to tell her everything. I want to tell her that I told my father he could take everything from me and I wouldn't care if I still had her. I'd still choose her. That the only reason I'm not fighting him this time is because I can't let him destroy her career.

My father is a cold-hearted bastard, and I will destroy him for this, but I cannot let it impact Erica. She's going to walk away from me and go straight to Hollywood. The Oscars. Super-fucking-stardom. I will not get in her way. I will sacrifice everything so her dreams can flourish.

"You're right," I say. "I did, and it was unfair. But I gave you all I had to give. My heart is yours. I'm pretty sure it has been all this time. And it will be, even after I'm married. I love you, totally, completely, obsessively. For years, I waited for you to think I was good enough. For you to want me too, but you never fucking did. So this was it for me. This was my last chance to ever have you, and call me a bad fucking man if you want to, but I took it."

She swallows hard, looking as though she's holding back more tears. For a second, hope swells that she might give in. That I might be able to take her in my arms. But her next words are spoken with such vitriol that I know I can't.

"How could you do this to me? If you really cared as much as you say you do, you wouldn't have let this happen. You wouldn't have hidden this from me. You humiliated me in front of everyone. Your whole family. The whole world. You think this won't be in the media as soon as word gets out?"

"I'm sorry. I'm so, so sorry." I step towards her but she steps back, maintaining the distance. "If it were up to me, I'd give you everything, forever. This was never fake for me. Every fucking moment was real, and even though I knew you didn't feel the same, and I'd never really have you the way I wanted, it was worth it. Worth every moment of agony, knowing I loved you and you didn't feel the same. Worth every moment, because you'd never have had me any other way. I would have done anything for you. I still would. I love you. I'll always love you."

She draws in a shaky breath, shoulders trembling, and locks onto me with such a potent stare that I feel myself tied to her. Chained, heart to heart. "Then call it off."

It's as good as a confession from her, but I can't meet her halfway. "I can't."

She lets out a wail, clutching her chest. "Is she pregnant? Is it yours?"

"What? No. How can you ask that?"

"Oh, I don't know. Because you fucked me without a condom. Maybe you do it all the time. Maybe there are hundreds of tiny Sebs running around the world, and you don't know any of their mother's names."

The accusation hits like a punch to the gut, nearly taking me out. "That's ridiculous."

"I don't think it's ridiculous," she snaps, then her chin quivers, and she repeats it, much quieter this time. "I don't think it is ridiculous." She crumbles, finally breaking and sobbing real fucking tears that run in makeup ridden tracks down her cheeks.

Her heartbreak cracks through my chest as though it's mine. It probably *is* mine. A sharp, painful agony that tears at my lungs, rising up my throat with each breath. I cross the sand, taking her in my arms.

"No," she says, pushing me away. There isn't a hope in hell she could actually shove me off, but she keeps trying. "Fuck you, fuck you. *Fuck you.*"

"You love me," I say, and she stops, looking up at me. "Tell me you love me."

The air swirls hot around us.

She yanks herself free. "You bastard. You heartless bastard." She launches herself at me again, shoving both hands into my chest, tearing at my shirt with her nails, but then her arms collapse, and she folds, sinking against me, sobbing into my shirt. "I love you. I love you. Of course I love you. And I fucking hate you for this. All of this."

A raw, aching groan escapes me, and she reaches up to my face with trembling hands, cupping my cheeks, stroking a thumb over my cheekbone, wiping away a tear I wasn't aware had fallen. She kisses the same spot, again and again, and then moves to the other side, kissing deliberately as though there are more fucking tears she's trying to get rid of. Pain courses through me, swelling and receding with the reliability of the tide, each crest of it worse than the one before. "Don't do it. Please, don't do it." She kisses my lips. "We could run away. You and me. We can go to Hollywood."

"Because no one would ever find us there," I say with a dry laugh.

"You could come with me," she continues. "Live with me. Leave your dad and all this shit."

I slide my hand to the back of her neck, and everything in me wants to say, *'Yes. I'll come with you. Live with you. Support you as you take this next step in your life.'* But if I go with her, there is no next step in her career. There is no Hollywood. No movies. And I know how much she wants that. Needs that. More than she needs me. "I can't."

Her hands skip over my face, fingers stroking every part as though she's trying to memorise my bone structure. Every curve and line of my face. It's not sensual or erotic, but desperate, as though I'm dying and any minute now she'll lose me forever. "So this is it? This is all I get?"

I nod, unable to force the affirmative from my lips. I hold her closer, burying my face into her hair, inhaling her scent, feeling her bare skin beneath my hands. *I don't want to let this woman go.*

"You're going to marry someone else? Raise a family with her?" A lone sob breaks free. "Do you even know her?"

"I've spoken to her, yes."

Erica's sobs spill out uncontrolled, painful to listen to, and the sound draws tears to my eyes too. My shirt is damp, black streaks of mascara marring the white fabric.

Inside, I'm breaking. "You're the only woman I'd want to marry," I whisper. "The only one I'd want to have children with. Raise a family. You. Only you." I lift her hand and press it to my chest. "Even if you hate me for the rest of your life, my heart belongs to you. Forever."

With a gut-wrenching scream, she pushes away from me. A fury I've never seen before swims in her eyes. "That means nothing. *Nothing.* I will never forgive you for this."

She turns, grabbing her shoes from the beach, and runs, feet sliding in the sand, racing towards our cabin.

"Erica, wait," I call.

She spins and flings one of her heels at me. "Fuck you," she yells as the shoe cracks across my eyebrow.

Pain shoots like fireworks through my skull, stars dancing in my vision. I cover my eye with my hand, my fingers coming away red with blood when I pull them back to examine the damage. The other shoe follows swiftly, but this one I duck, and it lands in the sand behind me with a dull thud.

Erica doesn't stop and I've halted long enough to give her a head start. I race after her, but she screams at me not to follow as she enters the cabin and slams the door.

Panting, I batter against the wood. "Let me in. Open the door."

"Fuck off," Erica yells. "Go back to the wedding. To your fiancée. Your family. They're probably missing you."

"Erica," I say, thumping on the door again. "Let me in."

"Never. *Never.*"

Muffled sobs sound from the other side of the door, and I slump against it.

"Please," I beg. "Please, open the door. Let me in."

"No. I will *never* let you in again."

She says nothing more, and every tiny fragment of misplaced hope burns to ash in my heart, because hers is closed to me forever.

44
ERICA

"**P**sst. Erica."

The noise rouses me from the bed, where I've fallen asleep fully clothed, head resting on a pillow that's stained with tears and makeup.

My head feels muddled. I rub at my eyes, but the room is still dark. *What time is it?*

A gentle tapping comes from the back door. "Let me in. It's Amy."

I hurry to the back door, undo the latch, and open it to find Amy standing in the moonlight. Her pink hair is more vibrant than ever, and she's wearing a full-length magenta sequinned dress, which hugs her curves and catches the glint of the outdoor lighting like a million tiny sparks.

"Oh, shit," she says, taking one glance at me as she steps inside and takes me in her arms. "That bastard. I can't believe he did this to you. I will fucking kill him." She releases me. "You know he's out the front? Just lying there in the sand."

"He is?"

My voice sounds hopeful, and Amy wags a finger in my face. "Nuh-uh. Don't even think about it. That arsehole is lucky I didn't throttle him. He doesn't deserve to see your beautiful face ever again. We're getting you the fuck out of here."

"How did you know where I was?"

Marie pops her head around the door, giving me an awkward wave. "Hey there."

"This one was worried about you," Amy says, nodding in Marie's direction. "Come on, let's pack your stuff. Everything. Don't leave anything. No reason for him to contact you whatsoever. Take the whole fucking room." She strides to the cupboard and opens it, pulling down all of my clothes and throwing them on the bed. "I've got a boat leaving in fifteen minutes, and when we hit the mainland, we can take the PJ to London. We'll be home tomorrow afternoon."

My stomach sinks while my heart thrums above it; the conflict makes me nauseous. If I go with Amy now, I might never see Seb again. And as furious as I am with him, that doesn't feel good.

Marie hauls my suitcase out from the hallway cupboard and together they start emptying all my belongings into it. Meanwhile, I sit, dazed, on the edge of the bed amidst piles of clothes as they get to work.

It only takes them a few minutes to pack everything up. *But the most important thing I came with is lying outside in the sand.*

The urge to cry burns behind my eyes, and I swallow to loosen the thickness in my throat.

"Who the fuck is she, this Diana woman?" Amy says as she forces my suitcase closed, huffing as she zips it. "Where did she come from?"

I raise my hands, letting them drop a moment later.

"Old Mr Hawkston brought her," Marie fills in. "Kate didn't know she'd been invited. It was all pretty bizarre now I come to think of it."

She's right. It was bizarre. I can't make it make sense, not least because I'm too distraught to use any brain power to untangle the mess. I hang my head and start to cry.

"Oh, no," Marie says, rushing to the bed and hauling me off it with a firm grip on my forearm. "No tears. You don't have time. Boat's leaving. You can cry later."

Amy rushes to my other side, ushering me to the door, while Marie grabs the suitcase and rolls it behind us.

"I want to get out of here before Seb realises where we are," Amy says. "I don't want to end up in some James Bond-style boat chase when he finds out I've kidnapped you."

Outside the back door, one of Amy's bodyguards is waiting. He takes my bag, lifting it with ease, and the three of us follow him to the jetty where the boat is moored.

Marie hugs me. "You're better off without him."

I squeeze her and step back. "Maybe."

"Definitely. You wouldn't believe the Jacob's Ladder-related injuries we see in the hospital." She winks, and I have no idea whether she's joking or not, but the thought of Seb's dick has me weepy all over again.

"I lied," I say between sobs. "It's not pierced."

Marie frowns. "Oh. I did th—"

"It's perfect," I blurt, my voice cracking.

Marie's frown disintegrates as an awkward smile shifts in to take its place.

Amy puts her arm around me and pulls me close. "Oh, honey. It's just a dick. We'll get you another one. In fact, that's on the to-do list as soon as we get back to the UK. You're going to show the world you do not give a fuck about that man and his soon-to-be-wife by going out on a hot date with some celebrity. Fuck Seb and his perfect penis."

Marie sucks in a breath, and Amy squeezes her eyes shut for a second. "On second thought, don't do that," Amy orders. "Absolutely do not do that, ever again."

A few minutes later, we're settled in the boat and waving to Marie's shrinking figure on the jetty as we sail out to sea.

"So," Amy says, linking her arm in mine and leaning her head on my shoulder. "Did you fuck him before he fucked you over?"

"Yeah."

"Any good?"

A sob shudders out of me. "Yeah."

"Oh, babes. I'm so sorry. I promise you, we'll find you someone else. Someone better."

I let out a shaky sigh. "I don't think there is anyone."

She says nothing. I let my weight fall against her, and together, snuggled up in the boat, still robed in all our wedding finery, we begin the journey home.

45
SEB

A rough shake to my shoulder wakes me, the pounding in my head crashing into my awareness. Sand on my face; grains of it in my mouth.

What the fuck? Where am I?

I spit out the sand, wiping my lips with the back of my hand.

"Hey, Seb," comes a soft voice.

I roll onto my back to find Diana Marchetti staring down at me, eyes creased with concern, Erica's shoes dangling in one hand.

Erica.

I scramble to sitting, twisting to face our cabin. The door is ajar. I'm about to push to my feet when Diana says, "She's gone. I already checked."

The world tilts. "Erica's gone?"

"Yeah. Apparently Amy Moritz took her back to the mainland. They're probably on a plane back to London already."

She's gone. My body hollows, the space filling with a hopeless panic that roars as loud as the ringing in my head.

I grapple with the sand, half dizzy as I run to the cabin and fling open the door, needing to verify for myself. I stumble from room to room, but it's empty of her belongings. Her clothes, her shoes, her makeup; all gone.

How did I miss her leaving? I waited out here for hours. I must have fallen asleep. *Or passed out?* Amy and Erica must have walked right over me.

My legs weaken, and I clutch at the wall, wanting to sink to the floor. *I've lost everything.*

Given Diana is waiting outside, I can't lie on the bed and weep, which is all I want to do. I step back outside, but as soon as I do, I start sprinting towards the jetty.

"Unless you're planning on sprouting wings and taking off at three hundred miles an hour, you're not going to catch her," Diana yells. "She's probably halfway across the Atlantic already."

I stop, tilting my head back to the sky and raking both hands through my hair. *This is a fucking nightmare.*

Diana walks towards me, and when she reaches me, she sits in the sand, then taps the space next to her as though she expects me to sit too. Not knowing what else to do, and not wanting to face my family, I drop down next to her, Erica's shoes between us.

"I found them on the beach," she says, nodding at them. "She really is like Cinderella, running away without her shoes."

I give the slightest rumbling hum in response.

"You look like shit," Diana murmurs. "You should get someone to clean you up. You might need stitches for your eyebrow."

Stitches? I run a finger over it. It's crusty, gritty with sand, and still weeping blood.

Maybe I did pass out. Or maybe I drifted off and Erica knocked me out with another whack to the head with her shoe before she left. I wouldn't put it past her.

Guilt churns. I missed the whole wedding. Dad will be furious, and Nico... *fuck.* Weddings are supposed to be a time of joy and celebration, and I spent my brother's lying in the sand with a minor head injury.

No one came to find me except Diana. Did anyone give a shit? Judging by the low morning light that speckles the sea, it's after dawn now, so no one did.

"You really love her, don't you?" Diana's voice interrupts my thoughts.

My heart twinges at the question. *This is too raw.* "Who?"

Diana sighs. "Erica, of course. You don't have to pretend. I know you do."

I catch her gaze and hold it. How much can this young woman take? She seems robust, sitting here next to me, looking completely unaffected by the fact she found me passed out in the sand outside another woman's room the morning after our engagement was announced. She must be robust to be the daughter of Antonio Marchetti. Yet at the same time, there's an innocence to her. Perhaps it's because she's only twenty, and it's more youth than innocence. Maybe her bright eyes and flawless skin are confusing me, but to agree to an engagement to a man who's in love with someone else, signing your life away to please your father... that's a terrible burden. I'd pity her if I weren't in the exact same situation.

"Arthur Knatchbull said you brought him a photo of Erica in a high street catalogue seven years ago, and that you told him you'd found the woman you were going to marry."

I press my palms over my eyes. "I did say that."

"If I fell as hard for someone as you fell for Erica, I'd never let them go. I'd fight for them."

"You sound very idealistic."

"And you sound like a condescending dickwad." A laugh escapes me, but Diana plunges on. "How did he threaten you?"

An eerie awareness prickles my skin. "Huh?"

"Your father. I assume you didn't agree to marry me willingly, seeing as you're completely besotted with another woman."

I grimace, clenching my teeth so hard that my jaw aches. "I'm sorry."

"Don't be. Do you think you were the only person threatened into this engagement?"

She was threatened too? It's obvious, I suppose, but I never thought about it. Diana Marchetti and I have more in common than I realised. We're both here, manipulated and coerced into doing something we don't want to do. I wasn't aware she had a boyfriend or a partner, so I can't imagine what her father held over her head. "What did you stand to lose?"

"My social media accounts."

A surprised laugh escapes me and I conceal it with a cough. "You'd get married to save your social media accounts?"

She leans away from me, kicking her feet out into the sand. "Who are you to judge what's worth saving to me? I run everything through those accounts. It's my business. I built them up from scratch. It's my income. My money. My freedom from both my father and you. He also threatened my mailing list, and I have 75,000 people on that. He was going to close it all down."

"He could do that?"

"Yeah. He has access to all of my content. He's super paranoid. He watches everything. There's nothing that happens in any of his homes, his businesses, without him knowing about it. Controlling it. He knows what my accounts are worth and how I run them. He knows *everything*. He could have taken me down in seconds." She inhales. "So yes, I would marry you to save my livelihood. And everything I earn, I'll spend on divorce lawyers to get rid of you."

I frown. "That makes no sense."

"It does to me."

I blow out a breath. "My father threatened to release photos of me with underage women." Alarm spreads in her gaze and I'm quick to add, "Deep fakes. Not real. AI images. But—*fuck*—those things look real. He had a girl lined up to testify it was her. He was going to have me sent to prison. Probably for the rest of my life, which wouldn't have been long because someone would have come and strung me up in my cell, and that would have been the end of it."

She touches two fingers to her lips, a furrow forming between her brows. "So you gave in? Just like that?"

My eyes pop. "Just like that? I'd like to at least see my fortieth birthday."

"Forty is old."

The randomness of her comment makes me chuckle. "Not that old. Anyway, I didn't give in. I told my father he could release whatever he wanted. Told him I didn't give a fuck because Erica was the most important thing. But then he threatened her career. I refuse to be the reason her life falls apart."

"So you let her go?"

I trace a small infinity symbol in the sand before I wipe it away. "Well, she's gone, so I suppose so."

We sit in silence, but it doesn't feel awkward.

"I deserve to be loved," Diana says eventually.

"I'm sure you do."

She shuffles to face me, waiting until I give her my full attention. "You don't believe you're worthy of it, do you?"

Her words crackle like a fire that singes my skin. "Where did that come from?"

"You'd rather marry me and flay yourself for the rest of your life than go after what you want. *Who* you want. To bind yourself to me might actually be easier for you, in some fucked up, twisted way."

"You don't know me well enough to say something like that."

She shrugs, the fingers of one hand diving deep into the sand. "I'm right."

I snort. "Okay, then."

But her words linger. Is that my issue? I don't feel worthy of Erica? Fuck it, I know in my bones that's true, but am I letting her go too easily? Would she ever take me back after this? Is it too late? Anything I do will result in Dad destroying her career, so if I were to make a move, I'd have to move with stealth.

How the fuck would I do that?

I flop back on the sand, staring up at the sky, my mind sifting through everything that's happened. Dad, the threats, the bribery... I can recall that meeting in the restaurant with a clarity I'd rather forget.

The restaurant. *Holy fuck*. Diana's father's restaurant.

I jerk upright, causing Diana to jump.

"What did you mean when you said your father watches every-thing? What does he watch?"

She blinks, tilting away from my overzealous questioning. "I meant *everything*. He has cameras everywhere. Recording devices. He stores them in the basement at home. It's full of recordings of all the famous people who have ever stepped inside one of his restaurants. There are devices in the booths—"

"In the booths?"

"Yeah. Like I said, he's extremely paranoid, and when I did the interior design, I had to take all of it into account. There's not an inch of that place that isn't covered. He stores all the recordings in case he needs them to... you know..." She does a little head shuffle.

"Bribe people?"

"Yeah."

"So, when we came to meet you at lunch—"

"All recorded. Definitely. I don't think he trusts your father."

"That's totally illegal."

She turns her palms upward, sand trickling through her fingers. "I don't know how often he uses any of it."

My heart thumps. "Could we get hold of it?"

"What for?"

"I have an idea, but I don't know if it will work. In theory, could you get hold of the footage and recordings from that lunch?"

"Yeah. Easy." She gives a coy smile. "I'm very friendly with one of my dad's bodyguards."

I arch an eyebrow. "*Very* friendly?"

"Yeah." She wafts the back of her hand in my direction. "We had a thing. It's over, but he'll do whatever I ask him to do. He manages Dad's digital stuff. He'll know where it is."

"Brilliant. When we get back to London, let's work out how to use it to get the fuck out of this engagement."

She dusts the sand off her hands. "I'll do anything to make that happen. I don't want to spend my life shackled to a lovesick puppy like you. I deserve to be with someone who loves me. And so do you."

I don't believe it, but I hope to God she's right.

She gives me a half smile, mischief twinkling in her eyes. "So tell me, is it true your dick is pierced?"

46
ERICA

Five days after the wedding, I got my period. I've never been so upset to see the blood. I felt so stupid, feeling sadness over a streak of red on a tissue. Did I really want to carry Seb's child and raise it alone? Without him?

I want to say no. My head says no. But my heart... it ached the week of my period as though I was losing something precious... some last piece of him and me. Which, of course, I wasn't. I'd never been pregnant. There was no child to lose, but that tiny flicker of hope that maybe I'd taken some part of him with me—that some lasting piece of me and him existed within me—was dashed with that first spot of blood the week after I got home.

It signified that it was really, *truly*, over between us. There was nothing left at all. Nothing but tormented dreams where he kissed me on the beach and tossed me aside, leaving me lying in the sand.

I sent him one message that read, ***I'm not pregnant, in case you were wondering.***

His reply came instantly. ***I was. I'm sorry.***

I don't know if he meant he was sorry about everything that happened, or sorry that I wasn't pregnant. I didn't ask, and he didn't send anything else.

I cried for two weeks straight. Didn't leave the house. Cancelled all my appointments and photo shoots. I pissed a lot of people off.

Even now, on day sixteen, I still feel like shit as I curl up on my sofa with a tub of dairy ice cream.

Bang.

The thump on the door is so loud that the spoon I'm holding clatters to the floor.

"Erica! Let me in." Mum's shrieks sail through the apartment, and my hackles rise. I've ignored every message she's sent to me since the wedding, deleting them all without reading them. I don't need to hear her say *I told you so*.

Bang.

But I can't avoid her any longer. I slop off the sofa like I'm made of jelly and slouch to the door, peeling it open.

Mum stalks in, doing her usual scan of my appearance, which brings her up short. "I was going to tell you that you need to leave the house, but if you look this bad, perhaps it's wise that you don't."

My heart is broken. Can't you see? Don't you care?

I shuffle back towards the kitchen without granting her a response, but Mum is quick to follow.

"I told you he'd destroy you. I knew it. If only you'd listened to me." She dumps her huge designer handbag on the island as though she's moving in. "What are we going to do now?"

We?

There is no more fucking *we* here.

"*We* are going to do nothing," I say. "I'm going to get up tomorrow and go to work. They're expecting me on set."

Mum bristles. "You're still doing this movie thing then?"

"I am. And I don't care what your opinion is on the matter. It's no longer relevant. I don't want anything to do with you."

She presses a hand against her décolletage. "Erica. How can you say such a thing? We have the business to think about. The company. The—"

"I don't want to be in business with you. I'm going to sell my half." I haven't thought this through, but my body is vibrating with rage. I put my heart and soul into that company. I don't want to give it up, but to extricate myself from Mum and sever all ties feels like the right thing. Without the company, she has no hold over me. *Freedom.* As much as it would break my heart to do it, I will. "I'll ring up Arthur Knatchbull and make him an offer—"

"You think a man like that will have time for you?"

Irritation sparks behind my ribs. "The way he had time for you? When you took him my portfolio? When you orchestrated my big break?" Mum's expression turns wary. "Oh, yeah. I know it wasn't you. I met him at the wedding and he told me he'd never met you. And you know what else? He told me it was Seb who convinced him to choose me. *Seb.* Not you. You lied to me. All this time, you claimed it was your doing, when it was him. You said Seb was awful, too dreadful to be seen with in public, and really, he's the only reason I've got this far. And he never tried to claim the glory. He did it quietly, without making a fuss. In all the years he's been my friend, he never once tried to take any of my success from me or claim it as his own. Not one time did he throw that in my face. And he could have. He—"

"Erica, wake up. He doesn't care about you. If he did, he wouldn't have humiliated you the way he did. You're nothing to him." She sighs. "At least you didn't sleep with him. That's one blessing, I suppose."

The air fills with an energetic charge that raises the hair on my arms. "Why do you think I didn't?"

"Because that's not something we'd ever do."

"Who the fuck is this '*we*' you keep referring to?" My voice trembles, my rage barely controlled. "There is no '*we*'. There is you, and there is me. Separate. And I did sleep with him. He popped my hymen like a fucking cherry. Blood everywhere. And after that, we did it again. And again. I had a lot of sex with Seb. And I *enjoyed* it."

Mum pulls herself up tall, sneering down at me. "Good for you." Her voice is like ice. "But that doesn't mean he cares. I have no idea why you're still defending him."

Because I love him. I will always love him. "I know you think men are animals and all they want is sex, but they aren't. They're human beings with thoughts and feelings and a history that explains why they do what they do. And Seb is a good man. At his core, he is good. His heart—"

"He dragged your name through the mud." Mum glares at me. "Why did he do that? What explanation could he possibly give?"

My throat chokes up. *I don't know why he did it.* If Mum were a different mother, I could fall into her arms and weep for everything I've lost. For Seb, and for our imagined child that I wiped away on a piece of tissue. For the humiliation. For the fact I hate him as much as I love him, and part of me agrees with her and now it feels like I have nothing at all.

But I can't tell her any of that, because she has no sympathy. She can't see me in a way that means anything. I'm little more than a puppet to her, and when she can't control my strings, I'm worthless.

I'm cutting those strings. She will never influence me again.

"Get out," I say, pointing to the door. Mum lets out a little squeak. "I mean it," I tell her. "And don't come back. I don't want your lectures or your I-told-you-sos. I don't want your opinions or your criticisms. I don't want to see you at all. Consider yourself exiled."

She huffs and snatches up her bag, hiking it onto her shoulder. "Exiled? Who do you think you are? The Queen?"

"Of my little kingdom, yes. That's exactly what I think."

A nasty laugh huffs out of her. "Don't come crying to me when it all goes wrong."

"It already went wrong, and I didn't come to you, did I? You came here. I will never come to you with my tears. You don't deserve them." Clenching my teeth, I nod at the door. "Get out."

Mum strides towards the exit, back straight and head held high. I expect her to pause at the threshold and throw a snide comment at me, some parting gift to make me feel even worse. But she doesn't. She passes out into the hall and the door gives a soft click as it closes behind her.

Silence engulfs me, and in Mum's absence, loneliness sinks through my skin and corrodes my flesh.

Unable to bear it, I grab my phone from where it's plugged in on the table by the sofa and flop back onto the cushions. My ice cream has melted, so I push it away and call Amy.

After she brought me back to London, she went straight to Paris for a series of intimate concerts in an old music hall, so she didn't witness the way I fell apart. She saw enough on the journey back from the Caribbean, and I didn't want to pester her with more of my tears, not when she was so busy.

"Babe," she says when she answers. "How are you holding up?"

At the sound of her voice, I break, sobbing into the phone, and for several minutes I can't get a word out as Amy purrs comforting platitudes down the line.

When I've composed myself, I tell her about Mum, and then she asks about Seb. I tell her I haven't heard from him since I told him I wasn't pregnant.

"I'm so sorry I'm not there," she murmurs. "I hate that he did this to you. I'll cut his fucking balls off and flay his dick if I see him. And I'll do it with pleasure."

I roll my eyes, even as sobs are still heaving my chest. The image she paints is so visceral. So disgusting. *So Amy.* And yet the mention of Seb, even in this context, sends a fluttering thrill through me, as though his name alone could put me back together and make me whole. "Please don't do that."

"Sorry, babe," she soothes, a hint of laughter in her apology. "I think he deserves it though."

Me too.

"You need to go out," Amy says. "Have you found someone to date yet?"

"No."

"You have to. Get out there. Be seen. Show Seb that you're moving on. He does not impact Erica Lefroy."

"Okay," I agree, but it sounds half-hearted.

"Promise me?"

I sniffle, wiping my tears on the sleeve of my hoody. "Yeah. I'll go out with someone."

"Someone high profile."

"Uh-huh."

"Good. I have to go. I'll call you tomorrow. Love you."

When the line goes dead, I decide to change my phone number so Mum has no way to contact me. And then I eat ten cherry tomatoes in a row.

———

The following weeks drag by, but I stay focused. I set up a meeting to sell my half of the business to Arthur Knatchbull. He's interested, but who knows if he'll buy it or not. It's small fry compared to what he normally deals with.

I hear nothing from Seb, but it's hardly surprising given I changed my number. If he had tried to contact me, which I doubt, I wouldn't know. It's been hard, but it's what I needed. A clean break. As clean as it can be when the tabloids are continually looking for juicy gossip, and Seb ditching me for Diana Marchetti at his brother's wedding is about as juicy as celebrity gossip gets.

Theories run wild. *What happened between Seb and Erica? Was Seb seeing Diana all along? Was it a publicity stunt after all?*

I keep my head down and get to work. Filming is a new experience, but I immediately know I'm going to love it. *I made a good choice.* It keeps me busy, and even working with Michael Drayton isn't as bad as I thought it was going to be. He's very talented, which makes my job easier, and he's complimentary about my acting, which, as it turns out, isn't nearly as wooden as Mum claimed.

Every day, when I wake to a world where Seb is no longer mine and my heart aches like a bruise from the loss, I pledge that I will not allow him to ruin me. This is not going to destroy me, and going forward, he will not factor in my decision making.

Seb Hawkston is not going to impact me at all, just like Amy said.

So when Michael Drayton asks me out, I say yes. He ticks all the boxes. High profile. A Hollywood powerhouse. One of the most famous men in the world with more clout on the other side of the Atlantic than Mike Tyson in a boxing ring. I'm not a fool; I know he doesn't care for me, and I feel nothing for him. Well, nothing beyond the admiration for a decent colleague who's brilliant at his job. In terms of dating, he's all about the image, and it's good publicity for us to be seen together. A real life relationship between the actors who play the main parts in a movie can do wonders for box office numbers.

So when he suggests the Hawkston Mayfair as the venue for our first dinner date, I say yes to that too. After all, I'm emotionally done with the Hawkstons, so what does it matter if I darken the door of one of their hotels?

It breaks my heart to even think it, but it doesn't fucking matter at all.

47
SEB

The Hawkston Mayfair is buzzing tonight, teeming with people dressed in all their finery, and Diana and I are no exception. I'm in black tie and she's in a full-length peach silk gown and another pair of Erica Lefroy shoes. She has them in every colour, and every time she wears a pair it's another fucking arrow to my heart, and I have to pretend I'm not dripping blood with every step. I take a breath and focus again on Diana. *My fiancée.* Her blonde hair is in a tight updo. She looks beautiful, and I've told her so, although I don't think she believes me.

"This is it," she whispers as we take the steps to the grand entrance. "After tonight, we'll be free. You can tell Erica you love her and live happily ever after. Cinderella and Prince Charming."

I don't dare hope this is the case. Diana might have all the evidence we need to prove that my father is a ruthless prick who'll go to any length to get what he wants, even screw over his own children, but there's no guarantee Erica will ever take me back. Either way, we have to get through tonight's event first to find out. My father and Antonio Marchetti are presenting the new hotel to the board and shareholders at an elaborate dinner. I will not celebrate before we've pulled this off.

"And you?" I ask Diana. "Will you be all right?"

Something uncertain flickers in her gaze, but she chases it away. "Oh, yeah. I'm a big girl. I'll be fine. Let's stick to the plan."

In the lobby, Matt and Aries greet us. Jack Lansen and Elly are here too; Elly's even ditched her cowboy boots, and she looks less pop star and more society girlfriend. Kate and Nico are still on an extended honeymoon, which is probably just as well because, although Nico's forgiven me for my behaviour at his wedding, I'm not entirely sure he'd approve of what I'm about to do.

Diana begins chatting with Matt, allowing Aries to sidle up to me and whisper, "Have you heard from Erica?"

"She's not talking to me."

"When are you going to tell us what really happened? Matt's been pestering me about it ever since. Said you refused to explain."

I could have gone to Nico and Matt, but something held me back. Pride, most likely. I didn't want them to know how my father had played me, using me in a way he would never have done to them. Tonight, Matt will find out and he'll likely let Nico know too. But at least it'll be because I've chosen to do it this way, and I'm not going to them with my begging bowl, asking for help. Diana and I have done this ourselves, with a little assistance along the way from the members of her father's household that Diana has charmed or won over and convinced to help us.

Everyone takes a glass of champagne, except for Aries, who opts for water, and we take our seats in the ballroom, where circular tables surrounded by gilded chairs are set out, and elaborate floral arrangements decorate each table. Diana and I part with the others as we go to the front of the room to take our seats with Dad and Antonio Marchetti.

Dinner is an awkward affair, my thoughts distracted the whole time as I try to make conversation with anyone but Dad. Diana, on the other hand, is chatting away, smiling as though she's completely at ease. If she's nervous about her dad discovering what we've done, she doesn't show it.

Dad and Antonio take the stage, and a hush falls over the room as they run through the plans for the project, huge images flashing on the double screens behind them. I have to hand it to Dad—it does look amazing. The Hawkston Mayfair is impressive, but this new hotel will dwarf it.

Too bad he'll never fucking get it.

When they finish, returning to their seats at the table with us, the applause is profuse, and for a sliver of time, guilt pervades me for what I'm about to do to my father, to Antonio, to Diana, and to everyone here. But the toxic hatred I feel for the man sitting opposite me overrides it. Dad might be old, and likely to die of a heart attack at some point, but I hate him with a fury that would burn bone to ash. Aside from the love I feel for Erica, it might be the purest emotion I've ever felt.

I catch Diana's eye, and together we stand. Dad glances at me, a questioning eyebrow disappearing beneath his grey hair. I offer no explanation and escort her to the stage. The applause falters, then slows. I glance over to Aries and Matt, Jack and Elly, who are watching with curiosity. *Fuck, this room is full of people.*

"Good evening," I announce. "Diana and I are honoured to be here. As you may or may not know, our union was an essential piece in the execution of this deal. We owe it to our fathers for bringing us together." I raise my champagne glass and Diana does the same. "So we'd like to formally thank them both."

Glasses are raised and cheers ripple through the ballroom.

"Unfortunately," I continue, "Diana and I have some bad news. We don't want to get married, and we want no part of this dirty hotel deal." Gasps sound and whispers begin. "We think it only fair that you are all informed of events that took place in the run up to the agreement of this deal, and how Diana and I ended up involved. But before we begin, Diana." I turn to her. "Is there anything you want to add?"

She steps forward. "Only to say that I agree with everything Seb's said. And Dad," she says, glancing over at her father, whose steely expression rivals my father's for coldness. "I won't marry a man who has been forced or manipulated into it. If I ever get married, I want it to be for love."

Another round of shocked murmurs begins as I press the button on the remote control hidden in my jacket pocket. It might not be a gun, but it's a trigger I'm willing to pull, and it'll all but kill Dad. Glossy images of the new hotel flicker on the big screens behind us, changing to the images we've loaded up in advance.

I don't turn. I know what's there. Me and Dad, seated in the booth at Diana's father's restaurant, flicking through the fake images he had made up. Diana's father's had high quality camera footage from every angle in that restaurant, and I'm sure the audience can see the images. We blurred out the offensive parts and identifying features on the young woman, but left enough to make it obvious exactly what was intended. Beside me, Diana turns to see the footage, squinting and recoiling from the screen.

Dad's voice booms through the room. '*They look real, don't they? The girl is real. A living, breathing woman. Very compliant, especially for a fee. A talented actress too. Very convincing. She's eighteen, but she'll testify to say she was underage when this took place. I have witnesses who will testify to it too...*'

I zone out, watching the horrified faces of the people in the audience. Dad glares at me, a furious redness colouring his neck and cheeks. His gaze sears my skin like an open flame, but I don't look away.

He rises from his chair, thumping the table with a fist. "Stop this!" he bellows, and from all four corners of the room, his dark-clothed bodyguards move as one.

Diana edges closer to me, but the footage continues rolling, Dad's voice echoing around the domed ballroom from the loudspeakers in the ceiling.

'All I need to do is press the button, and they'll string you up... I won't use any of it, if you agree to the marriage. Say yes, and I'll torch the lot right now... marry Diana... Pump her full of pretty little Hawkston babies to secure this fucking hotel deal. After that, you can walk away. Give her a nice divorce settlement. And as a kicker, I'll leave you the hotel in my—'

The screen flickers and the video finishes, but one final image follows. It's a picture of the note dad handed me at the wedding, warning me that if I didn't marry Diana, he'd ruin Erica's career.

The room falls silent. For a space so full of people, there's very little movement, aside from the bodyguards approaching Diana and me.

I grab her hand and hold it aloft as we descend the few steps from the stage. "You've witnessed the dirty tactics William Hawkston used to bring about this deal," I shout. "We're officially calling off this engagement."

We slow as we pass our table, where Dad is still standing, red in the face, gripping the back of his chair with one hand. He looks like he might have another heart attack, and if he did, I wouldn't be fucking sorry.

Matt rises from his seat as we pass and glances at Dad, who is now clutching his chest, then at me. I give the barest shrug. There's no way I am pausing to check that fucker is okay. Matt acknowledges my choice with a sharp nod before he strides towards me, keeping pace with us as we move through the tables. "Jesus, Seb. Why didn't you tell me?"

"I had to do this on my own."

He frowns like that's the dumbest thing I've ever said, but the judgement slides away almost instantly, replaced with a tender concern that I've rarely seen on my brother's face. He lays a hand on my shoulder, slowing our pace. "I would have been there for you, if you'd told me. Nico too. He'll be devastated when he hears what you were dealing with." He tips his head back in Dad's direction. "Even if that bastard dies tonight, we would choose you. We would choose you over him every *fucking* day. I know Nico would say the same. We're on your team." He thumps a fisted hand into his opposite palm. "We would have had your back, if you had let us."

I swallow the surge of emotion that threatens to submerge me. "Thank you. But this was my burden." I give him a tight smile and continue walking.

"Where are you going now?" he asks, moving with me.

"I don't fucking know. Away from here." Diana is still trotting at my heels, her small hand gripping mine, growing tighter with each step. I have no idea what the consequences will be for her; I barely even looked at Antonio Marchetti's reaction. I was too focused on my own father.

"Holy moly," Aries says, running up to us and shoving Matt out of her way. "That was insane. I can't believe he did that to you." She grips my forearm with both hands and shakes it. "Erica. You have to go tell her you love her. That's what you're going to do now, right?"

"If you let go of me, yes."

She releases me and presses her hands over her heart. "This is so romantic. I think I might faint."

"Oh, Christ," Matt says, putting his arm around her shoulders and wishing me good luck before he guides her off to a seat.

I quicken my pace because the bodyguards are closing in, and I want to get the fuck out of here before they reach us. We dash through the lobby, dodging past guests and the wide reception desk, heading towards the exit.

"We did it," Diana says, exhilarated glee threading through her voice as we trip out into the evening air, gulping it down like freedom.

"We did."

"We really did!" Diana throws her arms around my neck. Her elation is catching, and I pick her up, spinning her round in a moment of maddening joy. *We're free.*

"You were amazing. Wonderful. Thank you," I say, laughing, "I could never have done this without you."

Diana's smile vanishes as she catches sight of something over my shoulder. "Oh, shit," she mutters.

My stomach sinks, doom spreading through me as I lower her to the ground. I knew this had been too easy. *Too fucking easy.*

Releasing her, I turn to see what's upset her.

Erica is standing a few feet away, staring at us. Her gaze is colder than an arctic winter. Beside her is Michael Drayton, his arm around her waist, guiding her towards the crowds who are begging for their autographs.

I can't move, and yet my insides are splintering, painfully ripping me to shreds.

Diana looks anxiously between me and the celebrity couple.

Erica drags her gaze from mine, and the connection breaks with a chill that freezes my core. She turns her gorgeous smile on people nearby, chatting and laughing with Michael and their fans as they sign the last few autographs and move as one up the steps towards me and Diana.

"What do you want to do?" Diana whispers.

They approach in slow motion and my heart rate decelerates to match, thumping a slow toll as Erica passes right by. I catch her perfume on the breeze. *Infinity. Love that lasts forever. Passion across lifetimes. Desire that can never be exhausted.*

As Erica and Michael enter the hotel together, the hope that had so briefly flickered to life starts to die.

I'm too late.

48
ERICA

As I pass through the doors of the Hawkston Mayfair, there's a tugging in my chest; a tearing pain, as though I've left my heart outside the doors in Seb Hawkston's hands.

My knees feel weak and pinpricks skim my skin. *I can't do this.*

He was not supposed to be here tonight, and he's here with *her.* The way he froze, unmoving, holding my gaze like a lifeline, tugged on my heart, and not in a good way. I need to sit down, lean against the wall, *anything* other than keep walking across the lobby as if nothing happened. There's a buzz inside my skull; every memory of Seb has reignited, and his voice hums through my mind with a million previous conversations.

You're the other half of my soul.

"That was awkward," Michael murmurs, and it doesn't surprise me that he knows. *Everyone knows.* "He could at least have said hello."

"I didn't."

He doesn't stop, eyes focused on the entrance to the restaurant, where our table is waiting. He offers me the barest glance. "Didn't what?"

"Say hello. I didn't say hello either."

Michael frowns, then his brow smoothes as he looks around. "Busy in here tonight," he says, indicating the reams of people leaving the ballroom in their evening wear. His lack of concern for me and what

I might be experiencing reminds me how stupid and shallow this date is. The casual way he can shrug off the encounter with Seb is another wound, albeit struck without intention. He's already forgotten about it because seeing Seb didn't shift his world off its axis the way it did mine.

I'm alone in this agony.

I shouldn't have agreed to this date. I'm not ready, on any level, to be out with someone else. I don't want to be. I only agreed because Amy suggested it, and I know it makes sense for the movie and my future as an actress. But the sight of Seb lifting Diana off her feet, swinging her around as though they had some real, genuine connection, caused a riot in my stomach.

I might throw up.

But I don't. I stick on a fake smile and follow Michael to the restaurant because he's one of the most influential actors in Hollywood, and if I can't have Seb, I will damn well have this career.

I will not fall apart. I refuse to fall apart.

My heart is thundering like it means to shatter my ribs. If I were to throw up, it might dislodge from my chest and spew itself out onto the restaurant floor with the remains of my last meal. In a daze, I follow Michael to our table, my legs shaky and my hands trembling as I take my seat.

The sound is muted in the restaurant. Conversations are quiet and respectful, whispered amidst the gentle clink of cutlery on fine porcelain crockery, but I'm hardly aware of any of it because Seb has taken up residence in my mind, occupying every available space.

Reminding myself to slow my rapid breathing, I focus on Michael sitting opposite me. "Let's have some red," he declares, perusing the wine list. Before I can respond, he summons the sommelier and orders a bottle of red, which arrives promptly, and once Michael has tasted and approved it, the sommelier fills a glass for both of us.

I don't drink—*haven't touched the stuff since the wedding*—and he didn't even ask.

I'm about to tell him, but his gaze rises to something behind me. Every vain hope fills my lungs and I can't draw in a scrap of air. *Please, let it be Seb.*

"Lefroy."

Oh, God. Even though I wanted him, Seb's voice has a panicky heat unfurling through my chest. He's behind me, and if I turn, I could see him. Touch him. Speak to him.

Michael flashes a sleazy grin as he leans back in his chair, gaze fixed over my head. "Well, as I live and breathe. The man himself. Seb Hawkston."

"I'm going to have to ask you to leave," Seb says, and I finally turn towards him, needing to know if he's talking to me, but his gaze is fixed on Michael.

"Dude, what? I'm a paying customer. I just got here," Michael replies.

"You're in my seat," Seb says with calm determination.

Michael's mouth opens a fraction, features twisting with a sneer as he crosses his arms over his broad chest. "Your seat?"

"That's what I said." Seb gestures to Michael's chair. "My seat." He raises both hands to take in our surroundings. "This is a Hawkston Hotel. My fucking name on the door." He gestures to me. "No one brings my woman here but me."

My woman?

Michael glances at me. "Babe, what?"

I have no idea what's going on, but hearing Seb refer to me that way doesn't make me mad. I know it should, because *how dare he*, but it sets my soul alight and butterflies fluttering in my stomach. Michael calling me *babe*, on the other hand, has no such effect.

"Don't call me babe," I tell him, and he rolls his eyes.

A muscle twitches in Seb's jaw and he directs himself to Michael. "My brother broke your nose once. Let's not make it twice. I need to speak to Erica, alone."

Michael raises both hands. "Nah, man. We're on a date."

A cool, violent expression descends over Seb's face. "If you're genuinely interested in Erica, tell her now, and she can choose between us. But if you're in this for the PR, for the movie, because you look good together, then get the fuck out before I have you dragged out."

Michael glares at Seb and the moment crystallizes, ready to shatter. My heart pounds and I look around, noting that the other diners are watching the interaction and whispering.

Michael throws his napkin on the table, lifts his wine glass, and swallows the contents before he stands. "Fine. She's all yours."

I feel nothing as he walks away, even though every head in the room turns to watch him. He might be the most gorgeous man in Hollywood, the Brad Pitt of our generation, but he's not the one for me. In a world where Seb Hawkston exists, Michael could never be the one for me.

Seb doesn't sit in the vacated chair, but continues to stand at the side of the table, perfectly attired in his tailored black tie suit. It's only been a few weeks since I saw his face, but my memory of it holds nothing to the real thing. His jaw is so strong it looks like someone carved it from stone, and there's a softness in his eyes that makes me want to cry.

He slides one hand into his pocket, and although the gesture is casual, tension lines his shoulders.

"Hey, Lefroy," he purrs, and a pressure grows at the base of my throat as though all the tears I haven't shed are waiting right there for me to let them out as soon as he says another word.

"Hey." My voice is barely a whisper.

"Are you with Michael Drayton?"

"If I was, I'm not anymore." Seb's jaw clenches at my response, and I swallow to clear the lump in my throat before I continue. "What's going on? Weren't you with your fiancée outside?"

"She's not my fiancée."

I briefly close my eyes to tamp down the swell of emotion that's crashing, wave after wave, against my ribcage. When I open them, Seb is still staring at me. "She's not?"

"Not anymore. It's over. That's what we were celebrating. That's what you saw out there. That's why I was hugging her."

"It's over?"

"Yes. It's over. It was never real to begin with, but it's over now."

My upper body slumps, and I prop my elbow on the table to catch it, hand cupping my mouth. "How? Why?"

"There's a lot to explain. But ever since the engagement was announced, and you left the island, I've spent every waking moment trying to work out how to get out of it, so I could choose you. You are, and always will be, my only choice. I'm sorry I couldn't tell you at the time, but my father threatened to have me charged with soliciting underage women."

My pulse beats faster. "What?"

"It was all false, but he'd had photos made up, grotesque images of me and a girl I didn't know, and he had people ready to act as witnesses and testify against me. She was ready to give evidence too. And I really thought he'd do it. He was draining money from my accounts. I'm pretty sure he had people watching me. Watching *us*. He was responsible for our stuff being stolen from the photo shoot."

I can't process everything he's telling me. It's too much, and I have a million questions, but I settle on the most obvious. "Why?"

Seb rakes a hand through his hair. "He wanted to convince Diana's father to let him build a hotel on his land, and the engagement between Diana and me was part of the deal. I didn't tell you because I didn't think you'd ever want to be with me in a way that wasn't fake or for show, and I justified it to myself by thinking that our arrangement would be over before the news about Diana came out. I could help you with your career for three months, and then we'd go our separate ways and I would do what my father needed me to do. But as soon as we slept together, I knew for sure that this thing between us wasn't all pretend, and that I couldn't go through with the marriage.

"When you told me Dad was on the island, I went to him and told him that I wasn't marrying Diana because I wanted to be with you. That I was choosing you. That he could do whatever he wanted and I would fight him on it. But then, the night of the wedding, he threatened your career instead. Your role in the movie. Your future in Hollywood. He has contacts that would have shut you out of all the major production houses. You would have lost the role in *Taming the Beast*."

I give a pitiful laugh that morphs into a sob. "God, Seb. You can be so stupid sometimes." He frowns, and I continue, "If you'd told me what was going on, I would have given it all up. In a heartbeat, I would have given the whole thing up. I would have chosen you."

He holds my gaze a beat too long before he speaks. "I could never have lived with myself for making you choose. I know how much you wanted it. How much you needed it."

"Did you think about how much I needed you?"

Silence descends like midnight frost. His jaw hardens, eyes closing for a fraction of a second, but it's enough to let me know he never considered that factor. Never thought that I might value him more than my career.

"I wanted you to have everything you'd ever dreamed of," he says, voice soft but a little broken.

I dreamed of you.

"So you took my choice away?" Sobs weave through my words, rendering them unsteady. "Do you know what gives us power? Freedom? It's the ability to make our own choices. You should have let *me* choose. That's what I was really fighting for."

"I didn't mean to do that. I was hardly thinking when it happened, and then you left before I'd found out that there was a way to undo it all. But he can't touch us now."

"What do you mean? What did you do?"

"We exposed him. Diana's father records every interaction in his restaurants, especially if there are people of note dining there. Totally illegal, but I couldn't be more thankful because there was footage of everything my father did and said to me the day he threatened me. Diana sourced it and we showed all of it just now, in the ballroom, to the investors and board members who were there to hear about the new hotel. Everyone knows what he did to me and what he was planning to do to you, and that the engagement with Diana was coerced. Everyone knows it's you I wanted."

My chin quivers, and I press my fingertips to my mouth to contain yet more sobs that want to spill.

Seb steps towards me, taking both my hands in his before I can stop him. "I've missed you, Lefroy. *Fuck*, I've missed you. Knowing I couldn't touch you or hold you, or kiss you..."

His voice fades, and the pain in his eyes is almost more than I can take. The lump in my throat is so big, it's almost choking me. Tears seep from my eyes and shaky breaths slip between my lips.

"Thinking that I might never do any of those things again felt like someone had stuck a knife right through my heart," Seb continues. "Since we've been apart, I've dreamt of you every night, and in the mornings, for a second or two between waking and sleeping, I forgot that you were no longer mine, and life was perfect. I could roll over and find you there, lying next to me. But then reality crashed in and destroyed the illusion. You weren't there, and it was like waking into a nightmare I couldn't escape every *fucking* morning. There isn't a second that's gone by that I haven't longed for you. Pined for you. Ached for you. *Jesus*. Missing you is slowly killing me." His voice is breaking. "I love you. I want to spend my life with you. And I am deeply, deeply sorry for everything that happened, and every way I hurt you. You didn't deserve any of it, and I will spend every second of every day making it up to you. I'll—"

"It was so painful," I say, between sobs. "You publicly humiliated me. You—"

"I know. I'm sorry. God, I'm so fucking sorry." He gets down on his knees next to me. "I'm begging you to forgive me for everything I put you through. If I could take all of it back, I would. You're the only woman I ever want to be with, and to think I could spend my life with someone else is beyond crazy. I can't. I couldn't. I'm choosing you now, and I've been choosing you every fucking day for years. It might not have looked like it from the outside, but in here"—he thumps his chest—"I chose you every single moment. I didn't know how to tell you because I didn't think you'd want me. Not like that. And then you did want me, and *fuck*, that made me so happy... and regardless of what you choose today, I will continue to choose you until the day I die."

I wipe away my tears with the heel of my hand, but they keep coming. My throat aches and my nose stings.

"I love you," he murmurs. "And you don't have to do this fucking PR shit anymore with men like Michael Drayton, because I am here, telling you that I love you. I fucking love you. I love the way you smile, I love the sound of your laugh and the taste of your mouth. I love your focus, your ambition, and your drive. I love how you never give up. I love everything about you, and I always have. I loved being your friend. Every second in your presence was precious, and if I had believed it was possible for us to be together without you losing your career, I would never have given it up. Not for a moment. If you don't feel the same way, I'll walk out that door." He thrusts his arm back towards the exit. "And I won't come back. I'll let you choose. This has to be your choice. What do you want?"

My eyes close as I struggle to regain control, but my chin keeps quivering, and tears crest on my lower lids, rolling over and down my cheeks.

"What do you want, Lefroy?"

"You make it really fucking hard to hate you," I croak out.

"Then don't. Let me love you. I'll give you everything. Anything. I meant it when I said you're the other half of my soul, and I'm half a man without you. I don't want to live my life without you in it. Tell me you don't feel the same, and I'll walk away if that's what you want. But if there's even the slightest hope that you feel something similar, let me show you that I'm worthy of you and your love, and I will move mountains to deserve it."

I blink, pressing my fist to my lips.

"Do you still love me?" he asks, so gently that the words tear at my heart.

I lean forward in my chair, reaching out to touch his face, fingers stroking his cheek. "Of course I still love you. I'll only ever love you."

Relief washes over Seb's face, and he tilts to meet me, sliding his hand around my neck, pulling me closer. Every cell in my body lights up. *He's here. I'm here.* After all this time, I'm folding into his arms again, surrendering my body to his.

"You're the one," he whispers against my lips. "The only one. Nothing fake about it, Lefroy. There never was."

Before I can tell him the same, he swallows the possibility of any words leaving my mouth, his lips meeting mine.

It takes only a second for the kiss to shift from one of love and relief to one of desperation. If it had words, it would be screaming, *don't leave me again, don't ever leave me* from both sides. I tangle a hand in his hair, tugging the strands like I want to punish him. Or keep him, forever.

I pull back, and my breaths come in pants. "If you let me down again, I will cut off your balls and flay your dick. And I'll do it with pleasure."

His eyes narrow, head tilted to one side. "That sounds like something Amy would say."

I can't help smiling. "It is. But that doesn't mean I won't do it."

He pulls me to my feet so we're both standing and kisses me again. The glide of his tongue against mine makes heat unspool low in my belly like ribbons of fire. He breaks away and says, "I'd prefer if you just sucked them. I guarantee it would be better for both of us."

Laughter filters through me, unfettered joy mingling with relief. *I love him. He's mine.* Seb starts to laugh too, squeezing me tight against him.

"What the fuck are you doing?" Matt's voice booms from the other side of the restaurant, and I glance over to see him racing towards us while simultaneously beckoning us with both hands. "You need to get out of here. You've kicked off some serious shit. The board are demanding that Dad step down. His career is over. You fucking killed it." Aries appears behind him, sees Seb and I embracing, and claps like a giddy school kid.

Seb tugs me by the hand. "Let's go."

"Where are we going?"

"Home?" he asks. "Will you come back with me? I have this really huge apartment and it misses you."

"Does it?"

"Yeah. A lot, actually. I thought we could go there and eat cherry tomatoes all night."

Matt scowls and rolls his eyes. "Come on." He waves us to the door again. "I have a driver outside. We'll take you."

Seb looks eagerly at me. "Will you come?"

"Yes." I grip his hand and squeeze it tight. "Yes, yes, yes, yes, *yes*."

He smiles that beautiful smile, his glorious dimple popping, and everything in the world feels right.

Fuck it, it doesn't just feel right. It feels *perfect*.

EPILOGUE

We're lying in my bed the morning after the London premiere of *Taming the Beast*. Erica's dress lies in a heap on the floor, alongside my black tie suit. She wore one of the dresses Dominic DeLacey sent over for the occasion. He called her a few weeks ago, profusely apologised for throwing champagne on her at the Tate Modern, and begged her to wear one of his designs to the premier. He sent masses of flowers and more clothes than she could ever wear, as well as ten different ballgowns for her to choose from. Erica, not wanting to hold a grudge, chose the one she liked best and wore it. She looked incredible in it too. It was hard to keep my hands off her all night.

The film was better than I could ever have imagined, and Erica's performance had me desperate to get her home so I could have her to myself. Which I did, many, *many* times. I coaxed as many orgasms from her body as I could, relishing every tremor and whimper, eating them up like treats, before we both fell asleep in a tangle of sheets.

Erica, her hair mussed and eyes heavy with sleep and sated desire, kisses my hip, where there's a tiny tattoo of an infinity symbol. She traces it with her tongue, and a burst of arousal pumps through me, right to my dick, but we've already fucked twice this morning, so I try to contain myself. I disabled all the cameras in here, seeing as Erica's pretty much moved in and I no longer need to hide the huge picture of her in the bathroom from anyone anymore.

She teases the tattoo again with her tongue and my dick jerks. She looks up at me, brow rising as she deliberately looks between me and my dick. "You like that, huh?"

"Pavlovian response. You lick me, my dick's gonna jump."

She runs her tongue over the tattoo again. "I love this. I didn't think you were a tattoo kinda guy."

"I'm not. But I thought I was going to live my life without you, so I got it done to keep you with me."

She smiles, then leaps up and slaps a hand over my bare chest. "Why not on your heart then?"

I chuckle. "Because I'm not a tattoo kinda guy. Besides, you were already in there. You've been in there since I first saw you in that high street catalogue. You don't need to be on the outside too."

"I still think you should have put it on your pec," she says, her tongue sliding out and licking my nipple like she's some kind of sun-soaked reptile.

"Nah. I should have got it on my arse. Then you'd be licking that all the time."

She laughs. "You're ridiculous." She might be mocking me, but there's an indulgent gleam in her eye as she dips and gives the tattoo another long, lingering lick. "But this is sexy as hell."

I pull her up the bed, so our faces are on a level, and kiss her. "Maybe we should get you a matching one. The Hawkston logo, right here." I grab her arse with one hand and squeeze.

She yelps, then rolls over. "Nope. What if you sold the business? I don't want that logo on my bum if it has nothing to do with you." She nods at my hip. "I sold my half of my company to Arthur Knatchbull, so now you've got a tattoo that refers to him and my mother. It's nothing to do with me anymore."

"That's not what it means to me. To me, it's you. Forever. Also..."

She perks up at my tone. "What?"

"It wasn't Arthur who bought it, it was me."

She squeaks. "Really?"

"Yup. He just fronted the deal. I also bought your mother's half—I offered her a price she couldn't say no to."

She bounces on the bed, looking as excited as a little kid as she slams her hands down on the sheets. "No! Did you? I knew Arthur paid a crazy price for it." She swats playfully at my chest. "It was you all along. You idiot. I should have known."

"Yeah, it was me. I also set your mum up with a new business. A modelling agency, based in Geneva."

"Geneva?"

I shrug. "Yeah. Far away, but not too far. You know, in case you ever want to talk to her again. She seemed pretty happy about the deal to be honest."

Erica's eyes widen. "You exiled her."

I let out a bellowing laugh. "No, I didn't. She went willingly." I pause, reassessing. "With a little encouragement. I don't want anyone around who's going to upset you, but if you want to re-establish contact one day, I know where she is." I press a kiss to her lips. "And now the entire Erica Lefroy company is under my ownership, so if you want it back... it's all yours."

She leaps on me, smashing a sloppy kiss on my mouth. "You're the best."

"There is one condition."

"What's that?"

"You have to do a photo shoot with Diana for her social media accounts. She bloody loves that *Taming the Beast* book, and she idolises you. After everything that happened, and how essential her assistance was in taking Dad down, it's the least I could do."

"The least *I* could do, you mean?" she teases.

"The least *we* could do?" I suggest, and she smirks and kisses me again. "Without Diana, we might not be here. I'd do the photo shoot for you, but people would notice that I'm not Erica Lefroy. Your shoes are great, but they're not really my style."

She shakes her head at my joke. "Of course I'll do it. Thank you. I was really sad to let the company go." A cunning look whisks through her gaze. "You should do the shoot with me."

I grin, remembering how she straddled me all those months ago for the cameras. "Not this time."

"Spoilsport." She sighs, stretching her arms over her head, letting out an '*eee*' that's half yawn, half excited squeal. "Any news from your brothers?"

I roll over and grab my phone, checking the messages. I find one from Matt and another from Aries. "Yup. Baby was born last night."

Erica leaps out of bed. "What the hell are we waiting for then? Let's go meet your niece!"

"Nephew. They had a boy."

Her smile widens, and as much as I want to go and meet the new Hawkston baby, I can't take my eyes off Erica. She's a goddess, standing naked at the end of my bed. I can't believe she's here. Every day she's here, every night, every morning. I fall asleep next to her and wake up beside her. The reality of a life with Erica exceeds every hope and expectation I ever had.

"You're even more beautiful than the picture in the bathroom," I say. Erica's been pestering me to get rid of it. She complains it freaks her out having to pee in the same room as a huge image of her, but there's no fucking way I'm getting rid of it. It's here to stay, just like she is.

She grabs a t-shirt from the chair and tosses it at me. "Move it, Hawkston. I want to meet this kid."

———

Forty-five minutes later, we're showered and dressed and standing outside the suite at the Portland hospital with Nico and Kate.

A midwife exits the room and allows us to pass inside, where Aries is propped up on pillows, a tiny newborn cradled in her arms. She looks tired but happy. Matt sits on a chair at the side of her bed.

Aries smiles at us, but her eyes only leave the baby long enough to murmur, "Hey."

Nico and Kate enter behind us, and Kate coos and clasps her hands. "Oh, look how tiny he is."

Nico smiles, wrapping his arms around Kate from behind, hands protectively cupped over her stomach. He whispers something in her ear, and I instantly know she's already pregnant.

"Come here," Matt says to me.

Erica, who's been holding my hand until now, lets go so I can approach the bed.

"Do you want to hold him?" Aries says, passing the bundle of baby to me without waiting for a response. I haven't held a baby since Matt's daughter Lucie was born, and that was years ago. "He can't hold his head up," she reminds me, her own hand cradling his head until she's confident I have him in my arms.

I stare at his little face, all scrunched up and swollen. He's only a couple of hours old, and it blows my mind that the child we've all been waiting for is finally here. His tiny hands escape the swaddle, exposing wrists that are soft and wrinkled. Miniature fingers grip my index finger, and an unexpected sense of awe that sweeps through me. I'm choking up out of nowhere. Adjusting my hold, I accidentally knock the little cotton cap from his head, revealing a shock of red hair.

"Wow," I murmur. "Congratulations. You had a ginger baby."

There's a ripple of laughter.

"Yeah. I must have nuked Matt's dark-hair genes," Aries replies. "Pretty cool, huh?"

"He's gorgeous." I run my finger over his tiny nose and bend to pick up his hat and fit it back on his head. "Congratulations. What's his name?"

"Seb," Matt says.

My name sends a jolt through me. "Yeah? What?"

"No, stupid," Matt replies. "We named him Seb."

"Sebastian?" I ask.

"Nope," Aries confirms. "Just Seb. We know you hate Sebastian."

"We'd like you to be his godfather," Matt adds.

"Me?" It's a stupid question, which is appropriate given how stupid I'm sounding at the moment, but it's a lot to take in. I can't believe Matt would offer me something like this, or call his son after me, and I can't say anything sensible because my throat gets choked up again. "Oh, fuck," I mutter. "I'm gonna cry."

Nico steps up behind me, a hand on my shoulder as he peers around me to see little Seb's face. "He's nearly as wrinkly as Dad."

The mention of our father causes a chill in the air. The board ousted him after Diana and I exposed him. He's powerless. A lot of shit went down for Diana after that night at the Hawkston Mayfair, but eventually her father agreed to do the deal with Nico at the helm instead of Dad, and Diana didn't have to marry anyone for it. It was a win all round, for everyone but Dad. He'll still get the family name over the door, but his health is failing and whether he lives to see it happen is another issue entirely.

"Fuck off," Matt says, but his eyes are bright and there's no anger in the words. In fact, he looks deliriously happy. *In love*, I suppose, is how he looks. In love with Aries; with his kids, Charlie and Lucie; and now baby Seb too. With his whole perfect life. He deserves it though, after everything he went through before he met Aries.

Erica puts her hands over the baby's ears. "You all need to watch your language around this innocent soul."

"Oh, it's already too late for that," Aries says. "He's a Hawkston."

"So you accept, then?" Matt asks me.

"Of course. I'm honoured. I might have to start going back to church, but yeah."

Nico takes baby Seb from me, and he and Kate peer down, mesmerised by the tiny little guy.

We spend a few more moments congratulating Matt and Aries, and watching Seb's tiny movements, before we leave the room and let them rest. Nico offers to take Erica and me to lunch with him and Kate, which we agree to, but before we go, there's one thing I need to do before I lose my nerve.

"Erica?"

She's walking down the corridor ahead of me and Nico, chatting to Kate. At the call of her name, she pauses and turns back. I sink to one knee, causing her brows to rise and her mouth to drop open.

I pull the ring box from my jacket pocket and flip it open. "Will you marry me?"

"What?" she blurts.

Nico's looking down at me with an amused curl of the lip, and Kate's watching too, her face lit with a grin.

"'*What?*'" I repeat. "That's your answer?"

Erica gives a little shimmy and bites her bottom lip to contain a smile that I know promises to be enormous. "Ask me again."

"Will you, Erica Lefroy, make me the happiest man in the world and marry me? Spend your life with me? Let me keep you forever?"

"Oh, that's so cute," Kate mutters. Nico puts an arm around her shoulders and guides her away, so we no longer have an audience.

Erica sinks to the floor opposite me, throwing her arms around my neck. "In a hospital? You are the most unromantic romantic I've ever known," she whispers. "What's wrong with you?"

"It was the baby. He was so damn cute, and I didn't want to wait to ask you to marry me. I want to make babies with you."

Erica's shoulders shake as she laughs. "You told me you loved me in a toilet and proposed in a hospital corridor. Where do you want to impregnate me?"

"How about the Hawkston NYC? I think it's about time I took you to one of my hotels."

She takes my face in her hands and kisses me. "Yes. The answer is yes."

THE END

Want more Seb and Erica?

You can find the wedding night bonus scene here:

https://dl.bookfunnel.com/73u1yp0ztl

KEEP IN TOUCH WITH RAE

Join my Facebook reader group, Rae's Romantics, where you can discuss my books, characters, and get information about upcoming releases.

You can also find me at my website
www.raeryder.com
And on Instagram and Tiktok
@raeryderauthor

Thank You

I am so grateful to all the readers who have taken the time to read this series. I cannot thank you enough for coming on this journey with me. For years, I thought that writing books was a pipe dream that would never happen. I used to stand in Waterstones and panic that I would never write a book, and never have one on the shelf. I really wanted to be able to browse in bookshops without feeling like I was going to shit myself. (I'm not joking). But little by little, those things became less frightening and more achievable. (You'll be pleased to know that I can now stand in a bookshop and feel relatively calm about it). This series has been read by thousands of people and I can hardly believe it's real.

I must also give thanks to my editor, Sarah, who put up with my crazy voice notes; my book coach, Emily, who has helped me batter these stories into shape; Sido, who probably deserves an editing fee for how many scenes she helped me adjust (even post editing, when I was anxious I hadn't hit the mark), and all my beta and ARC readers, and the members of my Facebook group, who feel like a support group.

Please know that I have plans for other series that connect to this Hawkston world, so while we may not get another Hawkston story, we might get to see some of the characters perform cameos here and there in future books.

And of course thank you to my wonderful children and my husband. You are the best team in all the world.